Deadly Treasure Hunt

DONALD R. RICHTER

Gotham Books
30 N Gould St.
Ste. 20820, Sheridan, WY 82801
https://gothambooksinc.com/
Phone: 1 (307) 464-7800

Published by Gotham Books (date published May 15, 2022)

ISBN: 978-1-956349-22-1 (sc)
ISBN: 978-1-956349-23-8 (e)

Library of Congress Control Number: 2022901928

CHAPTER ONE

Setting Up the Game

One day, in a backroom of a Vegas casino, a group of older gentlemen were placing bets on what color the weatherman was going to be wearing. One guy said, "We need something a little more exciting." An older man named Frank said, "How about a good old-fashioned treasure hunt? Bear with me now, we could make it in a two-hundred-mile radius. We could hide clues, bet on teams, whoever gets to the end first wins." A younger man named Lance asked, "No rules and we all get to set the clues." Another asked, "Do we get to pick the teams?" A woman named Nancy asked, "What is the winning prize?" Frank, the old guy, said, "Winner takes all; we will need a prize for the players in the game." Lance said, "A chance of a million dollars to the winning team if they come in first on all ten clues." Nancy said, "So each clue is ten grand for first place, second place twenty-five hundred, and third a thousand." The old man Frank said, "Ten thousand for a clue to the clue." The younger guy Lance said, "That's a good idea. That way they won't get stuck."

Nancy asked, "What are the rules going to be? And I think the game will pay out a million in prize money, split between the teams." Frank said, "They can't work together. All the clues have to be within the two-hundred-mile radius, they can't be buried. And they must sign a waiver that we are not responsible for anything." A man stood up with his drink and said, "We are going to need a few people in on this, real-time cameras, trackers. Now they're going to be teams, you said four teams of four."

Lance asked, "Where is this going to take place?" Frank said, "We throw a dart at the USA. Ten-thousand-dollar bet on where it lands." Lance said, "I'm in. Who wants to help me set this up?" Frank stood, and so did Nancy. One of the men walked up and asked, "When are you planning to start this treasure hunt?" Lance said, "The first of next month. That gives us almost a month." Three men walked over and asked, "How much to get in?" The old man Frank said, "Million. We are going to need a minimum of five investors." Nancy said, "We have five right here. What is the maximum?" One man said, "I can probably bring in three or four more." Another man said, "Give me more details. I will take it to the club next week. Maybe I can get a few onboard." Nancy said, "You do know the more money the more cheating there will be, so we have to hold this close to our chest."

Lance went and made arrangements with Frank and Nancy to have a meeting and plan out the game. They met in two days. Frank said, "I have found some keyed markers. It takes five keys to open. The keys are located so one person cannot reach two key holes. The first ones who get to the marker and turn all keys at the same time, the top door will open. That would be first place of ten thousand. The second team to reach it gets twenty-five hundred. It needs five keys but we are only going with four players." Nancy asked, "Can it be reprogrammed for four keys?" Frank smiled and said, "Who cares four or five? They just split it up one more time." Lance said, "I have found four lime-green vans. We can put trackers in them." Nancy said, "If we are adding a player, we are going to have to cut the teams down to three. Then we just have to make up some clues to somewhere we don't know." The old guy said, "I have some of the investors. We call them in tonight, we throw the dart, and see where this will be held."

That night twenty-five people showed up for the dart throwing. They each paid ten thousand dollars to get a map. They marked their map and handed it in. A showgirl came out. They spun her around twenty-five times, once for every person there, and she threw the dart, hitting the large map of the US. One guy jumped out of his seat and yelled, "Wisconsin! I picked Chicago, am I the closest?" A man in a tux shuffled through the papers and said, "Yes, you are. The next closest is Nebraska. You have just made $210,000, forty goes to the house." Frank said, "There are a few rules. There are three teams of five. No contacting your team. If you do, you will forfeit your million dollars. The teams cannot work together. The clues must be left the way they were. The clues cannot be buried. There are ten markers. The clues are in machines shaped like question marks. And the payout is in markers that look like the Washington Monument. They take five keys that need to be turned at the same time. The one to get to the last one is the winner. Now we know the game has to be played within two hundred miles of a town called Wausau, Wisconsin."

One guy said, "Can we help you pick the points of interest and then you can make up the clues?" Frank smiled and said, "Okay. In three weeks we pick teams. I will put out a help wanted, must have driver's license and medical insurance." One of the guys laughed. "That's a must. Remember that game to cross Yellowstone Park? They had to collect flags. Three died and thirteen were injured." A skinny guy said, "That was one of the greatest games. We did live-action streaming." A man said, "That reminds me, no bringing in wild animals." The skinny guy said, "You heard the rules. We're not going to change them."

Another man stood and asked, "Do we get to know who is betting on what team?" The old man said, "Not at the start. After that, who cares." Nancy smiled and said, "Everything will be in place. We meet back here in three weeks. We will get you their résumés and you can bet for what team you want." Frank stood and raised his martini and said, "There are three of us that will pick the teams, then you can put your money on the team you think will win." Lance stood and said, "I have talked to some neutral employees. Seven of them will pick the location for the clues and machines to be hid. There are three of us, so that will give us ten people to pull this together. I gave them two days to research, so start thinking where in that two hundred miles you want to hide one." Nancy said, "We have to figure out where we want the locations of each clue and each marker to be.

This is going to have to be top secret. I have a feeling there is going to be a lot of money riding on this. Twenty-five people showed up just for a dart toss. In three weeks there might be a hundred. At a million apiece, that's a large prize."

In two days they had a seven-hour meeting and knew where the markers were going to be. They contracted out getting all the markers placed. That was a job in itself. They met in three days for another long meeting, getting all the clues to where the markers were. There were around fifty clues to the ten markers, which made it interesting. There were ten people with all their views on what clue and where to put them.

They interviewed the applicants over the computer, took their résumés and their medical cards. They met at the casino in the back-room to divide them into teams. The old man Frank, he took all the jocks. The woman, Nancy, took the geeks. The younger man, Lance, took the last group. The regular guys, they were put into the last group. Nancy asked, "Would you like to take a side bet? Ten grand, my team kicks your jocks' ass." Frank held out his hand and said to a man in a tux, "You hold the cash." They both wrote ten-thousand-dollar checks out for cash. Lance handed in a check also and said, "I think my team will win. I think they will work harder." The old man laughed. "They are uneducated, a bunch of unskilled workers." The woman asked, "Who do you think will be the first to find a clue?" Frank held up his hand and said, "Be patient. We will bet on this when the time comes." Lance smiled and said, "We have two days. Tomorrow we rehearse the presentation. It has to be a good sell. I have hired a professional speaker." They worked late into the night to get the presentation to where they wanted it. Then they rehearsed it the next day. The speaker walked through it and rewrote a few parts of it so it flowed.

The big day was there to launch the game. They had an open bar and the wait staff from the hotel was there. Lance and Frank were in tuxedos, Nancy was in a sparkly floor-length gown, their speaker was in a white tux. He started out with the rules of the game, approximately how long it was going to take, what the buy-in was, and 10 percent of the winnings was going to run the game and 10 percent to the house.

The overhead came on and a picture of a very fit man came on. The speaker said, "Team number one. Jack here is a thirty-two-year-old man. He has an MBA. He played corner back in college. He swims, skis, and runs. The next one here is Robert. He is thirty-five and he has run in two triathlons, sixteen marathons. The third in this team is Joseph, thirty-two, and he was a hockey player in college. He has hiked across the Grand Canyon, climbed Mount Olympus. The fourth is a twenty-eight-year-old girl, Cherry. She was in soccer and was nominated for the Soccer Hall of Fame. She does weight training, rock climbing. Last is a gal, Dawn. She is thirty-four. She is a weight lifter. She has gone to nationals, shot put and discus."

Most of the people were taking notes as the guy spoke.

The presenter said, "Okay. Team Two is quite different. The first one is a guy, Richard. He is twenty-eight. He has a master's in engineering. He is one of the leading chess players in the country. The next is Scott. He graduated head of his class in middle, high school, and in college. He is a math wizard. He is big into coding. The third is Jeremy. He is twenty-two. He has three masters' in technology, and has worked with NASA for the last three years. Now we have two women. The first is Gloria. She is thirty years old. She has a doctorate in computer science. She has an MDA in history and interned in the Smithsonian. The last one on this team is Sara. She is a thirty-six-year-old college grad with a bachelor's degree in computer science. She won the nationals High Q contest.

"Now last but not least, we have team number three. This is Mark. He is a thirty-seven-year-old forklift driver. He likes to fish and hunt. Next is Sam. He is forty-four years old. He is a factory rat. No, that's what it says. He has worked for the same company for thirteen years now. They just gave him the axe. The company now buys everything from China. Here is Charlie. He is a fifty-two-year-old physical ed teacher. He taught for twenty-four years. The next is a girl named Jane. She is thirty-eight, a waitress, and she says she needs a change. The last but not least is Sue. She is thirty-one. She has a degree in business and she worked in car sales. Those are the teams.

They may change as the game plays out. They must keep at least five to open the marker."

Lance stepped up and asked, "Did everyone get their packet?" He held up a handful of papers and walked around handing them out. The speaker told them, "Now the house will hold your bet. There are side bets going: how long it will last, who will get the first marker, the first injury, the first to drop out, really the first death, there are a lot of side bets going on."

Frank stood and raised an arm and said, "We set out a hundred chairs. Whoever isn't going to get in on this, would you please leave so the investors can sit?"

Six people got up and left. There were at least thirty people standing. Lance stepped over to Nancy and said one word, "Whoa." She smiled and nodded.

Frank walked over to the two and said, "Okay, you two, you had better pull this off." Lance smiled and said, "Tomorrow at eleven we talk about our pay. I am not going to run this for free you know." Nancy said, "I am getting a quarter of a million." Lance said, "Well, let's enjoy the night and we will see what the odds are after the betting is over." Frank asked, "Are you really going to bet on Team Three? They sound like a bunch of losers." Lance said, "The middle class, they are the workers that keep this country running. They are the back bone of our society, working two and three jobs to make ends meet." Nancy smiled and said, "I bet one of them is going to be the first to die." Lance said, "Why do you people think there is going to be a death?" Frank said, "During games there always is." Nancy said, "With this much on the line we have to hire more people to watch the teams." Frank said, "I had the cameras set up, and they are streaming. I think I will add more. This is a lot bigger than I thought it was going to be. And let me tell you, there are some crazy places these markers are set up." Nancy said, "You're not kidding. Now Lance is going to get the teams together and start the game on Monday morning." Lance said, "We are staying at the Holiday Inn. I like the Holiday chain. We will stream the start. All the vans have cameras and GPS. Everything is to be handled right here. This computer has the encryption. It should be unbreakable." Nancy said, "Oh, they will try. These games can get nasty."

CHAPTER TWO

Start of the Game

Lance left early on Wednesday morning. He had a two-hour layover in Chicago. It turned into a seven-hour trip. He got to the hotel and went to the front desk and said, "Hello, I booked a room for a meeting. I have it for the weekend. It should be under the hunt." The girl behind the desk said, "Oh yes, you have the smaller of the two event rooms. Would you like it catered?" Lance said, "And I need my room key, Lance Link." She asked, "May I see your card?" Lance said, "Bill the meeting room to me also and start a tab." She handed him his key. He was already shooting off e-mails to everyone to meet downstairs, and he asked, "What is the name of the room?" She said, "It is the small room. It is called the Bluegill." He typed in *the Bluegill* and shot off the e-mail, then another, and the last one. He said as he followed the gal, "Three teams, three texts. If it is possible, can we keep these teams apart?" She smiled and said, "It's not that big of a hotel. And here we are. If you need anything, just ring the front desk and I will see what I can do." Lance said provocatively, "Well, maybe later," and he raised his eyebrows. She rolled her eyes and headed back to the front.

The teams started to come down. Lance started to move tables around. Each team had their own table and were as far apart as he could get them. Lance took three sheets of paper from his briefcase and folded them in half and took a marker and numbered them, and set them on the tables. As the people walked in, he asked their names and told them which table, Team One, Two, or Three. The tables started to fill. They could see who was in their team. Lance said, "We are waiting for one more . . . and here she is. Sue, I would take it. You're on Team Three. Now the first thing you do is to think up a name for your team." He walked over and dropped a notebook on each team's desk. "You should take notes." Team Two had notebooks and their phones. Team One was videoing the meeting and putting notes on their phones.

Lance said. "Okay, you people signed up for a treasure hunt. Rule one, there are three teams. You do not work with the other teams. This would be bad. You have to sign the waiver. If you lose a player, you will have to find another. There are five keys to be turned at the same time on the markers. This is your payday. First ones to the marker it is ten grand. Second place is twenty-five hundred, third is a grand. The clues and markers are to be left the way you found them. And if you get stuck and need a clue, it's ten grand. I have your vehicles out in the parking lot, the three lime-green vans. This is what you are to drive. They have cameras and GPS. This is just for the game. And we will have cameras at the clues and markers. This is not a TV show, this is gambling on who will win. I have money on one of the teams. I can't say which team, but there is no quitting. Got it? The investors cannot contact you under any circumstance. You all have my number. I am running the game. I only want to hear from you if you need a clue."

Cherry asked, "Where is this going to take place?" Lance said, "I am getting to that. This game shouldn't take longer than three weeks max. It starts here, and you have a two-hundred-mile radius. I know Lake Michigan is off to the side and it goes into the upper peninsula of Michigan—I didn't even know that existed—and it goes into Minnesota. The clues can't be buried. I am not saying they can't be underground or underwater, just not buried." He then said, "Sign the waivers. I will collect them. Oh yes, ten grand for supplies. Get your shit together. The game starts Monday morning at ten. We will meet down here tomorrow at ten. I am going to need one team at a time."

Lance took his suitcase and briefcase up to his room unpacked, did a quick shower, and went downstairs to the bar. He had a snack and a beer. Sam of Team Three came down and chatted. A man with a monkey came in. The monkey was wearing a diaper. It went from table to table looking at people, then it climbed up on the pool table, started to play with the balls, and swallowed the cue ball. The bartender yelled, "What the hell!" He threw the guy and the monkey out. Lance chuckled and said to Sam, "That's something you don't see every day. Well, it's been a long day. See you tomorrow."

The morning came. Lance went down to breakfast and wouldn't talk about the game at all. Before you knew it, ten o'clock came and he started his interviews. He called in the first team. It was all streamed live to Vegas. He asked, "What are you calling your team?" Jack said, "We are Odin, the most powerful and wisest." Lance asked, "The captain of your team is . . . ?" Robert stood and said, "I have been chosen to lead." Lance then asked, "Do you have a plan?" Cherry said, "We don't have the first clue. Once we get that we can start the game." Joe said, "We are going to start the day with a daily two-mile run that will clear everyone's head." Lance asked, "Did you run this morning?" Dawn said, "Yes, we did. It wasn't a race. You learn a lot about a person when you run with them." Lance asked, "Have you bought supplies? And what have you bought?" Joe said, "We bought some climbing gear, hiking boots, gloves, some diving equipment, maps, lights, and we still have five grand left." Lance asked, "Is your team ready to play? We meet down here tomorrow at ten." Robert stood and said, "We are ready to play, and we will do everything in our power to win." Lance said to the camera, "Okay, this was Team One, called Odin."

He ushered them out and Team Two in. Lance said to the camera, "This is Team Two. What are you calling the team?" Gloria stood and said, "We are the Intelligentsia, a group of intellectuals." Lance said, "Okay then, we will call you Intel for short. So who is your captain?" Scott stood and said, "I am the captain and Richard is the driver. Gloria is the stenographer, Jeremy is the supply clerk, and Sara is our strategist." Lance asked, "Do you have a plan?" Scott stood and said, "Yes, we have a very good plan. I cannot tell you the plan, but we do have one in place." Lance asked, "Have you bought supplies?" Richard said, "Well, we really don't know what we are going to need, so we will pick it up when we need it." Lance asked, "Are you ready to start the game? We meet down here at ten." Scott said, "My team is ready. All we need is the first clue." Lance turned and said to the camera, "This was Team Two. They call themselves the Intelligentsia—did I pronounce that right? I call them the Intels."

He brought in the next group. He looked at the camera and said, "This is Team Three. And what do you call yourselves?" Jane stood and asked, "It is either Fifth Dimension or the Pentagon. What do you think?" Lance said, "Who cares? Just pick one." Charlie said, "Fifth Dimension just rolls off your tongue, but the Pentagon represents five sides." Lance asked, "Who is your captain?" Sam stood and said, "I guess I am." Lance asked, "Well, captain, what is your team's name?" Sam turned and looked at the table and shrugged his shoulders and said quietly, "The pentagon." The table nodded. Sam turned and said louder, "We call ourselves the Pentagon . . . That just doesn't sound right. How about Team Three?" Jane said, "The Third Team." Sam said, "That's it, we are the Third Team." Lance asked, "Do you have a plan?" Sam said, "Yes, we do. We are going to outwork everyone and we will be the first to the markers." Lance said, "Have you bought your supplies?" Charlie stood and said, "It will be here tomorrow. You have to love next-day delivery." Lance asked, "Are you ready for the game? We meet tomorrow down here at ten." Mark said, "We are as ready as we could be." Lance said to the camera, "This is the Third Team. Okay, place your bets."

The three teams went out and did their thing. Team One went hiking, played a round of disk golf. Team Two went and checked out the museums, worked on their computers. Team Three went through their supplies as they came in, went out and checked on the van. That night Lance went back down to the hotel bar. He ordered some pub food. The waitress recommended the brandy old-fashioned. To his surprise it was good, crushed fruit on the bottom and brandy, a couple of drops of bitters, and a few ounces of 7 Up. He sat and worked on his computer. The guy with the monkey came back in the bar; he took the cue ball out of his pocket, set it on the bar, and apologized for the monkey. The monkey climbed off his shoulder and sat on the bar. This time he wasn't wearing a diaper. The man set some peanuts on the bar. The monkey picked one up and shoved it up his ass then ate it. The bartender said, "That's just gross." The owner of the monkey said, "Ever since he swallowed that cue ball he checks everything he eats if it will fit coming out." Lance burst out laughing. He said, "That is the funniest thing I have ever heard."

He finished his snack and drink and went back up to his room. Then he walked to the cinema and took in a movie. It was a nice night for a walk. He stepped into a bar. There was Team One getting their drink on. He went to the bar and got a brandy old-fashioned and walked over to the table. He asked, "Odin, are you guys ready? I have a million dollars riding on this game." Robert said, "A million, whoa! That's one hell of a bet. Who did you bet on?" Lance smiled and said, "Can't tell you about that, but it is a million to get in and there are over a hundred bets. So you had better be watching your ass." Jack said, "You're talking sabotage. You think someone will try to take out a team?" Lance said, "It has happened in the past, at least that is what I hear. This is my first game." Joe asked, "So you are betting on the game and you are running it?" Lance said, "Yes, I am getting paid a quarter of a million, so I only have $750,000 invested in it. Once it starts I am going back to Vegas to work it from that end. There are three of us running the show."

Robert excused himself to go to the bathroom. He walked in, started to take a piss at the urinal, then a short little guy came in. His head was just above Robert's belt. He pulled out this huge cock and started to take a piss. Robert looked down and said, "With a dick that big, you must be a leprechaun." The little man looked up, slapped his dick alongside the urinal, and said, "Yes, I am. And if you would like a cock this size, I could grant your wish." Robert look down and said, "Hell yes." The little guy said, "Step into a stall with me and I will take you up the ass. Tomorrow morning you will have a dick bigger than this one." Robert said, "Ah, sure, let's do it." They went into a stall. The little guy climbed up on the toilet and had Robert turn around and face the door. The little guy pounded him hard. Robert had to put his hands on the door so his head didn't get pounded into it. When they were done, Robert said, "I can't believe it. Tomorrow I am going to have a huge cock." The little guy said as he walked away, "I can't believe you think I am a leprechaun." Robert's face went white. He knew he had just been had. He washed up and went out to the table and made a mistake. He told the table the story. Dawn asked, "So he was a short little guy with a cock this big?" She held her hands a foot apart. Robert said, "At least that big. He said he was a leprechaun."

Dawn chuckled and walked away. Cherry set down her beer, looked him right in the eye, and asked him, "Now what you are saying is you thought you could get a great big dick if you let this guy fuck you in the ass?" Robert blushed and said, "Okay, if you put it that way it does sound silly." Jack chuckled then asked, "Do you really believe in leprechauns?" Robert said, "No . . . yes . . . well, for a minute. This guy had a huge dick. I thought . . . well, okay, I was wrong." Cherry asked, "Are you gay?" Robert said, "No, this was the first time, and my ass is killing me." Joe asked, "Did he wrap that rascal? How about lube?" Robert said, "He spit on it. My goodness, it hurts." Lance held up his hand and said, "Tequila, six shots." Twenty minutes later Dawn showed up with a sly smile on her face. She leaned in close to Cherry and whispered, "His cock wasn't that big, eight inches. It just looked bigger on a small guy, it hung to his knees."

Now Team Two, Intel, met in Scott and Jeremy's room. They had a computer running, pages printed of the city maps and charts, history of the city. They each had a Power Point Presentation. Scott had snacks and wine, Gloria took notes. Richard said, "We got the keys to the van. We can load it in the morning. There is no GPS but we can run off our phones." Jeremy asked, "When do we get our first clue?" Scott said, "We are to be down at the meeting room at ten, so I figure that will be the start of it. A big thing to do around here is skiing, Rib Mountain. There is a very nice theater. They grow a lot of ginseng around here. We just need a clue to start." Gloria asked, "What about the history? Do you think the clues will work off the history of the towns?" Scott said, "This was a lumber town, started back in the mid-1800s. Now they have 124 restaurants and ninety taverns, but we don't know if all the clues will be in the city." Richard said, "The rules are pretty vague." Gloria asked, "How much did we spend on supplies? Do we have enough to buy a clue?" Scott said, "We are going to buy supplies as we need them. How can you tell what we will need?"

In the morning, Team Odin got up early and went for a run. When they met before going down to the meeting, Robert said, "I could have sworn I saw that leprechaun in the hall this morning." Cherry looked at Dawn. She shrugged her shoulders and smiled. Cherry just rolled her eyes and shook her head.

All three teams met in the meeting room. Lance asked, "Are you ready?" They all agreed they were ready to play. Lance walked around and handed an envelope to each team and said, "You all get the same clues and you can look at the camera. Now open your clue."

They opened the envelope to fine one word: Michelangelo. They all pulled out their smart phones. Lance said, "Get out of here. Go to your rooms or something. You can't be here."

CHAPTER THREE

First Clue

Team Two headed out to the van. Every one of them had their cell phones on. Scott said, "As team captain, there will be no talking until we get into the van. One of the Third Team was following us in the hall."

Sam turned and walked back and caught up to the team. He said, "They seen me. Let's go up to our room and figure this out."

They went to their room and Sam turned on his laptop. Everyone else brainstormed what Michelangelo had to do with Wausau. Charlie said, "Okay, what do we know about Michelangelo? He painted the ceiling of the Sistine Chapel. He was a great painter. He also was a great sculptor. He did the *David*, that huge marble statue. I saw that in Vegas. I think it was in Caesars." Sam said, "Intel is on the move, let's go." Sue asked, "How do you know that?" Mark smiled and said, "We put a LoJack tracker on the vans. Surprising, it was a little over fifty bucks, and it took Charlie about five minutes to wire up." Sam said, "Let's move." Jane asked, "Are we checking out?" It got really quiet for a minute, then Mark said, "Five minutes. Meet in the hall, get packing."

In less than five minutes everyone was out in the hall and heading for the elevator. Mark asked, "Sam is team captain, who is our driver?" Sam said, "We will take turns and see who the best driver is." They got to the van. Mark took the wheel and said, "I have tens of thousands of hours behind the wheel." Sue laughed and said, "That was driving a forklift in a building." Mark said like a pirate, "Arrr, captain, do we have a heading?" Sam said, "That we do, ye matey. Head south on 51. Now, we don't want to catch them. This tracking them has to be kept a secret." Sue said, "This is cheating. We are going to get caught." Charlie said, "You heard the rules, putting a tracker on their van was not one of them." Jane asked, "How many clues before the payout?" Charlie said, "Now that would have been a good question to ask when Lance was here."

Sue said, "I think I know where they are going. There is a place called Sculpture Park, it's just off the highway." Sam said, "Team Intel has parked. What is this park?" Sue said, "It looks like just a park with sculptures. It has walking trails, but the park is only twenty acres." Jane said, "This is great. We studied about Wausau and now we are in Stevens Point." Mark asked, "How do we know this is the place?" Charlie said, "It does make sense, Michelangelo made great sculptures." Jane said, "Well, let's hope so. We won't be first but we won't be last." Sam said, "Twenty-five hundred a piece is a lot better than a thousand. And maybe those jocks won't figure it out and this will knock them out on the first clue." Sue said, "Or they are going to the right clue and are going to be the first." Sam said, "I trust the eggheads." They pulled into the parking lot and parked right next to the other van. Mark said, "We aren't too far behind, so we should be able to catch up to them." Sam said, "Well, we know it's not right here or they would be back to the van." Mark said, "Okay, let's just go and find out what is going on. We can still be the first to find it."

Jane said, "Let's not lollygag. This could be ten grand." She got out and everyone followed her. Mark stepped over to a map. "This park has the Brickyard trail running through it, it's 1.2 miles long." Sam said, "Let's just walk through the park. Keep an eye out for the question mark."

They strolled through the park and found the Intel team looking up at a small question mark on top of a flagpole. Sam said loudly, "Well, you found it. How are you going to get to it?" Scott, the captain of Team Intelligentsia, said, "Ah, Team Three. What a nice name, may I add. We are working on it."

Jane asked, "Only one key is needed to get the clue, right?" Charlie said, "I think so. It takes all five to open a marker." Jane said to Sue, "Here, hold my stuff. I can climb it." Sue said, "No, you can't. It has to be thirty feet in the air." Jane took off her shoes and socks. To everyone's surprise, her pants too. She said to Sam, "Give me a boost." Sam picked her up from the back and lifted her over the first four feet to where the pole was. Jane wrapped her legs around the pole and quickly went up the pole, all the way to the top. Sam said, "Be careful." Mark said, "This is crazy. She should have a safety harness on or something."

Jane wrapped her arm tightly around the ball on top of the flagpole and stretched out, getting the key into the question mark. A slip of paper came out right above the key. She took the key out and hung it around her neck, then took the piece of paper and stuffed it in her bra. Sue yelled, "Great job. Be careful coming down."

Jane took her time coming down. She would hold tight with her arms, drop her legs a couple of inches, then do it over again. When she got close to the bottom, Sam put his hand on her butt and lifted her off the pole. He gave her a big hug and said, "That was great." She started to dig out the paper from her bra. Mark said, "Let's read that inside the van." Sue handed her, her pants and said, "That was great." Jane asked, "Didn't you do that when you were kids?" Sue said, "Oh hell no. I am glad you did." Jane gave her a hug and a kiss on the lips. Sue's face blushed bright red. Everything went quiet, the birds even stopped chipping for a minute.

Sara from the other team came up and asked, "Can we get you to go up and get our clue?" Sam said, "There are not too many rules to this game, but that is one of them. We can't work with the other teams." They got back to the van. Jane leaned over to Sue and whispered, "Sorry about the kiss." Sue smiled and whispered back, "That's okay. I am not . . . you know . . . that way." She lightly kissed her on the cheek. Charlie said, "Hey, you two. We have work to do. So what did the clue say?" Sam sraid, "Jane, I can't thank you enough. That was great." Mark said, "Well, the Intel team has seen it done, but I don't think any of those guys are going to climb that thing." Jane said, "Those jocks will be up and down that pole in a minute."

Sue said, "You're right, one of them is a rock climber." Jane cleared her throat and read the clue, "Dinosaurs, that is it. That is all it says." Mark asked, "In Wisconsin, is there La Brea Tar Pits or something like that here?" Sam said, "Point is a big college town, maybe they are starting a Jurassic Park." Charlie said excitedly, "Got it! God, I love Google. Jurustic Park. It's like forty miles away west on Highway 10, north of a town named Marshfield." Mark said, "Captain, we have a heading. Buckle up, we are on a mission."

Sam said, "I don't think team Intel will be far behind. That was pretty easy." Charlie said, "We are just lucky to have Jane here. Who else knows how to climb a flagpole?" Sam said, "Point well taken. That might slow them down a few hours." Sue said, "They were talking drones, but how would you turn the key?" Jane said, "I have seen people actually run up a pole." Mark said, "So have I, a clown. He pretty much ran up one and did a swan dive off the top and tightened his legs to stop a few feet from the ground." Sam asked, "What is this Jurustic Park?" Charlie said, "This old guy, he welded a bunch of stuff together and made dragons and stuff. It should be neat."

They pulled into a small parking lot. At the entrance to the park you could see two huge steel dragons. Jane asked, "I wonder where this question mark will be." Sam said with a chuckle, "It will probably be welded inside one of the dragons." Sue said, "Let's just go in and ask." They went inside the park and walked around, looking everywhere. Mark said, "Look for something new, like it was just welded." Sue said, "I am going into the hobbit house, maybe I can find someone in there to ask." She went inside. It was their workshop and studio. There in the corner was a question mark. She walked over and put her key in and a slip of paper came out. A voice from an older lady said, "So that is what that is." Sue turned to see the lady standing there watching her. She said, "It is a clue for a treasure hunt. You have so many beautiful things here." The lady said, "Thank you. I am Eve. So what is the prize for the treasure hunt?" Sue said, "Just money. By the way, I see everything here is for sale. Can I buy the question mark?" The lady smiled and said, "Now that wouldn't be fair, would it? That is the only thing that is not for sale."

Sue came out of the house and skipped down the trail to find her team. Mark was crawling under a huge turtle. Sue said, "A Polish rock." Jane looked at her and asked, "What?" Sue walked up and said, "That is the clue, a Polish rock." Sam asked, "Where did you find it?" Sue said, "It was in the corner of their studio. Come, I will show you." Sam said, "No, that is fine. I believe you." Mark said, "No, please show us. I would like to put my key in and see if we get another clue." Jane said, "I don't think that is the way it works." Sue took Jane by the hand and said, "It is this way." Jane looked down at her hand and pulled her into a hug, and said quietly in her ear, "They think we are a thing. That lightens things up a bit. That Charlie would like to get me in the sack." Sue kissed her on the lips. This time, she added some tongue. Sam said, "Get a room. We don't have all day." Sue started back to the hobbit house and said, "It's not far from the van."

They all went in and Sue introduced them to Eve. She showed them the question mark standing in the corner and said, "It's not for sale." Sam said, "That's against the rules. We must leave the markers and the question marks the same way we found them." Mark put his key in the question mark and nothing happened. He said, "It was worth a try." Sue looked at the old woman and asked, "Does Polish rock mean anything to you?"

She said, "I am sorry but that doesn't ring a bell." Sam said, "Let's get a hotel room and work on it from there." Jane said, "I think we should find a restaurant, sit down for a meal, and figure out our next move. The next clue could be a hundred miles from here. We are in the lead." Sam said, "You are right, and it sounds like a simple clue." Sue said, "There are Polish rock bands here. Are you sure it didn't say polish rock?" Jane said, "Nope, it said Polish rock with a capital P. That makes it the country Poland." They went to a bar and grill to think about it and get a bite to eat.

Team Two brought in a high lift. They had the operator of the lift go up and get the clue. When the lift was leaving, Team One came in. Robert asked, "What should we do? Should we chase after the lift?" Joe said, "This is a piece of cake. I will run up there and be down in five minutes." He pulled out his key and hung it around his neck. He climbed up to where the flagpole started and wrapped his hands around it and walked right up the pole; he got the clue and slid all the way down. He got a round of applause when he got down. He said, "Now that is the way you clean a flagpole." Jack asked, "So what is the clue?" Joe pulled the paper out of his pocket and said, "Dinosaur." They all pulled out their phones and searched the internet for it.

Meanwhile, Team Three was sitting in a bar eating burgers. Sam said, "Since I am the captain, the girls will work on the rock, the guys will work on the Polish. Let's sit at separate tables." After they were done eating, the two girls came over and made a presentation. Sue said, "Red granite is the state rock. And if you Google *granite Wausau*, you come up with Granite Peak Ski. It's a state park, and if you think of it, Polish names end with *-ski*." Mark raised his glass and said, "Good work. And do you know why Polacks end their names with –ski? It's because they can't spell *toboggan*." Jane rolled her eyes and asked, "What did you guys come up with?" Sam smiled and said, "We like what you came up with. Let's check out the ski hill. Is that the one you can see from the city?" Sue said, "Yes, it is. It has seventy-four runs, a vertical drop of seven hundred feet." Charlie said this could be like looking for a needle in a haystack." Mark said, "I suppose the chairlifts are not working. How the hell are we going to get up there?" Jane said, "If you look at it with Google Earth, there is a big parking lot on the top. The clue could be anywhere." Mark said, "The park is fifteen hundred acres; there is an observation tower on the top, that would be a good place to start." Sam said, "We still have sunlight, let's go."

They got into the van. Charlie said, "Intel is on the move. They have figured out the Jurustic Park clue." Jane said, "If we get this clue, we will be ahead of them by a day." Mark said from the driver's seat, "It didn't take them that long to figure out the clue, like the first clue to sculpture park if we didn't have Ms. Jane here to climb up that flagpole." Jane said, "I still can't believe you put a tracker on their cars." Charlie said, "I can't believe LoJack is that cheap. If I knew about that I would have put it on the wife's car, could have caught her cheating on me a year earlier, the bitch." Sam asked, "How long ago was that?" Charlie said, "Three years." Mark asked, "So have you forgiven her?" Charlie growled one word, "Never." Jane said, "Okay then, how far?" Mark said, "We get off the highway, a couple of miles, then up to the top."

Sue said, "We have to stop and get a state park sticker." Sam asked, "How much is that?" Sue said, "Well that depends. Do you want a daily or a yearly? It is eight dollars a day or twenty-eight for the year." Sam said, "Let's get the year. I have a feeling we will be in a few state parks." Mark pulled up to the window at the entrance to the park. He said, "We need a yearly sticker." Jane said loudly, "How was the bluegrass last night?" The ranger said as he handed Mark the sticker, "There was seventy-three cars. They said it was good. Have a good time up there, and remember, don't leave a mess." Jane said, "They have concerts in the clouds, that's what they call it."

They climbed up the hill slowly, up to the parking lot. Charlie said we have maybe an hour of sunlight." Sam said, "What a nice place to catch a sunset." They got out of the van and went to the observation tower. It was a big wooden thing, sixty foot tall. When they got to the top, there was the marker. Sam said, "Well, this is what we are looking for. Find a keyhole and we do a countdown."

They all got their keys into it. Sam started counting ten, nine, all the way to one, then they all turned their key. A door opened at the top, five bundles of hundred-dollar bills were inside." Jane squealed, "Cash, I love cash." Sue said, "There is supposed to be a clue in here." Sam handed out the bundles of cash and said, "Here it is, the next clue. One word, Jonah " Sue said, "Jonah, what the hell does that mean?" Jane said, "There are a few Jonahs, nothing out of the ordinary." Sam said, "Let's find a hotel. We will sleep on it."

Meanwhile, at the Intel's hotel, they met in Scott and Jeremy's room. They were watching the internet. Gloria and Sara came in and they were waiting for Richard. On the computer screen, three nuns were talking in a car. One screamed as a semi crossed the centerline and hit the car head-on. They floated above the smoking wreckage. One said to the other, "I think we are dead." The third one said sarcastically, "Ya think? Let's just head for the light and see if we can get into heaven." One of the nuns asked, "What light?" The first nun said, "Come on, sister," and she floated skyward toward a light.

They got to the pearly gates and St. Peter met them there. The first nun asked, "You must be St. Peter." The man said, "Well yes, I am. Don't mind the other angels, they are in training. For some reason, nobody likes this job. Well, let's get started. As you can see, sister here has a pure soul, as do the other two. Now, sister, I am going to ask you a question. Get it right and you will enter heaven." The sister said, "I didn't think there was going to be a test." St. Peter said, "Now don't let them talk too much. Sister, who was the first man on earth?" The sister said, "That's an easy one, Adam." A bell rang, lights flashed, and the gate opened and she stepped through. St. Peter said, "Next. Your question is who the first woman on earth was." The nun said, "That is an easy one, Eve was the first woman." A bell rang, lights flashed, and the gate opened and she walked through. St. Peter said, "Next. Your question is what was the first thing Eve said to Adam." The nun thought and thought then said, "Boy, that is a hard one." A bell rang, lights flashed, and she walked through the gate.

Scott looked at the women and asked, "Did you get it? She was talking about his penis." Gloria rolled her eyes and said, "Yes, I got it. Richard is here. Let's discuss this next clue, Polish rock." Jeremy said, "There are a few Polish rock bands in the area and polka bands, but we think it is something else if you take a look at the different kinds of rock in the area." Richard said, "It is Granite Peak Ski Resort. The granite is the rock and the ski is what is on the end of most Polish names." Sara said, "It opens at ten. There is a parking lot on the top with a sixty-foot observation tower. I hope the clue is there." Richard said, "Scott, you are the captain." Scott said, "We meet down at the front door at nine. Have your luggage and be checked out."

Now the first team, Odin, met in the hotel bar. Jack, Joe, and Robert were there waiting for Dawn and Cherry. Robert went to the bar to get drinks. When he went to pay the bartender, the bartender said, "Hey, why don't I do this? If you can go over to that guy with the beer and the pitcher, if you can make him laugh, drinks are on the house. His name is Jim." Robert asked, "The guy in the tie? Sure, why not." The bartender said, "Has hit a rough patch. Wife threw him out. He lost his house, his kids; the bitch ripped his heart right out of his chest. He has drunk a pitcher every night for the last three weeks and never says a word to anyone."

Robert walked up to the man's table and said, "You're Jim, right? Boy, you are a big guy. Hey, I bet I have a bigger dick than you." The guy smiled and chuckled. He lifted his beer and gave a salute to the bartender and said, "Nice try, but I don't think so. My nickname in school was HD. That stood for Horse Dick."

Robert turned and walked back to the bar. He said, "Did you see that? It wasn't a big laugh, he smiled." The bartender said, "Okay, they are on the house. If you could get him mad, I will buy the next round." Robert took the drinks to the table then went over to Jim's table and said, "I think I know you. Do you know why I am getting fat? Every time I fuck your mother she makes me a sandwich." Jim didn't even move, his hand was wrapped around the beer glass. He rolled his eyes up to meet Robert's. Robert said, "She liked it up the ass, just like your old man. Picture it, me slamming your mother as she did dishes in your kitchen." Jim raised his glass, took a big drink, and said, "You are one sick man. Now leave me alone." Robert shrugged and said, "Hey, dude, snap out of it. You have to get on with your life. There are more fish in the sea." Jim just stared at him as he took another drink.

Cherry came down to the bar and walked over to the team. Robert said, "Come with me." Cherry followed him to Jim's table. Robert said, "This man needs to get laid. His wife kicked him out of the house and he lost his kids, his house. His whole life is in the crapper. What do you say? Would you throw him one?" Cherry asked, "Are you fucking crazy? Sorry, it's not you, but it is something I just don't do." Robert said, "This is Jim. There, you're not strangers. And you said you needed to get laid. Just talk to the man." Cherry said, "Okay, I can talk to him. He is cute." Jim asked, "Don't I have a say in this?" Cherry said, "I like his voice. We are going upstairs and will be down in a half hour. If not, come and get me."

Cherry took Jim upstairs to her hotel room. Jim said, "I am not ready for a relationship. My wife will come back." Cherry said, "Sit, let's just talk." Jim said, "This has been hell. She left me because she said she needed a change and she doesn't love me anymore." Cherry rubbed his neck and into his hairline, massaging his head. She pulled his head into her cleavage, then started to rub down his shoulders to his chest and said, "Let's do it. I want your cock in me."

She pulled off his tie and unbuttoned his shirt. Jim stood and said, "I don't know if this is a good idea." Cherry unsnapped her bra, slid out of her shirt, and planted a huge kiss on him, rubbing her breasts on his bare chest. She reached down and took hold of his bulge in his jeans and said, "Someone is getting excited." Jim said, "It has been such a long time." He unbuttoned her pants and slid his hands down her pants, cupping her butt cheeks. She kissed him down the neck, down the front of his chest, and she unbuttoned his pants and dropped them to the floor. She reached inside his underwear and took hold of his penis and pulled down his underwear to his ankles with the other hand. She looked up at him with his dick in her hand, then took a lick. Jim sighed, "Oh my god." His dick throbbed. She put both hands on it and just could get the head in her mouth. Jim's hands went to her head.

She stood naked and kissed him full on the mouth, driving her tongue passionately into his. She turned him and pushed him onto the bed. Jim said, "Oh my god, you are so beautiful." Cherry said, "I am going to ride your ass like it has never been rode before." She climbed up on his belly and started too slide down. He grabbed her gently by the waist and pulled her up. She grabbed onto the headboard as she sat on his face. Soon she felt the waves of an orgasm running up her thighs as she came. She slid back down and grabbed onto his rock-hard member and slowly lowered herself on it. Jim moaned. Cherry said, "It is so big. Oh, I am cumming again. Holy shit, man." She started to ride him like a horse, rocking back and forth, faster and faster. Jim croaked, "I am cumming, oh my god."

Cherry slowed and enjoyed the feeling. Her eyes rolled back as she rode him. They both took a shower. Jim couldn't keep his hands off of her. He kissed every part of her body. He thanked her a dozen times. Cherry said, "I have to get downstairs or they will be up here." Jim said, "I will be down in a few minutes. I have some calls to make." Cherry went down and sat at the table. Everyone looked at her. She blushed. Dawn asked, "So, did he have a big dick? I heard he did." Cherry said, "It was huge." Joe said, "So you did do him, a guy you don't even know, and you won't do me." Cherry said, "Damn straight. He is a very nice guy. His wife really hurt him."

Jim walked over to the table, hair combed, wearing a different tie, smelling of cologne. He asked, "Do you mind if I talked to Cherry?" Dawn stood and said, "Yes, I do mind. Robert, order me a ribeye and baked potato. I will be back before it is here." She grabbed Jim by the tie and dragged him toward the elevator. He looked back at Cherry, who threw him a kiss. Jim asked, "What the hell is going on?" Dawn said, "I hear you have a big dick and I want to find out if it is true. And you need a good fucking." Jim said, "I have just had the best sex I have ever had. Cherry is such a lovely girl." Dawn said, "Yeah, yeah." She reached down between his legs and slid her hand up his thigh. Jim said, "Really." Dawn said, "Oh yeah, we are going to do it, and you are going to like it."

As soon as they were in the room, Dawn stripped slowly, showing off to Jim. She rubbed her pussy and grabbed onto his hand and put it between her legs. She said, "I am going to rock your world," and started to undress him. She said, "We will use this tie later, big boy." Jim rubbed her, sliding two fingers inside her. She pushed against his hand and arched her back. She whispered, "Oh yeah, boy, I can't wait to have that big dick up my ass." She bit his ear and sucked his neck as she pushed his hand harder between her legs. Jim said, "Don't leave marks." Dawn said, "Shut up and take it like a man." She dropped down and slid a condom on him and jumped into his arms, sliding onto his huge member. She yelled at him, "Now fuck me, slam me against the wall. Don't be a pussy." Jim said as she was humping him, "You want . . ." She grabbed him by the back of the hair and pulled his head back, and said forcefully, "Don't talk. Do as I say, you fucking girly man."

Jim stepped to the wall, leaned her against it, and started to pound away. You could see the veins in his neck. His body was tight as he slammed her against the wall. She bit into his neck. He let out a howl and said, "I am going to cum." She grabbed him by the shoulders and lifted herself off of him and slapped him across the face. She put her finger in his face and said, "I told you not to speak." He asked, "Why did you stop?" Dawn took three quick steps over to the TV and grabbed the remote that was taped to a one-inch board. She grabbed it and said, "That's it, over my knee. I told you if I want you to speak I will tell you." She bent him over and started to spank him, and I mean wailed on his ass. He grabbed the remote and threw it toward the wall, sticking it in the drywall. He picked up Dawn and slammed her down on the bed and mounted her. Dawn grabbed onto his neck and started to choke him. He asked, "Do you want me to stop?" Dawn wrapped her legs around him and squeezed and moaned, "No talking." She let go of his neck and slapped him across the face. Jim cried out, "Jesus Christ." He started to take longer strokes, slamming her head against the headboard. Dawn said, "That's it, you fuck pussy. How could you let your wife steal your kids? Be a man. I want you to act like a man." She arched her back, enjoying the sex. She dug her fingernails into his back and scraped them down to his waist. He cried out, "Fuck, I am cumming. This time you're not stopping me." He held her down and picked up speed, then shuddered as he blew his wad. He collapsed on her.

Dawn said, "That was a good one." Jim rolled over and asked, "Can I talk yet?" Dawn got up and said, "No, I will be right back." She walked into the bathroom and took a bottle of baby oil and ripped the shower curtain right off the rod, curtain rings flew everywhere. Jim got off the bed when he heard the noise. Dawn said as she threw the curtain at him, "Tuck this under the mattress and be quick about it. I already ordered my lunch." Jim opened his mouth then shut it and did what he was told. Dawn unscrewed the baby oil. She got on the curtain that was on the bed and poured the oil on herself. She said, "Get your ass over here and grab another condom." Jim climbed on the curtain and slid right up to her. Dawn rubbed oil on him and started to hump his leg and she asked, "So you want to fuck me?" Jim nodded, rubbed her breasts. His manhood was fully erect. She rolled him over on his back and rubbed the oil all over him and slid her body up and down his with ease. She then slapped him hard across the face and said, "What kind of pussy are you to let your wife steal your house, your kids, and your life?" She grabbed onto his cock and slid it inside her, then dropped all her weight, taking the whole thing right to the balls. She started to ride him hard; she moaned hard. Jim reached up to touch her. She slapped his hands away. He said, "Jesus Christ, you're going to break it off. Oh, here I cum." Dawn thrust four fingers up his ass. He let out a primordial yell. She rode him slow with him deep inside her, feeling his rock-hard cock throb as he came. Then she flopped down on his chest, sliding her body onto his in the oil until he went soft.

She lay there for a minute then quickly rolled off and said, "Well, that was fun. My meal should be there by now." Jim was breathing deep, his hand on his chest. He said, "My god, that was amazing." Dawn gave him a good slap on the inner thigh. She shook her hand from the sting as she said, "So, pussy, are you going to just roll over and let your ex-wife screw you? Because if you like it that way, I can get a strap-on. Hey, are you okay?" Jim said, "I actually thought I was going to have a heart attack. My heart will not stop racing." Dawn said, "I am going to hit the shower quick, see if I can get some of that shit out of my hair." She walked to the bathroom. Her body just shimmered from the oil. She looked over her shoulder to see him watching her. He said, "Can I help?" Dawn said, "What the hell? Do you have to ask? Do you want to wash me? If so, do it. You don't have to ask. Act like a man."

Dawn got down to the bar. The team was already eating. Cherry said, "You're late. We went up to get you, but we heard you had everything under control." Joe said, "Wow, and I do mean wow. If you ever want to go around, I am willing." Cherry said, "You were growing wood. All three of these guys had a little tent growing in their pants." Robert said, "Well, we have been discussing the clue." Cherry said, "He had a big cock, didn't he? And such a sweet guy." Joe said, "You have red marks on your neck. They look like they could be turning purple. And a lump on your forehead. Your arms are bruised. What the fuck did that asshole do to you?" Dawn said, "That was a good one, and his dick was too big to take up the ass. It was a nice size, two or three inches bigger than normal." Robert said, "Let's get down to business, discuss the Polish Rock clue." Cherry said, "We have to get up early tomorrow. The park opens at ten in

Wausau." Robert asked, "Shouldn't I be told what is going on? I am the team captain." Dawn said, "The clue, Polish rock, is Granite Peak ski hill. It is a state park, we might be able to sneak in early." Jack asked, "Are you sure? I would hate to lose time. What does a Polish rock have to do with a ski hill?" Cherry said, "Granite is the state rock, and Polish names like Adamski, Kowalski . . .

see how it fits?" Dawn said, "The park opens at ten, so we need to be there at ten." Robert said, "We can't be last. We need the money. Get some sleep. It is an hour's drive in the morning."

A waitress can up and set down a champagne bucket. Joe said, "We didn't order anything." The bartender stepped up with a bottle wrapped in a cloth. He said, "This is a 2004 Dom Pérignon, the best we have in the house." He started to uncork the bottle. When he saw Jim walking up he said, "What the hell happened to you? I have never seen you without a tie." Jim was wearing a white tee shirt and shorts. He walked up to the table and said to Cherry, "Thank you so very much. Here is my card. After you finish your game, I want you to come and see me or I will come to you." She asked, "What the hell happened to you?" Robert said, "There is something different about him. The eyes they are colder, the way he sets his jaw . . ." Dawn said, "Hi, lover. That was a good time." Jim said, "Dawn, you are an animal, I can't thank you enough." Dawn said, "Don't thank me. Didn't you learn anything?" Jim said, "Other than sex was great, I never thought it could be like that." Cherry said, "Are you okay? You are walking funny." He winced and said, "Oh, my ass." Dawn said, "I might have spanked him a little hard." Jim said, "Spanked? You almost shoved your hand up my ass." Dawn asked, "Did you like? It got you were you wanted to go, didn't it?" Jim said, "Okay, that was the best orgasm I ever had, thought I was going to have to call the EMTs." Cherry said, "My god, you are bleeding." Jim asked, "Really? Where?" Robert said, "Someone raked your back. Blood is coming through your shirt. You have a bite mark on your leg, a couple on your neck, a lump on your forehead. Looks like someone tried to choke you." Dawn said, "Good times. Hey, thanks for the champagne. This is some good shit."

The bartender said, "Oh no, here comes your wife." Jim looked at Cherry and said, "Really, I want you to be part of my life." He turned and took a few steps closer to his oncoming wife. She screamed, "What the hell is wrong with you?" Jim shrugged. She said, "You turned off my phone." Jim said, "Quiet down now. I thought you would be pissed at me putting a hold on all your credit cards. I paid everything up to the day you kicked me out. You owe me the rest, by the way. You should have been served. You can't be within a thousand feet of me." She stepped up and slapped him hard. Dawn was out of her seat, screaming, "You can't do that, get away from him." Jim grabbed her as Dawn was on the attack. He said, "Don't do it, she'll kick your ass." His wife said "Is this a whore you have been sleeping with? Let her go, I will kick her ass." Jim said, "No, she will kick your ass. I would walk away."

Cherry came up and stepped right up to Jim's wife and said, "She fucked him and I made sweet love to him, you fucking bitch. You don't deserve a man like that." Dawn looked up to Jim and said, "Now she is in for it." Jim said, "Cherry, don't. She is twice your size." Jim's wife took a swing, Cherry blocked it and stepped in, hitting her right in the tit, three quick blows to the gut. She jumped back and did a roundhouse kick to the head. She hopped back with her fists up, doing a boxer's dance, yelling, "Get up." A cop walked up and said, "Don't do it. I will Taser your ass, Mary Linstrome." He held out an envelope and said, "You have been served. Your children have been put in their aunt Jackie's protection, court order." Jim said, "By the way, you did sign a prenuptial agreement. I owned the house before we were married, and did own the business. I shall not take this lying down. Talk to my lawyer." The cop said, "I need a copy of that fight. Mary did swing first. Do you want to file charges?" Jim took Cherry in his arms, hugged her, and asked, "Where did you learn to fight?" Cherry said, "College. I did a bit of kickboxing. So that was your wife, hey?" Jim said, "Ex-wife, so there is an opening." Cherry said, "We can talk about that later." Robert said, "Okay, guys, this is the game plan. Six tomorrow down here for breakfast. Be packed and ready to roll."

CHAPTER FOUR

Team Three Has the Lead

Team Three figured out what *Johan* meant. Mark said excitedly, "Yes, we have a heading. You just have to word it right. Jonah was in the Bible. He was swallowed by a whale. Freshwater Hall of Fame in Hayward has a big fish and you can stand in the fish's mouth." Jane looked at her phone and said, "It's a giant musky." Mark said, "That would be three and a half hours, 150 miles. Sam said, "It's wind-down time. Pack tonight. We leave at sunrise. We will stop and catch breakfast on the way." Sue said, "Sunrise, that really helps." Sam said, "Okay, we leave at four thirty, so we should be there by ten." He looked at Mark. Mark gave him a small nod. They all headed to their rooms. Next thing you knew the front desk was sending out their wakeup calls at four in the morning.

Everyone met down at the front door. Mark had the van sitting there idling. Jane said, "Now what the hell would happen if someone stole the van?" Sam held up a set of keys and said, "It is locked. I have the spare set. And here comes Charlie. I guess I am buying breakfast." Mark smiled and said, "He bet Sue was going to be the last down." Sue shot him a dirty look. Mark said, "I filled the van last night. We are going to stop for breakfast at six, so that should be the halfway mark." Charlie said, "If the other teams wait for the park to open, we will be there before they even get the clue." Jane said, "I bet Odin wakes early and jogs up the hill." They all piled into the van and headed north to Hayward. Sam, who was studying the map, said,

"We could stop in Winter. It's probably a cool place." Mark said, "That's lame. It's big country up there. I have a feeling we are going to do a lot of hiking." Charlie muttered, "That's great."

Meanwhile, back in Wausau, Team Odin drove to the gate of the park and jogged up the hill to the observation tower and was the second one to get the payday. They each got twenty-five hundred dollars and they received the same clue. Cherry said, "Jonah, what the hell does that mean?" Robert said, "Well, we can think about it on the way to the van. The most famous Jonah is the one in the Bible." Dawn was running and looking at her phone. She said, "There is an aquarium named Jonah, not a lot of things." Joe said, "We will look at it at breakfast." They jogged downhill to the van, then back to the hotel, showered, and had breakfast. Cherry said, "Google Fishing Hall of Fame, Hayward, Wisconsin." Dawn said, "That's it. That musky is as big as a whale." Jack said, "And you can walk in it. I think you are right." Robert said, "Okay, we will have to plan a route. Let's go up and pack. Can we be out of here within a half hour? We should be on the road by nine."

The Intels waited for the park to open and drove up to the observation tower. Scott said, "Let's fan out, check the ski lift. Richard, you go up the tower. I will take a hundred-yard circle. Sara, you check the buildings. Anyone finds anything, call." Richard quickly went up the tower and called the crew to open the marker. Gloria took the cash and handed out the small bundles of ten one-hundred-dollar bills. She read the clue. "It says *Jonah*. That would be the big musky in Hayward, right?" Richard said, "I was there a couple of years ago. I don't remember any question marks. They must have just placed them there."

Team Three arrived in Hayward. They drove through the city and went to the Freshwater Hall of Fame. They walked through the place, went up into the musky, stood looking out its mouth. Jane asked Charlie, "Would you run down and take a picture of Sue and me?" She handed him her phone. Mark talked with Sam and said, "What do you think? Did we go to the wrong spot?" Sam said, "We will just have to walk through every foot of this place and search. The question mark could be any size." The girls posed for their picture in the mouth of the musky. Sam said, "Okay, let's go down. Look in every corner, under and above everything."

They went down and looked through the whole museum, looking in the outboard motors. Charlie came in and said, "Found it. The clue is 165 foot." Sam said, "Great, what the hell is 165 foot?" Jane said, "It's time for a burger and a beer." Mark said, "We can't sit still. If we get stuck on one of these clues, they are going to catch us." Sue asked Charlie, "Where did you find the clue?" Charlie said, "Follow me." He led them to a large fiberglass sunfish. This thing had to be sixteen feet tall, twenty feet long. He said, "If you stand over by the trout, you will just see the question mark in its mouth. I dragged the garbage can over and stood on it." Sam jogged over to the trout and gave the thumbs-up sign. Charlie asked, "Does this help? It was in a mouth."

Mark said, "One hundred and sixty-five foot . . . the musky is only forty-five feet." Jane asked, "How about a tree?" Mark said, "The tallest white pine was 167 feet, that could be it." Sam said, "Let's go and grab a burger." They went to a restaurant, ordered, and Mark asked the waitress, "What is 165 feet?" She looked at him and said, "The Big Manitou Falls is 165 feet tall, the tallest waterfalls in the state." Mark said, "Really? How far is that?" She said, "It's around an hour." Jane said, "From Hayward, California, it's 2,052 miles and will take thirty-one hours to get there. Here we go, it's sixty-five miles."

They finished breakfast and headed toward the waterfalls. In a little more than an hour they pulled into Patterson State Park. There was a huge parking lot. Charlie said, "Hell, it's going to be a hike just to get to the falls."

They got out of the van and hiked through a tunnel under the road. The trail was a half mile long or so. They took the overlook trail. Charlie was complaining it was all uphill. When they got to the overlook, Jane said, "Look on the other side, under that bush halfway up. There is something light green; it could be a pop can." Mark pulled out a small pair of binoculars and said, "Nope, you're right. It is our question mark stuffed into a crack in the wall." Jane said, "Okay, we only need one person to get up there." Sam said, "Or down. There is a trail above it." Jane said, "That would be safer. Did you bring rope?" Sam said, "I have fifty feet. There is more in the van." Jane asked, "Are you going to pay my fine if we get caught?" Mark said, "Sure, we will." Sam said, "Let's get going. Time is ticking."

They crossed the pedestrian bridge and went up the other side to a viewing platform. Sue asked, "How the hells are we supposed to know if we are right above it?" Mark said, "Give me five minutes." He took off at a light jog down the trail. They saw him run across the bridge, then Sam got a call. Sam said, "I have a half a bar, the reception up here sucks." Mark said, "Move farther downstream. Keep going. Okay, you are right above it. Wait a couple of minutes, there are people coming." Jane tied the rope around her, just under her arms, and started her way down the rock face. Sam slowly gave her slack. She went down quickly and she slipped once, almost pulled Sam off his balance. Charlie took the end of the rope. Jane reached the clue and put her key into the slot, turned it, and took the clue. She then climbed back up again. When she got to the top she said, "Thank you. If I didn't have the rope, I would have gone swimming."

Sam asked, "Okay, what is the clue?" Jane took the clue out of her bra and read it. "Sea caves, that's it." Mark said, "Apostle Islands, always wanted to do it." Sam asked, "Do what?" Mark said, "Do the sea caves with kayaks. I seen it in a magazine. They also do them in the winter, there are called ice caves. People from all over go to see them." Sue asked, "How many islands are there?" Charlie was looking at his phone and stepped off the path, slid down the hill a few feet, and screamed.

Sam quickly went down the hill to find Charlie lying down the hill with his leg stuck in a hole in the rocks, his pants leg was covered with blood. He yelled, "Ah shit, I need some help down here. Charlie, we are going to get you out of here." He worked his way down to Charlie and wrapped his belt around Charlie's leg. He said, "You're bleeding, I don't know how bad. We will get you out of here and take a look." Charlie passed right hunt. Sam said, "Dammit, I need the rope." Mark asked when he got to him, "So what do we have here?" Sam shouted, "What the fuck does it look like? He broke his leg." Mark said, "Well, it looks like he snapped that sucker right off." Jane was right behind him with the rope. She said, "Oh my god, I am going to be sick." Sam said, "We don't have time for this. Mark, get your ass down here and help me lift him. Jane, you pull his leg out of that hole. We get him turned around and drag him up to the trail." Sue said, "What should I do?" Sam said, "Run and get a ranger. We need a cart or something, get an ambulance." Sue jogged quickly back to the ranger station.

Sam and Mark lifted Charlie. Sam asked, "Why couldn't this be you?" Mark said, "What?" Sam chuckled and said, "You're damn near a hundred pounds lighter." Jane said, "Would you guys shut up and lift him higher? There, his foot is out. The bone is sticking through his jeans." Mark said, "That is just gross." Sam said, "We have to turn him and point him uphill, turn him on his back. This is going to be a pain in the ass." Mark said, "Dead weight. Let's get that rope tied around him then Jane take it up and wrap it twice around that small tree, just keep it taut. We will drag him up. You just keep him from sliding backward."

The two men worked together to get Charlie up to the trail. Sue came riding up with a six-wheel all-terrain vehicle with a ranger driving and one in the back. The guy who was riding in the back ran over to Charlie and took a look at Charlie's leg and yelled to the driver, "Tom, cancel that ambulance. Call for a chopper. This is a bad one." Sam looked at Jane and said, "Shit." She said, "Oh, he will live." Mark said, "That's not it. We need to find a replacement. We can't open a marker without him." Sue went over and knelt by Charlie and said, "You will be alright. We will leave your luggage with you." Sam leaned over and said, "Could you grab the key?" Sue opened her hand and showed him the key. He said, "Okay, let's get him to the helicopter pad. Mark, get his luggage." The ranger said, "You're going to help us get him on the gurney then lift him onto the ATV." Sam said, "Yes, sir. Tell us what to do." The ranger said, "Roll him to his side." Sam and Mark rolled him to his side.

Charlie started to wake. He started to moan and said, "Damn that hurt. What is going on?" Sue said, "Nothing to worry about, you broke your leg, we are taking you to a hospital." The ranger started to strap him to the gurney; he put soft blocks on both sides of his head and strapped him to the board. The four men lifted Charlie and slid him on the back of the six-wheeler." Sam said, "We need you to take his luggage." The ranger asked, "Really, you're worried about that?" Mark held out a fifty. The ranger took it and said, "We will meet you next to the parking lot." Sam said, "Bring my backpack." He took off at a full run down the path. Jane said, "I have never kayaked before." Sue said, "What, you're thinking of the game? Charlie could have died. If his leg didn't get caught, he would have dropped thirty feet." Mark said, "Now, you stop to look at your phone from now on." Jane said, "How are we going to replace him?" Mark said, "Well, we only need him to open the markers." Sue said, "Would you look at that. Sam made it to the landing site before the rangers got there." Jane said, "I hear the chopper." Mark said, "We might as well meet Sam at the van." Jane said, "Don't you think we should at least say goodbye to Charlie?" Mark said, "Why? He is in good hands. Besides, Sam is almost to the van."

They got to the van and Sam said, "There are twelve large islands, twenty-one altogether, almost seventy thousand acres, and the key could be in any." Sue said, "If it is in any, it could be close to the sea caves. These are very vague clues." Mark said, "It's almost a two-hour drive; we can stay at a casino, the Red Cliff." The chopper landed. Sam said, "Goodbye, Charlie, hope you make it." Jane said, "He lost a lot of blood." Sam said, "Dammit all to hell, I lost my belt."

Mark pulled out of the parking lot, heading for Lake Superior. A call came to the van. Mark pushed the button on the steering wheel and said cautiously, "Hello." Lance said, "Hello, Team Three. We see you had a bit of an accident." Mark said, "Oh that. Yes, we did." Lance said, "Tell me who was it and what happened." Mark said, "It was Charlie. He wasn't watching where he was walking and slid down the rocks and snapped his leg." Sam said, "It was a compound fracture; he lost a lot of blood." Jane asked, "So how do we get another player?" Lance said, "First of all, I have to congratulate your team for being in the lead. You have to find someone to take his place. Now, Charlie is going to live, is he not?" Sam said, "I would think so. Like I said, he lost a lot of blood. They might have to take his leg, but he should live." Sue asked, "Do you think so?" Lance said, "I will monitor the situation from my end. Good luck. By the way, you wouldn't have video or pictures?" Jane said, "What, really?" Sam said, "I took a couple of pictures. Would you like me to send them to you?" Lance gave him his number and Sam sent him the pictures of Charlie stuck in the hole with his bone sticking out of his pants leg. Mark said, "Okay, I ended the call. So they are watching us." Sam said, "They are betting on us. Whoever had Charlie to be the first injured made money."

Team Odin made it to the Freshwater Hall of Fame. They were looking all over. Intel pulled up and parked right next to them. Scott, the team captain, said, "Okay, we go in, spread out. They might not see us." Jeremy said as he pointed to the musky, "They can see the van from there. Let's get inside and keep an eye on them. This is just a clue. If they find it, we want to see." Gloria said, "I have to pee. That's my first stop." Richard said, "Check for that question mark in the ladies room." Scott said, "Good idea. I am going to keep an eye on Team Odin. This is only a four-acre park, it shouldn't be that hard." Richard said, "Okay, I am going in the fish. The two of you spread out and check the grounds. Sara, you come with me and act like you're my girlfriend."

They got inside the grounds. Jeremy said to Scott, "I thought you were the captain." Scott smiled and said, "Does it matter? Let's spread out. This clue must be hidden. If it wasn't, Team Odin wouldn't still be here." Gloria caught up to Scott and asked, "How is it going? We are being watched you know." Scott said, "I figured that." Gloria pointed to the fish's mouth and said, "Cherry from Team Odin, she hasn't moved since I came out of the restroom." Scott answered his phone. He said, "Great, we will be right there." Gloria asked, "What's going on?" Scott said, "Let's go over by the trout and talk to Jeremy. He found it."

They walked over to find Jeremy walking around the big blue-gill. He pretended he had it on a pole. He handed Scott his phone and said, "Take my picture from over by the trout." Scott walked up the path and stood by the trout and took his picture. He came down and handed Jeremy his phone. Jeremy said, "Told you so. Here, let me enlarge the fish's mouth. There you go. That is not a lure in its mouth, it is a question mark." Scott said, "No shit, good job." Gloria said, "Let's go inside. I want to go in and stand at the fish's mouth." Scott asked, "You want me to take your picture?" Gloria said, "That would be great." She and Jeremy went into the fish. Five minutes later, the team was standing in the fish's mouth. He took the picture. They all stood there and waved. He waved them down. When they got together, Richard said, "How are we going to do this? They are going to see." Scott said, "Richard, you take Sara over to the bluegill. You wait for the right time, lift her up, she gets the clue. Jeremy, you and Gloria go the other way, make a small distraction. I am going to distract Cherry. I will give you the signal." They all walked in different directions.

Cherry pulled out her phone and was talking when Scott got up there. He tapped her on the shoulder and introduced himself. "Hi, I am Scott from Team Two, the Intels." As soon as she turned, Scott raised his arm. Richard lifted Sara. She put the key in the question mark and waited a couple of seconds for the clue. Cherry turned quickly and saw Richard lowering her to the ground. She shot Scott an "I could kill you" look. Scott smiled and said, "The game is a-foot." He turned and ran down the stairs, then jogged to the parking lot.

He got into the van and said, "They will be right behind us. She seen you lowering Sara." Jeremy said, "We solved the clue. It was an easy one, 165 foot and Google says it is Big Manitou falls, it is a state park and is a hour away. They got there in just over a hour and Gloria asked the park ranger "Have you a Question mark." The ranger asked "are you on a treasure hunt." Gloria said "well yes We are." The Ranger said "Yesterday a team was here, boy was that something a guy broke his leg we had to airlift him to the emergency room, oh yes there is a question mark half way up the hill, it holds a clue of some kind." The team headed out towards the waterfalls. Randy said as he pointed "up there see where all the leaves are moved under the trail, a light green thing it must be the clue." Gloria said "ok lets take the low trail, and climb up to it." They walked through the tunnel under the highway to the trail along the river. Gloria asked a couple of young guys, "hey you want to make fifty bucks." The two walked up and said "what do we have to do." Gloria pulled out her key and said "see that green thing up in the rocks, put this key in it and get the clue." One kid said "sure we will be right back, the two ran up the hill to the rocks and started to climb." Team Odin pulled into the parking lot and started to jog down the trail, Joe said "look there are the Intels, and two guys rock climbing, they got to the clue." Cherry said "well we are not far behind." The two boys came down and said The clue is sea caves, That would be up on Lake Superior." Scott said, "There is no sea around here." Gloria said, "The Apostle Islands. There are twenty-one islands, twelve of which are large. That is why they are called the Apostles." Team Odin waited until the Intels left, Cherry said "I will be right back, I can free climb this thing in a minute." She headed up the hill to the rocks and up to the clue." When she got down to the trail she said "sea caves." Robert said "ok it looks like we are going kayaking."

Team Three got to the casino. The first thing they did when they got to the hotel was to interview a bunch of kayakers. Sam talked with the cute girl in the bikini. She told them, "There was a question mark in one of the caves on the northeast side of Devil's island. It is like ten miles from shore, so it would be too late to go there today." Mark said, "I will see about rooms. You find a boat, make it a fast one." Sam said, "Ask about a guide." Mark called Sam and said, "The guide is on his way, and we got the last four rooms. Rented two kayaks. I will meet you on the docks."

Their boat guide pulled up with a twenty-three-foot fishing boat. He said loudly as he pulled up to the dock, "Today it is calm enough, but if it is rough, the caves are dangerous. They will crush you to the ceiling. The cave we are going to is not that high, and you have to go in a quite a long ways." Sue said, "I am not the best swimmer in the world." Jane said, "I'm in. This should be fun." Mark came jogging out onto the dock. They handed the boat guide the kayaks. Sam asked, "Have you done this before?" The guide held out his hand and said, "Oh yes. When it gets hot out, the tourists come in. I make better money ferrying around rich folks than I do fishing. Devil's Island is like ten miles out. It is a long paddle."

They got on board. The man held out his hand and said, "Well, I am Luke." Sam said, "This is Jane, Sue, Mark, and I am Sam." Mark held out his hand and, "Shook it." Luke looked in his palm. Mark said, "We are in a bit of a hurry." Luke said, "Well, shove off. We will be on our way." Sam asked, "Do you mind getting paid in cash?" Luke smiled as he shouted, "Hang on." The boat jumped up to a plane and he held the throttle down. Everyone stared at the beauty of the islands, the clear blue water. Luke pointed out the islands and said, "It is a little over twenty miles from here, ten miles from the mainland. We should be there in less than an hour."

When they got to the island, Luke helped slide the kayaks into the water off the swim platform. He asked, "Do you have flashlights?" Mark asked, "Do we need them?" Luke smiled, "Only to see. Here, I have some headlights. Strap them on." Sam asked Mark, "Have you ever paddled one of these before?" Mark said, "No." He smiled and said, "How hard can it be?" Jane said, "Just follow me." She slipped into her kayak and started toward the island. Sue said, "Hurry now. I am hungry and I could use a drink." Mark got into his kayak and said, "Damn, these things are tippy." Luke said, "They are sea kayaks; you should try the racing ones."

Mark started to paddle. After a few yards he started to move, catching up to Jane. She asked, "Would you like to take the lead?" Mark said, "That is all up to you." Mark followed her in the cave. It got narrower, the ceiling slowly dropped. She turned on her light. The boat scraped the sides, she had to duck. Then it opened to a small room. There was the question mark strapped to the side of the cave. Mark asked, "Can you reach it?" She said, "You do it." Mark maneuvered the boat around and said, "This is creeper than shit. Let's get the clue then get out of here. One big wave when you are in the narrows could drown your ass." He took the key from around his neck and stuck it in the hole, turned it, and a slip of paper came out. He read it, "A small gun." Jane said, "A small handgun, like a .38 special." Mark said, "Go, I will be right behind you."

When they got to the narrow section, Mark ran right into Jane's boat. He pushed off the rocks and shoved them right through. They didn't take their time going out. They quickly got to the boat. Sam said, "Okay, I paid for the boat ride. Luke here says this is an all-day excursion if you kayak from the mainland." Jane said, "A small gun, that is what the clue is." They loaded the kayaks. Jane said, "That was beautiful. I would love to come back and take my time and just slowly paddle through it." Mark said, "I would never go that far in that one again." Luke said, "See what I mean. You get some good-size waves. That wouldn't be good." Sam asked, "How is the weather tomorrow?" Luke said, "There should be a little chop, not too bad three- or four-footers." The lake was like glass, they sailed right through. When they got to the hotel, Sam said, "Let's freshen up and then meet down at the restaurant and we will figure out this clue."

Twenty minutes later, Sam met Mark in the bar. They could see who goes into the restaurant from their point of view. A man around forty was sitting in the booth next to them watching the news and having a drink. He overheard them talking about the clue. He watched them for a couple of minutes; both of them had their phones out. He said, "Sorry about eavesdropping, but the word you are looking for is Dillinger. And what that means around here is where he had a shoot-out with the FBI. That was at Little Bohemia. It has to be like fifty to sixty miles away." Mark said, "It's ninety-five miles and about two hours." Sam said, "Hey, it's Wednesday. The place opens at ten." Mark said, "In 1934, the FBI and Dillinger had a shoot-out."

Mark asked the man, "If you don't mind me asking, what brings you up here?" He said, "Just doing a little rest and relaxation, a small vacation kayaking through the sea caves." Mark asked, "Are you up here with your wife?" The man smiled and said, "I am Edward, and no, I am up here by myself. I don't need to be fixed up with some broad. This is a stress-free week." Sam asked, "Well, Ed, do you like games? Because we are in need of a player." Ed held up his glass and caught the waitress' eye. He asked, "What kind of games are you playing?" Sam said, "We are doing a treasure hunt. We need five people on the team. Charlie, the idiot, wasn't watching where he was walking and broke his leg." Ed said, "Well, I flew into Duluth and rented a car." Mark asked, "How far is Duluth?" Ed said, "A couple of hours. What would I get if I played this treasure hunt? There must be a prize for the winner." Jane said over Sam's shoulder, "Each marker is worth ten grand for the first team to get there, second is twenty-five hundred, and third is a grand." Ed said, "Ten grand split five ways." Sam smiled and said, "No, that would be fifty grand split five ways, ten grand apiece." Ed said, "Okay, I am in. How am I getting my car back to Duluth?" Mark said, "Let's eat. Early to bed, early to rise. We leave at four, be there by six, back here by eight, and at Little Bohemia by ten." Susan said, "I thought we were meeting in the restaurant." Jane said, "Okay, I am Jane, this is Sue, Mark, and our team leader is Sam. Sue, this is Edward. He is our new team member."

CHAPTER FIVE

To Dillinger's

At quarter to four in the morning, Ed and Mark met by the front door. Ed said, "I want to transfer some stuff from my car to your van." Mark said, "Sure, whatever. We will catch breakfast after we drop your car." Mark said, "Let me see your cell phone." Ed handed it to him. Mark put his number in it and called his phone. He said, "Just in case we get split up. Ten grand, that's a nice payday."

They walked out to the parking lot to find the two other lime-green vans. Ed said, "We could disable the vans." Mark said, "We LoJacked them, Team Intel, which is short for Intelligentsia—whatever that means—they're a bunch of college-educated guys. The other team is a bunch of jocks. They are called Odin. Our team was the leftovers. We are called Team Three." Ed said, "I am parked up near the hotel. We can drive to your van." Ed pulled up behind the van and asked, "Would you give me a hand?" They lifted a wooden box with rope handles out of his trunk and put it in the back of the van. Mark said, "This is a heavy one. What do you have in here?" Ed said, "I bought a rock collection." He threw his luggage on top, and they were off.

Four hours later Mark had everyone standing in front of the hotel waiting for them. They pulled up, packed the luggage, and were on the road in five minutes. Two hours later they were at Manitowish Waters and pulled into Little Bohemia. Jane said, "This is where Johnny Depp filmed *Public Enemies*." Ed said, "Yeah, I saw that movie. They went around shooting Thompson machineguns. That must have been a fun movie to make." Sam said, "We are looking for a question mark. It could be six inches or six feet. Did anyone give him Charlie's key?" Mark took a lanyard from the glove box. It had dried blood on it. He said, "You might need a new lanyard. Don't lose the key." Jane said, "Charlie's broken leg was a compound fracture, bone stuck right through his pants." Sue asked, "I wonder if he lived."

They went into the restaurant. Sam asked the girl that was there, "Miss, we are looking for a question mark." Mark held out a hundred-dollar bill. She took it and said, "This way. If you would look, we still have the bullet holes from that Sunday, April 22, 1934, at ten o'clock in the morning. The FBI sprayed this place with lead. Now Joe Gillis, also known as Baby Face Nelson, he helped Dillinger escape from prison. He was a shooter. He kidnapped a few people and escaped, later being killed in a shoot-out outside of Chicago."

They followed her through the place, upstairs to a small room. "This is John Dillinger's bedroom and there is your question mark." Sue said, "Ed, since you are new, put your key in it and read the next clue." The girl said, "So that's what it is for." Ed put his key in and a clue came out. He read it and said, "Syphilis." The girl said, "Al Capone, he died of syphilis." Ed said, "I have always wanted to go there." Mark held up a fifty and said, "There are two more teams in this treasure hunt, please don't give them any clues." A sly smile slid across her face as she took the fifty. She said, "Okay, Al Capone's hideout, that is a two-hour drive, just east of Hayward."

Back at the Red Cliff casino, Team One was out in kayaks trying to make it to Devil's Island. They rented boats off the point of Eagle Bay. It still was a ten-mile paddle. All five of them were paddling led by Cherry; she set the pace. Team Two, the Intels, rented a guide to take them to Devil's Island. They talked with the locals and were told where the question mark was. When they got out there, they had a young man hired to go in and get the clue. He brought along dive gear just in case it was too rough to enter the caves. The guide pulled close to the island where the cave entrance was. Scott said, "If it is too dangerous, don't do it." He smiled and said, "The swells are around two feet. It will be tight. If I have to, I can swim. It's only thirty feet or so, then it opens up. It should take ten minutes or so." He climbed down to the swim deck. Jeremy slid the sea kayak down to him. The captain said, "Don't screw around. Get in and out."

The young man quickly paddled into the cave. In less than ten minutes he was out. He paddled to the boat and threw the rope from the kayak up onto the deck. Richard, Scott, and Jeremy pulled the boat aboard and tied it down. The young man came aboard and said, "Your clue is a small gun." He handed the clue to Richard. Richard read it aloud, "Small gun, and it has a two on it. Dammit, they must have got here earlier or last night."

Everyone pulled out their phones and started Googling *small gun*. They got back to the hotel still trying to figure out what the clue meant. When they got to the hotel, Gloria went to the front desk and asked, "Where is there a place that means small gun?" A girl said, "Little Bohemia. John Dillinger had a shoot-out there. Try the Bohemian pavos. It's chicken breast wrapped around shrimp then baked, my favorite." Scott said, "We are checking out. Let's go, we are behind. Dillinger, I wonder what he was doing up here in no man's land." Richard said, "Just think what this place was back in 1934, dirt roads, no electricity, pit toilets, no running water."

Meanwhile, Team Odin was out battling Lake Superior. The swells were getting three feet high and were starting to break. They worked hard just to gain a hundred yards. They got to Raspberry Island then skirted Bear Island. They were checking all the islands, slowly paddling around them looking for the clue. Dawn paddled up to a group of kayakers and asked, "Hey, guys, has anyone seen a question mark? I know it is a weird question but we are looking for one." One man said, "I think it is on Devil's Island. I have not seen it but I was talking to a group at the lodge and they said someone put a question mark way back in a cave, and, Devil's Island is out by itself, a two-mile shot of open water." They got there and found the cave. The wind was in their favor. It wasn't blowing in, so the cave was safe. By the time they got back to the hotel it was getting dark. Team Three was at Al Capone's hideout. It was in the middle of nowhere, on a small lake Capone used to fly Canadian whiskey across the border during Prohibition. He would land in the lake where they had a pump house. They would pump it right out of the plane up to the house. A young girl came out of the place and said, "We are not open right now." Mark held out a hundred-dollar bill and asked, "Can we get a quick tour?" She took the hundred and said, "This is going to be a quick one. Follow me." Sam asked, "You wouldn't have a question mark that was recently added?" She stopped and said, "Now that you say that, they put one in the cell." Sam smiled and said, "That is what we are looking for." She said, "Let's go back by your car. Now, this was all cut off. You could see for miles. The guards would sit in the towers with machine guns whenever Al came to visit. This over here was a cell. They say he brought men from Chicago to talk to and he would lock them up in here."

She opened the door and went inside. Right around the corner was the question mark, fastened to the wall. Ed said, "It sure helps if you ask." Mark smiled and took his key and put it in the slot. Out came the next clue. He read it aloud, "Meteor." Jane asked, "You did say meteor, like a falling star?" Mark spelled it out for her, "That's what I think it says, M-E-T-E-O-R. That's meteor, right?" Sue said, "There is a town called Meteor. It's in Sawyer county, population of 170." Mark said, "Well, let's check it out. It is like twenty miles to the south."

Team Two was on their way to Little Bohemia. They pulled into Manitowish Waters around supper time. They put in their names for a table and went on the tour. Scott asked about the question mark. The girl said, "Well, the other team gave me fifty dollars not to show you." Scott pulled a fifty from his wallet, handed it to her, and asked, "Well, do we have a deal?" She smiled and said, "Right this way please. It is up on the second floor, in the room John Dillinger was staying that night."

They walked in and Scott got the clue. He read it. "Syphilis. Now what the hell does that mean?" Their tour guide smiled and said, "I might know what it means." She held out her hand. Scott pulled out a twenty. She smiled and said as she took it, "Al Capone died of syphilis. He had a hideout in Couderay." Gloria said, "Well, thank you very much. I am hungry. Can we eat now?"

They followed the girl down for a nice sit-down meal. Richard said, "I have booked two rooms at the Pines Resort. It is thirteen miles from Couderay. That's the nearest city to Al Capone's hideout." Sara said, "That is weird. They got him on tax evasion. He was called Al 'Scarface' Capone. He did the Saint Valentine's massacre, one of the first to go to Alcatraz. That's amazing. They shipped him all the way to California and he died at the age of forty-eight in Florida, complications of syphilis, a stroke and pneumonia."

They got to the hotel late that night. They met in Scott and Jeremy's room. They had the TV hooked up to their laptop and were watching three holy men in Africa. They were held at spear point. The chief said to one of them, "Death or bungwana?" The man thought about it and said, "Well, I don't know what bungwana is but it has to be better than death." Two tribesmen grabbed him by the arms and dragged him out to a fallen tree. The chief yelled, "He said bungwana." A line of well-endowed men formed a line. The tribesmen pulled out their manhood and worked on getting their penis hard and the men had their way with him. The chief then asked the second man, "Death or bungwana?" He smiled and said, "Bungwana." The men grabbed him. He said, "Relax," and handed the first eight of them condoms. They looked at him. He said, "You don't know where I have been." They all quickly put on the condoms. The men had their time with him. He whooped and hollered, spanking them on the ass. The chief looked to the sky and rolled his eyes, and then he asked the last one, "Death or bungwana?" The man stood tall and said, "I won't disgrace myself. God is my savior, I do not fear death. I choose death." The chief said, "Death by bungwana." A line formed with tribesmen with huge cocks. The last one in line was pulling a horse. Gloria asked, "What the hell are you guys watching?" Scott said, "Just some internet. Did you see the size of those guys' dicks? My god." Gloria said, "Turn that shit off and let's start the meeting."

CHAPTER SIX

To the Meteor

Team Three stopped at the small town of Meteor. It was more like the crossing of two highways. There was nothing there. Sam said, "I am going up to this house and ask." Mark pulled into the driveway. Sam got out and walked up to the door. A large dog came up behind him as he stood on the porch. Sam knocked on the door, introduced himself, and asked, "You wouldn't know of a question mark around here?" The young man asked, "A what? A question mark, like the one at the end of a sentence?" Sam said, "Yes. We are on a treasure hunt. It could be six inches high or six feet." The young man said, "Nope, no question mark around here." Sam smiled and thanked him, then asked as he bent down to pet the dog, "Does your dog bite?" The young man said, "No, sir."

Sam reached out to the dog and the dog lunged at Sam, grabbing him by the face, knocking him to the ground, biting him in the neck and shoulder, dragging him down the steps. Mark ran from the van to the house. The young man was beating the dog with a broom. The dog started to run away and there was a loud *boom* as Edward squeezed off a shot. The dog folded up and took a roll, lay there kicking in the yard.

Sam rolled over in the yard, blood was oozing through his shirt. He got to his hands and knees. He looked up and his face was full of blood. He said, "I thought you said your dog doesn't bite." The young man said, "That's not my dog." Mark reached down and helped Sam to his feet. Sam said, "Oh my god, I don't feel very well." Jane said, "Get me a wet washcloth and a couple of towels now." She turned and ran back to the van. Edward took Sam by the other arm and said, "We need to get him to a hospital now."

They started to lead him back to the van. The young man came out and handed Jane the washcloth. She took it and stopped the men. She wiped the blood from Sam's face and put a piece of duct tape, holding a large cut together. She said, "We need to get his shirt off and stop the bleeding." They worked on him for a couple of minutes; they slowed the bleeding. Edward and Mark got Sam in the van; Jane put the towels on the seat. Edward ran over and grabbed the dead dog by the leg and dragged it to the van. He yelled, "Somebody hold this bag open for me." Sue stepped to the back and asked, "Why do you want the dog?" She held open a garbage bag and Ed lowered the dog into it. He said, "They need it to check for rabies." Mark yelled, "Where is the nearest hospital?" The young man said, "Hayward, straight up 27. It is like thirty miles." Mark said, "Let's move. Get your seatbelts on."

Everyone got into the van and Mark put the hammer down; the speed limiter kicked in at a hundred and five. Mark said, "Shit, I hate these new cars." Ed said, "Keep it under a hundred." Sue said, "When we get there, pull into the emergency parking. They will meet us with a gurney. You have to drive through town. Highway 27 runs with 77, then take the second Hospital Road, not the first one. It is called Hospital Road, we want Hospital Drive."

Mark slowed down, driving through town. He pulled into the hospital and into the emergency room parking. Sure enough, they met the van. Ed jumped out and opened the door. Sam was still awake and he bitched as they helped him out of the van and got him onto the gurney. Edward said, "We have the dog." He went to the back of the van and took out the garbage bag and carried it to the door.

A half hour later, Jane was questioning the nurse. She asked, "How is he? Will he be able to walk?" Edward held out a hundred-dollar bill and asked, "Would you please go in and see what is wrong with him? And ask the doctor when he will be ready to be released." The nurse took the hundred and said, "I will see what I can do." Five minutes later she came in and said, "He is being sewed up. He has a dislocated shoulder, some of the bites are quite deep, and it will take some time to check the dog for rabies. He isn't going anywhere today." Jane said, "Mark, get his luggage. We leave him here." Ed asked, "All in favor say *aye*." The four of them said, "Aye." Ed said, "Those opposed say *nay*." Nobody said anything. Mark said, "I will get his luggage." He turned and walked down the hall. Sue asked, "Can we see Sam?" The nurse said, "When he is out of x-ray, I will see what I can do."

Mark came in with the luggage and the nurse came out at the same time. Mark said, "This is Sam's luggage. We are going to have to leave him here." The nurse said, "If you will follow me, they have him waiting for a Dr. Kakapoo. He will set the shoulder. He is not to be moving about, and that dog bite to the head punctured the skull."

They filed into the room. Sam's eyes were glassed over. He looked up and chuckled, "It wasn't his dog. I can't believe that son of a bitch bit me." Mark asked, "Do you have your key?" Sue said, "I have it, it is covered in blood." Jane stepped up to him and stroked his cheek and said, "We have to move on. You are in pretty bad condition." Sam smiled and said, "I understand. You guys go." The nurse said, "If you want to say something to him, you better write it down because he isn't going to remember anything."

Sue pulled out a small notebook and wrote, "We are sorry but we have to leave you here. Get better. Give us a call." She zipped it into his luggage. Jane said, "There is nothing we can do here, let's go." Mark said, "The cell service up here sucks." Sue said, "There is an SS *Meteor* museum in Superior." Jane said, "That has to be it, set a course." Mark asked Sue, "Would you plan a route? I have no bars here at all." Sue said, "It is seventy miles. Go west of Hayward a few miles, then north on 53." Ed said, "If you find a hotel on the way, stop. It has been a long day."

Mark pulled into a hotel in a small town; they all agree it would do. Everyone checked in. Mark got a room, Jane and Sue shared one, Ed got his own. They met down at the bar. Ed asked for the keys of the van; he wanted to check out the town. Ed took the van to a service station and made a deal to use their parts washer. He took the wooden crate from the van, put it on a dolly, and went into the garage. He borrowed a crowbar and pried open the box. It had pistols packed in cosmoline. He started to pull back the canvas bag. A mechanic said, "There is a pair of gloves in the washer. What do you have in there?" Ed said, "It is supposed to be twenty-four Colt 1917pistols." The mechanic said, "Nineteen seventeen? I don't think cosmoline was made back then." Ed said, "It was made back in 1911, then reformulated in '14." Ed pried one of the guns out of the goo. He sprayed it, cutting through the heavy grease to show the pistols. They looked brand new. In a half an hour he was done.

He parked in the back and walked to the back door. He noticed a car with a light on in it. There was a young boy watching a movie. You could tell he lived in the car. He tapped on the car window and made a "roll down the window" motion. The kid powered down the window. Ed asked, "You want to make twenty bucks?" The kid's eyes popped open and then he said, "I better not." Ed said, "You don't have to do much. Does your mother work here?" The boy said "Yes, she does. Right now she is waitressing." Ed asked, "Should we go talk to her?" The boy said, "I can't go inside, that will get her in trouble." Ed smiled and said, "You are my guest. By the way, I am Edward. And you are?" The young boy said excitedly, "I am Johnny." Ed said, "Well, Johnny, let's go and find your mom and see it is alright if you help me clean some equipment."

They went into the restaurant. Johnny pointed out his mom. Ed slid in a table that was in her area. She noticed Johnny. She shook her head and rolled her eyes, and she stepped up to the table and asked, "Okay, what did he do this time?" Ed held out a room key and asked, "May I use your son for a couple of hours? I have some parts that need to be cleaned and he could help me." Johnny said, "He is going to pay me twenty bucks." She looked at Ed and said, "It would be faster to do it yourself." Ed smiled and said, "Oh, I know, but this will be a good lesson for him, and I would like the company." She reached out and shook his hand and said, "I am Mary, and I will check on you guys every half hour." Ed said, "Well, Mary, this should be interesting. Has he eaten? Are there any food allergies, anything

I need to know?" She said, "Johnny, you just behave." He said, "Yes, Mom." Ed said, "Well, we have to get to it. This is my cell number," and he handed a card to her. She read it, "Edward Nole, antiques. Is there any money in antiques?" Ed smiled and said, "More than you would think. I am retired, this is just a hobby."

Ed got up and headed for the front door. They grabbed a luggage rack and then headed for the back door. Ed had Johnny ride the cart. As he walked down the hall, he waved to Jane and Sue, who were in the bar.

They went outside and got the crate onto the luggage cart along with six rolls of paper towels and headed to his room. Ed said, "Okay, now don't tell your mother, we are cleaning guns. These are World War I 1917 Colt revolvers. The story is they were stolen off a train on the way to the war; brand new, never fired. They are worth a lot of money." Johnny said, "Cool." He jumped on the bed. Ed took a roll of paper towels and ripped off five sheets and had Johnny watch how he set everything up just so. Then he had Johnny wipe off the gun and hand it to him. Ed disassembled each, shot the trigger mechanism with brake cleaner, then WD-40. He then wiped it down and reassembled it. Johnny watched the first two then got bored. Ed turned on the cartoons.

Mary stopped by. It was about fifteen minutes and saw what they were doing. She said, "Guns, you are letting him play with guns." Johnny said, "Mom they are not loaded." Mary said, "That's what you said last time." Johnny said, "That was an accident, it wasn't my fault." Ed looked over and asked, "What did you do?" Johnny said, "I shot a hole in a police car." Mary said, "I told you not to play with it." Ed said, "Not to worry, I don't have any ammunition here. These are worth at least three grand apiece. Just beautiful guns, he is helping me polish them. I ran them through a parts washer." Mary asked, "How long is this going to take?" Ed said, "I have two queens; he could sleep here till you get off your shift." Johnny said, "You can sleep with me, Mom." Mary said, "Well, they want me to waitress in the bar until one, so I guess that would be fine."

Ed finished cleaning the guns and doing one last inspection; he took Johnny down and put the guns back into the van. They stopped at the bar and ordered hot chocolate and cookies; he was talking to the bartender getting the scoop on Johnny's mom. Ed sent Johnny to go and wash his hands; Ed asked the bartender, "Okay, what is up with Mary living in her car?" The bartender said, "This is the way it went down. She was married to a Bart, he up and left her. His brother runs the bank. He foreclosed on her. He owns this hotel, she can't get enough money to get away from here. Oh crap, here comes the chief of police. He is her ex-husband's brother. He threatens her with taking away Johnny if she doesn't do what he wants." Ed said, "That's not right." The bartender said, "Watch, he will have a burger, then he will take her in back. It's just disgusting."

Ed pulled out his wallet and took out a small guardian angel pin, then took out his phone and linked them together. He walked over to Mary and said, "Miss, you dropped this. Let me put it on you." He whispered, "Camera," and he winked. Johnny was sitting there eating cookies. Edward put an earpiece in and watched the phone as he had his hot chocolate and cookies. He said to Johnny, "Give me a minute, I have to make a call. It's going to be a good one."

The chief took Mary into a closet and he threatened to have Johnny put in a foster home if she didn't go down on him. He dropped his pants and she knelt down in front of him and said, "You know this isn't right. You could get in a lot of trouble for this." He reached down and said as he grabbed onto the back of her head and forced his cock down her throat, "And you're an unfit mother. Do you want to lose Johnny?" He then grabbed her by the hair and had her stand. Then he slid down her panties and lifted up her shirt over her head. He bent her over and he grabbed onto her hips and just slammed away. He said, "You're just a dirty whore, and you will do whatever I say. Do you understand?" She made sure the camera on her uniform was pointing at them.

Ed called the governor and said, "Robert, sorry about getting you up, but we have a problem. Yeah, it's one of your cops. I am going to stream you a video. You are going to call Bernie, the head of the state police, and get some cops here right now or this is going to the news. You got that?" The governor said, "Now what the hell is this about?" Ed said, "You see the video. This is rape, and this is the chief of police." Robert said, "It will be done." Ed walked over to little Johnny and said, "Let's go to the front desk and get you a toothbrush, then it's off to bed with you." They got into the elevator and Ed answered his phone and said, "Come in quiet. Call right before you get here." Ed smiled and said to Johnny, "Get in and brush your teeth, then to bed with you." Johnny fell asleep right away.

Ed slipped downstairs to meet the state police at the front door and brought them in. They walked up to the chief, who was having a cocktail. They read him his rights, put him in handcuffs. Ed stepped over to him and showed him a little bit of the video and said that pin was a camera and a microphone. He said, "My lawyers will be contacting you. Your brother the judge and your other brother, the banker, and the IRS are now involved. This is going to be a shitshow." Mary, who was standing behind him, asked, "Who are you?" A state cop said the same thing, "Who are you? And I do mean let's see some identification." Ed took out his wallet and handed the cop a card. The trooper handed it back and said, "I am sorry, sir. We will take care of this."

Ed said, "Why don't you come upstairs and have a good night's sleep?" She said, "You don't know what you have done. I will never get a job in this county again." Ed smiled and said, "Don't worry, everything will be taken care of, trust me." Mary said, "I am the only one here; I will come up in a couple of hours." In the middle of the night, Mary snuck into bed with Johnny. Ed played like he was sleeping. Six o'clock came. Ed got Johnny and Mary up and said, "Downstairs in ten minutes, in the restaurant."

Mary and Johnny came down to find Ed sitting at a table with Mark, Jane, and Sue. Ed stood and said, "This is the girl I was talking about. She just lost her job and she could use some money." Mark said, "She has a kid." Ed said, "Oh, this is little Johnny. He won't be a problem, I will take care of him." Jane said, "Well, we do need somebody, and I don't give a rat's ass who it is." Sue said, "But the little boy should be in school." Ed said, "You are right. Why aren't you in school?" Johnny said, "Well, the teacher was doing an exercise. You reach in a box and you explain what you felt, like Jim reached in and explained a round ball with dents in it and the class guessed it was a golf ball. And I asked the teacher to guess what I had in my pocket. I said it was round, hard, and had a head on it. I got suspended for a week." Jane said, "Well yeah." Johnny said, "It was a quarter. Boy, you have a dirty mind." Ed said, "And he is funny. Johnny's deadbeat dad up and left. His brother is the chief of police, who was arrested last night. We don't want to get into that. His other brother is a judge and owns this hotel." Ed said, "All in favor of Mary joining the game say *aye*." Everyone said *aye* except Mary. He then said, "Anyone opposed?" Mary asked, "Don't I have a say in this?" Ed said, "You can win a hundred thousand dollars in three weeks." She said, "Oh, I am in. What do I have to do?" Mark asked Ed, "You didn't tell her what the game is? Really?" Ed said, "It is a treasure hunt, ten thousand for first place. So far we are in the lead. There are ten markers or pay-days. Second place is twenty-five hundred and third is a thousand." Ed said, "We have to get going, so you need to pack and store the rest of your stuff." Mary asked, "When are we leaving?" Jane said, "As soon as you get your crap in one bag, we leave." Sue asked, "Have you been to the Meteor, a museum in Superior?" Mary said, "No, I haven't. How much stuff can I bring?" Mark said, "A suitcase. Oh, I guess two, one for the kid."

Ed stood and said, "We leave in a half hour. I will make sure she is ready. Come on, Johnny." Johnny asked, "Why do you need another person to play the game?" Mary stopped and looked at him and said, "That is a great question." Ed said, "There are five keys, they have to be turned all at once." Johnny said, "What happened to the last guy?" Ed said, "He got his face ripped off by a dog; he is in the hospital in Hayward." Mary said, "Oh come on, he didn't get his face ripped off." Ed said, "We are wasting precious time. Do you have luggage?" She said, "Whatever I own is in that car. Let me make a call. I will have Lisa take the car to her place. We are already packed." Ed said, "I have a lawyer working on this. You should get a very nice settlement; that was just so wrong. And by the way, what grade is Johnny in?" Johnny said, "I am in third grade and it sucks." Ed chuckled and said, "You only have nine more to go."

Team Intel got to Al Capone's early; the place was closed. Scott said, "Drive in. All we want is a tour of the place. If we ask, maybe they know where the clue is." Richard pulled into the long drive up to the mansion. They got out and a young girl answered the door. She said, "I take it you would like a tour. You are looking for the question mark, right?" Scott said, "Yes, we are. Would you show us where it is?" She said, "The last team gave me two hundred dollars not to show you." Gloria asked, "How much is it going to cost for you to show us, a hundred? They will never be back to know you showed us." The girl paused. Scott said, "We will match their two hundred." The girl smiled and said, "This way, it is just inside the cell."

She led them across the parking lot to the cell and into it. She said, "It says Meteor. What that means, I haven't a clue. There is a small town not far called Meteor. One team was talking about that." Scott put his key into the question mark and took out the clue. Sara said, "There is a ship in the city of Superior; it is a museum. That has to be it." Richard paid the girl and said, "Thank you very much." They went into the van. Scott asked, "Okay, what do we think?" They all had their phones out. Gloria said, "The ship is called SS *Meteor*; it is the last whaleback design." Scott asked, "Sounds good to me. Let's go."

Team Three was already there waiting for it to open at ten in the morning. Mark said, "Eight bucks, not bad. The clue must be inside." Ed asked, "Who pays?" Jane said, "It comes out of the kitty. They gave us ten grand for supplies. That is what we have been using for fuel and stuff like that." Little Johnny said, "I have to take a piss." Sue said, "That's not a nice way to say that. The word you are look-ing for is *urinate*. Try using *urinate* in a sentence." Johnny thought and said, "You're an eight. If you had bigger tits you would be a ten." Mary rolled her eyes and looked at the sky. Ed clamped his hand over his mouth, and Mark just laughed and said, "Damn, that was a good one kid." Ed looked at him and said, "Don't encourage him." Jane said, "Come on, they are open. Let's go."

They filed in and Ed found a bathroom for Johnny. He said, "That was a good one." They went on the tour through the wheel-house into the cargo hold. Jane said, "It's a marker. Up on the ceiling over there, strapped in the rafters." Mary asked, "How are you going to get up there?" Ed smiled and said, "It is how are *we* going to get up there." Mary's color drained from her face. Mark said, "This is a marker; we must all insert our key and turn it at the same time." Mary said, "Right, like I am going to climb up there." Ed said, "It's a ten-grand payout." Sue said, "Give me a moment. Hey, tour guide, here is two hundred bucks. Look the other way while we climb up to that marker. We are on a treasure hunt." The tour guide said, "You know, that is the first time I have seen that. I guess if you are not looking for it . . . Well, I guess you can. Just don't get hurt."

The team walked halfway down the hold, took a ladder up three stories to the roof, and started across the I-beam to the clue. Everyone got around it and they discussed how to get the keys in it. Ed said, "Okay, everyone get their keys in it, then I will hang one handed and get my key in the top back side." Mark said, "I think Jane should do it. She is the most agile." Ed said, "She doesn't have the reach; this is the only way it will work."

Everyone got their keys in the marker. Ed climbed over it and hung upside down to get his key in it. Then he said, "Okay, three, two, one, turn," and the door opened and five bundles fell out, down three stories to the floor of the hold." Little Johnny yelled up, "I got it." They climbed down and little Johnny had the five bundles sitting there. He asked, "Can I climb up there?" His mother said, "No, are you kidding?" Ed shrugged his shoulders and said, "You have to listen to your mom." Jane handed out the bundles of cash. She said, "Mark, you have the clue." He said, "Let's finish the tour and read it at the van." Ed said, "I take it you don't trust the tour guide." Mark smiled, "Well, we have to keep this close to our chest. If they don't get the clue, we are one step ahead of them." They went back to the tour guide and gave him an extra hundred, and then they finished the tour.

CHAPTER SEVEN

The Mall of America

Mark pulled out his bundle of cash. He broke the band holding it and read, "Mall, Brutus; that's it." Jane asked, "Brutus as in a man's name?" Mark spelled it out for her, "B-R-U-T-U-S. That is Brutus, right?" Sue said, "It's a fricken hundred-and-sixty-pound snapping turtle at the Mall of America." Jane said, "It's a two-and-a-half-hour ride, a hundred and sixty-two miles." Sue said, "There are 520 stores, fifty restaurants, and the nation's largest indoor theme park." Mark said, "Book some rooms; we will spend the night there." Jane asked, "How many rooms?" Mark said, "I want my own." Ed said, "I'll take one, the kid snores." Johnny protested, "I do not." Jane said, "Me and Sue will share one, so that is four. The Country Inn and Suites, it's a hundred and ninety, and it's a quarter mile away. If we stay a mile away, we can stay at a Comfort Inn for eighty bucks." Mark said, "They probably have a free shuttle." Ed said, "Let's spend the hundred bucks and stay close to the mall. Hell, the place sounds huge. We might be there for a few days. That sounds like one hell of a turtle." Jane said, "The behind-the-scenes tickets for the aquarium are twenty-six dollars. And, little Johnny, this is one big aquarium. You stay close."

Team Two, the Intels, got to the SS *Meteor* at three thirty; it closes at four. The tour guide said, "I am sorry, there just isn't enough time to take the tour." Gloria said, "We are on a treasure hunt, looking for a question mark." The guide said, "Oh, there was a team here early this morning." Scott asked, "Did they find the clue?" The guide said, "They all climbed up there. It took a while, you don't have enough time." Sara said, "Two hundred bucks, do you think you could get us there?" The guide said, "You still will have to pay the entrance fee. That is eight bucks apiece." Richard handed him a fifty then said, "Let's do this. We don't want to wait till tomorrow."

The guide bypassed everything and took them right to the bottom of the hold and said, "Up there, strapped to the I-beam." Scott asked, "How did they get up there?" The guy said, "There is a ladder. They went up and one of them hung from a beam, some scary shit." Richard said, "You wouldn't have a high lift or something?" The guide said, "You do know I shouldn't be letting you do this?" Richard held out two more hundred-dollar bills. The guide said, "The canvas over at the end of the hold has a high lift under it. It will reach the ceiling. Be quick about it."

The team went over and uncovered the high lift and moved it under the marker, then went up safely and got their payout. Richard read the clue, "Mall Brutus. What the hell does that mean?" Sara said, "The Mall of America isn't that far from here, that thing is huge." Gloria said, "Brutus is a huge alligator snapping turtle. They are doing renovations to the aquarium, and someone bought the place." They dropped the scissor lift and re-covered it. Sara said, "There are over five hundred stores in the mall." Richard said, "Are we all in agreement? To the mall we go." Soon they were on the way to the Mall of America.

Team One got to Superior late that night. They got to the hotel and Joe went to the bar. They had time to kill, the museum didn't open till ten in the morning. He sat at the bar having a manhattan. A man sat next to him and ordered four shots of tequila. Joe asked, "Are you celebrating something?" The guy said, "Yeah, my first blow job." Joe smiled and said, "Give me a shot and another for this guy." The guy said, "If four shots don't get the taste out of my mouth, nothing will." Joe's jaw dropped; he didn't know what to say.

Morning came. They met down for breakfast. Robert said, "I could have swore I seen that leprechaun in the hall this morning." Dawn said, "Oh, you fancy him?" Cherry shot her a look. She smiled and shrugged her shoulders. Robert said, "If I find that little son of a bitch, I am going to kill him." Jack asked, "Is your ass still sore?" They finished breakfast and hurried to the harbor.

Team Odin was standing waiting to get into the museum. They got in and went for the tour; they were looking for the question mark. The guide was three-quarters through the tour. He said something about a treasure hunt. Cherry was the only one listening to him. She asked, "What do you know about this treasure hunt?" The tour guide said, "Yesterday there were two teams here. They were looking for something, they called it a marker." Joe asked, "Did they find it?" The guide said, "Oh yes, both teams found it." He held out his hand palm up. Robert pulled out a twenty and handed it to him. The guide looked at it and said, "Really?" Jack slid him a hundred. The guide said, "Okay, let's go back down to the hold." They followed him back down to the hold. He said, "Now, if you look up on the I-beam in the middle of the ship . . ." Cherry said, "There it is." She pointed.

The guide said, "You do know I can't let you go off the tour route." Jack pulled another hundred and slipped it to him. He said, "Be quick about it." The team ran over to the ladder and quickly climbed it to the ceiling, then crawled across to the marker. Soon they were back down with their payday. Dawn said, "We have to stop being last place. This sucks." Jack asked the tour guide, "Okay, just get us out of here. The tour is over." The guide took them straight to the deck. Jack said, "Okay now, this Brutus is an alligator snapping turtle, a big one, a hundred-and-sixty-pound guy, in an aquarium at the Mall of America. I just Googled it and that is what popped up." Cherry said, "I have been there, big place, a girls' weekend." Robert said, "Let's get to the van. The other teams were there already last night and are probably in the mall as we speak."

Team Three met downstairs and had breakfast at the hotel, then stood outside waiting for the mall to open at ten. Ed was questioning little Johnny, "So, Johnny, has your mom told you about the birds and the bees yet?" Little Johnny wiped a tear from his cheek. Ed asked, "What's wrong?" Johnny said, "At age six I learned there was no Santa Claus, age seven I learned there is no Easter Bunny. This year

I learned there is no Tooth Fairy. Now, if you are telling me there is no sex, what the hell do I have to live for?" Ed said, "Oh, you are such a drama queen. There is plenty sex and heartbreak. There is plenty to live for. Look, today we are going to see a beautiful aquarium, we had a great breakfast and you didn't have to pay for anything."

Mary came up to them and asked, "What are you two talking about?" Johnny said, "Nothing, just that he bought us breakfast." Ed smiled and said, "Sure, why not." Ed asked Johnny, "So where is the English Channel?" Little Johnny said, "I have no idea, we never had cable." Ed looked at Mary and said, "Johnny is eight years old, right? He should be in third grade, right?" Mary said, "I know he is falling behind. He is acting out because of the trouble we are having." Ed said, "I will find out what he is supposed to have learned in the third grade and get him up to speed."

They took the shuttle to the mall. Mark said, "Team Two is here." Mary asked, "How do you know that?" Mark smiled and said, "We LoJacked the other teams' vans." Mary said, "That's not fair, is it?" Johnny asked, "What is LoJack?" Ed said, "It is a global positioning system—GPS for short—so we know where they are at all times." Johnny said, "You can't do that to a boy, can you?" Ed said, "Oh yes, most smartphones you can put a tracker on them, or we can get you tennis shoes with GPS." Mary said, "That's a great idea." Cherry said, "Cut the kid some slack, we need some freedom." Sue said, "This place is huge. Johnny, you stay close to Ed. We don't want to lose you." Jane said, "I downloaded a map. Follow me. We will go straight to the aquarium."

They started to power walk. Ed put Johnny on his shoulders and they walked a half mile to the aquarium. Sue said, "Last night I booked a behind-the-scenes tour. I expect to be reimbursed for that." Mark said, "Just ask when we get back in the van; the cash is in the glove box."

They got to the aquarium. Sue handed the girl her phone. She scanned it and gave them stickers to put on. Those were their day passes and behind-the-scenes tour. Mark led the way to another desk. They had to wait a few minutes, then a tour guide took a dozen people at a time. Ed asked as the tour guide was doing his presentation in the lab about the food they use, "Is this a timed tour? If so, we are looking for a question mark by the snapping turtle—Brutus, I believe his name is." The tour guide said, "Yes, this is a timed tour. We have ten minutes here explaining how we keep this place running and what we feed and do to keep everything alive. And the question mark is in Brutus' tank."

Ed stepped to the tour guide. He held out his hand and showed him a fifty-dollar bill palmed in his hand, then he shook the man's hand. Ed turned back to the tour and said loudly, "Okay, people, five of us are on a treasure hunt. This man knows where our clue is, so we would like to skip a lot of this information stuff. I will give you twenty dollars apiece for your inconvenience." He took out his money clip and started to peel off twenties and hand them out as people walked by. The tour guide asked, "Is everyone okay with this? Good, if you will follow me. Now, we can't get ahead of the tour in front of us, but we will go right over by Brutus and I will show you the question mark and fill you in as we go." Jane said to Ed, "That was great. This is a forty-five-minute tour. How the hell are we going to get the clue if it is in the tank?"

The tour guide stopped and had a girl feed the sea turtle. He said, "This will just take a minute," and he explained how everything worked, talking quietly. He said, "We are not supposed to be here yet. As I said, it is a timed thing. This is Brutus, he is a hundred-and-sixty-pound alligator snapping turtle. They will reach up to four hundred pounds and live up to two hundred years; in captivity, up to seventy years. Their range is from up here in the northeast down to Florida. The females venture onto land to lay eggs."

Mary said, "There is the question mark; it has to be six feet under water." The team discussed how they were going to get the clue. Ed stepped up to the guide and held out his hand and asked, "How are we going to get this key into that slot and retrieve a slip? It must be a waterproof clue." The guide said, "Now we take this stick here and put a piece of fish on it and rub his nose with it to get him to eat. He is a lazy guy."

The tour guide took the key and strapped it to the stick with a rubber band that was in a container next to the tank. Mark said, "Flat side up, and we need to turn it to the right." The tour guide kept talking as he tried to get the key into the slot. Everyone was watching him. He slowly rubbed the front of the question mark then got the key started in. He asked, "So what happens if I snap off the key?" Ed said, "Just don't do that, be careful." It slid all the way in. He lifted it and a slip of paper came out and floated in the tank. The tour guide got the key back out. Jane said, "Now, how the hell are we going to get that?" The tour guide said, "That's an easy one." He grabbed a long piece of PVC tubing, put his hand on one end, and put the other end into the tank. When it got close to the paper, he took his hand off the end of the tube and the paper got sucked up into it. Ed said to Johnny, "Just like a straw, the water will fill to the level." The tour guide lifted the pipe to the catwalk. He asked, "Could you hold that strainer for me please?" Mark picked up a net with a fine mesh. The guide left the water flow through it and the only thing left in it was the clue. Sue said, "Thank you so very much."

Mark took out the clue and read it, "Ceiling of a tree." Jane said, "Now what the bloody hell does that mean?" Sue asked, "Does it mean it is in the mall?" Ed said, "Let's just finish the tour, then we can figure out what the clue means." Mary asked, "How many clues before a payout?" Mark said, "The first was two, the second was four. I don't have any idea." Jane said, "This treasure hunt is supposed to last up to three weeks." Sue said, "We have lost two guys already. Speaking of that, did you sign the release? We need that signed and emailed to the overlords." Mark said, "That is right. Do you have proof of insurance?" Mary said, "That I do. With Johnny here, I need it."

Mark said, "Look through the tank. That is Team Two." Ed asked the guide. "Hey, can people see us up here?" The guide said, "Not really. They are looking into the lights. We can see them, they can't see us." Mary said, "I wonder how long they have been down there?" The guide looked at his watch and said, "I have to get back on track here. If you will follow me." They finished the tour. As they headed down the hall to the elevator, Ed thanked everyone. Mark said, "We should go to a restaurant, get a cup of coffee, and discuss this clue." Ed said, "You guys go ahead. I am going to take Johnny here through the aquarium and then maybe to the amusement park. You have my cell number." Mary said, "Do you mind if I tag along?" Jane said, "This isn't how it works; we are on a hunt, not a vacation." Ed said, "You're right. We will quickly run through the aquarium and then catch up to you."

The team split up. Ed said, "Okay, this shouldn't take long." He took Johnny by the hand and said, "Stay close to me. There are a lot of people in here." Johnny asked questions about everything. They stopped and watched a quick video of a professor showing the evils of liquor. He took a glass of water and a glass of whiskey. He dropped a worm in the water and it wiggled around, not harmed. And he dropped one in the whiskey. The worm writhed in pain and sank to the bottom and died. Ed asked Johnny, "So what did you learn from that?" Johnny said, "That was cool, and I learned if you drink whiskey you'll never get worms." Ed just shook his head and said, "Let's go find your mom."

Johnny was just amazed at the sharks and the sea life. The rays would skim right over the glass. They got out of the aquarium and to hall. Johnny asked, "Why do they call these Jellyfish? Are they made of jelly?" Ed pointed to a sign and said, "Well let's see. A group of them are called a bloom, a swarm, or a smack. They use the tentacles to sting, which are painful and some can cause death. They are considered plankton, so no, they aren't made of jelly. And there are two hundred different kinds of jellies."

Ed said, "I called your mom. They are in the Rainforest Café, looking at all the trees. I had her order us a sparkling volcano and we can split it." He put Johnny on his shoulders, that way he could make time walking the half mile to the restaurant. Ed called and asked what table they were at. He told the waitress and she brought them there. Mark said, "We have looked at all the trees, haven't found the clue. There must be more trees in this place somewhere. We are going to split up and take a lap." Jane slid close to Sue and said, "You can sit by us, we don't mind."

A waitress brought the dessert. It had a sparkler lit on top of it. Johnny's eyes got really big. He said, "This reminds me of when me and Pete stuck a firecracker up a frog's ass." Sue said, "You mean its *rectum*." Johnny said, "Wrecked them. Fuck, we blew it to pieces." Mark looked at Mary and said, "It's your kid." Ed said, "That is very poor manners. You don't talk like that at the table. And watch your swearing. There are ladies present." Mark said, "Mary, you come with me. Jane and Sue, you go left, we will go right. We will meet you in the middle." Jane said, "Top floor right, the trees need the sunshine." Ed asked Johnny, "Now, the aquarium was fascinating. Can you use the word *fascinate* in a sentence?" Johnny thought for a second and said, "My mom's sweater has ten buttons on it. She has such big tits she can only fasten eight." Ed said, "Oh my god, this is going to take longer than I thought. Just eat and we will get going."

Team Two, the Intels, took the behind-the-scenes tour and asked the tour guides about the question mark until they found the guy that got the clue. The tour guide said, "Yes, I turned the key and got the clue." Scott asked, "Could you do that again?" The guide said, "Well yeah, I don't see why not." Jeremy asked, "Did you hear them read the clue?" The guide said, "Not only did they read it, they asked me if I knew what it meant." Richard asked, "Well, what did they say?" The guide said, "They gave me two hundred bucks and everyone on the tour twenty, so that was like a hundred and forty. So that's like three hundred and fifty bucks." Richard pulled out his wallet and counted four one-hundred-dollar bills and said, "You all owe me a hundred," then he handed him the money.

The guide said, "I have no idea what this means but they read 'ceiling of tree,' that is what it said." Jeremy said, "Can we still go on the tour?" Gloria said, "Come on, let's figure this out." Sara said, "Look at your map, the log chute. It's a ride in the Nickelodeon amusement park." Scott said, "Well, that is a start. I was thinking the Rainforest Café."

They went down to the amusement park and talked with some of the kids that came off the ride and asked them if they'd seen a question mark on the ride. One young girl said, "We sure did. It is in the tunnel, it is strapped to the roof." Sara smiled and said, "Shall we go for a ride?" Scott said, "I will go on the ride. See if you can find out who is running the ride. Maybe we can get them to stop it right under it." Jeremy said, "Great idea. I am going to go with you, looks like fun." Gloria said, "We will work on getting it stopped for you." The two paid the admission fee and went on the ride. They saw the question mark; it was at the top of a hill, so the log was moving slow. When they got off, Scott called Richard and said, "We found it. Can you get them to stop it for thirty seconds?" Richard said, "I am talking to the engineer of the log chute right now. Just tell me when." Scott said, "I am in the log now. I will leave the phone on when we get close. It's like a five-minute ride."

They got to the part where they start chugging up the hill for the big forty-foot drop. They started into the tunnel. Scott called and had the ride stopped, then had them move it forward a couple of feet. He stood and put his key in and got the clue. He read it quickly as soon as he sat. "Tennis, cricket, python. We are ready." The ride went fifty feet then fell forty. Richard, Gloria, and Sara met the two as they got off the ride and said, "We discussed this. It is ball, cricket ball, tennis ball, and ball python, that is what they have in common." Sara said, "There is a place called House of Balls here in town. That's where we want to go."

Ed took Johnny on the log ride. He only had to be three feet tall with a guardian. The ride stopped then started then stopped again. They sat for a few seconds, then started again. Ed said, "This isn't right. I hope we don't get stuck." Johnny looked up and said, "Really? Could that happen?" Ed said, "Well, these things run every day. It is very unlikely something will go wrong. Oh, here we go." They saw the question mark right before the big drop. Johnny screamed all the way to the bottom. They hit with a huge splash. When they got off, Ed called Mary, "Hey, Johnny and I went on the log chute. We found the question mark. All we have to do is to get them to stop the ride for a couple of seconds. I think the other team has the clue already."

Twenty minutes later, everyone met. Ed asked, "What the hell took so long?" Mary said, "This place is huge. You could shop for a week." They found the control room. Ed said, "A couple of people were just in here to get you to stop the log chute. We would like you do the same." A man said, "I have no idea what you are talking about." Ed pulled a hundred-dollar bill from his money clip and asked, "Can you do that again please?" A young man stood and said,

"Not a problem. Treasure hunt, hey?" Ed said, "You guys stay here. Johnny and I will go for a ride."

Ed jogged and Johnny ran full speed to the ride. They stood in line for ten minutes then got onto the ride. They called when the log was chugging up the hill. The engineer stopped the ride at the top and Ed got the clue. Ed read it to the team, "Tennis, cricket, and python; that's it, here we go." The log dropped forty feet. You could hear Johnny scream.

Ed and Johnny met the team in the mall. He asked, "So what does tennis have to do with a cricket and a python?" Jane said, "Google talks about a python eating a tennis ball." Sue said, "That's it, a ball python, a tennis ball, and a cricket ball." Mark said, "That's it, there is a House of Balls right here in town." Jane said, "Let's go, we are falling behind." Little Johnny said, "I have balls there right under my penis." Mary said, "Just ignore him. He is just looking for attention." Jane said, "But it is funny."

Team Two got to the House of Balls. Scott said, "Oh, this should be easy. It's a small place. Look at the giant polar bear." Gloria said, looking at her phone, "It's an art studio. There is stuff all over in the yard; inside, just a bunch of weird stuff." Richard said, "Art can be anything, even a question mark. Let's hope it's a marker." Sara said, "Let's go in and ask about the treasure hunt, maybe they know where it is."

They went in and paid. The young man had no clue about a treasure hunt. Jeremy said, "Captain Scott, how would you like to handle this?" Scott said, "Okay, you and Richard check the outside grounds and me and the ladies will split up and look in here." Two hours later, Gloria called Scott and said, "Found it in a metal totem. It is only six inches tall. Back room, against the wall." Scott said, "Stay right there, I will get the team." He quickly called everyone and had them meet at the totem. Sara said, "Well, we are all here. Get the clue." Gloria put her key in and turned it. A clue came out. She read it, "It says '*Amorphophallus titanum*,'" Richard said, "That's the corpse flower; it has to be a green house." Jeremy said as he was looking at his phone, "How about Marjorie McNeely Conservatory? It's a big place." Sara said, "It opens at ten tomorrow morning." Team

Three pulled into the parking lot and quickly went into the place. Mark said, "There they are, Team Two, the Intels." Ed said, "Mary and I will go over and see what they are doing; they have never seen us before." Jane said, "Good idea, take the kid." Mary said, "Johnny, stay here and be quiet." Ed said, "Come on."

They walked right up to the Team Two and looked around; he listened to their conversation. Team Two left. Ed said to Mary, "They're going to some conservatory and zoo in Saint Paul, the clue must be here." The rest of the team came to them and Mary said, "There is a small question mark on the back of this tin man." Jane said, "Put your key in it and get the clue." She did and said, "I have no idea how to pronounce this, *Amorphophallus titanum*." Johnny giggled and said, "You said *tit*." Sue said, "It is the corpse flower, and there is a conservatory close to here." Ed said, "In Saint Paul, it's a park with a zoo. Team Two knows." Jane said, "With cell phones, this treasure hunt is easy." Johnny said, "This place is cool." Ed said, "It defiantly is different, a lot of busts, just odd stuff." Mary said, "Well, let's go. Maybe we can find the clues before the smart guys do." Jane said, "It opens at ten tomorrow." Mark said, "Right, let's hang here for a half hour then back to the hotel, dinner, and a good night's sleep." Sue smiled and wrapped her arm around Jane and said, "We don't know where we will be tomorrow." Johnny said, "Look, real teeth. And over here there's tons of doll heads." Ed said, "I will watch him and make sure he doesn't break anything."

Team One, Odin, got to the mall. They found Brutus the turtle and went on the backstage tour. Joe made a plan with Cherry. She was going to hold the turtle with a stick and Joe was going to swim down and get the clue. The rest of the team distracted the tour guide and Joe slipped into the tank and got the clue. The turtle wasn't even interested in him. Joe read the clue, "Ceiling of a tree." They figured out it was in the ceiling somewhere. They were up searching. Jack watched the log ride go whipping past. He said, "Log, tree, I have to go for a ride." He went down and took the ride and found the question mark. It took three rides to get the key into the slot and get the clue. They got the clue. Jack read it, "Tennis, cricket, python, that's it." Joe said, "Tennis ball, cricket ball, and ball python." Dawn said, looking at her phone, "The House of Balls, opens at nine."

They went on some rides then went to the hotel. It was getting late already. They got to the hotel. Jack went down to the bar for a drink. The guy next to him ordered a double martini, and he had a light conversation with him. Five minutes later, the guy looked in his shirt pocket and ordered another. Ten minutes later, he looked in his pocket again and ordered another. Jack asked, "So what is up with looking in your pocket before you order a drink?" The guy smiled and said, "I keep a picture of my wife in there. When she starts to look good, I know it's time to go home." Jack said, "Okay, that's just weird. It's time I get some shuteye," and went to his room.

Team Three went to a restaurant. Ed asked, "In second grade, Johnny needs to know basic math, write, and know what the seven continents are. Okay, Johnny, if I give you two bikes, then two more, then two more, how many bikes will you have?" Johnny said, "Easy, seven." Ed said, "Now listen, if I gave you two bikes, then two more, then two more after that, how many bikes would you have?" Little Johnny said, "Seven." Jane said as she placed bread sticks in front of him, "Try this. I give you two, then two more, then two more. How many do you have?" Johnny said, "Six." Ed said, "Okay, you got it. So if I gave you two bikes, then two more, and two more, you would have . . . ?" Johnny said, "Seven. Two plus two plus two is six, and I already have a fricken bike. That makes seven."

Ed shook his head. "This is going to be a challenge. Okay, Johnny, if you can name the seven continents, you can skip dinner and go right to dessert." Mary shot him a look. Johnny smiled and said, "Oh, let's see, North America, South America, Antarctica, Australia, Africa, Asia, and let's see . . . oh yes, this one doesn't make sense because it is part of Asia, Europe." Ed said, "Ah yeah, I didn't see that coming." Mary said, "I am telling you, he is going to turn my hair gray before its time." Johnny said, "I will have the lava cake and vanilla ice cream." Mark said, "That sounds good; I will have a small steak and the lava cake also."

Ed got a text. He looked up and excused himself from the table and met a guy at the bar. He returned to the table and said to Mary,

"This won't take long." He left with the man. Ten minutes later he returned with a black smudge on his cheek. Mary asked, "Did everything go well?" Ed said, "We will see. Johnny, I will need your help after dinner." Johnny smiled with a spoonful of dripping chocolate. He said, "Don't ask, don't tell." Mary leaned over to Ed and whispered in his ear, "What the hell are you doing?" Ed said, "I got a deal on some Civil War stuff. I paid ten grand, the three 1853 Sharps should be worth more than that. And I think I can make around twenty grand." Her eyes opened and said, "Really?" Ed said, "It's a cash thing. He isn't reporting the sale, nothing is registered. I have to move some numbers around and it will be legal when I am done." Mark asked, "Is that what you do, arms dealing?" Ed said, "No, it's a hobby. I am retired, military." Johnny asked, "Twenty bucks." Ed said, "He is saving his money to start a stock account." Jane asked, "So how much do you have set aside?" Johnny looked at his mom and said, "Four hundred. I am going to invest it and take care of you, Mom." Sue said, "That is just so sweet." Mark said, "If we can get the next clue before the Intels, we have a chance at another ten grand." Jane said. "Where is the Odin team?" Mark pulled out his phone and said, "They are at the mall. I highly doubt they found the two clues last night." Ed asked, "Do you know when they got there? The aquarium closes early, and they need that first clue to get the second."

They finished dinner. Ed and Johnny went out to the room. There was a huge wooden crate right in the middle of the walkway. Ed said, "First thing, we need to get some towels. Let's go down to the manager's office, see if they have some they are going to throw out or we can buy cheap. If not, we are going shopping."

They went and talked to the gal at the desk. Ed showed her his hand with a fifty showing in his palm. He reached over and shook her hand and asked, "Now, if I had a crate, what would I do with the wood?" She said, "Go out the back; there is a dumpster." Ed said, "Great. Now I am in need of some used towels, about twenty, bill it to my room." She made a call and said, "Would you like them delivered to your room?" Ed said, "Now that would be great."

They walked into the pool area; there were Mary, Jane, and Sue, sitting in the hot tub. Ed whistled a wolf call softly. He said, "Your mom is kind of cute." Johnny said, "She has her good days." Ed said, "We will be in my room." As they were walking down the hall, Johnny asked, "Are Jane and Sue rug munchers? You know, are they queer?" Ed said, "*Queer* . . . that is out of the ordinary. Well, it's getting more ordinary. Are they sexually involved? That is none of our business. And where did you come up with rug munchers?" Johnny said, "Oh, my dad. He was a bit rude."

They got to the room and started to break into the crate and unload it. The towels got there. Ed slipped the man a twenty and had Johnny lay out the towels on the beds. Then he laid the weapons on the towels, and they then disassembled the crate and took it to the dumpster. Came back and started to wipe down the swords and guns. Ed said the numbers of the guns and Johnny wrote them down. He then took pictures of each and put them into his laptop.

Mary stopped in and the beds were full of weapons. Johnny said, "Mom, look. Real swords. These have killed people." Ed said, "Well they could have. They are from the Civil War, and some are worth five, maybe six grand apiece." Johnny said, "This is an 1848 Springfield. It is worth two thousand dollars." Mary asked, "Really?" Ed said, "Could be a bit more. The prize so far is this revolver. It is a WP9 Leech & Rigdon Confederate .36 caliber and is worth twenty-six thousand." Mary said, "Why are you doing this hunt? It doesn't look like you need the money." Ed got up, rubbed Johnny's head as he walked by, and said, "It's kind of fun." Mary said, "You were on vacation when you joined." Ed interrupted her and said, "Technically I am retired, so I am always on vacation. I flew up here to do some kayaking around the caves, and in the winter I go to Saint Lucia."

Mary said, "It's almost nine o'clock, your bedtime." Johnny protested, "But, Mom, Ed is going to let me shoot one of the guns." Mary's eyes popped open. She asked, "Why would you say that?" Ed said, "Well, maybe not one of the old ones. It should be perfectly safe. The shotguns with the Damascus barrel can't be shot with smokeless powder, and I would hate to blow up a thousand-dollar gun." Johnny asked, "What is the difference?" Ed picked up a gun and said, "See the markings on the barrel? It is how it was made back in the day. I have shot thousands of rounds out of a double barrel; that was my favorite trap gun. And your mom is right, you should get to bed. We have a long day ahead of us." Mary said as she was leaving, "I would double check those numbers." Ed smiled and said, "Have faith. I will see you in the morning."

Team Two, the Intels, got up early and met in Scott and Jeremy's room. They were watching the internet. A woman walked up to a priest and said, "Father, I have a strange problem with my two girl parrots. All they say is, 'Hi, we're prostitutes. Do you want to have some fun?'" The priest said, "Well, you know, I have two male parrots. I have taught them to say the rosary, and they listen to me practice my sermon every week. We should get them together." Gloria asked, "What the hell are you guys watching?" The woman brought the parrots to the church and put them in the cage with the other two. The girl parrots said, "Hi, we're prostitutes. Do you want to have some fun?" One male parrot squawked, "Put away the beads, Frank, our prayers have been answered." Richard said, "I have no idea what I walked in on, but what the hell are you two watching?" Scott looked up and said, "Okay, we are all here. Is everyone packed? We go down for breakfast then head over to the zoo." Gloria said, "I thought we were going to the conservatory?" Scott said, "It's a big complex, three hundred acres. And the conservatory is beautiful. It was built back in 1915, back when they put pride in what they built. And it's free."

Now Team One, the Odins, were up. Robert went down the bar and had a bloody Mary, waiting for the rest of the team to come down. A guy sat right next to him and ordered eleven shots of tequila. The bartender set them out and filled them all. The man looked at Robert and winked, then started to pound them one after another. The bartender said, "I don't think you should be drinking those so fast." The man said, "You would if you had what I have." He threw down shot number eleven. The bartender asked, "So what do you have?" The man got off his barstool and said before he bolted to the door, "Fifty cents." The bartender said, "You bastard, get your ass back here." Robert slammed his hand on the bar and roared, "My god that's funny. Don't worry about it, put his drinks on my bill." Joe and Jack came down. Jack said, "We have an hour before the House of Balls opens." Robert said, "It doesn't open till noon." Jack said, "For a hundred dollars they are opening at nine. That's eighty bucks apiece." Joe said, "We need to get a bigger payout; we are here to make some money." Robert said, "Well at least there is a minimum a thousand." Joe said, "We need a nest egg of ten grand. If we miss a clue it costs ten G's."

The girls came down; the guys were eating breakfast. Dawn asked, "So what is the plan?" Joe looked at his watch and said, "Fifteen minutes we roll. Are you girls packed and ready to go?" Cherry said, "We will meet you at the front door." They turned and back in the elevator they went. In a half hour they were on their way to the House of Balls.

To their surprise, it was a lot smaller than they thought. They got there and sat and waited for someone to come and let them in. Jack said to Joe, "Come on, let's look inside that big polar bear. What the hell kind of place is this? There is an eyeball on top of a set of dentures. That thing has to be twelve feet tall." Cherry said, "I have read all the reviews and a question mark has never come up, and there are a lot of oddities here."

A car pulled up and two men got out, one was a midget. Robert said, "Okay, they're here. Let's make this quick." Dawn got out of the car and yelled to the boys. They met the two gentlemen at the door. Cherry asked, "Have you gentlemen seen a question mark? It could be six inches to six feet." The taller man said, "Hi, I am Dick and this is Mike. I don't remember seeing a question mark but there is a lot of stuff in here." Dawn said, "There are two more teams and I think they are ahead of us. Do you have many people working here?" Dick said, "Well we are part owners, we really don't work here. Mike calls himself an artist. I believe we have four people hired to run this place." Mike said, "Did you get the four hundred bucks? Let's get these assholes in here, find the stupid shit, and get to breakfast." Dick said, "You know little people, they have short tempers." Mike said, "That's fuckin' hilarious."

They went into the place. Joe said, "Robert, you're the captain. How would you like to work this? Jack and I can do a quick sweep of the outside. There is a lot of stuff to look though, tons of bowling balls." Dick said, "You know, I have always wanted to count them. We could put that on the website. And now, what the hell are we looking for?" Dawn stepped up to Mike and scratched behind his ear. She said, "The question mark can be anywhere from six inches to six feet. It is metal with a key hole in it." Mike said, "Your hair smells nice." Joe said to Jack as they headed for the door, "When a midget says your hair smells nice, isn't that sexual harassment?" Jack said, "Not when you're talking to Dawn. She was asking for it."

Dawn said, "We should split up. Cherry, you go with Dick. I will go with Mike. And, Robert, you check in this room. This shouldn't take long. Dawn got Mike in the back room and asked, "What do you do for a living?" Mike said, "Not much, I own a few places, play the stock market. I am sorry about being rude before." Dawn said, "Let's see, there was Doc, Dopey, Grumpy . . . I thought you were horny." Mike said, "So you're into short guys?" He reached around her and grabbed her by the ass. She lifted her skirt, showing him she wasn't wearing any underwear. He stepped in and gave her a kiss right on the puddy. He climbed up on a display, dropped his drawers. Dawn handed him a condom and then bent over. He quickly slid on the condom and said, "Yeah baby," and they started going at it. When Cherry yelled, "I found it, come on," Dawn said, "You had better pick up the pace. I have to leave."

In five minutes everyone was gathered around the steel totem. Mike was sweating, still trying to catch his breath. Dick said, "Hey, Mike, are you going to be alright?" Mike smiled and said, "Oh hell yes." Dawn gave Cherry the eyebrow lift, she just rolled her eyes. Joe said, "So where is it?" Cherry said, "It's right behind the totem, just lift the cape. I found the clue on the ground and looked around. Here it is." She put her key into it and out came the clue. She said, "Oh, this will be good. It says *Amorphophallus titanum*." Robert said, "May I see that? I will Google it . . . Here we go. It is also called the corpse flower. Add in *Minnesota* and out comes St. Paul, the conservatory." Dick said, "That's a big place, it has a zoo."

Cherry stepped close to Dawn and asked, "Did you do him?" Dawn smiled and said, "Oh yeah, I shagged him, baby. I shagged him rotten," She looked down at Mike and gave him a wink and said, "We have to go, lover." Dick looked at her with his jaw hanging. Cherry asked, "Why?" Dawn said, "I felt like it. Their cocks look so much bigger on them." Cherry said, "Well, was it?" Dawn said, "No, just a standard six inch or so. But it was fun, we both got off. Kind of neat when he doesn't have to go down on you, he was at eye level."

CHAPTER EIGHT

The Conservatory

Team Three parked in a side parking lot next to a big truck. Mark said Team Intel was on its way and Team Odin was at the House of Balls. That should take them some time . . . Ah crap, they are on their way here." Ed said, "That place doesn't open till noon. How would could they get the clue?" Jane said, "Here comes Team Two. That green van sure sticks out." Mark asked Johnny, "So I heard you got expelled from school." Johnny said, "Yes, I got an F in math." Mark asked, "So how did that get you expelled?" Johnny said, "The teacher asked what is two times three, I answered six. Then she asked what is three times two." Mark said, "It's the fucking same thing." Johnny said, "That's what I said. I got kicked out for three days."

Jane leaned over and kissed Sue lightly on the lips and said, "For luck." Mary looked at Ed. He just smiled. Johnny said, "Rug munchers." Mary just looked at her lap and shook her head. Mark put his hand over his mouth and tried not to laugh, then said, "Okay, this is what we are going to do. Mary, you come with me. The child behaves better with Ed. And, Jane, take Sue. We all split up. I am hoping the clue didn't mean right at the corpse flower, because if it did they are going to get there first." Sue said, "The first thing we do is grab maps." Jane said, "Give Intel five minutes, then we go in and make a plan." Ed said, "Okay, Johnny. Let's go, we are going to spy on Team Two. We will keep in contact. They don't know us." Ed jumped out and started to jog, little Johnny was at full run to keep up.

Mark said, "Okay, that will work." Jane said, "Ed is more of a leader, but you are our captain." Mary said, "There is something about that guy." Sue said, "It's like you want to trust him but you know he is playing you, like he tells you what he wants you to hear." Mary said, "Like a cop or a lawyer." Jane said, "That's it. He can switch it on and off. I think that is why Johnny has respect for him." Mark asked, "Does anyone really know who he is? All I know he is retired." Mary said, "I really don't know. He said he was in the marines. He is a gun dealer." Jane said, "A gun dealer." Mary said, "There is over fifty thousand dollars in rare guns in the back here." Mark said, "Really?" Mary said, "Don't say anything. The time we met in the hotel, he had Johnny cleaning dozens of pistols. And he got the governor to call out the state troopers on the chief of police. My god, who is he?" Jane said, "Okay, everyone is going in now. Ed and Johnny are in line with them." Mark said, "Let's go. And I wouldn't worry about Ed. Johnny is in good hands, that kid is a card." Sue said, "He sure is." Jane said, "Yeah, a joker."

Team Two went straight to the corpse flower. Everything was roped off and there was no question mark. Scott pulled out his map. Ed grabbed Johnny by the hand and led him right next to Scott. He explained the smell of the rotting flesh, it is to attract insects for the flower to capture and consume. Scott said, "Richard, you take this corridor. And, Gloria and Sara, you go down this one. Jeremy and I will take this one and the front entrance." Ed took Johnny around to the backside of the flower and asked, "What did you learn?" Johnny said, "They split up so they can cover more ground." Ed said, "That is true, but we also know their names and who is the captain. Did you notice they just looked at the flower and around it?" Johnny asked, "And your point is?" Ed said, "Look up. Is it in the rafters? Let's look at the exhibits around here and look close, it could be a small one." Johnny said, "They're going to catch us looking." Ed said, "Now think about this, where we are and what do people do when they come here." Johnny looked up and said, "Everything is glass, this is the coolest place." Ed said, "Now, this flower blooms for just a day or two every few years." Johnny said, "Come on, we have to keep up with the other team." Ed said, "Let's just do it slowly, keep an eye on the girls." Johnny said, "Why are we following the girls?" Ed smiled and said, "They're cute, and if any of their team finds the clue they will lead us there."

Ed's phone rang. He told them they were following Team Intel. Ed said to Johnny, "Keep an eye out for Team Odin, they are here." Johnny said, "I don't know what they look like." Ed said, "Do you see the girls? They are looking for the question mark. Are they looking at the exhibits? Not really." Johnny said, "They are going into the palms room. This place is huge."

Team One, the Odins, came in and went straight to the corpse flower. Once they got there Joe said, "We need to split up. There is a zoo, an eighteen-hole golf course . . . This place is huge." Robert said, "I think we spend our time here." Dawn said, "Well, you are the captain. Should we look for leprechauns too?" Cherry said, "Okay, we split up. I am going to the visitor's center. Joe, you go to the fern room. Robert, you go to the palm dome. Dawn, you go to the children's. And, Jack, you go to the Ordway gardens."

They quickly spread out, looking around everything. Ed asked Johnny, "Have you noticed anything new?" Johnny said, "That man, he is looking for something." Ed said, "He must be from Team One. And there he goes, he is in the bushes." Johnny said, "He's going to get in trouble." Ed said, "Come on, Johnny. Let's go and see what he has found." Ed jogged over to the spot where Joe had gone into the ferns. Johnny had to run full bore to keep up to him. Joe came out to the path and took out his phone and read the slip of paper, "Talk to Jesus, that's it." He quickly headed for the front entrance.

The team met and discussed the clue. Cherry said, "There are a shitload of churches here. Number one is the Cathedral of St. Paul, huge church, still on a hill overlooking the city. It was built back in 1904 and it has 43,560 square feet." Robert said, "But how do we know that's the church, and does the clue mean a church? It could be a grave yard." Joe said, "Oh my goodness, are there a lot of churches here? I would love to do a church tour. It could be in the Basilica of St. Mary, that's a big one too and it was the first in the United States." Joe said, "We are killing time. Should we go to the cathedral?" Everyone agreed that would be a great starting point.

Ed said to Johnny, "You stay right here. See that lime-green reflection on the water? That is the clue." He stepped off the sidewalk into the ferns, went around a small pond and to the back side of a large twenty-foot fern, then was back in a minute, holding a slip of paper. He said, "Call your mom." Johnny pulled out his phone and called his mom and said, "We found it, we found the clue." Johnny looked up at Ed and asked, "What is it?" Ed said, "Talk to Jesus. Tell her to call everyone and meet at the entrance. Crap, here comes Team Two." Johnny told his mother and followed Ed toward the front entrance. They met in front of the doors.

Mark said, "We will start with the Cathedral of St. Paul. It is the top church in the area. There are so many. What did the clue say word for word?" Ed said, "All it says is 'talk to Jesus,' that's it. Does it mean a church?" Sue said, "What the fuck—excuse my French. That was supposed to be a payout. Now Team One is ahead of us." Ed said, "If we don't get moving, Team Intel will be too. They seen Team One run out of the fern room and he was still holding the clue."

They started for the van and Johnny asked Ed, "So what is a cathedral?" Ed said, "It is a big church where the bishop hangs out. And when you are in church you have to be quiet." Little Johnny said, "Oh, I remember. You don't want to wake the people sleeping in there." Ed said, "Well, you're not supposed to sleep, you are listening to the priest. By the way, what religion are you?" Mary said, "He was baptized a Catholic, but we haven't made it to church lately." Ed said, "Well, you were living in your car trying to make ends meet." Mary said, "We hit a rough patch." Jane said, "This is going to be clue number five. It should be a payout, right?" Mark said as he entered the cathedral into the GPS, "I thought this one was going to be a marker. The rules are a bit vague." Jane said, "Step on it. Team Odin has a half-hour lead on us." Ed said, "A big open church. They are going to see us as soon as we walk through those doors. My god, the place is huge. See it up on the hill."

Team Two, the Intels, slowly walked through the fern room. It was dense, there were some little wood chips on the sidewalk where someone stepped out of the garden. Scott looked closely and saw a footprint inside the garden. He looked both ways and stepped in, followed the prints to the clue, and got back out with the clue. He called his teammates. Gloria was the first one there. She said, "See the lime-green in the reflection in the pond?" Scott said, "No kidding, how did I miss that?"

Scott waited for everyone to get there then he said, "Now look at this, see the reflection. You cannot see the clue, just the color. Okay, the clue is 'talk to Jesus.'" Everyone pulled out their phone. Sara said, "There is a song, chat rooms, Bible verse, there is even an app." Scott said, "It's a church. Where do you talk with God?" Jeremy said, "There are some beautiful churches. I think it would be in the basilica. It is the first one built in the States." Richard said, "Boy, there are a lot of churches here, and it doesn't say where. I mean, what the hell kind of clue is that." Jeremy said, "The other teams will be going to the Cathedral of St. Paul. It is the number one church in the area, and the place is huge." Scott said, "Should we take the chance and head to St. Mary's? If we are right, we could get the big payout. This one must be a marker."

Team One was doing a quick run-though of the cathedral. There was a tour going on. Richard said, "The pipe organ up there; the marker is strapped to it." They hurried to find the staircase to get up to the pipe organ. Scott said, "This is going to be tricky."

They got up to the pipe organ and looked at the marker. It was stuck way off to one side. You would have to walk out on the banister to get to it, and one could sneak between the pipes in the back. It was a slim marker but tall. One of the key holes was seven feet from the banister.

Jeremy said, "Okay, Scott and Gloria, you two see if you can come in from the back. Richard, you go first across the banister. Sara, you follow me then you get on my shoulders to get the top key." Scott said, "Let's try it. Gloria, are you with me?"

They walked around the backside and crawled on their hands and knees to get to the back corner of the pipes, and then worked their way through to the marker. Richard said, "I don't like heights." Jeremy said, "Just don't look down, and have three contacts at all times." Richard stepped on a chair to step onto the banister, then slowly worked his way to the marker, followed by Jeremy and Sara.

Everything worked out well. Sara was on top of Jeremy's shoulders. She counted, "Three, two, one, turn." The drawer slid open and took the five bundles of money. Team Three stood off to the side watching and listening to a tour guide talking, explaining how the church was built. Ed said to Mary, "We just lost seventy-five hundred. Second place is twenty-five hundred apiece."

Team Odin huddled together up in the loft. Sara handed out the cash. She kept the one with the clue, broke the seal, and pulled out the clue. She read it to them, "Man-made Polish hop." Cherry sat flipping through her pile of cash and said, "Fricking ten grand, ten thousand dollars. I have never held so much money." Dawn kissed her lightly on the neck and asked, "What bank do you use? Not too smart to have fifty grand in the van. Hey, I am a poet, and I don't even know it." Robert said, "Let's get our head back in the game. A man-made Polish hop." Dawn said, "When we were in Wausau, the clue was Polish rock; it ended up to be granite ski hill." Jack said, "A manmade ski jump. There is one in a town called Westby. It is 161 miles, but there is a bigger one in Iron Mountain, Michigan, that is 290 miles." Joe said, "That one is over the two-hundred mark." Dawn said, "Not from the two-hundred mark from Wausau. In fact, it is 126 miles from our starting point." Joe said, "Okay, you're right. What the hell was I thinking?" Joe said, "Is the one in Westby on the way?" Jack said, "Not really, Westby is south and Iron Mountain is all the way across the state. It is a six-hour drive. We pick the wrong one we are screwed." Cherry said, "Let's look at it this way. We drive down to Westby, check it out, and if it isn't it is six hours shot. But if we drive to Iron Mountain and it's not it, that is twelve-hour shot. I vote for Westby." Joe said, "All in favor of Westby say *aye*. All opposed say *nay*." Jack said, "Nay, the Pine Mountain is made to walk up, but I do see your reasoning to check the one the closest."

Johnny was getting impatient. He was playing in the holy water. Mary said, "Stop that." Ed said, "Now go wash your hands. Do you know how many people put their hands in there?" Ed dipped his finger in it and made the sign of the cross and said, "At least a thousand a day." Mark said, "I will take him. Come on, Johnny, we have to make this quick." Jane said, "My god, this place is just beautiful."

Team One made their move down from the loft. They headed out the door. Ed said, "I don't understand, they are going to see our van anyway." Sue smiled and said, "Mark moved it and parked on the other side of the church." Ed said, "But really, who cares?" Jane said, "The less they know the better." Mary said, "The coast is clear. Another tour is starting, and we might have to wait to make our move." Ed said, "Well, we know how to do it, and it isn't as bad as the one at the SS Meteor So three in front and the two must come in from the back."

They headed up to the choir loft and figured out how to do it. Ed said, "Let me see if I can squeeze in behind the pipes." He did and he climbed the pipes to where he could reach around and get his key in the top slot. He came back and said, "The only one that has to climb on the outside is going to be Mark, maybe Jane. She has big tits." Mark said, "Well, we are going to have to wait for the tour to leave. I am sure they will call the cops if we are climbing around." Ed said, "Give Johnny your key, we can do this. Follow me."

They squeezed between the pipes and the wall then got down on their hands and knees and crawled under the next set. Ed said, "Mary, Johnny, and Sue, turn sideways, slide down a few feet. There is an opening. Then come back to the marker. Now, Jane, follow me, tight against the wall. I will climb up for the top slot, you get the one in the back near the floor." A few minutes later, Ed said, "Okay, Johnny, when I say turn the key you turn it clockwise." Johnny said, "Clockwise, what the hell is that?" Mary slapped him in the back of the head and said, "You're in church." Johnny said, "What the fuck did you do that for?" Mary said, "I am going to wash your mouth with soap." Johnny said, "And I will blow bubbles out of my ass." Ed said, "Clockwise, turn it toward the right. And three, two, one, turn." The second drawer opened.

Ed took out the five bundles of cash and stuck them in his shirt. He said, "Done. Now carefully turn the key back and take it out, straight out." Johnny pulled it out and showed Ed the key. He was proud of himself. They met and Ed handed out the bundles of cash. He gave Jane the bundle with the clue. She read it and said, "Man-made Polish hop, that's it." Ed said, "Now what is a Polish hop? The polka." Sue said, "In the beginning of the hunt, one of the clues was Polish rock. It was a ski hill, and you know the Polacks end their name with ski." Ed said, "Hey, Johnny, do you know why Christ wasn't born in Poland? It's because they couldn't find three wise men and a virgin." Mark said, "Stay on task, a man-made ski hill." Jane said, "No, a man-made ski jump, as in hop." Mary said, "There is a big one in Iron Mountain, Michigan. Does this treasure hunt go into Michigan?" Ed said, "Da UP dar, yeah hey." Mark said, "Two hundred miles from Wausau, so I do believe that takes a large part of the Upper Peninsula. There is a smaller one down to the south, it's called the Snowflake." Mark said, "Well, I think we should head over to Pine Mountain. You can climb to the top of that one."

Team Two made it to the cathedral after spending an hour at the basilica. They found the clue and brought up climbing gear, roped everyone off. By the time they were ready to turn the key the place was having an evening mass. The church held three thousand people. It wasn't full but still there were over a thousand there. Scott had four of them walk out on the banister and Sara climbed behind to get the key in the bottom slot. They got their thousand-dollar payout and read the clue.

CHAPTER NINE

Pine Mountain

Team Two headed toward Westby, the Snowflake ski jump, and teams One and Three headed for Pine Mountain ski jump. Ed sat way back with Johnny and did some schoolwork. Ed asked the car, "Could you guys tell us what your father did for work and spell it? Mine was a P-O-L-I-C-E O-F-F-I-C-E-R, police officer. If he was here, he would arrest Mark for driving ten miles over the speed limit. Back it down to eight over." Mark said, "Mine was a T-E-A-C-H-E-R, and if he was here he would tell you to mind your own business. He was a history teacher." Jane said, "Mine was a F-A-R-M-E-R, and if he was here he would put you to work." Johnny said, "Mine was a B-O-O-K-I-E, if he was here he would give you a twenty-to-one odds of our team winning this thing." Ed asked, "Mary, is this right?" Mary said, "Oh, he was a loser alright. He owed so many people, and he gambled away the house, the car, everything we had." Johnny said, "And when Mom caught him with Mrs. Lee playing the tube-snake boogie, he left and we lost the house." Mary said, "And we were lucky my car is in my name."

Johnny said quietly to Ed, "You want to know the real reason he left?" Ed said, "Yes, tell me more." Johnny said, "I looked at her driver's license. She got an F in sex." The car broke into laughter. Ed said, "No, that is F for female. That means she is a girl." Johnny said, "Oh, that makes sense." Ed said, "Let's try this. Mary, can you use *fascinate* in a sentence?" Mary said, "Disney World is fascinating." Ed said,

"No, I said *fascinate*." Johnny said, "I got it. Jane's tits are so big, she can only fasten eight of ten buttons on her shirt." Mark said, "Good one. Last time you said your mom had big tits. Jane does have a bigger rack." Mary just shook her head. Ed said, "Let's try this one more time. Use *defiantly* in a sentence." Jane said, "This kid is defiantly going to need help." Sue said, "I am defiantly hungry." Johnny asked, "Do farts have lumps in them? If not, I defiantly shit my pants." Mary turned and shot him a look and started to speak. Ed cut her off. "That was a good use of the word." Ed asked Johnny, "You kind of know about sex education. Have you learned it from the internet?" Little Johnny said, "TV. I watched a John Wayne movie. The Indian attacked him; he killed them all." Ed asked, "What has that to do with sex education?" Johnny said, "Well, it taught them not to fuck with John Wayne." Ed said, "Mark, stop somewhere to eat. This kid is killing me."

Team Two went to Snowflake ski jump. There was a golf course there. They went to the bar, had a drink. Scott asked the bartender as he slid a fifty across the bar, "Is there any way we could get a tour of the ski jump?" The bartender said, "For another fifty I will be able to find someone." Scott slid another fifty across the bar. The bartender stepped to the kitchen and said, "Rob, these guys want a tour of the ski hill." A young man came out of the kitchen and said, "Sure, why not. I hope you have your walking shoes on. It's quite the hike." Sara said, "You boys go ahead. You don't need us with. It is just a clue."

The three guys followed Rob across the parking lot and started up the hill. Richard said, "We are looking for a question mark. It can be small or big. It is for a treasure hunt." Rob said, "I haven't seen anything like that." Richard asked, "Can we go into those buildings?" Rob said, "Whatever you would like. Those were built for the judges. We have had international jumps here." Scott said, "Let's go to the top of the jump first."

The four climbed the hill to the ski jump. Jeremy looked up at the thing and asked, "How tall is that thing?" Rob said, "A hundred and eighteen meters." Scott said, "Four hundred and seventy-two feet." Jeremy said, "Okay, I am going to sit this one out. Just climbing the hill tuckered me out." Richard said, "I am not feeling this.

No tire tracks, no footprints; I think we have the wrong hill." Scott asked, "Have you ever been to Pine Mountain?" Rob cut him off and said, "That is one of the tallest, if not the tallest, manmade jumps in the world. I seem to remember it is like ten stories, one hell of a nice bar." Richard said, "We are here, so we're going to give it the once-over." They climbed to the top, nothing. Scott said, "Isn't this a great view? Well, let's head down." They went down and Rob took Jeremy up into the judges' box. When he got down he said, "I think we made a mistake. This isn't the one; beautiful ski hill though."

Team One did a marathon drive, stopping twice in five hours. They got to Pine Mountain with plenty of light. The team ran up the steps, right up the ski ramp. Everyone was trying to catch their breath; it was like running up a ten-story building. There in the corner was the clue. Robert took out his key. Cherry said, "Wait, it is pretty dam windy up here. If we lose the clue we're shit out of luck." Robert smiled and said, "You're right. What do you suggest?" Dawn stepped to his side and put her hand on where the clue should come out and said, "Do it." Robert turned the key. Dawn grabbed it as it came out. She read it and said, "Mine, that's the clue, mine." Cherry said, "Okay, let's take our time and climb down. One slip and it would be a long fall." Jack said, standing there with his arms in the air looking down the jump, "This would be great. Do you know records have been broken here?" Robert said, "I would do it, hell yes." Joe said, "I have skied in Colorado, Arizona, California, but this is way too much for me." Dawn said, "Let's go down, have lunch, and figure out our next move."

Team Three made it to the ski hill right before sunset. They pulled up to the jump. Mary said, "This is a clue, right?" Jane said, "Yes, it should be." Mary said, "Well I think we shall be sitting this one out." Ed said, "Oh come on, you just sat on your ass for the last six hours." Mark said, "We better do this; I don't want to come down in the dark." Sue said, "Good point. Of course, wouldn't it be a beautiful sunset?" Ed said, "Fall down go boom. Let's do this and get back down."

Johnny was the first one out of the car. Mary said, "Oh no you don't." Ed said, "I will take him to the top." He said to Johnny,

"Quick, let's get going before she stops us." Johnny ran behind Ed, followed by Mark and the girls. Halfway up Johnny started to whine, "My legs hurt. I can't do it, it's too far." Ed looked down at him and said, "You big pussy." He picked him up and put him on his shoulders. It was like climbing a ladder, you walked on all fours.

They got to the top and the rest of the crew was right behind them. Mary said, "I told you so." Ed said, "But what an experience, we are on top of the world. Look at this view." Jane said, "Let's get the clue. It's like climbing a ladder." She walked over and put her key and took the clue. Johnny was spitting off the tower. He asked, "Can I pee off this?" Ed looked over the side. He didn't see anyone. He smiled and said, "Okay, let's." He pulled his out and started to pee with Johnny at his side. Mary yelled, "What are you two doing?" Ed turned his head and said, "Pissing in the wind." Jane said, "Mine, that's all it says."

Mark said, "Okay, we should start to head down now." Ed asked Johnny, "Have you ever watched a sunset over the ocean? You can see it just disappear, drop off the side of the earth." He said, "Nope, I have never seen the ocean." Ed said, "Well, you're not going to see the sunset here, too dangerous. Climbing down." He took Johnny by the hand and started down the ramp. Johnny looked up at him and asked, "Do people really slide down this?" Ed said, "Yes, really fast. I read the longest jump was over four hundred and fifty feet. They must just fly down this thing. That's not for me. Have you ever skied?" Johnny said, "I went sledding."

Jane said, "We will be right with you. We want to just take in the sunset. We will start down before it gets too dark." She slid her arm around Sue's waist and looked at the setting sun. Johnny looked at the two with the sun's last light. He asked Ed, "What do you call a lesbian dinosaur?" Ed said, "I don't know. What do you call a lesbian dinosaur?" Johnny said, "A lickalotopuss." Mark said, "Oh, that is bad. What do you call a gay dinosaur? A megasoreass." Mary said from behind them, "That is enough of that." Mark turned and looked up, seeing Jane and Sue's silhouettes kissing in the last light of the day. He muttered, "They better start down." They got to the ground and Mark had his phone out and Googled Iron Mountain mine. He said, "Oh, Johnny, you're going to like this. It has a train underground. It is 2,600 feet long and is four hundred feet below ground." Mary asked, "When does it open and how far is it?" Mark said, "It's like ten miles, in a town called Vulcan, and opens at nine." Ed said, "Really, Vulcan? Like in *Star Trek*?" Johnny looked up and asked, "What is *Star Trek*?" Ed said, looking at Mary, "What, your mom hasn't showed you *Star Trek*? That is a classic. How are you raising this kid? Do you know what *Looney Tunes* is?" Mark said, "The girls have started their descent." Johnny looked up and said, "That is so high." Mark said, "One slip and it's a long fall."

Mark played with his phone and asked, "Do you mind sharing a room with Mary and the kid? It has two queens. Either that or you have to stay at a different hotel." Ed said, "Why don't you put Jane and Sue together?" Mark said, "There are three rooms available." Mary said, "That's right, they are having a big car show this weekend. I don't mind." Ed said, "Yeah, that's fine, as long as she doesn't snore." Johnny said, "Great, cookies and milk." The girls got down and Mark said, "Let's go. We are going to stop at a bat-viewing place." Mary said, "No way, those things carry rabies." Jane said, "It's too late anyway. It says to be there at dusk. And they got the white nose disease, so a lot of them died." Mark said, "I just thought the kid would have enjoyed it."

They got to the hotel. Once inside the room Johnny asked, "Where is the door to get out?" Mark said, "It's right over there." Johnny said, "That door says 'do not disturb.'" Ed said, "Boy, is he overtired." Mary said, "He is taking a shower." Ed said, "It's been a long day. Let me put on some cartoons, have milk and cookies." Mary said, "Did you have the porn disabled?" Ed said, "You are one sick girl. Do you like disabled porn? I mean people with MS or missing limbs." Mary blushed and said, "You know what I mean. Have it turned off." Ed motioned to Johnny, who was fast asleep. He took his shoes off and gently picked him up and put him under the covers. Mary said, "You might as well cancel the milk and cookies." Ed said, "You thought those were for him." Ed said, "I am showering tonight. That way you can have the bathroom in the morning." The morning came and Ed took a run for a few miles. He came up to the room at six in the morning. He grabbed the sheets and ripped them off the bed and said, "Get up. We have a meeting in an hour downstairs for breakfast. I am going to do a quick shower." Five minutes he was out, wearing nothing but a towel. He said, "Mary, get in there so I can get dressed. And pack your suitcase, bring it down for breakfast." Johnny asked, "Where did you go?" Ed said, "A quick jog. There is a beautiful lake here, Lake Antoine; a historical church. This is a nice little town." Johnny asked, "Are we going on a train?" Ed said, "Not only a train, this is a small underground train. You get showered and brush your teeth. I will meet you guys downstairs."

Ed went down to find Mark, Jane, and Sue sitting at a table. Ed said, "Team whatever is at a hotel down the street about a mile." Mark said, "That is Team Odin. Team Two is at the ski jump right now, so everyone is going to be at the iron mine at the same time." Jane asked, "What the hell happened to our lead?" Mark said, "We have lost two of our team members, and the clues haven't been that hard." Sue asked, "But Team Two went to the wrong ski jump." Mark said, "They must have driven half the night because they just pulled in at two this morning."

Team One was up and working out before breakfast. Robert said, "I could have swore I seen that leprechaun in the hall this morning. He is driving a Ford. I am going to kill that little fucker." Cherry whispered in Dawn's ear, "You have to stop this." Dawn said, "He was in the area, it was just a booty call." Jack said, "I have been researching the area. There is a large Cornish pump here, one of the biggest built. I think that might be holding a clue. It is in a museum, so we can't get into it to check it out." Robert said, "Hey, we have to bank this cash. It isn't safe in the van." Joe said, "This is true, but we are limited on what banks are around there, mostly local. You are in the Upper Peninsula." Cherry said, "There are a thousand places to hide your body up here." Jack said, "But wouldn't it be great, fishing, hunting, skiing. That ski jump was wild. Could you see flying off that thing at like sixty miles an hour?" Dawn said, "And breaking every bone in your body." Cherry chatted with an older woman around seventy; she was sitting alone. The older woman said, "I was married four times." Cherry said, "I don't want to pry, but what happened?" The older woman said, "My first husband died from eating a poisoned mushroom." Cherry said, surprised, "Really?" The older woman said, "My second and third died the same way, poisoned mushrooms." Cherry asked, "What about the fourth? Are you still married?" The old woman said, "No, he broke his neck." Cherry asked, "Now how did that happen?" The old woman said, "He wouldn't eat the mushrooms." Dawn said, "Whoa, that was too much information. So you are well off then?" The old woman smiled and said, "Oh yes. Here comes my boyfriend. You have a good time." Joe said, "I didn't catch it all but that is one twisted broad."

Team Two, the Intels, went up the ski hill and got the clue. Scott said, "Let's wait a while. The boards are a bit wet. We should catch our breath and take it easy."

They sat on top and took in the beauty of the place. On their way down, Sara was looking at her phone and took a misstep, catching her shoe. And down she went, face-first, on the wood planking. She started to roll, taking down Richard. He caught the handrail. She kept on rolling, picking up speed as she crashed down finally, wedging herself into the railing. Scott said loudly, "Take it slow. I think we are going to need an ambulance." They made their way down. Jeremy said, "Be careful, there is some blood and it is slippery."

Scott was the first one down to her. Gloria was just sobbing. Scott asked, "Sara, are you okay?" Jeremy said, "Can we move her?" Richard said, "She is pretty banged up. What do you think?" Scott said loudly, "Sara, can you stand?" She said, "Help me." Scott got down next to her and pulled her arm out of the railing. She screamed and then tried to sit her up. Scott said, "Call an ambulance. We're not going to move her." She said, "My phone." Scott said, "We will find it. What did I say? Don't look at your phones when you are walking. Stupid, stupid people."

Richard said, "Her phone is at the bottom. I will get it. So what now, we just leave her at the hospital?" Gloria said, "Maybe nothing is broken." Scott said, "Did you see that fall? She went head over tea-kettles down at least fifty feet." Jeremy said, "Great, the cops are here; this is going to take a while." Gloria said, "She is bleeding from the ears." Scott said, "Here comes the emergency medical team."

They reached the team. One of the members asked, "What do we have here?" Richard said, "A stupid broad was looking at her phone while she was walking down." The EMT said, "No, what are the injuries?" Scott said, "Looks like a dislocated shoulder, skull fracture, maybe a broken leg." Jeremy said, "The way her neck is turning black and blue, it is probably broken."

They got her on the gurney and headed down the steep stairs to the ramp onto level ground. One guy yelled, "We have to get her to the hospital." They put her in the ambulance and took off. The cop said, "Okay, what happened?" They told him they were on a treasure hunt, she was looking at her phone as she was walking down and must have missed a step. The cop said, "If you will follow me, I will bring you to the hospital."

They followed the cop through town and to the hospital. When they got there the cop said, "Okay, this is now a death. I am going to need that cell phone and any personal affects. We are going to need statements from each of you." Scott got a call. It was from Vegas. Scott said, "I have video of the fall in slow motion. My god, would you look at that. She actually landed right on her head. Look at the blood splatter." The cop said, "Send that to me. We will take a good look at it and see if you can go." Richard said, "This is all her belongings. There is twelve thousand in cash in there, make sure it gets to her family."

Five hours later they were released from the cop shop. Richard said as soon as they got into the van, "Okay, we have to put this behind us. We have to find another player." Gloria said, "I have already posted the position and had an interview." Scott said, "That is great. Let's go to the hotel and discuss this."

Jeremy and Scott were up watching the internet, waiting for Gloria and Richard. Gloria was up and she asked, "What are we watching?" Jeremy said, "Okay, this farmer was having problems with his chickens; they weren't laying eggs. So he got this Italian rooster. The farmer woke up to hear the quacking like hell. He looks out the window to see the rooster having sex with the ducks. The farmer said one of these days he was going to fuck himself to death. The next morning he awoke to the turkeys gobbling, making all kinds of noise. He jumped out of bed, grabbed the shotgun, threw open the door. There was the rooster having sex with the turkeys. He said, 'One of these days you are going to fuck yourself to death.' The next morning the farmer awoke to silence. It was a bright sunny day. The farmer said to himself, 'What the hell happened to the rooster? He should have crowed.' He walked outside to see a couple of vultures circling out in the pasture. There lay the rooster. The farmer said, 'I told you one of these days you're going to fuck yourself to death.' The rooster opened one eye and said, 'Shh, they are about to land.'" Richard said from behind them, "How can you watch this shit?" Gloria said, "Great, you finally made it. I have the interview on my phone." Scott said, "Great, send it to me and we can watch it."

It was a young black man, Randy. He was working toward his master's in engineering. Scott asked, "Does he have health insurance?" Gloria said, "Yes, he does. This is his spring break, and working at a fast food restaurant that is sucking his life away." Jeremy said, "When can he start?" Gloria called him and said, "He will be here for breakfast."

CHAPTER TEN

To the Iron Mine

Team Three got up and met down for breakfast. Mark said, "Well, everyone is here. We will meet them all at the mine, I would suppose." Jane said, "What the hell happened to Johnny's hair?" Mary said, "He hasn't taken a shower in three days." Ed said, "He is pretty worn out at the end of the day." Mary said, "No, he is a stubborn little ass." Ed said, "Fine, order for us. I will take him up and shove him in the shower." Johnny rolled his eyes up to look at him. Ed grabbed him by the back of the shirt and lifted him right off the chair. Johnny complained, "Sure, fine, whatever. Just get your stinking hands off me." Ed said, "Let's get going. I want to be back before the breakfast is cold."

Mark said, "He is a good kid, just needs some tender loving care." Mary said, "Yeah at the end of my foot." Sue said, "And don't threaten to kick him in the ass. He will tell you it will take a week to get you shoe back." Jane asked, "So what is the game plan?" Mark said, "No game plan. We all know the clue is in the mine. Just hope we are the only ones to find it." Mary said, "This clue is too easy. There are a few mines around. Why do we think it is this one?"

Ed brought Johnny into their hotel room and said, "Okay, get undressed." Johnny said, "No way, I will get undressed in the bathroom." Ed stepped into the bathroom and turned on the shower. Johnny asked, "What are you doing?" Ed said, "Get your ass in there. You have three minutes to shampoo your hair, do a quick soap and rinse. Time starts now. If you are not done in three minutes, I will wash you. Got it?" Johnny's eyes opened wide. He quickly got undressed and into the shower. Ed got his clothes set out. He stepped into the bathroom and barked, "A minute and a half left. You need help?" Johnny turned off the water, stuck his head out of the shower, and said. "I am done. Get out of here." Ed said, "Your clothes are on the toilet. You have a minute to dry and to be dressed."

Ed and Johnny made it down to the table before their breakfast even arrived. Mary looked up and said, "I don't believe it." Ed said, "Motivation. I didn't even have to wash him." Jane asked, "Did he wash behind his ears?" Ed said, "I don't fricken know and I don't care. As long as he doesn't smell." Mark said, "That shirt doesn't match." Ed asked, "What did we miss?" Sue said, "I am playing the part of being Mark's girlfriend and you guys are playing a family. As long as they don't see us getting out of the van together, we should be fine." Mary said, "I still don't get it. What is the difference if they know who we are?" Ed smiled and said, "The less they know the better. We might need to get some information from them. If they think we are just friendly folks, they might just spill the beans."

Johnny looked at Ed and asked, "Okay, if Adam and Eve were made by God, why do they say humans have been on earth for millions of years?" The table got quiet waiting for an answer. Ed smiled and said, "Okay, this guy talked with God. He asked God, 'What is a thousand years to you?' God said, 'It is like a second.' Then the man asked, 'What is a million dollars to you?' God said, 'It is like a penny.' The guy then asked, 'May I have a million dollars?' God said, 'In a second.' Did you catch that? He would have to wait for a thousand years to get his money." Johnny said, "Adam and Eve, the timeline doesn't make sense." Ed said, "Okay, God created Adam and Eve. He put them in the Garden of Eden. So far so good. Eve, the bitch, ate from the forbidden tree. She was tricked by the devil and God tore down the walls of Eden, letting all the animals out of the garden along with Adam and Eve. Now who says the dinosaurs were not outside the garden or were they extinct already? Neanderthals bred with the sons and daughters of Eve, or they killed them off. They were the first of their kind. Life could have been here for millions of years. The crust of the earth had to cool, the universe is ever growing, and the Big Bang theory might be the way God is expanding, starting life on other planets. Does that answer your question?" Johnny said, "The devil has been here a long time." Jane said, "In some cultures, it is the balance of good and evil." Sue said, "The yin and yang." Mark said, "Well, that is our lesson for the day. Now we just stick with the tour and don't talk about the treasure hunt."

Team Two's Richard got up early and sat at the bar and had a bloody Mary. An old man sat next to him and struck up a conversation. He said, "That drink reminds me of something years ago. I was having trouble getting an erection. I remembered watching a breeder rub the pussy of a cow in heat, then walk over to the bull and rub her juices on his face, then leave them out in the barnyard. And the bull would go right through the herd and mount that one cow. I reached down and rubbed my wife's pussy while she was asleep, got her all wet, and rubbed it on my face. Boom, I had a rock-hard erection. I turned on the light and said, 'Look, honey.' She said, 'Oh my god, you have a bloody nose. Don't get it on the sheets.'" Richard took a drink and said, "That is disgusting." The old man said, "Ah, you would think. But it worked." Richard excused himself and went and sat down with the team as they came down from their rooms.

Gloria said, "I still haven't gotten a hold of the Iron Mine. I thought we could pay a couple of hundred to get in an early tour." Randy said, "You know what I miss up here? Chicken and waffles." Jeremy said, "That's not a black thing, it's a Southern thing. I have had it at the Pfister Hotel in Milwaukee." Randy said, "Good, right? So what are you whiteys doing?" Scott said, "We have a little time before heading to the mine tour. You do have your bags packed? We will be staying somewhere else tomorrow night." Randy said, "Where?" Gloria asked, "What part of *treasure hunt* don't you understand?" Richard said, "You were in college, didn't you do treasure hunts?" Randy said, "I was in college up in Houghton. They get like fifteen feet of snow up there, we drank." Gloria said, "You have to be shitting me. Fifteen feet of snow?" Jeremy said, "The record was 355 inches the winter of '78. That's like damn near thirty feet." Scott said, "Who would want to live up there?" Randy said, "Lake Affect, it just snows a lot up there. There are lots of snowbirds." Gloria said, "You mean people that leave for the winter and come back in the spring?" Randy said, "You're pretty smart for a white girl. We should hook up sometime." Richard said, "I just seen Team Odin run through the parking lot." Randy asked, "Team Odin?" Scott said, "That team is a bunch of jocks; Odin, the Norse god." Jeremy said, "And the other team is a bunch of lowlife workers, common folks." Gloria said, "They are in the lead." Randy asked, "Now what does that mean, the lead? The payout is at the end? I thought you got paid as you play." Gloria said, "If your team gets the ten grand every time, that is fifty grand, ten clues. That's a half million. The last payday is one hundred grand. That makes it a million for that team." Randy said, "Now we are talking." Scott said, "We haven't got a ten grand yet."

Team One came in. Jack walked up and said, "Hey, Team Intel, are you ready to have your ass handed to you today?" They went over and sat at the other side of the room. Dawn said, "Did you see? They have a cute black guy on their team." Cherry said, "Once you go black you never go back." Dawn said, "They're not all that hung, trust me. And if you want to be treated well, try a rich old guy." Robert asked, "So have you tried that?" Dawn had a sly smile slide across her face and then said, "Oh, it was nice. His wife didn't like it much. I was like his puppy. He took me all over and gave me treats, five-star hotels. I was the mistress, London, French Rivera, Vegas, and I had a condo in Washington." Jane asked, "Let me guess, you didn't save anything and he kicked you to the curb." Dawn said, "That was my mistake. I should have skimmed some off the top and made a nest egg. But we are talking good times. I got caught having an affair with a bodyguard. He was so frickin' cute." Joe asked, "This sounds like someone we should know." Dawn said, "I was paid never to talk about it, so that is as far as it goes. And I don't want to sleep with the fishes, do I?" Jack said "Okay, we will let it go. So we have an hour and a half to be at the mine. Just watch our tongues. Team Brainy Acts will be right there. We might have to go through the whole tour then go back in to get the clue." Robert said, "This clue was pretty easy, maybe too easy. All it said was *mine*. Could it have been a land mine or a ship mine? Is it mine or yours?" Jack said, "Let's not read too much into this. We are here and so is Intel, this has to be it." Dawn said, "You do know it was an easy clue." Robert said, "I am just saying, there are over ten million hits when you type in mines in Wisconsin. How do we know this is the one?

Team Intel left the breakfast and headed to the door, picking up their luggage at the concierge. Team Odin finished their breakfast and headed back to their rooms to get their luggage and off to the iron mine. Team Three got into the van and drove around the city, up to the Cornish pump museum. Mark said, "This could be a place for a clue. It is the largest steam-driven pump ever to be made in the United States, and it opens at nine." He pulled into the parking lot to the pump museum and World War II glider museum.

Mark said, "These gliders were made here in the 1940s at a Ford plant. They made more CG-4A gliders than any plant. And you're right, it doesn't open till nine." Mary asked, "Aren't we going to be late for the mine tour?" Jane put a little blush on Sue and said, "That is the point. We want to be late so they don't see us getting out of the van. Once they see us together, they will figure out who's playing the game."

Mark pulled out onto the highway and started the ride to Vulcan. Mark said, "Watch for signs. I have it in my GPS. We want to be a few minutes late but not too late." Johnny said excitedly, "There it is, a huge guy holding an ax." Mary said, "That is a mining tool. My god is that a big sign."

Mark pulled into the parking lot and said, "Well, the other two vans are here and there is no way we can hide this thing." Sue said, "We slip in, get the clue, and slip out. We need to get the lead." Mary asked, "Who is in the lead?" Mark said, "Well, we are all here, so we are starting over. But we have made the most money so far." Ed said, "Let's get on the same tour. I am going over to the sign to take a picture, then we can get inside." Jane said, "Take your picture after. Let's get inside."

They went in. Ed, Mary, and Johnny bought their tickets first. Jane, Sue, and Mark were last. Mark said to Ed, "Get close to Team Odin, those guys over there, and see what they are saying." Mark wondered by Cherry and Dawn were looking at rocks. The tour guide asked everyone to come over to the back. They all got rain jackets and hard hats. Ed handed Johnny a hooded sweatshirt. He said, "You're going to need it." The tour guide asked who has been on the ride before. Mark and Jane raised their hands. Ed leaned in and whispered to Mary, "They lied." She smiled and said, "This should be fun. Keep an eye on Johnny."

They all lined up and the guide told them about the mining equipment. He started up an old air compressor and showed how some of it worked. They were loaded on a small train. They were going into the mine 2,600 feet. And they got off the train and started to walk. Jane said, "It's bloody freezing in here." Sue said, "The tour guide said it stays between forty-three and forty-six degrees in the cave year-round."

The guide told them all about the mining process. They got to the point when they were overlooking a huge lake. The tour guide said, "We took seventeen five-gallon buckets of dead bats out this spring. They died of a fungus called white nose syndrome. Now you remember the sign of Big John out front of the mine. That miner is forty feet tall and twelve feet wide." She turned on a switch and a light came on showing a miniature Big John. She said, "That is a ten-foot version of the same sign across the lake."

Johnny was amazed. He asked, "Is there a boat to get across?" The tour guide said, "No, but when was the last time you were in complete darkness?" She turned off the lights in the tunnel and left the lights on Big John across the lake. There you could see a question mark right at his feet.

All of a sudden there was chatter. The tour guides asked, "Are you ready?" She turned off the light and it went dark. You couldn't see your hand in front of your face. Little Johnny said, "Wow, I am blind." Ed pushed his light on his watch and it lit half the tunnel. The tour guide said, "See how little light it takes to light the darkness. Someone turn on their phone." Five people turned on their phones and lit the whole tunnel in an eerie light. Mark stepped up behind Jane and Sue and wrapped his arms around them and said, "We told you it was going to be cold. She said it is forty-four degrees year-round."

The questions started to fly about how to get over to the sign of Big John on the other side. The tour guide said, "It is around six hundred yards across and very deep, the deepest manmade lake in the UP. Team Two asked, "How do you change the light bulb over there?" She said, "I don't have a clue. They switched to LED years ago and the bulbs are supposed to last for years." Jack flashed a high-powered flashlight on the wall of the cave next to the water. Mark and the girls were right next to him. Robert asked, "How much time is there between tours?" The tour guide said, "Around a half hour. We get you in here and out before you get to cold. Shall we continue our tour? We are going to make our way back to the train." Ed said as he picked up Johnny, "This is going to be interesting."

They got back to the gift shop. Each team huddled together and discussed what they were going to do. Ed said to Mary, "Count the members in Team Odin. One didn't come out. Shop around. I am going to talk to Mark." He stepped over to Mark and said quietly, "One of the Odins didn't come out of the mine." Mark said, "The bathroom is right over there." Ed said, "I am going to bribe a worker to tell us how to get over there."

Ed went back and checked pockets on a raincoat that was hanging in the backroom, and then slid into the door the tour guide went in. He walked up to her. She was sitting having a coffee, talking to a man. Ed held out his hand and said, "You were told not to tell us how to get across the lake to the question mark. I have five hundred dollars if you would take me over there." The man said, "Well, Sally, five hundred. We split it." She smiled and said, "Sounds good to me." Ed gave her $250 and said, "I will give him the other $250 when we are back. So is there a boat?" The man said, "Come on, we can ride right up to it. There is a shaft on the other side of the hill. We will take a four-wheeler." Ed took his phone out of his pocket and asked, "How long is it going to take?" The man said, "A half hour, forty-five minutes, depending on the tours. We can't be in there during a tour." Ed asked, "How many times do you go in here?" The man said, "Three or four times a season you have to clean the light." Ed said, "That makes sense."

He got on the back of a four-wheeler and the guy took off. He was driving around forty miles an hour and stopped in front of an iron gate. He got off and unlocked the door, swung it out of the way, and said, "Get on, we aren't walking. We have ten minutes to get in and out. They want the mine to be quiet."

The man hammered it going through the tunnels. They got to the Big John sign. He turned on a light and the sign was illuminated. It had three spotlights at his feet. Ed said, "This will take but a minute." He saw a light go out halfway across the lake. He put his key in and took the clue, and he quickly read it then put it in his pocket. Ed said, "We're good. Let's go."

They got back to the gift shop. Ed paid the man and shook his hand. He asked, "Is there a way I can get out of here without being seen?" The man showed him to an outside door. Ed called Mark and said, "Meet you at the van. I will call Mary." He called Mary and said, "Make sure Johnny goes pee, and meet us at the van."

Ed made it to the van and said, "The clue is 'piers.' What the hell is a piers? I know what a pier is. Are there somewhere with a bunch of piers, a lake or river?" Jane said, "Google says Piers Gorge, it is right off of Highway 8, just out of a town named Norway. We drove right by it." Mary showed up with two bags of stuff. She asked, "What took so long?" Ed said, "We had to go around to a side entrance with a four-wheeler and go in a service tunnel. Oh, and by the way, the guy from Team Odin is halfway around the lake." Mary asked, "So did you get the clue?" Mark said, "Buckle up, it sounds like we are going to do some climbing." Jane said, "Do you really think so?" Sue said, "There is Wildman Adventure, whitewater rafting, zip lines." Johnny said, "Let's go there." Mark said, "First we go hiking the state park."

Team Two started to ask about how to get to the other side of the lake. They devised a plan of sneaking in there at night using a raft and crossing the lake. Scott asked, "Did anyone see any wires? How did they get juice to the other side of that lake?" Jeremy said, "That is interesting. I guess I never looked." Randy said, "I will walk around the back and check if they ran wires out into the woods." Sara smiled and said, "No, that wouldn't be the best thing to do, a black guy out checking out the joint. Why don't we just ask?" Randy asked, "What are you implying, that I am a thief? Well, maybe it would be easier to ask." Richard said, "I will ask." He took out his money clip and pulled out a fifty. He asked the lady behind the counter at the gift shop as he slid the fifty across the counter, "Miss, I was wondering if I could buy some information. You see, we are on a treasure hunt and there is a clue at the big sign across the lake, in the mine. Is there another entrance to it?" She smiled and said, "The last guy paid five hundred." He looked her in the eye and said, "Three." She said, "Four and you have a deal." He shook his head as he peeled off four hundred-dollar bills and then asked, "Will you show us?" The woman said, "Stay right here, I will be right back."

A police officer came in and said loudly, "Mary, is Mary here?" The woman from behind the counter came back with the man who drove Ed. He walked up and asked, "Which one of you are going to see Big John?" Scott stepped up and said, "I suppose I could." The man said, "The guy that snuck around the lake is going to be charged with trespassing or work out some kind of payment."

Scott got on the back of the four-wheeler and they took their time getting to the locked iron door. They sat there talking. Scott was telling him about the treasure hunt. The man got a call and he said, "Time to go. The tour is on its way back." Scott got on the back of the four-wheeler and the man sped through the tunnel at around forty miles an hour. He came to the sign, jumped off, and switched on the light. He said, "Be quick about it."

Scott quickly stuck his key into the slot and took the clue. The man already had the four-wheeler turned around and his hand on the light switch. Scott sat down and grabbed onto the guy. They shot through the tunnels to the door. The man quickly slammed the door and put the padlock on it. They shot through the woods. Scott held on for dear life.

When they got back, Scott followed him as he jogged to the gift shop. Jeremy met Scott and said, "They arrested one of the Odins. They took him in the side room." Scott said, "They are going to shake him down. It's going to cost them a lot more than four hundred bucks."

CHAPTER ELEVEN

To Piers Gorge

Team Three was on their way to the gorge. It was just a short distance. There was one other car in the parking lot. Mark said, "I hope you have a good pair of tennis shoes on." Jane said, "It doesn't look like a hard hike, and it shouldn't be that swift." Sue said, "If there is whitewater rafting, it is going to be fast. And the clue probably will be a hundred feet up on a cliff somewhere." Ed looked at Johnny and said sternly, "If you have to go to the bathroom, go now." Jane said, "Oh, I hate those porta potties, I can hold it."

Mark led the way down the trail through the woods. Mark said, "I did bring bug spray." Ed asked Johnny, "Why did the elephant paint his toenails red?" Johnny said, "An elephant painting his toenails?" Ed said, "It is so he can hide in a strawberry patch." Everyone moaned. Mark asked, "How do you get a one-armed Polack out of a tree?" You could see Johnny was really thinking about that. Mark said, "You wave at him." Sue said, "What do you call a guy with no arms or legs on your doorstep?" Everyone said at once, "Mat." She asked, "In a hole?" Mark said, "Phil." Sue asked, "In your pool?" Ed and Mark said, "Bob." Sue asked, "Under your car?" Nobody said anything. Sue smiled and said, "Axel. How about in your mailbox? "Bill." "In a pile of leaves?" "Russell." "Last but not least, in a hot tub?" "That would be Stew." Johnny said, "How about a dog with no arms or legs?" Ed looked down at him and asked, "Why would you call him? He wouldn't come anyway." Johnny gave him a dirty look. Ed asked, "What? I heard that one already."

Mary said, "Shh, be quiet. You hear that? It is water rushing." Johnny cocked his head and said, "Yes, I hear it." Mark asked, "Can he swim?" Mary said, "Like a fish." Sue said, "You ask him but not the rest of us?" Jane smiled at her and asked, "Can you swim?" Sue said, "I never learned. I have tried a couple of times." Jane said, "Do you trust me? I will show you how." Ed said, "At least the doggy paddle."

They were on a trail high above the river and Mark said, "It's a big one." Sue said, "See the high cliffs? God, I hope it isn't a marker." Mary asked, "Why? We are the first here. It would be ten grand apiece." Mary said, "Why do they call it Piers Gorge?" Jane said, "The rock ledges or piers cause the water turbulence. There are four of these piers, the fourth one is small." Ed said, "Keep an eye out, that question mark can be anywhere."

They kept on walking father into the woods following the high path. Sue said, "There it is. How the hell are we going to get that?" Mark said, "Where? Oh, I see." Johnny said, "I want to see." Jane said, "Look in the middle of the river, on that rock." Ed said, "We might have to rent a rubber raft." Jane said, "Screw that, it's a clue. I can make that." Mary said, "You're shitting me, that water must be moving twenty miles an hour." Ed said, "There is no way you can make it out there." Jane smiled and said, "You want to make a bet?" Mark said, "It's too risky." Ed said, "Let's go down and take a look."

The team started to head down the trail to the rocks that stuck out into the river. Jane said, "You're right, the water is moving pretty fast." Ed asked, "Mark, you got that rope with you?" Mark said, "We aren't going to let Jane risk it; the water is just too fast." Ed said, "That's what I said. I am going to do it. I go up to that rock up there then swim across to that rock then to the clue. Then you guys pull my ass out of the river." Mary said, "There is no way you are doing that."

Ed sat down and took off his shoes, socks, pants, and shirt. Mary's jaw dropped. Jane said, "Damn, someone has been working out." Ed said, "Mark, I need a towel for when I get back." Mark said, "That's nice, I will pull one out of my ass."

Ed worked his way up stream above the clue. He started to walk across to the next rock and the current took him right off his feet. He swam as hard as he could and just reached the next rock. He walked up as far as he could go. This time he dove right in and swam like hell. He got behind the rock. The current got hold of him and brought him back up to the rock, smashing him against it. Instantly blood poured from his nose. He held on and pulled himself onto the rock. He got up and put his key in the question mark and took the clue. He was standing there bare-ass naked, his underwear got stripped off him in the current. He rolled up the clue and put it in his mouth. He gave the thumbs-up sign. He slid into the water and started to swim out of the back wash into the current. He was instantly pulled downstream. Mark wrapped the rope around a tree and started to pull. Ed went downstream but was pulled against the bank.

Mark walked down to him with his clothes and said, "I thought we were going to lose that clue." Ed took the clue out of his mouth and handed it to Mark as Mark gave him his clothes. Ed was completely out of breath. He said, "Glide, it has to be the glider museum." Johnny said, "You have a little dick." Ed said, "The water is cold, I have some shrinkage going on." Mary covered her eyes. She had tears streaming down her face and she said, "I thought you were going to die." Ed sat up and said, "We saved a lot of time. Let's get to that museum and get to the next clue." Jane said, "He is right you know. Mark, wind up that rope, let's get going."

Sue stood there waiting for Ed to put on his pants. Jane said softly in her ear, "He does have a nice body." Jane turned to her and kissed her full on the lips and said, "Yeah, but men are nothing but trouble." Johnny came up and said, "That was cool." Ed said, "Yeah, but I think I am going to get a black eye from it." Ed stood and put on his pants. Mary turned around to see the two girls watching. She said, "Turn around." Sue said, "Cheap entertainment. Oh, the water must be cold." Ed looked up and said, "Damn cold." Mark said, "Come on, we don't have all day." Ed got his shoes on. Johnny said, "I have to pee." Ed asked, "Who is stopping you? Step behind a tree.

You know what they say, the grass is always greener if you water it with your wiener."

As they got close to the parking lot, Mark said, "Jane and Sue, take the trail to the river. Stay there until they pass. Johnny, you ride on my shoulders. And Mary and Ed, act like lovers."

Team Two, the Intels, walked by.

Mary took Ed by the hand and looked at his injury to his face. She said quietly, "You are going to get a black and blue eye you know. That was really stupid. You could have drowned." Ed said, "No, I figured it all out. Everything worked well except the current was stronger than I thought."

Johnny asked Mark, "Did you ever have kids?" Mark said, "A long time ago. I had to kill them. They wouldn't listen, same with my wife. I fed them to my cats."

Team Two talked as they walked by, not even noticing them. They asked Ed, "Hey, how far to the waterfalls?" Ed said, "Take the high trail; it is a lot dryer, about a half mile."

Mary waved the girls up. They were sprawled out on the rocks, taking in the sun. Once they got back to the van, Mark said, "Let's roll. I can feel a payday coming." Jane said, "I think you are right. It is the fourth clue." Ed said, "It is the third clue. First was the ski hill in the iron mine, the gorge, now the glider museum." Johnny said, "That is four. Where did you go to school?" Ed said, "I am going to need some aspirin and a whiskey." Mark said, "Buckle up." He pulled out onto the road.

Johnny motioned for Ed to lean over. He whispered in Ed's ear, "Mark killed his kids and his wife, buried them in the backyard. He said they wouldn't listen to him." Ed chuckled and said, "No, Mark went through a bitter divorce. He lost his house, one of his cars, has to pay for the family's health insurance. He lost his job, his apartment, half of his retirement. Cashed in everything he owned just to keep from going to jail." Mark said from the front seat, "I never told you any of that. Who the hell are you?" Ed said, "Just someone that cares. And you fed your wife and kids to your cats? You must have had big cats." Johnny said, "He has good hearing too." Team Odin paid the mine not to press charges. They passed Mark going down the road. Mark turned down toward the whitewater rafting. As soon as he did he pulled into a side road and parked, waiting for them to pass them. He turned around and headed back toward Iron Mountain. He smiled and said, "Just trying to throw them off the scent. Now the Intels won't try, it is too risky." Jane said, "Odin might try to swim across, but they might rent a raft."

Team Two got down the trail to where they could see the clue. Scott and Jeremy said, "Oh, Randy, you're the last one to join. You swim out there and get the clue." Randy stuttered, "Yo, you want me do what, swim out there? Are you fucking crazy? I am not going down there." Richard burst out laughing. "No, dude, we will rent a raft. My god, you should have seen you face. It damn near turned white." Randy said, "Bunch of crackers." Scott said, "Now that was funny. Let's get out of here. We can't beat Team One in a boat race." Gloria said, "Well, they might still have one of theirs in jail." Scott asked, "Has anyone ever whitewater rafted before?" Randy said, "I did, the Grand Canyon, eight days, 188 miles, sixty-seven rapids. That was a trip never to forget or do again." Gloria said, "Never do again why?" Randy said, "Well if it was just guys, maybe. The drama of being with those people for eight days straight . . . I lost my girlfriend. Come to find out she was one crazy-ass broad." Richard said, "I have kayaked, canoed, water skied. This shouldn't be that bad. We have to hurry, the last trip down the river is at two." Gloria said, "They are holding one for us and we have the guide and a case of beer." Jeremy said, "Really, beer?" Gloria said, "It was an option. Would you like a shore lunch?" Richard said, "We tip him big up front, tell him what we are doing." Gloria said, "Done, we are getting a raft with a motor. It will cut the time in half." Randy said, "That was an option on the Colorado. Boy, I wish we would have took that option. Let me tell you, it was one of my best trips of my life. The walls of the canyon reached up a mile in places, beautiful waterfalls. You were out in the middle of dumbfuck nowhere listening to nothing but bitching." Scott said, "Sounds like a good time. Can you operate a raft?" Randy said, "We are getting a motorized raft with a guide; we shouldn't have to do anything." Gloria said, "Drink beer, have the guide park right at the clue. The whitewater shouldn't bother us."

Team Intel pulled into the rafting place. A tall blonde girl met them. She asked, "Team Intel?" Gloria said, "Yes? We booked the trip down the river." The gal said, "Hi, I am Bonnie. I will be your guide. Shall I help you with your things?" Richard got out and stepped close to her. He held out his hand, showing her a bill in his palm. He said, "Gloria here said she told you about our trip. This is to be a quick trip down the river." Bonnie said, "Sounds good to me. No thrills, just a ride to that question mark." Scott said, "Here is the fifty bucks apiece, that's $250, and a very good tip at the end. And we will see how you do." Richard said, "I already palmed her a hundred." Bonnie said, "Okay, let's go inside and get you helmets and life preservers." Jeremy asked, "Do we have a choice of beer?" Bonnie said, "Yes, and you picked Miller Highlife." Bonnie asked, "Has anyone rafted before?" Randy held up his hand. Scott said, "Don't ask."

A half hour later they were in the water. Bonnie sat at the helm. She said, "This is a bit unusual. People like the quietness of the river, the adventure. It normally takes five and a half hours. We can do this in about two and a half. We are going to shoot the rapids manually, so you have to work together." Richard said, "Hey, Randy, hand out those beers." Bonnie took one. She said, "Trust me."

She fired up the outboard and started down the river. They all got wet shooting the rapids. Bonnie was yelling orders. Soon they got to the question mark. Scott said, "Randy, take Richard with you and get the clue." The two walked to the other end of the rock pier and Richard showed him how to get the clue. They came back and Randy yelled, "Glider, that is all it said." Gloria put her finger to her lips and said, "Let's not tell the world. If they want the clue, they have to get it." Bonnie said, "There is a glider museum in Iron Mountain. Now push us straight off the rock. We are going to do a 180 and get our nose headed down the river." Jeremy yelled, "How much farther?" Bonnie said, "A mile or so."

Gloria stopped paddling and started to bail out the boat. There was a good six inches of water in the bottom. They pulled up to the landing. Bonnie asked as they were loading up the boat, "So how did I do?" Scott said, "Excellent, less than two hours. We shot the rapids quickly. It was fun." Richard said, "You did a fine job. Get us back to our van so we can get on the road." She smiled and asked, "Do you want the rest of your beer?"

Gloria asked when they got to the lodge, "Should we tip her a hundred?" Randy said, "Why? We are done. We will never see her again." Scott said, "Do it. She did a good job nice and quick. We didn't lose anyone."

Team Odin got to the state park, jogged down the trails to find the question mark. They stood at the shore looking out into the river. Cherry asked Robert, "You are the team captain. Swim your ass off and get the clue." Robert looked at her and said, "Screw you, we need a boat." Joe said, "That is some fast current. You have to do it right or you could miss it completely." Jack said, "Too dangerous; undertows, you get your foot caught between two rocks you drown. No question, we need a boat." Cherry said, "Oh, you need a boat alright; it only takes one person to get a clue." Jack said, "I will go." Joe said, "Right with you, brother." Robert asked, "Are we doing kayaks? Should we rent them and carry them in here?" Jack said, "There is a place to drop them in upriver like two miles. It won't take long, and the girls can pick us up here." Joe said, "Sounds like a blast. Let's get the kayaks."

They went to Niagara and rented three kayaks, strapped them to the roof, and the girls followed them down the trail to the river and took pictures of them going down the river. They drove back to the state park and hiked to where they could see the question mark. Twenty minutes later, the guys came down the river. All three of them landed on the rock pier. They got the clue and made it to the side, where they pulled the boats out and carried them up the hill to the trail. Joe asked, "Can anyone tell me some kayak jokes?" Robert said, "Knock, knock." Cherry said, "Who is there?" Robert said, "Canoe." Everyone asked, "Canoe who?" Robert said, "Canoe you tell me some kayak jokes?" Jack said, "Okay, here is one. Two blondes were kayaking., It started to get cold, so they started a fire and the boat sank, proving once again you can't have your kayak and heat it too." Joe asked, "What's the difference between a slut and a bitch? A slut will sleep with anyone and a bitch will sleep with anyone but you." Dawn said, "That's enough of the jokes, let's just get to the van."

When they got to the top by the girls, Joe said, "You should have come, it was great." Robert said, "Jack took a digger, sucked him right to the bottom." Jack said, "I thought I dislocated my shoulder for a second. The clue has a three on it, so we are the last ones again." They carried out the kayaks. Cherry and Dawn took Jack's; his back was bleeding through his tee shirt.

CHAPTER TWELVE

Cornish Pump and Glider

Team Three was at the glider museum. They went in and Jane walked up to an older lady that was working there. She said, "We are on a treasure hunt looking for a question mark." The lady said, "You have to pay admission to enter." Mark said, "Eight bucks apiece. Here is fifty, and if you show us that question mark, there is another fifty." The lady said as she took the fifty, "Right this way. They put a small question mark in a locker over here near the wall." Johnny said, "This is so cool." Ed said, "Come on, let's check this place out quickly before we have to leave. I can't believe how clean it is. The floor just shines. Johnny, no touching anything."

The woman took them right to the locker. She opened it and asked, "Is this what you are looking for?" Jane reached in her shirt and took out the key that was hanging around her neck. She handed it to Sue. Sue smiled and held it and said, "It is so warm, right next to your heart." Mary rolled her eyes and said, "We are waiting." Sue put the key in and turned it. Out came the clue. She read it, "Pump." The lady said, "That would be the Cornish Pump museum. We just walked through it, but we will be closing in fifteen minutes." Mary shouted, "We are leaving." Mark said, "Tell the old broad it will be worth her while to stay open a few minutes longer." Ed raced Johnny to the entrance; Johnny was right behind him.

The last ten yards, Ed slowed to let him win.

Mark said, "Lucky it's in the same building. Shall we try this again?" He stepped up to the admissions and said to the old lady, "Hello, we are on a treasure hunt and are looking for a clue." The old lady said, "I am old, not stupid. I just showed you the question mark. And we are just about to close, you will have to come back tomorrow." Mark put a hundred on the desk and said, "This is for your time." He pulled out a fifty and said, "This is for information. Now we are looking for a question mark or a small pyramid-looking thing with five keyholes in it." The old lady said, "That I have seen. It is at the top of the pump. If you will follow me."

She turned the sign in the window so it read "closed." The team went in. Mark was carrying his backpack. Mark said, "Johnny, this is a museum. You have to be quiet and don't touch anything." The guide started to talk while they walked, "Now this is the largest steam-driven pumping engines ever built in the United States. There are only a few this big in the world. It weighs 725 tons, stands fifty-four feet off the floor. The flywheel itself weighs 160 tons. Now this pump ran at ten revolutions per minute at 319 gallons per stroke or 3,119 gallons a minute, 190,400 an hour. That would be 4,593,600 gallons in twenty-four hours." Ed said, "Whoa that's amazing." Johnny tugged at Ed's shirt and gave him a dirty look.

The guide said, "The pump started in 1883 and ran until 1932. In 1934, the Oliver Iron Mining Company gave the pump to Dickinson County for people to see. Now if you look up, there is your clue hanging from the rafters." Sue said, "How the hell are we going to get up there?" Johnny said, "Holy shit, that's up there." Ed asked the guide, "How did they hang that thing?" The guide said, "Nobody knows. They came in one night, in the morning there it was." Mark said, "Okay, we don't have much time, let's do this." Jane said, "This is a rough one. It is hanging ten feet from the ceiling, fifty feet from both sides, and at least twenty from the far wall." Ed said, "Yeah, we can see that. How the hell are we going to get all five of us up there?" Mark said, "We could get an electric crane, just like the box they have outside to let people down into the mine. We go up to the clue." Johnny said, "Why don't we go up the stairs to the top of the pump and put a ladder up?" Ed said, "Too far, and we need to get five people up there." Jane said, "We could string a wire across." Mark said sarcastically, "What, and tightrope walk across?" Jane said, "Now who in the hell would hang that up there like that?" Ed said, "Makes you think, doesn't it?" Mark said, "It is hanging freely, so we can move it from side to side." Ed said, "We need all five of us. I think we drop it." Jane said, "That is against the rules." Ed asked, "What the hell are the rules?" Sue said, "The teams can't work together, and you must leave the clues like you found them." Johnny said, "How would they know?" Jane said, "This is live fed to Vegas. Right now people are betting how we do this." Ed said, "Or who dies trying. I think we get an electric crane, lower the marker to the ground and put it back up." Mark said, "You wouldn't have a crane in your pocket with a sixty-foot rope?"

Jane said, "Scaffolding. Dude, do you have any scaffolding?" Ed said, "Why the hell didn't I think of that?" The tour guide said, "There is a pile of it in the backroom. It's for changing lights, but I don't think there is that much." Ed said, "Let's see it." The guide said, "You know if I get caught I am going to lose my job." Mark said, "Okay, how about a couple of hundred and nobody will know we were here?"

They went and looked at the scaffolding and counted the pieces. Mark said, "It is going to be close. We put a couple of planks across the top, we should be able to do it." Mark and Ed grabbed an end piece and the girls grabbed cross members. The guys assembled it as fast as the parts were brought out. They used a rope to pull up the pieces. In two hours they had it built and the five of them climbed up to the top. Mark was right, they had to stand on planks on the very top. Mary did the countdown, "Five, four, three, two, turn," and the door on the top opened. Sue reached in and took out five bundles of cash. Ed said, "Slowly pull out your keys. Let's get this tore down and get something to eat."

Mark and Ed started to lower every part. Jane said, "Okay, everyone, give. Cough up a hundred. Without our guide we wouldn't have got this payday." Mark said, "We already gave her three hundred . . . oh, fine." He took a hundred out of his pile of cash. Ed said, "Not a bad night of work, ten thousand bucks." Mark said, "Let's go to the hotel and figure out the next clue. Who has it?"

Team One was watching from outside. Jack said, "We catch the old gal who is running the place and get her to keep it open so we can get a payday." Cherry said, "We can't miss her. They will not let us put that scaffolding up during the day." Robert said, "I just wonder how much they paid her to let them do this." Dawn said, "There is only one car in the parking lot. I will ether get in the backseat or sit next to it. Jack, you hide the van." Robert said, "No, that's not the way we are going to do this." He started to bang on the door. The tour guide said, "Who the hell could that be?" She answered the door. Robert said, "Stop what you're doing. We are going to have to reassemble the damn thing anyway." The guide asked, "And who are you?" Robert said, "We are Team Odin. How much did they pay you?" The guide said, "A thousand bucks." Dawn said, "Holy shit, a grand." Jack said, "Let's all go in. We are not working together, so we are not breaking any rules."

The guide said loudly, "Stop, we will put away the scaffolding. You guys get out of here. Team Odin will just pull it out anyway." Ed said, "Shit, they seen us. Mary, Johnny, get to the van. I am right behind you." Joe said, "We will get started on assembling the thing. This shouldn't take long." The guide asked, "How many teams are there?" Jack said, "Just three."

Team Three slid out the side door, not even speaking to Team One. Team Odin quickly climbed up and started to reassemble the scaffolding and got their payday. Cherry said, "What the hell is this pump thing?" The guide filled her in on how it worked, when it was built, how many people worked in the mine, and when the price of ore dropped after World War II it closed.

It took a good hour and a half to disassemble the scaffolding. They went to the hotel bar. Cherry Googled *fire* in Iron Mountain, Michigan. There was over 60 million hits but she didn't come up with anything. Then she put in *fire Wisconsin* and the Peshtigo fire came up. She told everyone. They discussed when they had to leave. It didn't open till ten o'clock. Jack said, "It is an hour and a half drive, so we leave at eighty thirty." Dawn said, "Hey, look at the TV. There is Dill Dump, the president. Turn it up." The presidential aide nervously approached him. Dill looked up and asked, "What is it?" The aide said, "It is the abortion bill, Mr. President. What would you like me to do with it?" Dill said, "For Christ's sakes, just pay it, make sure nobody finds out about it."

Dawn said, "Whoa, didn't see that coming." Joe asked, "Should I grab another round?" He walked up to the bar, ordered another round of drinks. A man in a lab coat stopped and talked with Joe. He said, "I am a scientist, and am looking for someone that is not from around here. We have found a female ape and would like to have it mate with a human. Five thousand dollars." Joe looked at him and said, "Okay, three conditions: my team must not learn about this. Second, the kids must be raised Catholics. And third, I have to pay you with a credit card." The guy said, "No. See, we will pay you." Joe slammed his beer and waved to the team. "See you guys in the morning."

Team Two, the Intels, they called the rafting company and got them to open early. They got the same girl to guide them to the clue in Piers Gorge. They got a room in Iron Mountain. They met in Scott and Jeremy's room. They were watching the internet again. Gloria was the first one to arrive. They watched an older couple walking on a beach. The man picked up an old crusty bottle. He brushed it off. *Poof.* Out comes a genie. He said, "I will grant each one of you a wish." The woman said, "I would like an all-expense paid cruise around the world." *Poof,* tickets appeared in the genie's hand. He handed them to her and asked the man, "And what is your wish?" He smiled and said, "I would like a partner that is thirty years younger than I am." *Poof,* the man turned ninety-three. Gloria laughed and said, "Good for you, he deserved that."

The next clip was a guy walking into a bar. There was a little tiny man standing on the piano bench playing the piano. He asked the bartender, "What is up with the little midget?" The bartender said, "Well, I have this genie here. He will grant you one wish." The guy said, "Cool, can I get a wish?" The bartender said, Sure, but I must warn you." The genie popped up and asked, "What is your wish?" The guy says, "I wish I had a million bucks." *Poof,* a huge cloud of smoke, then there were ducks all over the place. The man asked, "What the fuck is this?" The bartender said, "I tried to tell you. He is hard of hearing. Do you really think I asked for a twelve-inch pianist?" Jeremy said, "Oh, that is just sad."

The next one was three blondes on an island. They open a bottle. The genie pops out and says, "I will grant each one of you a wish." The first blonde said, "I wish I was smarter than these two." *Poof,* she turned into a redhead and she swam off the island. The second blonde said, "I wish I was smarter than her." *Poof,* she was turned into a brunette. She swam off the island. The third blonde said, "I wish I was smarter than both of them." *Poof,* she was turned into a man, so he walked across the bridge. Gloria said, "Okay, that's enough of that crap. Let's figure out what we are doing." Scott said, "We meet downstairs at seven. We will be on the water by eight. The guide said it will take a couple of hours."

Team Three got to the hotel. Sue said, "I have the clue. Let me read it. It says *fire,* that's it, fire." Mark asked the girl behind the desk, "What do you know about fire around here?" The girl said, "Nothing big about a fire around here." Jane said, "I got nothing. Wildfires, a truck on fire, building a new fire station." Mark said, "Let's just get a bite to eat and sleep on it." Ed said, "Yeah, it's past my bedtime. Johnny is already asleep. I got him. You just get checked in." Mark said, "Jane and Sue, are you sharing a room? I booked mine already. Mary and Johnny, all you should have to do is check in and pay." Ed said, "Great, is there a room for me?" Mark said, "I am sure the hotel isn't booked." Ed got out and picked up Johnny. He said, "Let him sleep. He has had a long day."

Sue said, "If you Google *fire in Wisconsin,* the great Peshtigo fire, the deadliest forest fire in history, killed between fifteen hundred to twenty-five hundred, October 8, 1871. Burnt 1,200,000 acres. Wow, that was a big one." Mark asked, "Where was it?" Sue snapped, "The hell if I know? Somewhere called Peshtigo." They went in and Mary said, "Ed, why don't you stay with us?" Ed said, "Ah, no thanks. I can get my own room. I will carry the little guy up to your room." He looked at the hotel attendant and asked, "You do have four rooms, right?" The guy said, "Oh, we have plenty." Mary said as she pulled out her driver's license, "It should have been called in about ten minutes ago." The man looked at her license and said, "Mary, you have room 320, two queens." Mary smiled and said, "That's great; he is a ninja in his dreams." Ed said, "Let's get him in bed, and then I can get my room."

Mary said as they walked down the hall, "You know we could have shared a room." Ed said, "I am going to sleep a lot better than you. And if he was in your bed, you wouldn't sleep at all."

Mark went down to the bar and ordered an appetizer and a beer. A man sat down next to him and ordered a triple scotch. Mark said, "That will knock you out." The guy said, "I caught my wife in bed with my best friend." Mark said, "Oh man, sorry to hear about that. What did you do?" The man said, "I told her to pack her stuff and get the hell out of my house." Mark said, "Well, you will see how that works. She probably called a lawyer. What did you do about your friend?" The man said, "I sat him down and looked him right in the eye and yelled, 'Bad dog.'" Mark put his hand on his forehead and said into his glass, "Why does this keep happening to me?"

Jane sat next to Mark and said, "So you're getting a beer and a snack." Mark said, "Let me tell you . . . well, forget it." Jane read the specials. "A two-dollar hamburger, three-dollar cheeseburger, and a ten-dollar hand job." She asked the bartender, "Are you the one that gives the hand jobs?" The cute bartender purred, "I sure am. Would you like one?" Jane said, "Go wash your hands. I want two cheeseburgers and two house wines, a soft red please." Mark said, "I thought that was a typo. I bet she gives a good hand job." He said, "Could you keep an eye on my beer? And a nacho plate is coming out. You can have a bite if you would like."

He went into the men's room. As he stood at the urinal, a guy stepped next to him with no arms. He pleaded with him, "Hey, buddy, can you help me out here?" Mark thought, then said, "Oh, what the hell." He took a deep breath and unzipped the man's pants, reached in, and pulled out the guy's penis. Much to his horror, it was hideous. It was moldy, bluish green, covered with pus-filled scabs. It reeked something awful. The man relived himself. Mark shook it and put it back into his pants and zipped it back in. The guy said,

"Thanks, man, I really appreciate it." Mark said, "No problem, but I have to ask, what is wrong with your dick?" The man poked his arms out of his shirt and said, "I don't know, but I sure the hell am not going to touch it."

Mark came out. Jane was sitting there eating his nachos. He said, "Sorry it took so long, I had to wash my hands like fifteen times." Jane looked at him and asked, "Why?" She took her cheeseburgers and wine, stood, and looked at him. Mark stared at her for a second and said, "It is just so frecking weird. I touched something nobody should touch. It's a long story. See you in the morning." He ordered a manhattan and sat down at the bar.

A drunken woman at the other end of the bar held up her arm, showing off her hairy armpit. She said loudly, "Smell it, I smell just like a man." An old man next to him said, "Bartender, I will buy the ballerina a drink." The bartender rolled his eyes and walked down to the other end of the bar. Five minutes later, the woman was doing the same thing, holding her arm up in the air, showing off her hairy armpits. The old man said, "Bartender, buy that ballerina another one." The bartender came up and said, "She is no ballerina, stop encouraging her." Mark asked the old guy, "Why do you think she is a ballerina?" The old man said, "Any broad that can lift her leg that high has to be a ballerina." Mark said, "Holy shit, dude, you need new glasses or you have drunk way too much."

The morning came and team Intel was up bright and early, heading to the raft company. Scott pointed out the window and said, "There is Team One out jogging." Randy said, "I used to jog, gave it up when the cops started to follow me around, got picked up a couple of times." Jeremy asked, "What time were you jogging?" Randy said, "Around midnight, just screwing with them." Gloria said, "You have a juris doctorate degree. All you need to do is pass the bar and you are a lawyer. What were you doing screwing with the cops?" Randy said, "Okay, that wasn't that smart. The college got wind of it and gave me the boot. I have to reapply at a different college, and I am so far in debt."

Richard pulled into the rafting company, a middle-aged woman stood next to a van with a rubber raft on the trailer. They got out and walked up to her. She said, "Get your ass in the van. You are in a hurry, so am I. We are going to motor right to your clue. Has anyone whitewater rafted before?" To her surprise, everyone raised their hand. She said, "Well that should save us a half hour." Scott asked, "What is the rating of the rapids?" The gal said, "We have one, two, and four. There is a ten-foot waterfalls we shoot." Gloria asked, "Can you motor through them?" The guide said, "No, we have to paddle. If you are good, it should be a quick trip."

They got into the raft and the guide fired up the engine. She stopped a hundred yards before the first rapids to feel out the crew. Gloria and Randy were up front, Richard and the guide were on one side, and Scott and Jeremy were on the other. The water was fast. They shot the rapids like a pro. The guide said, "Okay, this is going to work out just fine." The next rapids they stopped at, she pulled right up to it. In a half hour they were landing on the rock and got the clue. The guide said when they were done, "Just over an hour, that was amazing." Gloria said, "I really enjoyed that. Cut out all that paddling and the ten-foot drop, that was cool." They were on the road by eleven.

CHAPTER THIRTEEN

Fire Museum

Team Three was on the road to the small town of Peshtigo, Wisconsin. They got there and waited for someone to open the museum. Ed said, "This should take like five minutes, the place is small." Mary said, "Don't count on it, this clue could be strapped to the bell tower." Jane gave Sue a pat on the ass as they got out of the van. She shot her a sly smile. Mary said, "Have those two always been together?" Mark said, "No, it's something new. It will wear off." Mary said, "Johnny, this is a museum. No touching." Johnny just rolled his eyes.

They went inside. Ed put twenty bucks in the donation box. An older man told them about the fire. It was the deadliest fire in the nation. Fifteen hundred to twenty-five hundred people died. It burnt off 1.2 million acres. The fire jumped the bay of Green Bay and burned a large chunk of Door County and burned into Michigan. Jane said, "That's nice. We are here looking for a question mark. Have you seen one?" The old man looked up at the ceiling and hummed for a second, then said, "Nope, don't think so."

They looked there for an hour. Team One showed up. Johnny said, "Let's go play in the cemetery." Ed said, "Sure, let's go for a walk. Now you have to be respectful. You are on hallowed grounds." Johnny asked as he read a gravestone, "What do you mean?" Ed said, "You are walking on dead people." Johnny said, "This kid was eighteen months old." Ed said, "It was a fire, a big one, back in 1871. I thought the graveyard would have been much bigger."

Johnny ran up the hill and said, "Come on, there is a mass grave. What is that?" Ed made his way up the hill. There was a large marker up there telling about the fire. Johnny ran down to a fenced-in area. Ed said, "Read it, there are up to 350 people buried here. They were burnt so bad they couldn't tell who they were. And I am sure time was of the essence. There was no refrigeration back then. It was the horse and buggy days." Johnny said, "You mean they dug a hole and threw them in all together?" Ed said, "Yes, that is what I am saying. Now you stay here."

Ed stepped over the fence and walked around to the back side of the memorial. He came back with a smile on his face. He said, "Go inside and quietly tell your mother we have the clue." Ed went quietly to the van. The team slowly came out. Once they were in the van, Ed said, "Spared by the fire." Jane said, "Where did you find it?" Johnny said, "It was at the mass grave." Sue said, "Chapel of Our Lady of Good Hope, it was in Robinsonville. It is called Champion now. Whatever, here is the address." She handed Mark the phone. Ed said, "Ah crap, they noticed we are not inside anymore." Mark said, "Yep, I guess we should have left right away." Johnny said, "They're going into the graveyard." Mark said, "This will be like an hour and a half drive." He pulled out and headed for the highway.

When they got to Green Bay, there was a huge bridge going over the Fox River. Jane said, "That must be Lambeau Field, big place." Mark said, "The chapel is like a half hour from here." Mary said, "Now, Johnny, this is a place where a woman seen and talked with Mother Mary." Johnny asked, "The mother of Jesus? But she has been dead a long time ago." Mary said, "The lady that talked to her has been dead a long time too." Ed asked, "Do you believe in life after death?" Johnny said, "I believe in death after life." Ed said, "Now that is a fact. I believe that your spirit goes on. If you are a really good person, you really don't die." Johnny asked, "Are you a really good person?" Ed said with a smile, "Oh no, I am going straight to hell." Mark started to pull into the parking lot and said, "This is going to be a madhouse. There are four buses and there is a boatload of people here." Jane said, "And it is out in the middle of nowhere." Sue said, "Let's go in the gift shop and ask. This place isn't very big." Ed said, "Johnny and I are going to take a piss, we will catch you later." Mark said, "I am going to church and see if there is a service going on."

Jane, Sue, and Mary went into the gift shop. Sue went up to the counter and asked, "Hi, we are on a treasure hunt. Do you have a question mark here or have you had someone recently do some work?" The lady said, "No, I don't know of any question mark, and we haven't done anything around here for a while." Jane said, "Thanks, we will look around." Mary said, "They have coffee in the lunchroom; maybe we can grab a sandwich." Jane said, "I think we can wait for a proper sit-down meal."

Ed took Johnny down to the shrine. There was a display of crutches where people put them saying they were healed. Candles lined the room. A life-sized statue of Mary stood there. Ed put his finger to his lips, pointed to a pew. They sat for a second, then Ed knelt and said, "Pray for forgiveness." After a couple of minutes they got up and lit a candle. Ed knelt in front of the candle and prayed.

They went back outside then up to the church; they went inside to listen to some of the mass. Ed took Johnny back outside and went to the Stations of the Cross. Johnny looked up at him and said, "Mary downstairs is freaky. Her eyes follow you wherever you go." Ed said, "You just remember that. Let's cut across the field to the crucifix." The two of them walked across the field to the back corner. There was a small question mark strapped on the back of the base. Ed saw it but waited for Johnny to spot it. Johnny looked around. He said quietly, "It's right there, on the bottom of the cross." Ed grabbed him by the shoulder and said, "Good job. See, there is a reason to keep you around."

Ed took the key off from around his neck and put the key into it and took the clue. He read it to Johnny, "Gravity, H_2O. What does that mean?" Johnny said, "Gravity, that is what holds everything on the earth." Ed said, "Come on, we have to get back to the team. And you are right, gravity is what holds us to the earth. Without it, we would fly into space. But what about H_2O?" Johnny shrugged and said, "To hell if I know." Ed said, "You should know this. Two parts of hydrogen and one part of oxygen makes what?" Johnny had to jog to keep up to Ed as he power walked back to the church. He had his phone out and said, "We meet at the van." Johnny stopped. Ed said, "Come on, get the lead out." Johnny whined, "My legs hurt. This is a long way." Ed said, "For Pete's sake." He stepped back and picked him up and put him on his shoulders.

When they got close to the van, Johnny asked, "What is that H_2O thing?" Ed said, "Water. Now watch, everyone will know what this clue means. Oh, there is another van." Mark said from behind them, "It is Team Odin, they pulled in a couple of minutes ago." Ed said, "I hope they didn't see us. In fact, you go to the van, pick us up on the other side of that bus." Johnny asked, "Why don't you want them to know we are on the team?" Ed said, "If they knew they would be watching us. I bet they followed Jane and Sue."

Ed waved Mary over; she looked at him then turned away from the van. Mark and the girls drove over and picked up Ed, Mary, and Johnny. Ed asked, "Okay, everyone, what is H_2O?" The team said, "Water." Ed said to Johnny, "See? I told you so. Now the clue is gravity and H_2O." Jane said, "We passed it on the way in here, some 'Indian name' falls, a county park." Sue said, "Wequiock Falls. Looks really cool when it is frozen. It is at Brown County Park." Mark said, "You are really quick with your phone. Have you Googled me?"

He pulled into the parking lot fifteen minutes later. Ed said, "Let's all go to the falls first then we spread out. The other team is right on our ass." They all walked down to the falls onto the boardwalk down the stairs. Mark said, "Well, it's not here. I am going to follow the river down through the culvert. On the other side there is a trail." Jane said to Sue, "We should go and check around the bridge and the monument." Ed said, "We are going behind the falls." Johnny looked up and said excitedly, "We are?"

Ed climbed over the railing, took Johnny by the hand. He looked over his shoulder and said to Mary, "Are you coming?" She climbed over and caught up to the two. It was a slippery path to the falls, but sure enough, you could walk right behind it. There up on the wall, about twenty feet up, was the question mark. This one was painted gray to match the wall.

Ed called the team to figure out how to get to it. Mark came up and said, "I will get the rope. We can throw it off the bridge and someone can climb up." Everyone looked at Jane. She rolled her eyes and said, "I guess. But I am not climbing. Your sorry asses can pull me up."

Jane and Sue went behind the waterfalls. Sue leaned in and kissed her full on the lips and said, "I wonder how many kids were conceived here." Jane grabbed her right by the crotch and said, "God, you make me hot." Sue pushed her away and said, "There is the rope. How are we going to get it?" Jane said, "Hold on to my hand. I will reach into the falls and get it." Sue did and Jane got the rope and tied a loop in it so she could get her foot into it. Sue called Mark and said, "Pull her up and I will tell you when to stop." Mark handed Mary the phone.

Ed and Mark pulled Jane up to the clue. She got the clue and they lowered her. She read the clue, "Lingonberry and goats. What the hell does that have to do with anything?" Sue pulled her into a hug and said, "That was amazing. It is so romantic here." Jane said, "Let's get the hell out of here. I am wet and cold."

They got up to the top and told the rest of the crew the clue. Sue said, "Al Johnson, Swedish restaurant. It has goats on the roof, and lingonberry is a Swedish berry." Ed asked, "You just Googled *lingonberry goats* and it tells you about a Swedish restaurant?" Sue said, "Yes, sir. Well, I added Wisconsin." Mark said, "You have to love the internet." Mary asked, "Where is it?" Sue said, "Sister Bay, a small town of 876 people. About an hour's drive north on the peninsula."

Team One got to the falls an hour later. The team went down and looked at the falls. Joe hopped the fence and said, "There are fresh footprints. I am going to follow them." Jack said, "I have a pair going downstream, I will follow these." He walked through the water though the culvert to other side of the road. Five minutes later, Joe called on his phone and said excitedly, "I have found the clue. It is strapped to the wall under the waterfalls." The team made their way under the falls to decide how to get to the clue. Joe said, "Give me a boost. I think I can get a hold up a few feet and I can climb the wall." Cherry said, "Don't be fucking stupid. It's wet and slimy.

You're going to fall and break a leg." Jack said, "She is right you know. It looks about fifteen feet." Dawn said, "The internet says it is a twenty-five-foot falls, so I would say it is about twenty feet up." Robert said, "Okay, it's too high for a ladder. We are not setting up scaffolding. The bridge is too far. I say we put someone in a harness and hoist them up." Cherry said, "I am the lightest." Dawn shot her a look. Cherry said, "What? Do you want to get your fat ass up there?" Dawn smiled and said, "No, that's fine. But I don't weight that much more then you."

Joe said, "I am going to tie the rope to the harness then send it over the falls." He tossed the harness off the bridge and it flowed down over the falls. Jack stepped into the waterfalls and grabbed it. Cherry complained, "Dammit, it is wet and cold." Jack said, "Slip into it. This shouldn't take long. And besides, I think this is illegal." Dawn had her phone out and asked, "Are you guys ready?" Cherry said, "Let's do this." Cherry said into the phone, "Take her up . . . keep going . . . keep going . . . little farther . . . just a foot more. Good." Cherry was holding herself against the wall so she wasn't in the water. She got the clue. Jack was standing downstream in the middle of the river in case she dropped the clue. Cherry gave the thumbs-up sign. Dawn said, "Everything is good. Lower her slowly."

They lowered her and she got out of the harness. They met up by the parking lot. Cherry read the clue, "First of all, this clue is marked number two, so Team Three has beaten us here." Jack said, "We know that, we followed their tracks." Cherry shot him a look. She said, "Lingonberry, goats." Dawn said, "Got it. Sister Bay, a restaurant. They have goats on the roof. Lingonberry is a Swedish berry, and it is a Swedish restaurant." Jack asked, "Why do they have goats on the roof?" Dawn said, "They have grass on the roof and the goats eat the grass." Robert said, "This is a payday, right? It is clue four." Joe said, "It might be a payday. It seems three or four." They got on their way. Team Three had a couple of hours' head start.

Team Two got to the glider museum, went through it. Richard said, "Well, we didn't find anything. Let's go through the Cornish Pump museum." They walked in and found the clue. It was hard to miss, and the guide asked, "Are you on a treasure hunt?" Scott said,

"Yes, we are. Could you tell us how to get to that marker hanging from the ceiling?" The guide said, "The other two teams used scaffolding, and they paid a grand apiece for me to look the other way." Gloria said, "A grand, really?" Scott said, "Okay, we can pay you a grand. Where is the scaffolding?" The guide said, "You can't do it during hours. Come back tonight at closing time." Jeremy said, "Crap, we lost a day. Did you overhear the clue they read?" The guide said, "Something to do with fire." Scott said, "Well, we might as well finish the tour and hang around. It's three o'clock already, the place closes at five."

A man rushed up to them and said, "Call 911, my wife is having a baby. For Christ's sake, hurry." Scott asked, "Is this her first baby?" The man said as he turned to run, "No, I am her husband." Randy said, "For fuck's sake, how long are her contractions? She probably has a long time. I'm going to take care of this." He followed the man out of the museum.

Team Three got to Al Johnson's Restaurant. You could see the question mark right there up on the roof with the three goats. Mark pointed, "There on the roof. It's a question mark." Mary said, "Dammit, I thought it would be a marker." Jane said, "They weren't shitting, there are goats on the roof." Johnny squeezed up between the seats to get a good look. He said, "I want to go on the roof." Mary said, "No way are you going up there." Ed said, "Now how the hell do they get up there?" Sue said, "Every day they get loaded on a pickup and they are brought here. There are stairs on the back of the building." Mark said, "Really, you found that on the internet?" Sue said, "I just watched it on YouTube. Their barn is three-quarters of a mile away." Ed said, "Let me do the talking. It's time to eat anyway."

They went inside and Ed asked to see the manager. He talked with her and she took him outside. Johnny pulled his mom's arm and asked, "Can we go out and watch?" Mary said to the rest of the team, "Order a couple of cheeseburgers, fries, and a couple of Cokes." They went outside, and sure enough, there was Ed up on the roof. The goats were walking around him. He kept turning. One tried to head butt him. He grabbed it by the horns and turned him away. He was getting the clue and one butted him right in the leg. He quickly got the clue and got off the roof.

CHAPTER FOURTEEN

Cave Point

Once he was down, he got to the table and read the clue, "Cave. That's it, cave." Sue had her phone out and said, "cave Point, county park. This could be a bitch." Jane asked, "Why is that?" Sue said, "It is a long stretch of coastline with rock ledges. That clue can be anywhere." Mark said, "Well, we can rent kayaks." Ed smiled and said, "First we check it out. Maybe we can find someone who knows where it is." Mary said, "It should be a marker."

Johnny said, "That was cool how that goat hit you with its horns." Ed said, "When you are with goats, always face them. If they get a shot at your back, they will take it and a lot harder than that one did." Johnny said, "I am done. Can I get a candy bar?" Ed handed him a ten and said, "Hurry, we are going to leave as soon as possible." Johnny went and got four candy bars and was stuffing them in his face as fast as he could. A man across from him watched him eat three of them. He said, "Eating too many chocolate bars is bad for you." Johnny said, "My granddad lived until he was a hundred." The man asked, "Did he eat a lot of chocolates?" Johnny said, "No, he minded his own damn business."

The team headed for the door. Ed said, "My change." Johnny said, "You gave me ten bucks for candy bars. I ate them." The man across from them laughed and said, "Now I see. He did, he ate them all. Ha, that's funny. And he is a little spitfire, that one is." Mary asked, "Did you give him ten dollars for candy?" Ed said, "I thought he was going to buy one candy bar." He shot Johnny a look, then said, "You don't know what you just did, but you screwed yourself. I shall never really trust you again." Johnny looked up and said in a meek voice, "I'm sorry." Ed said, "No, you're not." He turned and power walked to the van.

Mark said, "This is like a forty-five-minute drive." Ed said, "I wish we had a drone." Johnny looked at Ed. He knew he had that small drone. Ed lifted a finger and shook it, telling Johnny not to mention it. Jane said, "I just hope it isn't like the caves in the Apostle Islands. If the wind is in the wrong direction, we might not even find it." Mary said, "This is ten grand cash, we have to find it." Sue said, "We are in the lead but Odin is right behind us. Are we going to rent kayaks or not?"

Ed said, "Mark, you're the captain, your call." Mark said, "We do a drive-by. We will spread out and question everyone, find someone with a drone or kayakers. Someone knows where it is." Sue said, "Okay, I messaged two rental places. We will see if they know."

Johnny crawled over the seat. Ed asked, "What the hell do you think you are doing? Sit down and buckle up, watch a movie or something." Johnny said, "I am getting you ten dollars." Ed said, "It's not the money, you know better." Johnny said, "Should I read about history?" Ed just ignored him. Jane asked, "Where are you going to park? Take North Cave Point Drive toward Whitefish Dunes State Park. We can walk from there, but it's a long walk. If you take Schauer up like two to three miles, there is a small parking lot that is in the middle of the bluffs." Sue said, "And watch the kid, there are blowholes. You can fall right through into the lake." Mark said, "Everyone, play safe. We don't need to be searching for another teammate." Mary turned to Mark and asked, "Do you think Ed will forgive Johnny?" Mark said, "Maybe or not, who cares? The kid needs to learn you don't screw people. Everyone has feelings."

They pulled into the parking lot. There was a good chop on the lake. The sky was blue. It was around seventy five but still a chill from the lake. Mark said, "Find some kayakers; ask everyone you see. This should be a marker." Johnny went right to Ed's side. Ed looked down and said, "Oh no, you don't. You go with your mother. I will do better by myself." He turned and jogged down a path. Johnny's smile turned into a frown. You could see he wanted to cry. He walked over to his mom, who was talking to Mark. Mark looked down and said, "Oh, for Christ's sakes." Mary said, "See what you did? Now stay close to us." Mark said, "I am going to the bathroom. Ask everyone."

Jane and Sue headed the opposite way Ed went and they stopped everyone they saw. Sue got a ding on her phone, she looked down at it. Jane said, "Stop, don't read and walk." Sue looked up at her and said, "It's not a marker. It is a clue and it is in a cave to the north." She called Mark and said, "It is to the north about a quarter mile from the parking lot." Then she called Ed, she said, "It is in a cave, a quarter mile north from the parking lot." Ed said, "I must have passed it. I will backtrack and look closer." Sue said, "He is come back; he was already a quarter mile up the trail." Jane said, "Yeah, the kid pissed him off."

Ed got off the trail and went to the edge, looking over. He crawled down in one place so he could look. He waved at a kayaker who was skirting the coast. He held out a bill and waved it. The gal in the boat came within shouting distance. Ed stepped out into the surf on a rock ledge. She pulled right up to him. Ed grabbed the bow of the boat and handed her a twenty and asked, "Have you seen a question mark?" She smiled and said, "Yes, that is weird, isn't it?" Ed said, "Where and can you reach it?"

Two more kayaks came up and parked just twenty feet away from them. The gal said, "Yeah, I can reach it, about fifty yards back." Ed took the key off his neck and handed it to her and said, "Put this key in it and get the clue. Don't drop either. There's a hundred bucks in it for you." Ed's phone rang. She said, "Sure, I will be back in a few minutes."

Ed gave the kayak a shove off the ledge. The waves were getting a bit higher. He stepped closer to the rock wall. The gal paddled out to her friends and they all headed back around the point. Ed answered his phone. He yelled to Sue; the waves were loud. "Yes, everything is under control. I hired a girl in a boat to go and get the clue."

He stood waiting for a good twenty minutes, then he saw his girl coming around the point. She came right to him and he pulled her in close. She handed him the clue. He put it in his pocket then she took the key off her neck and held it. Ed said, "Oh, I am sorry." He reached in his pocket and took out his money clip and peeled off the hundred-dollar bill. She exchanged the key for the money. Ed said, "I can't thank you enough." She said, "That was kind of a bitch with the boat moving up and down."

Ed climbed up the cliff to find the rest of the team. They could see him down there but he couldn't see them. Jane said, "Well that worked. What is the clue?" Ed pulled out the clue and read it. "Tall flower, large leaves." Sue pulled out her phone. She said, "There are lots of flowers with large leaves. Got it. Cana Lighthouse, about an hour north, just past Baileys Harbor. It has ninety-seven steps. This is a cool lighthouse." Ed looked at Mark and said, "What the hell would we do without the internet?" Sue said, "It is spelled different, but it is so close it has to be it."

Ed asked, "Where the hell is Johnny?" A worried look came over Mary's face. Jane said, "He just went into the woods to take a leak." Ed asked, "How long ago?" Mary yelled, "Johnny, we are leaving." Johnny came running from up the shoreline. Mark said, "This might be interesting. There are a few blowholes along there. He can swim, can't he?" Mary yelled, "Be careful of the holes." Johnny caught up to them. Mary grabbed him by the back of the neck and asked, "What did I say?" Johnny said, "I did stay close." Ed smiled and said, "Your mother is going to look nice with gray hair." Johnny looked up at him with a puzzled look. Jane said, "You're stressing her out."

They got to the van. Sue said, "We might have to change into shorts. The water might be over the causeway, a hundred yard walk or so." Mark asked, "What number is on the clue?" Ed said, "Number one, we are in the lead. This should be a ten-grand prize."

Ed said, "Why don't I ride shotgun?" Johnny looked like he was going to cry again. He squeaked out, "I am sorry, I will never . . ." He looked at his mom and then said, "Disrespect you again." Ed looked down at him. His face hardened. He set his jaw and hardly opened his mouth as he said, "You do know I don't take that shit from anyone. You screw me and I will never deal with you again. I don't need you, just remember that. You hurt my feelings." Ed climbed into the passenger's seat.

Mary had a tear run down her cheek as she guided Johnny into the van. Jane said, "That was rough but, Johnny, you brought this on. You have to pay for your actions." Sue leaned forward and said softly in his ear, "He is coming around, but I wouldn't do that again." Mark said, "Everyone buckled up, let's roll."

Ed took out his phone and looked up the address, then looked it up on Google Earth. He said, "Let's take the highway, then I will program the GPS. It is going to take us through all the back roads."

Team Odin was falling behind. They got to the Swedish restaurant. Robert said, "There it is, up on the roof." Jack said, "This should be a piece of cake." Dawn said, "Let me do the talking." Jack said, "That is a good idea; you could sweet-talk your ass out of anything." She smiled and said, "It's a gift." They went inside.

Dawn asked if she could see the manager. A woman came out. Dawn smiled and said, "I was wondering about that question mark on your roof." The woman asked, "Are you one of the teams in the treasure hunt?" Joe stepped up and said, "Oh, you know about that? Was there another team here earlier?" She said, "Early this morning. They paid two hundred to go up there." Jack said, "Fine, here is two hundred. You guys owe me." The woman asked, "Who is going up there?" Robert said, "I guess it doesn't matter." Joe said, "I will. Order me something and a Coke."

The woman had him follow her. He went up on the roof and walked right over to the clue. A goat reared up on his back legs and butted him right in the lower back, knocking him face-first into the grass roof. He bellowed, "Jesus Christ." He got to his hands and knees and another goat butted him right in the ribs, rolling him halfway down the roof. Joe was pissed. He asked, "What the fuck is going on?" He quickly got to the clue. The goats slowly walked around him looking for another shot. Joe talked to one of the bigger goats, "You motherfucker, I am going to kill your ass." He put the clue in his pocket and started back, looking behind him. He turned and deflected a blow from a smaller goat. Joe got off the roof as soon as he could. He stretched and moaned. The woman said, "You do know you never turn your back on a goat." Joe looked at her and said, "No shit, fine time to tell me." She led him to the table. Cherry said, "Looks like you took a digger. Grass is slippery, I take it." Joe said, "Those fucking goats are mean." Robert chuckled, "No way, they're cute little goats. You didn't turn your back on them, did you?" Dawn said, "What happens if you turn your back on them?" Jack said, "They will headbutt you, and those damn things will climb on anything." Joe asked, "Does everyone know this?"

Robert asked, "So what is the clue?" Joe pulled the clue gingerly out of his pocket. Cherry said, "You did get hit." Joe raised his shirt. His ribs were turning black and blue. He turned and his back was puffing up and turning color. Jack took the clue off the table and said, "Cave." Dawn was looking closely at Joe's injuries. Cherry said, "Cave Point. It is a section of rock-faced shoreline. We will have to rent kayaks." Joe said, "Oh god." Robert said, "Suck it up, buttercup. And you better eat, you have five minutes." Jack asked, "Are you going to be able to paddle?" Joe said, "You don't worry about me."

It was getting close to five o'clock. Team Intel was at the Cornish Pump museum, getting ready to start assembling the scaffolding to get their payout. Randy explained how he got the husband calmed down and got the pregnant woman in the car. The contractions were ten minutes apart; they had a lot of time. Scott asked, "I didn't know you had a medical experience." He said, "I have taken a few classes. I thought I wanted to be a doctor, but that's not my thing. Law is so much cleaner." Gloria said, "That is why you are so deep in debt. You took all kinds of classes, meteorology, film studies, biochemistry, liberal arts . . . and that's not all of them." Randy said, "Well, I didn't know what I wanted to do in life." Gloria said, "You have enough credits to be a professor, but they're not in one subject." Jeremy said, "He is jack of all trades." Scott chimed in and said, "Master of none. Now let's get going."

The tour guide gave them the okay. The team started to haul the scaffolding out. They went up sixteen feet, tied it off, then up another sixteen. And so on till they reached the top. The guide told them, "The other teams put planking on the top. That way all five of you can stand." Gloria said, "All that weight right on top will make it unstable." Richard said, "Let's just do this."

Everyone climbed up to the top and put their key in. They got down to the bottom. Scott read the clue, "Fire. That's it, fire." The guide said, "That reminds me. A German, a French, and a Polack were to be executed by firing squad. The German was brought up first. They brought him in front of a wall and said, 'Stand here.' The German thought as the squad readied their guns. He yelled, 'Flood. Do you hear the water? The damn must have burst.' Everyone was looking around. He snuck off in the confusion. The French guy watched this and when it was his time to be shot he yelled, 'Oh my god, it's a tornado.' He slipped out of there in the confusion. Now the Polack watched both of them, and when it was his turn he yelled, 'Fire,' and they did." Scott looked at him and asked, "You think that is funny? A guy lost his life." Jeremy said, "Now what the hell does fire have to do with anything? Let's look at all the clues, analyze them." The guide said, "Google 'fire Wisconsin.' The Peshtigo fire comes up. That's what the other teams did." Scott said, "Okay, let's go." The guide said, "Whoa, wait a minute. You have to take that scaffolding down." Richard said, "We paid you a thousand dollars, you take it down." Gloria said, "The museum is closed. We lost another day."

Team Three made it to the Cana Lighthouse. Mark pulled into the parking lot. Jane said, "We walk from here. If it is windy, which it is, the causeway might be underwater. It is a good half mile and we have an hour. Let's move." Mark said, "This is a clue, we all don't have to go." Sue said, "It will be fun. We can make it a race." Jane leaned in and kissed her on the lips. She whispered, "For luck." Sue blushed and they started for the lighthouse.

Mark started to jog down the road to find the causeway was completely underwater. Ed said, "Well, let's do this." Mark said, "Are you going to carry Johnny? I will go and get the clue." Ed said, "We have an hour. You get a move on, we will be right behind you." Mary was telling Johnny, "This is going to be too hard for you to walk through." Ed stepped up behind him, picked him up and put him on his shoulders, and said, "Let's go." He quickly started through the water. It was about a foot deep. It was all rocks, so he had to slowly pick his footsteps. As soon as they got to the other side, Ed put him down and said, "Run, we have to get there by five."

Mark was way ahead; Jane and Sue jogged behind him. Jane said, "We will catch him. He is out of shape." Sue said, "Speak for yourself, I am going to die. When we get there it's like ten flights of stairs." Mark got to the lighthouse, went around the buildings, then went into the gift shop. That's where you got to the tower. He started to climb the stairs. He slowed and knew he was already in the building. They had the next clue.

Jane and Sue got to the lighthouse and started their way up. Mark said, "Hey, you made it. I need a drink." When they got to the top, Mark stood looking at the view. He said, "That was just too much too fast. I have to wait and catch my breath."

Jane asked, "So what is the clue?" Mark said, "You get it."

Jane took the key from around her neck and put it into the question mark, then took the clue. She read it and said, "Movers. Okay, what do movers do?" Mark said, "They pack. It's the Packers, Lambeau Field, seen it going over the big bridge." Sue slid her arm around Mark and said, "You know, it is truly beautiful here." Jane slipped her arm around Mark from the other side and said, "It sure is."

Ed asked, "Did you get the clue?" Mark said, "Come here and just take in the view." Ed said, "Yeah, it's nice, but what is the clue?" Mark said, "It is the hallowed grounds of the Green Bay Packers." Ed said, "Imagine that. You do know I am not just a fan, I am an owner." Mark looked over at him and said, "No shit, how is that doing for you?" Ed said, "Well that is the only stockholders' meeting I have ever been to. They get more than twenty thousand people there, but they don't serve beer until it is over. That might have changed by now." Mark looked at the girls with a huge smile on his face. He asked, "So what do they talk about?" Ed said, "Ah, let's see. They recap the last year, do a financial talk, tell what charities they gave to, how many trees they planted for first downs. I think it is around five hundred a year, nice trees." Mary came up. She said, "Shit, that is a lot of stairs." Jane said, "Ninety-seven, kind of freaky-looking through the iron steps. So where is the child?" She said, "Oh, he is coming. He tried to keep up to Ed. That took the wind out of his sails."

Johnny crawled up the stairs and lay on the floor. Sue said, "Drama queen. Well, we might as well get going." Mary asked, "Could we wait for a minute?" Sue said, "I will book the rooms. Ed, do you want your own?" Ed said, "Yes, please. Nothing too fancy." Sue said, "Hilton Garden, Hyatt, Aloft . . . there are fifty-four hotels." Ed said, "All we need is four rooms and a bar." Johnny said, "This is cool." Ed said, "Mary, take his picture then in front of the place." Mark said, "I do like to see the 'one' on the clue. We are still in the lead." Ed said, "I will run down and take a picture of the five of you up here." He took his time down the steps then ran down and out a hundred yards to get the shot.

Team Odin rented four kayaks. Joe said, "This is just a clue. I don't really think I can paddle." They got to Cave Point and there were four-to five-foot swells. The waves were crashing into the shoreline, water spraying out of the blowholes. Dawn said, "There is no fucking way I am going out in that." Cherry said, "I'm in. This should be a challenge." Jack looked at Robert and said, "What do you think? It is a bit rough. Shall we wait till morning?" Cherry said, "It's not that bad." Jack said, "You are one crazy broad. Let's do this."

In two hours they found the question mark. When a wave pulled out you could see it, then another wave would come in and the cave would disappear. Jane got in close then pulled back away. She yelled, "Can't do it. We have to wait until it calms down." Jack called Joe and said, "Mark this spot. We will drop in tomorrow morning and get the clue."

They got a hotel that wasn't too far away. The team ate and started to drink a few. Dawn said, "Have you been outside? It really calmed down." Jack asked Joe, "Can you find that place in the dark?" Joe smiled. He'd had a few manhattans. He said, "Sure I can. I set my GPS on it." Cherry said, "Grab some ropes. I will go right over the side. I need a life jacket." Jack said, "Aren't you going to take a kayak?" Cherry said, "This will be a lot faster. It's deep there. I will jump off the cliff and you guys pull me back up." Dawn said, "Sounds like a plan."

They pulled into the parking lot. Joe said, "The other end, by the toilet. There is a trail that leads to the cliff." Everyone put a headlight on and they trekked through the woods to the lake's edge. Joe had his phone out and said, "This should be the place. See the arrow drawn in the dirt?" Cherry scanned the cliff with her light and said, "Well, here goes nothing," and she jumped. It was a good twenty feet to the water. She disappeared into the darkness."

The team trained their lights on her. Jack threw the lifejacket to her with the rope attached. She yelled, "I can see the clue." She swam out of sight. In three minutes, which felt like twenty, she yelled, "Pull me up." They pulled her out of the water and up to the cliff. She yelled, "Slow down, dammit." She climbed up the cliff and over the edge back onto dry land. Robert said, "Good job." Cherry said, "That was a rush. The water sure didn't warm up any." Robert said, "It's Lake Michigan, what do you expect?" She pulled the clue out of her pants and said, "Tall flower, large leaves." Robert said, "Let's get back to the hotel and we will figure this out."

Everyone got in the van and had their phones out, researching. Dawn said, "Lighthouse." Jack said, "Cana, as in canna the flower?" Dawn said, "It doesn't open till ten. Shit, we lost another morning." Robert said, "Where should we get the hotel?" Dawn said, "It really doesn't make a difference. Sturgeon Bay, Baileys Harbor, that would be the closest." Jack said, "We already booked a hotel. We have time to drive up in the morning."

Team Three stayed at the Hyatt. Ed said to Mary, "Let's go out to eat. I will get an Uber and we can go to Brett Favre's steak joint. Wait a minute, that's closed. How about Chefusion? A nice sit-down seven-course meal with linen tablecloths." She said, "That would be nice." She looked down at Johnny and said, "You had better behave." Mark said, "You can leave him with the girls." Jane said, "No way in hell. We are going down to a place called Hagemeister Park and have a few beers, take a walk on the river walk, then to bed. It has been a long day." Mark said, "It was just an idea." Mary asked, "What are you doing?" Mark said, "I can tell you what I am not doing. That is answering three hundred questions from a kid." Ed said, "This is just dinner, nothing romantic. I have been here before." Mary looked a bit depressed as she said, "Oh, I didn't think . . . well . . . I mean." Sue said, "Well, this is interesting. We will see you downstairs for breakfast at eight." Mark smiled and said, "Eight it is. I have to find a bank before we go to Lambeau Field. And it no longer is Brett Favre's. It was Hall of Fame Chophouse and that is closed, but the Chefusion looks nice. They have fine dining and casual. Great reviews and truffle fries." Ed said, "Really? It's been a few years and things do change. I hope the food is still good. Well, I am going to freshen up. See the two of you down here in fifteen." Mary said, "Fifteen? How about a half hour?" Ed said, "Fine, a half hour. Johnny needs to get some sleep." Ed pulled out his phone and made reservations and called a cab.

Jane and Sue started to walk to the bar. They saw a priest standing there overlooking the water. Dawn slid her arm around Jane and asked the priest, "Hi, Father, beautiful day. So are they going to let you guys get married?" The priest said, "The pope thinks it would be a bad idea. It would weaken our faith." Dawn asked, "How would that weaken your faith? The love of a family should strengthen it." The priest said, "After four years of marriage most people start to think there is no God." Sue asked, "Wow, I didn't see that coming. So how is the food at Hagemeister Park?" The priest said, "You do know they named that after the park the Packers first played in back in 1919, when the team first started. The food is good. Right now they have a crème brûlée cheese cake. Oh my goodness, it is so good." Dawn said, "You have a good day, Father," and the two of them headed for the river walk.

Mark went down to the bar, talked to the bartender, and asked, "Hey, where is a good place to catch a burger and a drink?" A woman that was working on her laptop said, "There is Al's Hamburger, it's only a few blocks away. It has a four-star rating." Mark asked, "Do you think a cab will know where it is?" The bartender said, "Everyone knows where it is, a couple of feet from the Meyer." The woman asked, "Are you going alone?" Mark said, "Yeah, dining by myself tonight. My team are hooking up." She said, "Really? Mind if I tag along?" Mark said, "Well sure, I will buy the lunch, you catch the cab." She smiled and said, "It's only like five blocks." Mark said,

"Well, would you like to walk? I still plan on paying for lunch." The bartender said, "You should go to Chefusion, it is a fine-dining place."

The woman closed her laptop and stood, held out her hand and said, "HI, I am Lisa." Mark stepped to her and took her hand and said, "I am Mark. Now this is just a burger and some nice conversation." She said, "That's the plan. I don't eat much when I am alone." Lisa said, "Let me get rid of this laptop and we can be on our way." Mark said, "I would freshen up but I have been living out of my suitcase, everything looks the same." Lisa said, "I plan out what I am going to wear, iron it, and hang it in the closet." Mark said, "Well, you do office work. You should look nice." Lisa said, "Let's walk, it really isn't that far."

She went up to her room and put on tennis shoes. They headed for the river walk. Mark looked up on the bridge. A girl was standing on the bridge, holding a large cinder block and a rope tied around her neck. Lisa said, "Holy shit, she is going to jump." Mark ran full bore to her and said, "Don't do it." The girl looked at him and said, "Why not?" Mark said, "Well, if you're going to do it, would you give me a kiss first?" She did; a long, deep, lingering kiss. Mark said, "Wow, that was one hell of a kiss. You would make any man happy. Why are you committing suicide?" The girl said, "My parents don't like me dressing like a girl." Mark said, "Oh for fuck's sake." He wiped his lips. Lisa burst out laughing. She said, "Oh my god, I have to pee. Don't worry about your parents. They will either come around or they won't. Who cares, you just be you." Mark asked, "Are you going to be ok?" The boy looked up at him, wiped the tears from his eyes, and said, "Yes, I think so." Mark pulled out his money clip and pulled off three hundred dollars and said, "Here, go do something for yourself."

They got back on the river walk. Mark asked, "Can you believe that shit? People are getting weird." Lisa said, "They are just being true to their feelings." Mark said, "Well, that is not normal." Lisa asked, "And how do you think normal is?" Mark said, "You know, a man and a woman. I know the rules have changed a bit, but not that much." Lisa said, "Hey, there is a public bathroom. I had better use it before you kiss another guy." Mark said, "I will be right over there talking with those two girls." He pointed to Jane and Sue.

He walked over to their table. A few people thanked him for talking the girl down. Jane said, "That was amazing. We all thought she was going to jump." Mark said, "Yeah, there is more to that story. So how are you guys doing?" Sue lifted her mojito. "Everything is good; good drinks, good company, and food looks delicious." Mark reached over and took Jane's martini, put it to his lips and sucked half of it down. He swished through his teeth and swallowed, then drank the rest. Jane said, "Hey, I was going to drink that." Mark raised his hand and said, "That was pretty good. What was it?" A waitress came to the table. Jane said, "Another martini with one shot of Cointreau. that is an orange liqueur." Sue said, "That was rude, you could have ordered one."

Lisa said from behind him, "He didn't tell you, did he?" Jane looked up. Mark said, "This is Lisa, we are going for a burger." Sue said, "He didn't tell us what?" Lisa said, "About kissing that boy." Jane said, "That was a boy? No shit." Mark said, "I didn't know." Lisa said, "It worked. He is just confused." Sue said, "That was a boy dressed like a girl?" Mark said, "I thought if I got her to give me a kiss it would get her mind off jumping." Lisa asked, "If you knew it was a boy and it still would have worked, would you have done it?" Mark looked at her and said, "Well yes, but I would have done something different. I sure the hell wouldn't have kissed him. But it did work and he was a good kisser."

They headed up the river walk and went up a couple of blocks. They stopped and watched a guy fish and chatted. A game warden stepped up to the fisherman and asked, "May I see your fishing license?" The fisherman said, "I don't have one, and I am not fishing." The warden said, "I saw you put fish in your bucket." The fisherman said, "Those are my pet fish. I bring them down here to the river and let them swim. When it is time to go, I whistle and they come right back. This fish are tired and want to go home. There still are a few that are out swimming." The game warden said, "You're full of shit." The fisherman said, "Here, I will show you." He picked up his pail and poured the fish in the river. The game warden asked,

"Well, aren't you going to whistle for your fish?" The fisherman said, "What fish?" Mark laughed out loud. The game warden shot him a look. Mark said to Lisa, "We should get going." They got close to a bridge. A funeral service drove over it. One man stood up, took off his hat and put it over his heart. He stood there until the procession went by. His fishing buddy said, "Earl, I didn't think funerals meant that much to you." Earl said, "Well, it is the least I could do. After all, I was married to her for thirty years." Lisa said, "That is terrible." Mark smiled and said, "At least he stood. I could see it but the fish aren't really biting." Lisa said, "Come on, I am hungry."

They walked a block away from the river and down the street past the old opera theater to the burger joint, very old school. Mark said, "It has been in business since 1934, they must be doing something right." He opened the door for her and she picked out a table. She said, "I would rather have a proper sit-down than eat at the bar." Mark asked, "Do they serve drinks?" Lisa said, "Milkshakes." Mark said, "I just want a quarter-pound burger, a half is just too much." They ate. As they were walking back to the hotel, Lisa said, "This was nice. Would you like to grab a night cap then tuck me in?" Mark smiled and said, "That sounds really nice."

Morning came. Team Two, the Intels, got to the Peshtigo fire museum and waited for someone to open the doors. They split up and searched the museum. Then an hour later Scott said to Jeremy. "Let's look in the cemetery." They walked through and read the facts about the fire and who died. Jeremy went to the mass grave and looked at the monument. He stepped over the short fence and walked to the back of it. Sure enough, he found the question mark. He got the clue and called the team and told them to meet him at the van.

Scott walked down to the mass grave and Jeremy read the clue. "Spared by the fire." Scott said, "The tabernacle, that was saved by the fire." Jeremy said, "I think it is a place." He took out his phone and started to walk toward the van. Scott got to the van and announced, "The clue is 'saved by the fire.'" Jeremy said, "*Spared* by the fire, but that should be close enough." Randy said, "I think it is the shrine in Door County. The fire burnt right up to the property but did not burn the place down." Richard said, "I will be right back. If it is the tabernacle, we don't want to drive back here." Richard jogged back in the museum.

Gloria said, "We just keep falling behind." Randy said, "Speaking of a nice behind . . ." She shot him a look and said, "You're definitely not my type." Randy asked, "So what is your type?" Gloria said, "Good-looking, successful, smart, and knows how to treat a lady for starters." Randy said, "I am all of that." Gloria said, "Oh yeah, and rich." Randy said, "What does money have to do with anything?" Scott said, "You do have more than a half million in student debt, you don't have a job, and let's face it, you're black." Randy said, "What the hell does that have to do with it?" Scott asked Gloria, "What color do you want for a husband?" She said, "I have dated an Asian. But you're right, I am going to marry a white guy and have white kids, live in a condo on the lake with three kids and a dog." Jeremy asked, "What kind of dog and what kind of car?" Gloria said, "A collie and a Caddy SUV." Scott said, "You see? She has her life planned out. Is it going to work that way? Time will tell."

Richard came back and said, "Okay, there is nothing special about the tabernacle. Let's go to this shrine." Scott asked, "How long?" Randy said, "Hour and a half."

CHAPTER FIFTEEN

Lambeau Field

Team Three got up and everyone met down for breakfast at eight. Sue asked Mark, "So who was the girl you had lunch with last night?" Mark said, "A very nice businesswoman. She is in sales." Jane said, "Are you ever going to see her again?" Mark smiled, "Nope, just two ships that go bump in the night." Ed asked, "Did the ship go bump, bump, if you know what I mean?" Mark smiled and said, "If you are asking if we slept together, no, we did not." Lisa said as she walked up to the table, "No, he wanted to sleep in his own bed. Mind if I pull up a chair?" Mark jumped to his feet and pulled out a chair for her. She said, "So you guys are on a scavenger hunt?" Mary said, "Well kind of, it's a treasure hunt." Jane asked Ed, "How did the child behave at the steak joint?" Ed said, "Oh my god, we went to Lambeau. They are having some doings down there. The place was a madhouse, some concert. They say they close the streets around Lambeau and have just a big street party the night before the game." Lisa said, "Oh, and the day of the game; tailgaters, music, drinks. The prices of the rooms double, if you can find a hotel. You have to figure the stadium holds eighty thousand, and a lot of people just come and party and not go to the game."

Jane said, "You didn't answer the question. How was Johnny?" Ed said, "Not bad. He is a bit burnt out. He didn't get to bed until eleven, had a few kiddie cocktails." Mary said, "Ed here was doing some business on and off all night." Ed smiled, "It's a big one. I am going to have to fly out to the coast. I am buying a White Tiger. It was found in Germany, never seen war. It was buried. These things had an eighty-eight-millimeter canon, and I am selling it to a tank museum in Virginia. Well, sell, trade, deal." Sue asked, "How do you move a tank." Ed said, "Jump in it and drive. It weighs around seventy tons. It's real name was Panzerkampf whatever. It's German. A real find. Chefusion, that was a good meal. I had the eight-ounce filet, the kid had had a burger, and Mary had a black and bleu New York strip, which was mighty tasty." Jane said, "We just did a manicure, pedicure, and a short massage at the Lodge Kohler, very nice. Next time, we stay there."

Mark said, "Well, everyone had a good night then." Johnny said, "They wouldn't let me play." Ed said, "We were at a restaurant." Mark asked, "Is everyone packed and ready to go?" Lisa said, "You have to go?" Mark said, "We have to be mobile. You don't know where the next clue will send us. It is in a two-hundred-mile radius of a town called Wausau." Lisa said, "Oh yes, I go there a couple times a year." Mark said, "I could call you and tell you were we are." She said as she walked up behind him, "Would you like me to help you pack?" Mark smiled and said, "I might have missed something." They headed toward the elevators.

Ed said, "Wheels up in twenty-five minutes." Johnny asked, "What does that mean?" Ed said, "He had better hurry. We are leaving in twenty-five minutes." Johnny said, "But he is driving." Ed said, "We want to be there at nine o'clock." Sue said, "Okay, are we all going on the tour?" Ed said, "Been there, done that. I will wander around the Packer Pro Shop, take a walk around the place. Last time I was there they were going to change the place up a bit, add a new restaurant. In fact, I think they upgraded the hall of fame tours." Sue said, "Maybe we could take a day off and rest." Mary said, "Are you shitting me? This is a race, ten grand is the prize. We are not slowing down." Ed smiled and said, "She is right you know. Team Odin, if they get the lead, they will kick our ass."

Team Odin got to the parking lot. They walked to the water on the causeway. There was a tractor and trailer hauling people across. It was a very bumpy ride. The driver hit every rock. Once you got to the other side you paid admission. They got to the lighthouse as soon as it opened and ran up the ninety-seven steps to the top. There was no room to pass. Joe stayed at the bottom; he could barely walk. Jack said, "Well, one of you ladies get the clue." Dawn said, "What the hell?" She took the key from her neck and put it in the question mark. She took the clue and read it. "It says 'movers.' Now what does that mean?" Cherry said, "Like Mayflower. Is there a ship or something?" Jack said as he looked at his phone, "There are a ton of movers around here." Robert said, "And if you look up *Mayflower* there is a bunch of them."

They walked down the stairs talking trying to figure out the clue. Joe asked them, "Was the clue up there?" Cherry said, "Yeah, it said 'movers.' We haven't figured it out yet." Joe said, "Okay, let's look at it this way. What do movers do?" Robert said, "They take your shit and move it from one place to another." Joe said, "First they pack your shit. And you could see the Packers stadium off that big bridge." Dawn said, "I will be damned. I think you are right." Jack said, "Now just think of this. What does the Green Bay Packers have to do with movers?" Dawn said, "Movers pack." Jack said, "Okay fine, let's look. But I have a bad feeling about this." Cherry said, "I bet fifty bucks." Jack reached out his hand and said, "You're on." Dawn asked Joe, "So how's the back doing?" Joe held up a fifth of whiskey. He said, "I am keeping my blood thin so I don't get blood clots." Cherry said, "Now that's a bunch of shit." Joe said, "Look it up, a Norwegian study. It thins your blood." Jack asked, "How long?" Robert said, "An hour or so."

Team Three was at Lambeau when it opened at nine. They all went in through the Packer Pro Shop. Johnny said, "Mom, I want this." Ed said, "I would give you twenty bucks but I wouldn't get any change back, would I?" Johnny shot him a pissed-off look. They split up and Ed headed for the restaurant. He walked in like he owned the place. A waitress asked, "Can I help you?" Ed held up a twenty, she took it. Ed said, "I am looking for a question mark." She looked at him funny, then asked, "A what?" Ed pulled out another twenty and said, "Go ask someone that might know." She reached over and took the forty bucks and said, "There is no guarantee." She walked away and came back with a man following her. Ed raised a beer he said, "This Spotted Cow is a nice beer." The girl said, "This is Bob. He might know where the question mark is." Ed smiled and took out his money clip, pulled a hundred off from it and held it up between two fingers, and asked, "Do you know where it is and will you take me there?" The man smiled and said, "Yes, for a hundred I will take you there." Ed tipped the bill toward him and he took it and said, "Keep up, it is in the nosebleeds." Ed said, "Does the tour go through there?" Bob said, "Oh hell no, you might be able to see it from the field. It's way up." Ed took his phone out and called Mary, "Yeah, I think I have found it. Just keep looking and enjoy the tour."

Ed followed Bob. He opened a few gates and they took the ramp. It wound all the way to the top floor. They walked around the stadium then started up the stairs at the north end zone. They went to the very top, then Ed followed Bob up through a doorway up on top, next to the huge megaton scoreboard. Ed said, "How big are these things?" Bob said, "They are from the Mitsubishi Corporation. They are a hundred and eight feet long and forty-eight feet high, and all in high definition." Ed said, "This is amazing." Bob said, "And here is your question mark, right on the other side. See how small the people look down there? I don't think you could see this from the field."

Ed walked over to the question mark and got the clue. He read it. "Elvis, zip. Now what in the heck does that mean?" Bob said, "The Zippin Pippin is Elvis' favorite roller coaster—well, *was* his favorite." Ed asked, "Is that the one just over that big bridge?" Bob said, "It's the only one in town." Ed said, "Okay, get me down from here. You have been a great help." Bob led him back to the ground floor.

Ed called and said, "When you are done with the tour, meet me in the bar." The team came up to the bar. Johnny ran over to Ed. He said, "That was cool. Do you know they wear jockstraps?" Ed said, "Yes, I know." Johnny asked, "But did you know they played a game they called the ice bowl?" Ed said, "Yes, I did. It was with the Cowboys." Johnny, trying to impress Ed, said, "They have trophies." Ed said, "I will show you a big one in a minute." The rest of the team got there. Ed asked, "Did you see the question mark?" Mary looked at him and said, "No, should we have?" Ed smiled and said, "It is right out in plain view, right next to one of the big monitor screens at the end of the field." Mark asked, "Was it six inches tall?" Ed said, "About three feet. Let me tell you that is the nosebleeds. If you ask the right person, it sure makes this easier. The clue was 'Elvis zip.'" Jane had her phone out. Ed said, "It is a roller coaster called the Zippin Pippin that was Elvis' favorite roller coaster. It is on the bay." Ed looked at the bartender and said, "Will a twenty cover this?" She nodded. They started for the door.

Ed said, "This way. We have to show Johnny the Lombardi trophy." Jane said, "We seen them, they're on display." Ed said, "Follow." They got to an escalator and they saw it. Ed said, "Now this is a four-and-a-half-ton statue, fifty feet tall, and is the largest thing ever to be chromed. Pretty impressive, hey?" Johnny said, "Wow, you can see yourself. Look, Mom, there we are." Ed said, "Then we go through the Pack Pro Shop and right out to the car." Johnny said to Ed, "I can jump higher than the goal posts." Ed said, "You cannot." Johnny said, "Bet you a dollar." Ed said, "Fine, let's see you." Johnny hopped and said, "Goal posts can't jump." Jane grabbed Sue by the ass and said, "He got him." Ed pulled out a dollar and handed it to him and said, "Fine, you got me. Now we are going to an amusement park. This is for business, so you don't get to go on rides."

Now Team Intel arrived at the Shrine of Our Lady of Good Hope. Richard asked, "Do you really believe in this stuff?" Scott said, "Sure. Mother Mary has been seen in different places in the world, why not here?" Richard said, "I mean God, the creator of the world." Scott said, "Believe what you want. There is a higher power. You believe in the Big Bang. What or who made the Big Bang? There will always be questions, where we came from and is there an afterlife. I would like to think my life force, also known as your soul, will live on." Randy said, "Hell yes, let's be very respectful. This is holy ground."

They got out of the van. Jeremy said, "Spread out. Gloria, check the woman's bathroom, I will check the men's, then go to the gift shop." Scott said, "I will check the church. I am sure it will be there." Richard said, "I will check the grounds."

Scott went into the church and scoped it out for the clue, then he knelt before the altar and said a silent prayer. Gloria went into the gift shop and started to ask questions about the question mark. A priest said, "Yes, there is a question mark out at the back of the property. What is it?" Gloria said, "It is holding a clue to a treasure hunt."

Scott went downstairs to the shrine. He lit a candle and knelt in front of it and said a prayer. Gloria caught up to Randy, who was walking around the outside of the church. She said, "I know where it is, come on." Randy followed her to the back of the church. Randy gave a whistle and waved Richard from the stations of the cross. They went across the field to the back corner to the crucifix. On the back of a monument there was the question mark. Randy said, "You found it. Get the clue." Gloria put her key in and got the clue. She read it. "Gravity H_2O. It's a waterfalls." Randy had his phone out and said, "Wequiock Falls. It is just a few miles from here." Richard said, "It is an Indian name meaning *bladder*." Gloria said, "Let's get moving. This clue has number three on it, so we are in last place." They got into the van and headed to the falls. Randy said to Gloria, "So you're sleeping with me tonight, right?" Gloria said, "There is no fucking way in hell I am going to sleep with you." Randy smiled and said, "Oh, you will. Do you want to know why? Curiosity. You want to know what it is like." Joe said, "You took that one right from Jack Sparrow." Randy said, "Just wait, you know it's true."

Richard pulled in and parked at the falls. He said, "I am going to run over to that statue. Let's do this quickly. We have to make up time." Everyone else went to the falls. The water wasn't running that hard. Scott said loudly, "Look through the falls, there is the clue. It is on the backside of the falls." Jeremy said, "That has to be twenty feet from the ground. How are we going to get it?" Randy said, "I have done a little rock climbing, but that is wet slimy rocks." Scott said, "Well, let's go down and see. Maybe there are steps." Gloria said, "Oh, I highly doubt that." They went down the wooden staircase and went over the railing. There were a couple of kids playing in the falls. Scott asked one of the kids, "Can you climb up there to that question mark?" One kid said, "Don't be stupid. You only can climb it when the water stops running." Randy said, "We go to the top. Scott, you hold onto me. I only have to get three feet over and I can reach it." Jeremy said, "And what if you fall?" Randy said, "Don't you know us black guys bounce? I am not going to fall." Gloria said, "Hold on, let me get a rope. We tie it to something so you only fall a couple of feet." Randy said, "You do care, that is nice. Now this is why your ass is in last place." Richard said, "We lost one, we don't want to lose another." Randy said, "That bitch was looking at her phone and walking. I'm not going to do that shit."

Gloria came with the rope. She tied it off to a tree and brought it down to them. Randy asked, "Do we have a harness?" Scott said, "Just tie it around your chest." Randy stood, measured off twelve feet, and tied it under his arms. He got down on his hands and knees then slipped over the side. Scott grabbed him by the back of his shirt. He was on his hands and knees, Jeremy was holding his legs. They worked over to the falls. Randy ducked under the water and took his key off his neck and got the clue. He inched back to where he could climb up. Randy climbed up the cliff and over the edge with a little help from Scott. Gloria asked, "So what is the clue?" Richard said from behind, "Give him a minute." Randy stood and took the clue from his pocket. He said, "Lingonberry goats. Yes, you heard it right, Lingonberry goats." Jeremy said, "Al Johnson's, goats on the roof. Up at a town called Sister Bay. It's way up north." Richard said, "Let's go."

Team Three drove to Bay Beach Amusement Park. There were hundreds of cars. Jane said, "Doesn't anyone work nowadays?" Mary said, "It is the middle of summer." Ed said, "Keep driving. There is a parking lot right at the roller coaster. You have to love Google Earth." Mark said, "Oh, there is a line. And look at that, it is an old wooden roller coaster." Johnny asked—well, begged, "Can I go, please? I will do anything." Ed asked, "Are you four feet tall? If not, you're not going. If you are, I will take you." Jane asked quietly, "Sue, do you do coasters?" Sue said, "No, but if you want to go, I will go with you." They smiled at each other. Mark said, "This is a run through. Find the question mark then we figure out how to get it." Ed said, "If it is on here, we aren't going to be able to get it until nightfall. They aren't going to let us climb the thing with it running. Crap, we need tickets."

Ed asked a woman who had two kids, "Miss, I really don't want to walk over and get tickets. Could I buy like . . . oh, I don't know . . .

I will give you fifty for your tickets." The gal said, "Fifty? They are only a quarter apiece." Ed said, "Can I have them all then?" The lady handed him all her tickets. Ed counted out sixteen, folded it in half, ripped them apart, and handed the rest back to her and said, "This will get us through this ride."

Jane said, "Let's just ride the thing. It's not like it's a big one." Ed said to Johnny, "Stand tall. You're going to be close." Jane and Sue went ahead of them. Jane said, "A whole dollar." Ed said, "That's what it should be. Here are your tickets. My god, they rape you everywhere. Have you gone to the movies lately?"

The girl that was working shook Ed's hand. He said, "Thank you for working, this is for luck. He has been growing." She had Johnny stand at the four-foot mark and he was just a bit shy. She smiled and said, "You just made it." Johnny smiled ear to ear. He squealed, "Yes." On the way up, Johnny started to scream. Ed said, "We didn't do anything yet." The first drop, he screamed all the way through. Jane had her arms up in the air the whole ride. When they were done, Sue leaned over and gave her a kiss and said, "Thank you. I would have never gone if you weren't here." Johnny said, "Again, let's go again." Ed said, "It's not on the rollercoaster. It is on the big slide, up on top, right-hand corner." Sue said, "No shit, you seen that? We could have

been looking for that all day."

Mary came up and asked, "Well, Johnny, what did you think?" Johnny had tears running down his face. "That was so cool. Come on, Mom, you have to try it." Mark asked, "Did you find it?" Ed asked, "Couldn't you see it from here?" Mark said, "We looked every-where." Ed said, "Look." He pointed at the coaster and slowly turned so his arm was pointing at the big slide. "Over there, right on top, in the corner." Mark said, "What the hell?" The clue said . . ." Sue said, "Now we know it could mean that it can be seen from the clue."

Ed said, "Mary, why don't you take Johnny up and get the clue?" She smiled and said, "I think you should take him." Sue said, "First of all, you have to buy tickets, and there are thousands of people." Jane said, "I will run and get the tickets. You two get in line." Ed said, "I got them. How many tickets do you think it will take?" Sue said, "Two, fifty cents each." Ed said, "Come on, Johnny, let's run." Ed took off jogging, letting Johnny lead the way.

Mark said, "I thought Ed was going to ditch the kid after that candy bar thing." Jane said, "Oh, don't worry. He will never forget that. I think he will make a good dad one day." Sue said, "He is just kind of weird. Like, what he does he do for a living? He has no past, and he bought a fucking tank." Mark smiled. "Everyone needs a hobby, and I think he is well-off." Mary asked, "Why do you think that?" Mark said, "He drinks top shelf. Did you see him slip the girl some cash? Johnny isn't four feet, he needed another inch and a half. And have you noticed he pays people off and never asks us to pitch in our share." Sue said, "Hey, you're right. And he has picked up the tab a couple times." Jane said, "Well, he has run into a bit of cash lately, and I thought he was on vacation up north." Mark said, "There again, he flew in, rented a car just to go kayaking around those sea caves." Mary said, "And he has been buying and selling guns."

Johnny beat Ed to the slide; he was huffing and puffing. Ed said, "Hey, I have been down one of these before. You see, you sit on a burlap bag." Johnny said, "I have never been on a slide this big." Ed reached down and patted him on the head and said, "Well that is two things you haven't done before. Did you like the roller coaster?" Johnny looked up and said, "Can we go on that again?" Ed said, "You know our mission is to get the clue. Now your mom needs all the money she can get her hands on." Johnny looked up and asked, "Do you like my mom?" Ed said, "She's okay. You have to like her, she is the only mom you will ever get." Johnny said, "Yeah, she is really trying. She works so much." Ed said, "Well we put a stop to that now, didn't we? What about your father?" Johnny said, "Well my dad was a bookie. He would give twenty-to-one odds that I will kick your ass on this slide." Ed said, "Then your father is a dumbass. It's a weight thing." Johnny said, "Wind resistance."

They got to the top. Ed took off his key and got the clue, and he quickly read it and put it in his pocket. Johnny said, "I am taking this lane; it is faster than the rest." Ed said, "Winner buys dinner." Ed sat down right next to him on his burlap bag. He pointed to Johnny's mother. Johnny waved and yelled, "Go," and pushed off. Ed sat down and leaned back and pushed off. He flew down the hill, holding himself from touching his back to the slide. He got to the end and quickly stood to watch Johnny come to a stop. He said, "Told you so." Johnny got up and whined, "Can we do it again?" Ed said, "We have completed our mission. We can't stay long in one place."

Johnny ran up to his mom and said excitedly, "Did you see me? I got air off that hill." Mary said, "Yes, dear. Did you get the clue?" Ed said, "Four-eight-eight-four. That's it, just a number. I think it is a locker number." Sue said, "Okay, what do we have? Well there is a train, Michigan state pension, Keystone electronics, and a flame soapstone." Mark said, "It has to be the train. They have the National Train Museum here, and it has a 4-8-8-4, Big Boy. Oh, and it is a big one, the largest in the world. It is 133 feet long and weighs 1.1 million pounds. I am excited to see the thing." Jane asked, "How far?" Sue said, "Just up the river, fifteen or twenty minutes." Ed looked down at Johnny and said, "This sounds like a big place. Our mission is to find the clue and leave; no train rides or looking around." Johnny said, "We could stay here and go on a train ride. They have two." Mark said, "This one is going to be a bit larger."

Team Odin arrived at Lambeau Field. They all took the tour. Robert, who was a big Packers fan, loved every minute of it. Jack said, "There is so much history here." Jane said, "This place is huge. How are we going to find a stupid question mark?" Dawn said, "After this tour I have to take care of some lady business."

The tour ended. Dawn snuck off. Robert said, "I seen him. I think I saw him, maybe not." Jane said, "Who are you talking about?" Robert said, "That fucking little leprechaun. I catch that son of a bitch I am going to kill him." Jane rolled her eyes. Jack asked, "Should we wait for Dawn before we eat?" Jane said, "No, let's eat. If she is doing what I think she is doing, it's going to take her a while."

Jack walked up to the bar and ordered a brandy old-fashioned, sweet, with green olives. He asked the bartender, "Hey, you wouldn't know of a question mark? It could be six inches to six feet." He pulled up a picture on his phone. The bartender said, "You know, I think I have heard someone say something. I will ask around." Robert said as he slid a twenty across the bar, "This might speed things up. Another twenty when you find out where it is." The bartender said, "Okay, I will get on that right away." He went and talked with a server, who went into the kitchen.

The bartender handed Jack his drink and asked, "Would you like to start a tab?" Jack said, "Yes, and I will be at that table over there." Robert said, "We are on a treasure hunt and are looking for clues. They are hidden in these question marks, if Jack hasn't told you." The bartender smiled and said, "I was wondering what the hell was going on. Oh, just wait here a second. Here comes Shelia."

A cute little waitress came up and said, "Bill, I found out where that question mark you were talking about is." Robert said, "Oh, do tell." The bartender asked, "I thought there was another twenty involved." Robert took two twenties out of his wallet and handed one to the girl and one to the bartender. She said, "It is right next to the big screen, on the north end zone." She said, "You really have to look, but it's there." Robert said, "How do I get there?" She put out her hand palm up and said, "That is a behind-scenes tour." He looked at her and asked, "How much?" She said, "A hundred." Robert said loudly, "What?" She said, "What choice do you have?" His hand went to his forehead, then he said, "Fifty now, fifty once I have the clue." She said, "Okay, let's go. I am on the clock here." Robert said, "Give me one minute."

He jogged over to the table were the team was. He said, "I found the clue. Order me a burger and a Coke. Oh, and fries." He turned and jogged back to Shelia. She led him to a ramp. They went up several floors then halfway around the stadium, up four flights of stairs on top of the seating srection. Robert was amazed. "This is super cool. You can see the whole city from up here." Shelia said, "Isn't it nice? Well, there is you question mark. It is a lot bigger than I thought." Robert walked over to the question mark. It was around three feet tall. He put in the key and said, "I should have seen this from the tour." The clue came out, he read it. "Elvis zip. Now what the hell does that mean?" Shelia shrugged her shoulders and said, "It could be the roller coaster."

Robert stood and took a couple of pictures of the field and said, "This is somewhere very few people will ever have a chance to be." Shelia said, "Let's get our ass out of here before we get caught. You have your clue, where is my fifty?" Robert handed her the fifty and followed her back down to the restaurant. The team had finished eating; his burger was sitting there. Dawn came strolling in with a big smile on her face. She asked, "Did you find the clue? I am starving." Robert said as he sat down, "The clue was up on top of the stadium. My god, what a view." Cherry said, "That's nice. What is the clue?" Robert took it out of his pocket and handed it across the table. He said, "Elvis zip. What the hell that means, I haven't the foggiest." Dawn said, "You haven't the foggiest? Who says that?" Cherry said, "They have a roller coaster here that is called the Zippin Pippin, it was Elvis' favorite coaster." Jack said, "Let's get going, it's not far."

They got to Bay Beach Amusement Park. Robert asked, "How does this work?" Cherry said, "If you look at Google Earth, there are a couple of parking lots. Drop Dawn and I off at the main lot. We will get tickets, then you guys get in line. I am sure they don't have fast passes." Robert pulled in and said, "Look at all the people. This is going to take a while." Joe said, "I hope they didn't strap the clue to the bottom of the track. Look at that thing, it a big old wooden coaster."

The team got in line. They scanned the track looking for the question mark. Dawn and Cherry got there right before they got on the coaster. Joe said, "I hope I don't throw up." Dawn said, "Why do you want to go on it if it is going to make you sick? It's a clue." Joe said, "You're right, you don't need me." He got out of the line.

The team went three times and could not find the clue. Joe stopped them from getting in line again. He said, "A kid told me the question mark is on top of the big slide." He pointed and said, "It is right there." Dawn said, "Well, why didn't you get your ass up there and get it?" Joe said, "Because I was waiting for you guys. Let's go."

They streamed to the big slide. Robert said, "That's enough of roller coasters for me." Cherry said, "I could do that all day." They got to the top of the slide and got the clue. It was 4-8-8-4. Jack said, "Train museum, big steam engine."

Team Three was at the train museum. They were loading a train for a ride. Johnny started to beg, "Can we go for a ride? The clue might be on that train." Ed said, "Stay on track. You get it? *On track*." Mary looked at him and said, "Really?" Jane said, "Come on, we have to keep moving. We don't know how far ahead we are."

Mark paid the admission and asked directions to the Big Boy train. They went in. Sue said, "Holy shit, this is a big place." Ed said, "Yes, it is. Whole trains inside. Let's spread out and head down all the walkways down to the Big Boy. Me and Johnny are going to go inside and work our way to the back." Mark said as he walked over to a train—he was reading an accident report—"My goodness, these things weren't that safe." Ed said, "What did you expect? They didn't have safety measures like nowadays. And stop reading, look for the clue."

They got to the big steam engine and went through it. They were looking all over for clues. Johnny went up behind Jane and pulled her shirt. He gave her a motion." She bent down. Johnny whispered, "I found the question mark, follow me." He put his finger to his lips and looked around. Ed saw what was going on but didn't move until they were out of sight.

Johnny led Jane up into the train, up to the engine, then past the roped off area. He opened the large coal chute and said, "Down in there." Jane stuck her head—well, most of her body in. She said, "You're right. Now can you climb in there and get the clue. Here is my key." Johnny said, "Sure." He took the key and slid down a pile of coal into the box."

Ed snuck up behind Jane and whispered, "Tell him to turn it to his right." Jane said into the box, "Johnny, when you put the key in, turn it toward the right, clockwise, okay?" Johnny said, "Clockwise? What is clockwise?" Jane said, "Just turn the damn thing to the right." Johnny said excitedly, "I got it." Ed whispered, "Put it in your pocket." Jane said, "Johnny, put it in your pocket. Don't lose it. And hang the key around your neck."

Johnny came out of the box and Jane shut the big cast-iron door. She said, "Oh boy, your mom is going to be pissed. You are blacker than the ace of spades." Johnny tried to wipe off some of the coal dust. Jane asked, "Do you have the clue?" Johnny pulled it out of his pants pocket. She read it, "Orville and Wilbur. Come on, we best get you cleaned up." Johnny said, "They can't see me, they will know I went behind the lines." Ed said from just outside the train, "I will take him." Johnny jumped. He said, "Did you see? I fell down." Ed said, "Sure you did. Let's get you cleaned up before your mother finds out." Jane said, "I will take the clue out to the team." Ed said, "It has something to do with flying. Orville and Wilbur Wright, they were the first ones to fly." Johnny looked up and said, "No shit." Jane said, "You might want to wash his mouth with soap." Johnny smiled and said, "And I will blow bubbles out of my ass." Ed said, "Come on, let's get you to the bathroom. I will get you a fresh pair of clothes out of the van. We have to be quick about it."

Johnny jumped down from the train and they snuck around the engine so nobody would see them. Ed said when they were walking toward the bathroom. "Okay, here's a joke for you. Three ducks were in a courtroom. The judge asked the first duck, 'Why are you here?' The first duck said, 'I was blowing bubbles in the pond.' The judge thought, 'That's not that bad.' He told him to go and sit back down. He called the second duck and asked, 'Why are you here?' The second duck said, 'I was blowing bubbles in the pond.' The judge had him sit back down. He called the third duck and asked, 'So why are you here? And don't say you were blowing bubbles in the pond.' The third duck said, 'No, your honor, I am Bubbles.'" Johnny stopped and said, "I don't get it." Ed said, "Just get your ass in the bathroom and start washing up. I will be back in a flash with your clothes."

Johnny walked in and an old man asked him, "Do farts have lumps?" Johnny said, "No, they're gas." The old man said, "Well, I shit my pants then. You're a cute little boy." Johnny said, "Stranger danger. And let me tell you, you're stranger than most." The man said, "What does a cow say?" Johnny said, "Moo." The man asked,

"What does a sheep say?" Johnny said, "Baa." The man asked, "Okay, smarty pants, what does a pig say?" Johnny smiled and yelled, "Up against the wall, motherfucker."

Ed stepped in and bellowed, "What the hell is going on?" Johnny jumped and his eyes snapped wide open. The old man grabbed his chest. Ed said sternly, "I just got a text from your mom. They are ready to leave. Strip down, let's go." Johnny asked, "Right here?" Ed said, "Yes." He got some paper towels, damped them, and gave Johnny a quick wipe down and told him to get dressed. He then wiped off his shoes. Johnny said, "She is going to know. I am wearing different clothes." Ed said, "Just play cool. You are going to need a shower tonight." Johnny asked, "What should I do with my dirty clothes?" Ed grabbed them, went through the pockets, and put them in the garbage. Ed said, "If someone asks, I didn't see anything."

They stepped out of the bathroom. Ed said, "Found him. He was in the bathroom. So what is the clue?" Jane said, "It's EAA, that stands for Experimental Aircraft Association. It is in some town called Oshkosh." Johnny said, "Oshkosh? What is that?" Mark said, "It's a city named after some Indian chief. You think they could change it to something easier to pronounce." Ed asked, "How far?" Mark said, "Hour, maybe a bit more." Mary said, "This should be a payout."

Team Intel got to Al Johnson's restaurant. Richard said, "Look, on the roof. There's our question mark. I wonder how you get up there." Gloria said, "There is a ramp in back. They bring the goats every morning and take them home every night." Richard said, "You guys go and order. I am going to sneak up there and get the clue." Jeremy said, "I wouldn't, maybe we should just ask." Richard said, "We don't have time for that." Scott said, "This I have to see. Order me something Swedish."

Richard snuck around the building and went up on the roof. He walked right over and got the clue. He said, "Cave." A ram reared up on his hind legs and hit him solid in the back. Richard went face-first down into the grass and off the roof. He landed on his face and shoulder. Scott just stood there with his mouth open. Richard rolled over onto his back and groaned, then blood just poured from his nose. His mouth was bleeding. Scott asked, "Are you going to need an ambulance?" Richard said, "No, I don't need no fucking . . . oh, wait a minute. Maybe you should call an ambulance." Scott said, "We are in never-never land. This should be interesting." He called and said, "Yes, I have a male at Al Johnson's. He fell off a truck, on his head, bleeding pretty bad. Looks like he dislocated his shoulder. He is right in the parking lot, about twenty feet from the front door." He said to Richard, "Hey, I hear the siren. They must be close."

An old guy stepped up and said, "Fell off the truck my ass. Young feller, you never turn your back on a goat. I'll go in and get him some napkins." Scott called Jeremy, "Hey, you got to get your ass out here. Richard is down. I called an ambulance. And the clue is cave."

Jeremy came running out the door, Randy and Gloria walked out." Jeremy said, "Oh my god, is he alright?" Richard said, "I can't move my head or my arm." Randy said, "Don't you touch that. Boy, he might have spinal cord damage, and it sounds like the ambulance is almost here." Gloria looked at him and said, "Randy, get his bags. He is done." Scott said, "Oh, I would think so." Randy knelt next to Richard and said, "You're going to be alright. They will just take you down and reset your shoulder and stitch you up, a couple of hours." Scott said, "The EMS guys are here." Randy said, "Did you get his bags? He isn't going nowhere for a while."

Jeremy said, "Now what the fuck are we going to do? What happens if the next clue is a marker?" Gloria said, "Cave Point County Park. That has to be it. Let's finish eating and get on our way." Randy asked, "What the hell was that white-assed dumbfuck doing?" Scott said, "He got the clue, but he turned his back on a ram and got butted off the roof." Randy said, "No shit." Scott said, "I will show you the video tonight." Jeremy said, "Really, you taped it?" Gloria said, "Come on, we have to get on the road."

Scott said as they raised Richard to go into the ambulance, "Stay strong. You have our cell numbers. Call when you are ready to come back to the team." Randy slid his arm around Scott and turned him away and said, "Come on, he might be paralyzed." Scott said, "Do you think?" Randy said, "Time will tell."

They quickly finished their meal. They had a quick vote who was going to drive. Scott got the honors. A half hour later, they pulled into the parking lot at Cave Point. Jeremy said, "I will fly the drone along the shore and search for the clue." Randy said, "Dude, that is cheating." Gloria said, "No, the rules are pretty vague; no team working together and no interaction with the Vegas guys." Randy asked, "That's it?" Scott said, "All clues and markers have to be left the way we found them." Randy asked, "Now how are they going to know?" Scott pointed to a camera in the roof of the van and said, "And they watch the clues."

A man's voice came over the speakers, "I see you have lost Richard, and you say you have a recording of the fall. Could you send it to me? Ours was a different angle. And you do know you're falling behind." Gloria asked, "Is this Lance?" The voice said, "Yes." She asked, "How is the game going?" Lance said, "Team Three is in the led, Team Odin is close behind, and your team is falling behind. There are bets when you are going to give up. By the way, there is a lot of money riding on this, you can't give up." Scott asked, "How far behind are we?" Lance asked, "Can I tell them? Oh, what the hell. Your team is six clues behind the leader. Now get to work and find another teammate." Gloria said, "That's easier said than done."

They got out of the van and walked to the lakeshore. Jeremy came with the drone. He set it on the rocks and put on the headset, and the drone took off. Scott asked, "How is it working?" Gloria said, "Leave him. He has to concentrate, we don't need a crash." Scott dropped the drone to six feet from the lake and started up the lakeshore. Randy whined, "Why does he get to fly it?" Scott said, "He has hours of experience, he has flown in competition." Gloria said, "Really? Do people make money at that?" Jeremy said, "Whoa, there it is. Dammit, it is in a shallow cave. Fuck, that's going to be a bitch to get to." Randy said, "Stay there, let me run up the coast and mark the spot." Jeremy said, "Give me a second. Here we go, and it is down." Gloria said, "Scott, go back to the van and get some ropes. Let's go and look at this cave." Scott asked, "Who died and left her boss?" Jeremy said, "While you are there, grab me a candy bar." Scott said as he headed to the van, "And I thought I was captain."

They got to where the drone was parked. Gloria said, "You can't see a anything. Randy, climb your ass down there and see if you can get to the clue." Randy said, "I don't know what the hell you're talking about but I am not climbing down there." Jeremy said, "The water looks deep enough jump." Randy said, "Screw you and your mother too, you jump." Scott said as he lay down the rope, "I don't know how deep it is." Randy said, "I can see the bottom." Jeremy said as he sat down, "Tie the rope off, it's plenty deep." Gloria said, "I don't think so. Randy is right, I can see right to the bottom."

Jeremy slid off his pants and took off his shirt. He was standing in his underwear. Scott said, "The trick is don't lose the key. And how high off the water is the question mark?" Jeremy said, "That could be a problem." He stepped to the cliff and jumped off. Gloria screamed as he hit the water. Scott yelled down, "So can you get to it?" Jeremy yelled up, treading water, "It is freezing. I think I can reach it. I am going to try." Scott looked at Randy. "How are you going to get him out of there?" Randy looked at him and asked, "Me? Why me?" Scott said, "Well, you're the black guy, the athlete." Randy said, "I don't think so." Scott said, "You want to sleep with Gloria, right?" Gloria said, "You just wait one goddamned minute." Scott chuckled, "It was a shot." He leaned over the cliff and yelled, "How is it going?" Jeremy said, "Tall flower, large leaves. Now pull my ass up. Better yet . . ." He swam out to a point and climbed the rocks and made his way back to the team.

Scott said, "Hey, your underwear is see-through." Gloria smiled. She held up her thumb and finger an inch apart. Jeremy said, "The water is really cold." Jeremy said, "What do you expect? It's Lake Michigan." Randy said, "When I was in college at Houghton they wanted me to go surfing on Lake Superior. Wow, is that motherfucker cold. Their wet suits would ice up in the winter."

Gloria said, "Get some clothes on. What was the clue?" Jeremy said, "Tall flower, large leaves." Randy said, "Oh boy, there are a lot of those. Try canna, from the family of *Cannaceae juss*." Gloria said, "You're right. There is a Cana Lighthouse, it has ninety-seven steps. It is eighty-nine feet high, it opened in 1869, and it is closed till ten tomorrow." Scott said, "The nearest town with hotels?" Gloria said, "Baileys Harbor." Jeremy said, "Hey, Scott, you want to carry my drone? And while we are there, we need a teammate." Gloria said, "I wonder how Richard is doing." Randy said, "You will never know because you're not family." Scott said, "That's right, they do not release any medical information unless you are family. I don't even think we can visit." Randy said, "We could stop by, but we don't know where they took him." Gloria said, "I guess it doesn't matter. He was our teammate." Randy said, "So was that Sara chick. What happened to her again?" Scott said, "She fell down a ski jump. She must still be in bad shape or she would have called one of us." Jeremy said, "She might have died. She was pretty fucked up, not pretty at all."

CHAPTER SIXTEEN

EAA

Mark said, "The experimental aircraft museum is open till five. It is fifty-five miles from here, so we should have a couple of hours there." Johnny asked, "Why can't Peter Pan fly in a plane? Because it would never, never land. Get it?" Ed asked, "So why don't ducks talk when they fly? Because they would quack up." Jane asked, "What keeps three whores from two alcoholics? A cockpit door." Johnny asked, "Why do they call it a cockpit?" Mark said from up front, "It's a guy thing. That's where you find the joy stick." Ed said, "That's funny. It is from cockfighting. The roosters were put into a pit where they couldn't get out but everyone could see." Sue said looking at her phone, "It was from the 1580s. It is an old word, and Ed is right. It is a pit they put roosters in." Mark said, "If they are woman pilots, it would be a box office." Jane asked, "Where do you get all this crap?" Mary said, "Enough of the dirty jokes." She asked, "Have you ever been to a cockfight?" Ed asked, "In a shower." She said, "No, what? I mean . . ." Ed said, "I am going to decline to answer, thank you very much." Jane said, "Oh hell, I had to picture that in my mind." Sue said, "Hey, I will give you a hundred each if you have a sword fight and we can watch." Mark said, "Only a hundred?" Ed said, "There is a no way in hell." Mark said, "I can truthfully say I have never done that." Mary said, "Okay, changing the subject." Johnny looked up at Ed and whispered, "Do you use real swords?" Ed put his finger to his mouth.

They pulled into the Experimental Aircraft Association. Sue said, "They have had a fly-in here for years. It brings in a half million people and ten thousand planes." Jane said, "Damn glad that's not going on." Sue said, "It is the busiest airport in the world during that event." Ed said, "I hope this is a marker." Mark said, "This is only the fourth clue, and the sixth marker." Mary asked, "How many markers are there?" Mark smiled and said, "There are ten. So you have been on what, three? That's thirty grand. Another four will give you seventy. That should help you out."

Ed said, "Sue, give Jane your good luck kiss. That seems to work." Sue blushed, turned to Jane, and planted one on her. This time it wasn't just a peck. You could see they were tongue wrestling. Johnny asked, "Are they girlfriend and boy—I mean girlfriend?" Mary said, "Yes, they are." Mark said, "Not officially, there is no ring on the finger. And we have to go, we don't want to lose the lead." Johnny asked, "What happens if somebody beats us to the clue?" Ed said, "That is just hot. Oh, if we are second we get a quarter of the money. We are talking each team member loses seventy-five hundred. And if we fall into third place, we lose nine thousand dollars apiece, right?" Mark said, "All I know is first place is ten grand, second is twenty-five hundred, and third is one thousand." Mary said, "We sure the hell don't want to drop to third place."

Mark said, "Next marker we are all going to have to pitch in. The pot is getting low." Jane asked, "Where is Team One?" Mark took out his phone and said, "Team One, Odin, is at the train museum. We just can't pull away from them." Ed asked, "And Team Two, the Intels?" Mark said, "They are at the lighthouse. That's like four clues back." Mary said, "That's a good thing." Jane said, "What the hell are we waiting for?" Ed said, "Well you guys looked like you were having a good time, we didn't want to rush you." Sue smiled and said, "Girls really know how to kiss. I love it when she sucks my tongue." Johnny stared at her. Sue apologized, "Oh, I am sorry. Did I say that out loud?" Ed said, "Oh, don't be. You're growing a little wood over here." Johnny asked, "She is what?" Mary said, "Ed is just getting excited, so am I. Let's get in there and find that clue." Mary looked at Ed's crotch to see a bulge.

They got to the admissions. The guy asked, "Five adults and a child. Is he five or under?" Johnny piped up and said, "I am eight years old." Mark said, "There you go. If you were five you would have been free." Jane and Sue took the lead. Mark said, "Okay, people spread out. I will take the perimeter. Look close, we want to find this thing and get out of here." Jane said, "We will head this way and you go the other. We will meet you." Ed said, "Look up and at the planes on the wall. Johnny, you come with me. Mary, you head down the center aisle."

Johnny said, "There are all kinds of airplanes." Ed said, "The problem is we can't go through them. And is it here or in one of the hangars?" Ed said, "Hey, I flew one of these. The De Havilland Mosquito, a British World War II plane. This is the one that won the war. Well, the nuclear bomb helped." Johnny turned and looked up at him and asked, "You can fly." Ed smiled and said, "I can do a lot of things. Now you crawl under the plane and look up into the bomb bay, the open doors under it. And be quick." Ed lifted the rope. Johnny quickly went the ten feet and quickly crawled under the plane. He ran back to Ed and said quietly, "It's there, give me your key." Ed looked around and took his key from around his neck and handed it to him. He whispered, "Be careful, that thing is old." Johnny said, "So are you." He watched his mother. As soon as she turned her back, he was gone. He crawled up into the plane.

Ed turned and walked away from the plane but kept an eye on it. Johnny's head poked out of the bomb bay doors. His head went back up. Ed said loudly, "Hey, what is that on the Spirit of St. Louis?" He looked down and Johnny was holding the clue. He said, "Now, Johnny, Charles Lindbergh made the first transatlantic flight. I believe it was 1927." Mary said, "You're right." Ed said, "Team Three, it is time to leave." Johnny looked up at him and said, "Escape artist." He handed Ed the clue. Ed snuck a peek at it before he put it in his pocket. Then nodded and said, "See, you can read." They got to the van. Ed said, "We found the clue." Sue asked, "Where?" Ed said, "It was in a plane. Now it said 'escape artist.' That would be Harry Houdini, right? He was from around here." Sue said, "He was an immigrant from Hungary. He was the son of a rabbi, came over in 1876. His name was Ehrich Weiss, changed it to Harry Houdini, trained to be an escape artist in the circus." Ed said, "Ah, now we're getting somewhere. Back to the Circus Museum. It is around here." Mark said, "There also is a Houdini Museum in Appleton. We drove through that town on the way here, and we can find a hotel there." Mark fired up the van and headed out onto the freeway.

Team Odin decided they didn't have enough time to go to the train museum, so they got a nice hotel and went down and ate at the restaurant. Robert excused himself and went to take a piss. As he was standing at the urinal, a big black guy stepped up next to him and said, "Hi, I'm six foot six. I have a thirteen-inch dick, weigh 370 pounds. I play ball for the Clean Bay Crackers. My name is Neal Brown." Robert's eyes rolled back in his head and he fell to the floor still pissing. Jack walked in and asked, "What the hell is going on here?" Robert said, "I don't know, I must have blacked out." The ball player said, "I just told him who I was and he passed out, must be a fan." Jack said, "You're Neal Brown." Robert said, "Oh, I thought you said 'kneel down.'" Neal burst out laughing. "That is a good one." Jack said, "Old Robert here had a traumatic incident in a bathroom not too long ago. A little man told him he was a leprechaun and fucked him in the ass. My god, Neal Brown. I love you, man. You have been on my fantasy team for years." Neal said, "A leprechaun fucked you in the ass? Now I have heard everything."

Jack went back out to the table, and told the story. Robert cleaned up and came out. He had to tell the story. He said with his hands a foot apart, "And he had a dick this big." Dawn said, "No way, just like you said that leprechaun had a foot-long dick." Robert said, "I bet you a hundred dollars." Dawn said, "You're on. Now how do you prove it?"

Neal walked over to the table and asked, "How are you doing? I am sorry for the bathroom mishap." Dawn said, "I hear you have a thirteen-inch penis." Neal shyly said, "Ah, yeah." She got up and said, "I have a hundred-dollar bet you don't. Come up to my room and prove it." Neal said, "I don't think so." She grabbed him by the hand and said, "Come on, it will be fun."

They got into her room. He said, "You do know I measured it when it was hard." Dawn took a Magnum condom from her purse. She knelt down in front of him and took his manhood into her hand. She said, "Wow, this is a big one." She worked the condom on and worked on him until he was hard as a rock. Then she had him lie back and she lowered herself onto him.

Neal said, "Be careful." She took him right to the balls and started to ride him like a horse. She got the rocking motion going, he could last long. She let out a loud, "Oh god, oh god, I am coming." He let out a primordial scream. She lay on top of him and said, "That was some of the best sex I have ever had, I just can't stop cumming." He stroked her back and said, "That was great. Really, I mean it. That was fantastic." Dawn got up and said, "Well I already ordered, so my food should be there." Neal got up and got dressed and wrote his number on a piece of paper and said, "Keep in touch. I would like to do this again." Dawn smiled and said, "Oh, so would I, again and again."

She got back to the table and handed Robert a hundred-dollar bill. She grabbed onto the table as she sat and moaned as she had an orgasm. Robert asked, "Was it thirteen inches?" She opened her mouth and her jaw cracked. She said, "All of that. It was a beautiful cock, not a thin one like Dennis'." Joe asked, "Dennis? Who is Dennis?" Dawn said, "Robert's leprechaun. He has an eight-inch dick. It just looks huge because it hangs damn near to his knees." Jack said, "How thick was Neal's?" Dawn said, "The size of your wrist." Jack said, "Hell, my dick is the size of your wrist." Dawn reached over and took Jack by the wrist and said, "Your wrist. This thing was huge, biggest I have ever rode."

A waiter came up carrying a bottle of champagne in an ice bucket and a glass. He said, "A gentleman sent over a bottle of 2004 Dom Pérignon, a very nice year, I would say. He said you would know why." Dawn said, "Could I have another glass? Cherry, when is the last time you had Dom Pérignon?" Team Intel got up and went down for breakfast. A man walked up and said, "I hear you are looking for a teammate." Scott stood, held out his hand. "Yes, we are. And you are?" The man said with a bit of an accent, "Boris Ivanov at your service." Jeremy asked, "How did you hear about this opening?" Boris said, "Let's just say we have mutual friends that would like your team to win." Scott said, "Now I get it. We lose, your employer loses." Jeremy said, "A million to get in isn't anything to sneeze at." Randy came down and Scott said, "We have found a new teammate. This is Boris. He is between jobs and is ready to go." Boris said, "This is four, we need five for a team, right?" Scott said, "Gloria will be down shortly."

Gloria came to the table. Boris stood and held out his hand and said, "You must be Gloria. I am Boris, your new teammate." She shot Scott a look, then said, "So I don't get a say?" Boris said, "No, you don't. You are over a day behind and you have lost two teammates, and are losing time as we speak." Scott said, "He has been sent by an investor in Vegas." Gloria said, "Just fucking great. He knows nothing about Wisconsin." Boris asked, "Have you guys thought about replacing her?" Randy smiled ear to ear and said, "That is an option, but right now that should be a marker on top of that lighthouse." Jeremy asked, "Do you know where the clues are?" Boris said, "That would be cheating." Scott looked into his eyes and knew that he was a man that was sent to get the job done. Jeremy said, "Okay, we have a half an hour then we get our bags on the van and get to the lighthouse." Boris said, "It is a bit of a walk from the parking lot across the causeway to the back of the island. Now you guys are four clues behind."

They quickly finished breakfast and got into the van. Gloria kept on trying to pry into Boris' life. He finally said, "Listen here, bitch, you don't need to know anything about me, who I am, where I came from. I am here to do a job. Is everyone okay with that?" Randy said, "I'm cool." Scott said from the driver's seat, "In fact, it is better this way. Stay focused on the job at hand." Boris said, "You guys have a problem; you have to ask where these clues are." Jeremy said, "You know, don't you? It sure would be nice if we got a couple of first places. I mean ten grand is a whole lot better than a thousand." Scott said, "I am fine with not knowing who you are; we just have to trust you." Boris said, "That is a two-way street, I have to gain your trust."

They took the first tractor ride across the causeway. The waves washed over it. They crossed it quickly and bought their tickets. They walked quickly to the other side of the island and stood in front of the lighthouse. The keeper opened and started his speech. "This lighthouse has been here for over 140 years." Boris said, "That's nice. We are doing a treasure hunt, and I do believe the clue is on the top." The man said, "Oh yes, you are the third team to come. When will they remove the . . .

what do you call it? Oh yes, the question mark" Gloria said, "After the game, I would suspect." Boris said, "Sometimes isn't it easier to ask?" They filed up the lighthouse to the light. Jeremy said, "What a view." Boris said, "Yes, this is beautiful. Now how do you do this?" They all took out their key. Gloria asked, "Boris, did you bring your key?" Scott handed him Richard's key. Randy said, "I replaced the lanyard, it was covered in blood." Scott said, "Turn clockwise all together, three, two, one, turn." The doors opened. Scott and took out the cash. He handed out five small bundles. Gloria took hers and said, "Movers, that's it." Boris said, "We go now. Green Bay, top of the stadium." Randy said, "If you know where the other teams are, can't we skip a few?" Scott said, "And get disqualified?" Boris looked at him and nodded. Scott asked Boris, "Hey, would you like to drive." Boris smiled and said flatly, "We

must go quickly. And no, I do not drive."

Gloria asked as they went down the stairs, "Do you mean you can't drive or you just don't like to? Do you have a license?" Boris said, "My life is none of your business. I am here to help you win this game. If anyone asks, I am a farmer." Jack said, "A dairy farmer just trying to pick up some extra cash, got it." Boris said, "Yes, that will do." Scott said, "There is paperwork, you have to sign a waiver. We or the game are not responsible for anything. And you have to have proof of insurance." Boris asked, "Are you kidding me? Fine, whatever." He took the iPad. Scott gave him a stylus, and he filled it out, not letting anyone see it.

They got to the van and in an hour and a half they were at Lambeau Field. Boris said, "We will go to the restaurant. I will order then get the clue." They followed in a young girl. Boris kept scanning the restaurant. When they got to the table, Boris picked up a menu and said, "Order me a bourbon barbecued pork sandwich and a Spotted Cow." Jeremy said, "What the fuck is a Spotted Cow?" Scott said, "It's a beer." Boris turned and jogged across the room to a young man. He put his hand into his pocket then shook his hand. Gloria said, "He is smooth. I think we have a chance with someone on the inside." Randy asked, "But do you trust him? I have this strange vibe at the end he is going to kill us all and rob us." Jeremy said, "My god, you are paranoid. Are all black guys like you?" Gloria said, "I am with you, there is something about him." Scott said, "Whatever, he has insider's information."

Boris left with the young man. He said, "Let's do this quick." The man said, "We have to take the ramp. The escalators are turned off for the top floors, and I don't have a key to the elevators." They went up to the top floor then halfway around the stadium. He popped in his key, got the clue, and was back down at the restaurant just as the food was getting there. He said, "You have five minutes to eat. Miss, bring us the bill please." Scott said, "So what is the clue?" Boris said as he took a long pull off his beer, "We are going to the amusement park. What's it called? The Bay Beach." Gloria asked, "What did the clue say?" Boris had a mouthful. He handed her the clue. She said, "Elvis zip. Now what does that mean?" Randy said as he looked at his phone, "It is the roller coaster, the Zippin Pippin. It was Elvis' favorite coaster." Boris slammed down his empty beer glass and said, "Where is that broad with the bill?" Jeremy said, "When you said five minutes you weren't kidding, were you?" The waitress came with the bill. Boris pulled some cash off his money clip and said, "Let's go." They left with half their meals on the table.

They pulled into Bay Beach. Boris told Scott to pull over to the parking lot near the roller coaster. Boris said, "I am going to get tickets. Look around and see if you can find the clue." Scott and Jeremy walked around the coaster, looking at all the crossbeams and the tracks." Randy and Gloria went the other way. They both were studying the coaster." Boris went and stood in line to buy tickets. He came back with strings of tickets, holding them so everyone could see. Gloria said, "How many fricken tickets did you buy? I thought you knew where the clue is." Boris said, "We are on camera. Let's make it look good. One ride on the coaster then we go and get the clue." Scott said, "We looked all over the coaster and didn't find it." Boris said, "When you are on the ride, point to the top of the slide. Let's make it look good." Jeremy said, "He is right, you can see it from here." Gloria said, "That is amazing. I just looked at the coaster." They went for the ride.

Randy had his arms up and was screaming like a little kid. When they got off the coaster, Gloria said, "Next time someone else sits with the kid." Randy said, "That was great. Can we do it again?" Scott said, "That actually was a nice coaster. Wooden ones usually are bumpy, but this was a nice ride." Boris said, "Straight to the slide. Ah crap, there is a line." Jeremy said, "It will go pretty quick. There are a lot of lanes." Scott asked, "Where next?" Boris said, "Train museum. I think we will catch Team One. What the hell do they call themselves?" Gloria said, "Odin, some ancient God."

Fifteen minutes later they made it to the top and got the clue. Gloria read the clue to everyone, "It's a number, 4-8-8-4." Boris said, "Let's slide down then everyone can look at your phones and we can get going." Randy said, "Twenty bucks I can beat you to the bottom." Scott said, "I am in." Jeremy lined up with them and they all went at once.

Scott beat them by a couple of seconds. He held out his hand and took the money from Randy and Jeremy. He said, "Wind resistance. If you sit up you are going to slow down." Randy said, "It still was fun. Oh yeah, we are supposed to look at our phones to make it look like we are trying to figure out the clue. Boom, there it is. It is the largest steam locomotive ever built. This should be cool." Scott said, "Twenty-five of them were made and it looks like eight of them still exist. These things are huge." Jeremy said, "Wait until you see it. Sometimes reading about things then seeing them . . ." Gloria said, "When I was a kid we went to South Dakota to see Mount Rushmore. I had myself all worked up to see this grand thing. We drove for hours. Sure, it is neat, but it is still just a fucking rock." Jeremy said, "I thought it was neat how they carved it. You had all those guys with air hammers hanging from ropes. It took them fourteen years, and they never finished it." Scott said, "Don't they have Crazy Horse going on out there?" Randy said, "That has been going on for generations. It's going to be twice the size of Rushmore." Team Odin was at the train museum. They went over the Big Boy train, couldn't find the question mark, walked around the whole place, took the train ride, spent two hours just walking around. Jack said, "It has to be on the Big Boy." He went into the locomotive. This time he crawled under the rope and opened the fire box. There it was, the question mark, but he was too big to fit in there. He called Dawn and said, "I need a small person to crawl down and get the clue." Dawn and Cherry came to the locomotive and looked at the box. Dawn said, "Not a problem." Cherry said, "I have jeans on. You don't want to get coal dust on that shirt." She crawled in head first, then crawled to the back and got the clue. She read it, "Orville and Wilbur. That must be the Wright brothers." Cherry held out a hand. Jack took it and helped her out of the box. She had a smudge on her cheek and her hands were black. Other than that, not bad. She said, "Whoever was in there before me wiped everything off. Looks like they even rolled on top of the coal." Joe said, "They have an Experimental Aircraft Association, also known as EAA, in some town called Oshkosh." Cherry said, "Oshkosh B'gosh, they make jeans and stuff." Dawn said, "Hey, you're right, they make baby clothes, little bib overalls." Joe said, "Come on, we are still trailing. The clue has a two on it." Dawn said, "Nope, we can't tour the company. It was started back in 1895. They closed the plant in 1997. It's all made overseas. Isn't that sad?" Jack said, "This free trade is killing our world. They send millions of tons of crap around the world, burning billions of tons of fuel to move it." Robert said, "Not only that, the third world countries don't have pollution control." Cherry asked, "Are we going to Oshkosh or what?" Jack said, "This clue took a long time to find. I hope it takes the other team as long." Cherry held out her hands and said, "I would like to freshen up first, if you wouldn't mind." Robert said, "Good idea, potty break. How far is this place?" Joe said, "It's around an hour, all highways." They headed for the visitors' area.

CHAPTER SEVENTEEN

History at the Castle

Team Three headed for Appleton to the museum to see the Harry Houdini exhibit. Johnny asked, "See that billboard? What is an adult bookstore? Do they have toys?" Ed said, "Mary, this one is for you." Mark turned off the radio. The van got quiet. Mary said, "Remember the babysitter Rachael? The drawer next to her bed? That's the kind of stuff they have there." Johnny said, "She had leather masks, handcuffs, and those things that hummed when you turned them on." Mark said, "You have to hook me up with her." Mary said, "She was a good sitter." Jane asked, "Did you do her?" Mary said, "Oh hell no, I am not that way." Sue smiled and said, "Neither was I. Kind of like it though." Jane said, "Kind of?" Sue said, "No, I love you."

Ed said, "Okay, next subject. What do we know about this museum?" Sue said, "It has a few exhibits, a lot of local stuff. It's not that big. Did you know that Houdini died of appendicitis? They don't know if the blow to his stomach ruptured it, but that is what he died of at the age of fifty-two." Johnny said, "It looks like a castle." Mark said, "Da, why did you think they call it 'History at the Castle'?" Mary said, "Houdini, this could be a hard one to find." They went up to the admissions. Johnny asked Mark, "Hey, are they going to have those gay dinosaurs here?" Mark said quietly, "No." Jane asked Johnny, "What gay dinosaurs?" Johnny smiled and said, "The megasoreass and the lickalotopuss." Ed asked Mark, "What are you teaching this kid?" Mary shot him a look and said, "Come on, can you act like an adult?" Sue smiled and said, "I thought it was cute."

They went right to the Houdini exhibit. There were a lot of hands-on stuff. Ed put Johnny in a straitjacket, had him hold on to some ice-cold pipes. Mark said, "Okay, let's split up. Sue and Jane, you go to the Asylum Out of the Shadows. Mary, come with me. We will go to the Stone of Hope. And, Ed, after you're done playing here, there is a Golden Age of Toys."

They looked all over the museum. Ed went to the front desk and asked, "Have they done any remodeling lately? We are on a treasure hunt, looking for a question mark." The girl said, "Let me give a call to Lucy. She knows everything about this place." Five minutes later she hung up and said, "About two weeks ago a couple of men made a donation to the castle if they could put a question mark up on the roof." Ed said, "Really? The roof? You're kidding me. Way the hell up on that turret?" She smiled and said, "I guess." Ed asked, "Can you take me up there?" The girl said, "I am sorry, it isn't on the tour." Ed showed her a hundred-dollar bill and asked, "Could you give us a private tour?" She smiled and picked up the phone and called someone to take over the desk.

She led Ed and Johnny up a winding staircase up the turret to the roof, and there was the question mark. Ed said, "Now this is a view not too many people see." Johnny picked up a used condom and said, "Look, a balloon." Mark said, "Put it down, you don't know where it has been. Look over the city. Isn't it beautiful?" Ed put in his key and took the clue and asked the girl, "Does 'wizard' ring a bell, anything around here?" She said, "Nothing I know about." Ed said, "Come on, Johnny, and leave the balloon. I tell you, kids these days."

Ed called everyone and told them to meet in the front. They met outside and Ed said, "Wizard, that is the clue." Everyone took out their phone. Johnny said to his mom as he pointed up, "We were way up there. You could see all over." Mary looked at Ed questioningly. He nodded and said, "It treas fine, flat roof." Jane said, "There is nothing in Appleton." Mark said, "The only thing I see is Wizard Quest in Wisconsin Dells." Ed asked, "How far is that? And wasn't that the fifth clue? It should have been a marker." Mark said, "It is a hundred miles away, so a couple of hours." Jane said, "It is open till eleven o'clock, so we have time." Ed said, "That's not good. It is open late, so the other teams could catch us." He took his laptop out, which he had never done before. Sue said, "Laptop, a bit old-school." Ed said, "This is more secure. You don't know who is hacking you."

Ten minutes later Ed said, "Okay, there are just over a hundred investors in this game, which means there is over a hundred million dollars riding on the winner without side bets." Jane asked, "How did you find that out? I have searched the net for hours trying to find out what this is about." Ed said, "My contact said there might be a leak. No more information, that would be cheating." Mark said, "Oh my god, this might not be good. That much money . . ." Ed said, "Yeah, I know what you mean." He knew more but won't tell.

Team Intel was on their way to the train museum. Gloria said, pointing, "There is the other team. We are going to catch them." Randy said, "We're going to get caught. We are catching up to fast." Boris said, "Do not worry, my black friend." Randy turned and said, "Did you hear that? I am his black buddy." Jeremy said, "Just chill, dude. We are getting close to a big payout." Randy said, "You honkies are so funny. What is white, orange, and beautiful? A white guy on fire. Do you know how white men satisfy their wives? They hire a pool boy. What do you call a bunch of white guys in a bowl? Crackers. How about a woman with a yeast infection? She is a cracker with cheese." Boris said, "I do believe it is time for you to knock it off." Scott said, "Oh, just one more, make it a good one." Randy said, "Okay, what is the difference between your momma and a mosquito? When you slap a mosquito it stops sucking."

Scott pulled into the train museum and said, "Okay, we are done with the jokes, right? We need five people." Jeremy said, "Or four people and a black guy." Randy said, "What the hell, dude, chill." Jeremy put his arm around him and said, "Come on." Boris stepped close to Scott and asked, "Is he gay?" Scott smiled and said loudly "Jeremy, gay? Well the jury is still out on that one."

The team went right to the Big Boy locomotive. Boris said, "See the cameras? They are watching us." Gloria said, "No shit, Sherlock, you're in a museum." Boris said, "Ah okay, you're right. Look for ones that look new. And you're going to have to get it." Gloria asked, "Why me?" Boris said, "Because you are the smallest one. The clue is in the fire box. You guys look all around the train and we will get the clue."

Gloria climbed aboard the train and slid under the ropes and opened the big steel door. There it was, down inside the box. She turned and said, "Hold this door open for me please. It's pretty dark down there but I can see it." Boris said, "Make more of a scene. Remember, people in Vegas are watching." She said, "You had better hope they don't have microphones on those cameras." Boris said, "Ah shit, you might be right." She slowly climbed down into the fire box. When she came out she was black. Boris gave her a hand getting out and smiled as he said, "Looks like someone forgot to dust." She said, "Just get me the hell out of here." Scott saw her and laughed and asked, "What in the hell were you doing?" Boris said, "We got the clue." Jeremy asked, "Well what is it?" Boris said, "Wilbur and Orville. They are the Wright brothers. We are going to a town called Oshkosh, to an air museum." Gloria said quietly to Scott, "I never showed anyone the clue. He does have insider's information."

As soon as they were in the van Randy asked, "So what happens if we get caught using your insider's information?" Boris smiled and said, "We don't get caught, did you hear me? We are going to win, and nobody says a word. Do you understand?" Scott said, "Fine by me, I can live with it." Jeremy said, "So do you know where the next clue is?" Boris said, after looking at his phone, "The van is bugged. We can never talk about this in the van." Randy said, "Oh boy, I hope nobody was listening." Jeremy leaned over to him and asked, "Do you think they will fire us?" Scott turned and said, "They will feed us to the fishes." Boris said with a worried look on his face and said, "Yeah, I shouldn't have taken this job. You're a bunch of fucking losers." Gloria said, "I have a doctorate in computer science, an MDA. I worked at the Smithsonian, Jeremy here worked at NASA, three masters in technology. Scott was a chess champion, top of his class, and is a big guy in math." Scott said, "Well actually it is a PhD from MIT, faculty of mathematics." Boris said, "Who gives a rat's ass? Let's just get down to Oshkosh and find the clue."

They parked close to the other van. Boris said, "Give me a second." He hopped out and slit all four of the van's tires." He jumped back in and said, "Okay, let's park over there behind that truck." They got out of the van and headed to the museum. Boris said, "The clue is in the belly of the Mosquito, a British fighter bomber. I don't know where the plane is, but I do know it is up in the bomb bay." Randy said, "You find it. I will make a distraction so nobody will see you." Scott said, "Gloria, you are filthy." She said, "Thanks, asshole. Oh, excuse me, Doctor Asshole."

They went in. Gloria said, "I don't see the other team. Wait a minute, it is Odin. That is Jack. He is a cutie." Randy said, "He has never seen me. I will go over by him." They walked through the place. Scott made the call to Randy, "Okay, I found the plane. Make your scene." Randy yelled, "Oh my god, I have found it. This is the plane I want." Scott stepped over the ropes and slid beneath the plane. In less than a minute he was stepping back over the ropes. Cherry pulled out her phone and called the rest of the team. She saw him. Team Intel headed for the door and out in the parking lot. Scott said, "Escape artist." Boris said as he looked at his phone, "Harry Houdini, a museum in a town called Appleton, just north of here." Gloria said, "The History in the Castle."

Team Odin got the clue and headed out to the parking lot. Four flat tires. Robert said, "Now what the fuck do we do?" Jack said, "Well shit, all four. Dammit all to hell." Joe said, "Okay, let's try it. I bought some tape and we have Fix-a-Flat. Whoever did this stuck a knife straight in, so there is a half-inch gash in the tire." Dawn said, "That's not going to work." Joe had the kit out and cut a piece of tape off the roll and stuck it to the sidewall, then pumped some air into it. Robert said, "It is holding. Let's do all four, then get to a gas station. A few minutes later there were a few pounds of pressure in each tire. Robert said, "Let's go." Jack said, "You do know the five of us weigh about a thousand pounds." Joe said, "Who cares? We get to a station and air these puppies up and get going." Cherry said, "You're not thinking of driving seventy miles an hour on slashed tires, do you?" Robert said, "It's not far. I drop you guys off at the museum and get four new tires put on."

They pulled into the gas station and debated how much air to put in. If not enough they will heat up, too much they might start leaking right away. They got to the museum in time to see Team Intel on the top of the turret. Joe asked, "So do we have to flatten their tires?" Cherry said, "Well if we seen them they have seen us. Just drop us off, we will get the clue." Robert said, "Well this is going to take at least an hour." Joe said, "Don't buy the cheapest thing you can get." Robert said, "Whatever they have will work."

Team Odin went into the museum. The guy at the admissions desk said, "Sorry, we are about to close." Cherry begged him, "We have to get up and get the clue from the roof." She started to cry. Jack showed him a hundred-dollar bill and said, "This is a tip if you take us to the roof." The man stepped to the door and turned the open sign around and said, "We are on camera, so you are going to have to pay for admission."

Team Intel left the building. Dawn said, "I wish we could have flattened their tires." The young man said, "If you would follow me, I have never been on the roof but I know how to get there." They quickly went up the circular staircase and were out on the turret. He stepped out and said, "Hey, this is kind of nice. By the way it looks, people have been sneaking up here."

Dawn pulled her key out of her shirt and handed it to Cherry, who put it to her cheek and smiled as she said, "It's still warm." Joe said, "What do you expect? We just went up four stories of stairs." Cherry put the key in and got the clue. She said, "Loser, there is a number three on the clue. The clue says 'wizard,' that's it." Jack said, "Okay, let's get this right. One missed clue could really put us behind." Dawn said, "I think it is Wizard Quest in Wisconsin Dells." Joe said, "Let's take our time; we have to do this right." Cherry said, "I think Dawn is right. There is nothing to do with wizards close by." Jack said, "Okay, that sounds good. It is open till eleven tonight, so hopefully Robert gets the tires on quickly." Joe said, "It is on the hoist right now, so it shouldn't be long." Cherry said, "Well I could use a drink. Let's go next door to Dr. Jekyll's." They all agreed and went to the bar.

As they sat at the bar, a guy came up and ordered three shots of tequila. Bartender said, "Rough day, Frank?" Frank picked up one shot and said, "Just found out my oldest son is gay." Bartender said, "Really? Well we kind of knew that." Frank picked up another shot and said, "Found out my youngest son is gay." Bartender said, "No fucking way, David is gay? What the hell, doesn't anyone in your family like women?" Frank lifted his last shot and said, "Yeah, my wife." He pulled out his wallet. The bartender said, "Oh hell no, those were on the house."

Joe said to the guy, "Now that's what I call a shitty day." Cherry said, "Well, maybe your wife will invite you to a threesome." Frank said, "I highly doubt it. She is dating her divorce lawyer. Looks like I might lose the house, half of my 401K, half of my savings." Jack said, "Dude, you are getting robbed." Frank said, "I would kill myself but she would get the life insurance." Joe said, "Suck it up, buttercup. Better times are a-coming. Don't know how or when. And you don't know if you have hit rock bottom but better times are a coming." Frank said, "Let's surely hope so." He got up and left. Bartender said, "Man, that sucks." Cherry burst out laughing. "Wow, that is fucked up, man. His whole family is gay. Do you think he had something to do with it?" Jack asked, "How long has he been married?" The bartender said, "Well, let me see. Both kids are in college, so maybe twenty years." Joe said, "Makes you think. Work your whole life and lose everything in the end." Dawn said, "Okay, but why was she seeing a divorce lawyer? He had to have done something." Bartender said, "Bowling team, my bar sponsored it. And they were on the team. Oh man, this sucks." Joe said, "Well, it's good for business. When you're happy you drink, and when you're sad you drink more." Cherry said, "Drink up, our ride is here." Robert pulled up with four new tires; they all piled into the van.

CHAPTER EIGHTEEN

Wizard Quest

Team Three pulled into the Wizard Quest parking lot. Sue said, "Okay, this is supposed to take an hour and a half." Jane read her phone, "This is a 13,000-foot labyrinth. We go through, find the clues, and rescue four imprisoned wizards. They are Air, Earth, Fire, and Water." Johnny said, "This is going to be fun." Mark asked, "Who is watching the kid?" Mary asked, "Ed, would you mind?" Ed whined, "Now why me? We have to do this quickly. Where are the other teams?" Mark took out his phone and said, "They are both in Appleton." Jane said, "What the hell? They're catching up to us." Sue said, "With this place open till eleven o'clock, they are going to catch us." Mary asked, "So what does second place pay?" Jane said, "Ten grand for first place, twenty-five hundred for second, and a thousand for third." Mary said, "Let's go, what are we waiting for?" Ed said, "Fine, I will take Johnny. Now there are different levels. We are going to take the easy. This should be a monument. Now, everyone has their key?" Mark said, "Keep an eye out. It could be on the outside of the building, up on those towers." Johnny pointed up and asked, "Is that one of the wizards that we have to rescue?" Jane slid her arm around Sue and said, "This will be fun. We are going to do a quick walk through." Mary said, "Good idea. You guys run through the place. We will take our time. And, Ed, you two play the game." Ed said, "We ask everyone we see. Someone knows where it is." Mark said, "Great idea. Who the hell would have thought to look on the roof at the history castle?" Ed said, "That's why I don't understand how they are catching up to us." Johnny said, "I am hungry." Ed said, "You're just going to have to wait." Mary said, "It is five o'clock." Jane looked at her and said, "Too late now. Let's get it done."

They went inside. They were given tablets to guide them through, and they started to look for clues. Mark stepped up to the assistant and slid him a fifty. He waved everyone to follow. They cut through some hidden doors, down a slide, across a ball pit, and down in a cell that was filled with fog. You could just see the top of the marker. Mark held out another bill as he said, "We need to get down to it and put in our keys." Johnny complained, "But we have to rescue the wizards." Mary said, "We will. First we need to do this."

The assistant walked over and lifted a fake rock that was a trap door. He said, "It's going to be tight, five people in that little cell." Ed said, "Johnny, now you stay up here. Make sure he doesn't close the door." Ed climbed down the ladder and everyone followed. They blew on the monument to find the key holes. Jane did the countdown, "Three, two, one, turn." The door opened and Mary took out the bundles of cash. She handed them out and up the ladder they went. Ed said, "I will be the last. The door needs to be shut tight, and nobody needs to know it is here." They climbed out of the trap door. Ed made sure the rock was set back in place.

The assistant showed them a quick way out. Johnny was pissed, "Mom, you said we were going to play the game and rescue the wizards." Mary said, "Well, that is just too damn bad. Get in the van and maybe we will feed you." Sue said, "The clue is 'longest and deepest.'" Jane said, "It has to be a water park." Johnny said, "We won't be able to play there neither." Ed took him by one of his shoulders and said, "Just wait. You don't know what is coming up. It might be fun." Johnny looked into his eyes. He had tears filling his eyes and said, "That would have been so much fun." He looked like he was going to cry. Ed said, "While they're figuring out what the clue is, let's go and grab an ice cream cone."

Jane said, "The Kalahari water park has the longest lazy river." Sue said, "Some of these water parks are insane. The Chula Vista has a 350-foot-drop water slide." Mary asked, "Did you see the Black

Anaconda at Noah's Ark? It's a quarter-mile-long water coaster." Mark said, "The Wisconsin River is the longest river in Wisconsin, but is it the deepest?" Ed said, licking his ice cream, "What comes up the most? The lost canyon." Sue said, "The lost canyon. Dr. R.O. Ebert started a carriage tour through the deepest, longest canyon in Wisconsin. You're right. That has to be it." Mark said, "Jane, book it. Let's get going. Tell them if they wait for us there is a huge tip." Ed said, "It's after five. I doubt they would still be open." Mark said, "Until seven. Everyone buckle up. It's not far and the tours are an hour long. I just hope there is room on the last one."

Sue read, "Some parts of the canyon have not seen sunlight in fifty thousand years." Ed asked, "Now what the hell does that mean?" Sue said, "That's what it says. It is a mile's ride in horse-drawn carriages. It looks beautiful." Jane said, "It's going to be dark. There is going to be moss all over, and they are not going to let us climb on the rocks." Johnny said, "Oh, why not?" Jane said, "Because we want to preserve the canyon. If you have thousands of people climbing around the beauty of the place would be ruined." Mark said, "This could be just a tourist trap." Sue said, "It stared back in 1956 and only changed hands twice. It has to be legit. And they will hold the tour up to ten minutes."

Mark was driving offensively. He said as he rounded a corner, "It's right off the road, three minutes." Ed said, "We are following the lake. Boy, there are some big resorts around here." Sue asked, "Are we staying in the Dells tonight?" Mary said, "That all depends on the clue. The other teams are breathing down our neck." Ed said to Johnny, "That means they are close to catching us." Johnny said sarcastically, "Ya think?"

Jane leaned over to Sue and blew lightly on her neck down to her cleavage. Sue said, "Don't be starting anything you can't finish." Johnny whispered to Ed, "Rug munchers." Ed asked quietly "Do you even know what that means?" Johnny shrugged.

Mark pulled into a parking spot and everyone jumped out and started for the ticket booth. They got there and the girl said, "Just in time, you have a five-minute wait." Mark slid her twenty and said, "This is a tip for booking us at the last minute. You wouldn't know of a question mark around here?" The girl asked, "You mean like a punctuation mark?" Mark smiled and said, "Yeah, it could be six inches to six feet." She smiled and shrugged her shoulders and said, "This is just a part-time job. I don't know of any around here."

They went to a huge horseshoe. People were getting their picture taken. Ed said, "Ugh, sign of bad luck." Mary said, "What, the sign?" He said, "A horseshoe pointing down, the luck runs out of it."

The wagon pulled up. It was painted a bright blue. It held fifteen people. The driver was checking over the harness on the horses. He came over and started to explain the canyon and what they could do and what they couldn't. One was climb on the rocks. Ed told Sue, "You're cute, ask the guy if he has seen a question mark." Sue popped a button, showing more cleavage. She stepped up to him and asked, "You wouldn't have seen a question mark? We are on a treasure hunt. The question marks are steel. They can be as small as six inches to six feet and can be any color." The young man couldn't take his eyes off her tits. He said, "No, I don't think I have seen anything like that." Ed stepped up and said with a low tone to his voice, "Have you noticed anything changed in the last three weeks? These clues are not light. Has there been any trucks in here lately?" The tour guide said, "No, but a couple of weeks ago we shut down for a morning. We scrubbed the carriages, fixed harnesses, and you could hear a helicopter in the canyon. They must have dropped in your clue." Mark said, "It has to be on the top of the cliffs." Jane said, "We might have enough light to see it, let's go." The guide said, "Yes, we can board now."

Ed sat with Johnny. He said, "Now, you listen to the tour guide and look to the top of the rocks for that question mark. If you find it, I will buy you a slingshot." Johnny said excitedly, "Really? A strong one?" Ed said, "Yes, you can pick it out." Johnny said, "A wrist rocket." Ed said, "Sure." Mary elbowed him in the ribs. Ed said, "Ouch, what the fuck? He isn't going to find it. Johnny, you're right. Your mother is a fun sucker." She shot him a look to kill. Johnny said, "Oh, you're in trouble now." The tour was beautiful. The wagon just squeezed through places. He kept the ride amusing, talked about the horse and the rocks. Johnny pointed and said excitedly, "There, up there, under the tree." Ed looked and said, "Son of a bitch, there it is." He bellowed, "Stop the wagon." The tour guide pulled back on the reins and said, "Whoa, hold on there." Ed hopped off and said, "Tony, come on over here." The guide said, "This is a timed ride, we can't get off schedule." Ed pointed at the clue and asked, "How do we get up there?" Mark said, "That is straight up fifty feet at least." Jane said, "Moss, it's a hard climb." Ed pulled out his phone and asked, "Can I come in from the backside?" The guide said, "That you could do, but it would be trespassing. It's all private land." Ed stepped in close to him and said, "Could you take me for a price?" Tony nodded and said, "For the right price." Ed said, "A couple of hundred." Tony held out his hand, Ed shook it. Tony said, "Just you. There are holes on the top, don't want to lose the kid." Ed got back aboard and said, "I got this." Johnny said, "I get a wrist rocket." Jane said, "This should be fun. When?" Ed said, "He is going to take me as soon as we are done with the tour." Mark asked, "How much?" Ed smiled and said, "Don't worry about it." Mary looked at him. You could see her thinking, "Does he really have money?"

They got off at the end of the tour. Ed walked up to Tony and said, "Are we doing this?" Tony said, "Give me five minutes. Stay here." Ed said, "Go into the gift shop, screw around. I will call you when I am done." Tony showed up and said, "I hope you can ride." Ed said, "Not a stupid horse." Tony said, "No, what do you have against horses? A fat-tire bike. It really isn't that far."

They got to the bikes. Tony looked at Ed and asked, "That was two hundred, right?" Ed took a hundred off his money clip and handed it to him and said, "The other hundred when I get the clue." They rode up and up to the top of the canyon. Tony said, "Stay on the trail. There are some deep veins that run from the canyon." They crossed some small bridges that were two feet wide and the drop was like fifty or sixty feet.

Ed kept right up to the young guy. He said, "Whoa, we are just about there." Tony said, "How can you tell?" Ed said, "I marked it on my GPS. Another fifty feet or so." Tony said, "Okay, this sounds weird, but tread lightly. They are really anal about signs people have been here. When we cut a tree, we have to remove everything. They don't want you to see a stump cut with a saw." Ed stepped to the edge and said, "Damn, should have brought a rope. Oh well."

He slowly made it down ten feet until he was under the tree the question mark was strapped to. He put in his key and got the clue. Tony said, "Be careful of the moss. It seems to give way. You fall I am in deep shit." Ed made it back to the top and said, "Okay, it's all downhill from here." He followed Tony back to the tour. Tony said, "Well that was nice. So the other hundred?" Ed peeled off a hundred and another, gave them to him and said, "Thanks a lot. Don't know how I would have done it without you."

Johnny ran up to him, wrapped his arms around his leg, and said, "I found the slingshot I want." Ed picked him up and looked him in the eye and said, "Okay, let's get it." Mary said, "I haven't seen him that happy in a long time. He actually hugged Ed." Ed said, "Fine, show me." Johnny grabbed him by the hand and towed him into the gift shop. There was a slingshot with Wisconsin Dells burnt into it. Ed said, "Are you sure you want that one? It's a toy you know." Johnny thought and said, "Yeah, this is it. I want this one." Ed said, "No, you don't." Johnny said, "Yes, I do. You said I could get a slingshot." Ed said, "Think about it. What were we going to get you if you found the clue?" Johnny said, "A wrist rocket, but I want the slingshot." Ed took the slingshot and said, "The deal was you get a wrist rocket. This is a toy." You could see Johnny was about to cry. Ed said, "We will get this but I owe you a wrist rocket. They have rockets that will shoot up to nine hundred feet per second. That is almost as fast as a .45." Mark said from behind him, "Are you out of your mind? He is too small for something like that, and it is too hard for him to pull."

Mary said, "Come on, you never told us the clue." Ed said, "Oh, sorry. It was Lucifer." He held out the clue. Mark looked at it and said, "Yep, that's it. Lucifer, the devil. Are we looking for some satanic thing?" They went to the van. Everyone was waiting for the clue. Mark said as he walked up, "Lucifer, all I got is a bar in Milwaukee and a TV show." Sue said, "Devil's Lake, founded in 1911, the third oldest state park. Magnificent views from a five-hundred-foot quartz-ite bluff, overlooking a 368-acre lake, blah, blah, blah." Jane said,

"That looks like the one. Is it close?" Sue said, "There is a hotel four miles from there, a Best Western. Should I book it?" Johnny said, "I thought we were going to stay at a water park." Ed asked, "What time does the park open?" Jane said, "Eight to eleven. If we get our ass on the road we can check it out tonight." Mark said, looking at his phone, "Better leave the kid in the van. This is some serious rock formations." Ed said, "He will be fine. It's only twenty miles away. Let's move."

They got into the van. Sue said, "Hotel has been booked. I told them we might be late." Johnny was pissed. There were kids in their swimming suits all over, and every time they drove by a hotel you could see kids riding water coasters, surfing huge wave pools. Ed said, "We are playing a game. If we stop the other teams will catch us." Johnny looked up at him with tear-filled eyes and said, "I know." Mark up front said, "Maybe the hotel will have a pool." Mary said, "That would be nice." Mark said, "But it won't be nothing like this. I mean look at the size of that slide." Sue said, "You're not helping." Mark laughed, "Really."

Ed asked, "Someone said you have head lamps." Mary asked, "Where are you from? Head lamps, are you talking flashlights?" Jane said, "This is a lot of rocks, big rocks, miles of trails. I sure hope there are no timber rattlers there." Mark said, "They were in Appleton, I saw their stadium." Ed looked down at Johnny and said, "Timber rattlers are rattlesnakes, but we drove by the baseball team called the Timber Rattlers." Jane said, "There are twenty-nine miles of hiking trails, and it is hooked up with the thousand-mile Ice Age trail." Mary said, "You have to be shittin' me. A thousand-mile trail?" Jane said, "That's what they say. I would think the clue is in the park. We just have to pick the right trail."

Sue said, "This is confusing; there are so many different trails." Mark said, "Well we go and question people. A metal question mark should stand out." Ed said, "This is true. We are going to be losing sunlight in a couple of hours, so I think we split up." Mark asked, "Are you taking the boy? This one might wear him out." Ed said, "You know, you are right. I will take the high trail." Johnny looked like someone just ran over his dog. Mark said, "I will take Mary and interview some campers." Jane said, "Sue and I will take the trail next to the water. Mark, go through the campground. That clue could be anywhere." Ed said, "It could be underwater. The rules, if I am correct, say they're not buried." Mark smiled and said, "Okay, we will look for some divers to interview." Johnny worked on Ed until he said, "Okay, you can come, but you had better keep up and stay on the trails. We are going up five hundred feet, and we are doing a power walk." Mary said, "Are you sure about this?" Ed said, "No, he will never keep up." Johnny begged, "I promise I will keep up."

Mark pulled into a parking lot. Jane said, "Come on, Sue. Ed, we can pick up the trail here. Mark, you and Mary go down to the campground and see what you can find out. There are a lot of trails." Ed asked, "What do you think? Should the boy and I take the lake-shore trail?" Sue said, "No, that is just fine. Get going."

Ed started up the trail. It was steep, just a worn dirt path in most places. Johnny said, "Look how high we are, those boats look so small." Ed stopped and called Jane, "Hey, that clue could be any-where up here. Maybe you guys should come up here." Jane said, "That is what I was thinking. You guys should be down here, it is like a maze of boulders. It's going to be a miracle to find this one. Sue is ten feet from me and I can't see her, and now everything is in shadows." Ed said, "Come on, Johnny, pick up the pace. Okay, good luck to you two. I am going to call Mark."

Ed jogged up the trail. He stopped and called Mark and asked, "So what did you find out?" Mark said, "Nothing. We have asked everyone we met and it is not in any of the buildings. This place is big, and to look up where you are that's a big area to look at." Ed said, "And the girls are in a labyrinth. They said there are huge boulders and it is getting dark down there. Come on, Johnny, we are going this way." Mark asked, "Is he slowing you down?" Ed said, "Well, it makes me stop and look closer at things. We are going to go to the Devil's Doorway. I will climb it. That would be a great place for a clue." Mark said, "I don't think it is there. I have talked with a few people who have been there. Nobody seen a question mark." Johnny caught up to Ed. He stood and said, "Down this trail. We are going to the Devil's Doorway." Johnny looked beat. He said, "That's not fair; you got to sit down and rest." Ed said, "When we get to the doorway you can rest."

They went down the trail to the rock formation. Johnny said, "Whoa, how did they build that? And why don't the rocks fall?" Ed said, "Okay, we are going to stop right here." Ed said as he opened his fanny pack and pulled out a small plastic box, "Now you have heard of glaciers. Well thirteen thousand years ago the glaciers stopped here and melted, leaving the rocks like they are. And it created the lake. This rock formation is called the Devil's Doorway because of the gap between the rocks. Now the reason the ones on top don't fall is because of their weight. It would take an earthquake to move them."

Johnny asked, "What is that?" Ed said as he slid an eye patch on, "I am a pirate. Do you know why pirates wore eye patches?" Johnny said, "Why are you wearing an eye patch?" Ed gave him a look and said, "It is to train the eye to see better in the dark. They weren't blind in one eye, they were robbers and murderers, anything for money."

Johnny didn't say a word as Ed set a small drone on a rock and flew it using his smart phone. It went up and around to the backside of the Devil's Doorway. It went down to where the trees were, then back up to the top, one slow circle around it, then back to Ed. He held out his hand then opened his other eye to see to catch it. Johnny said, "That was so cool." Ed said, "Okay now, you have to keep this a secret. Nobody needs to know we have this." Johnny said, "How about my mom?" Ed said, "Nobody, this is between you and me. Those rocks are over fifty feet tall and we don't have the gear to climb them."

Sue said to Jane, "Hey, there is paint on this rock. Somebody lately tried to squeeze something through here." Jane went back to look at it, she said "your right lets follow it," they went off the trail winding through the boulders, a good fifty yards, to a small cave." Sue said, "I have a penlight, follow me."

She led Jane into a short cave. There was the question mark strapped to a rock. Jane took out her key and handed it to Sue. She smiled and held it to her cheek. Jane said, "Come on, let's get out of here. Snakes will be coming out."

Sue got the clue and read it to Jane, "R-B-B-B, now what in the bloody hell does that mean? It's not even a word." Jane said, "Come on, you're the one with the flashlight. Let's get out of here."

Soon they were weaving through the boulders. When they got back to the trail, Sue called Ed and said, "We found it. The clue is R-B-B-B, whatever that means." Ed asked, "Are you going back or are you almost through? Because you guys should come up here and see the view. It is amazing."

Ed called Mark and had them come up on the bluff to watch the sunset. Jane and Sue came up with two other couples. Mary said, "This is stupid. Nobody has flashlights." Mark said, "We should get back before it gets too dark." Johnny said quietly to Ed, "Fun sucker." Sue said, "She is right, safety first." She turned and took Jane by the hand, pulled her close, and kissed her long and passionately. Ed said to the dozen people that were standing there watching the sunset, "Young love."

Everyone followed Mark down the trail. When they got to the bottom, Ed put Johnny on his shoulders. Mary stepped up close to him and said, "He can walk. You don't have to do that." Ed said, "It has been a long day. As long as he doesn't drool on me it's fine." Jane said, "Don't be looking at your phone while you are walking. It's dark and you could step in a hole."

They got to the van. Mark said, "Okay, it's off to the hotel." Ed took Johnny off his shoulders and put him in his seat. He was one dead soldier, didn't even wake. Mary said, "You didn't have to do that. If you let him sleep now, he is going to be awake all night." Sue said, "This clue doesn't make sense. There is all kinds of RBBB." Ed said, "Pull up a map or Google *R-B-B-B WI*." Sue said, "Circus World, Baraboo, Wisconsin. It is Ringling Bros. and Barnum & Bailey circus. It opens at nine. Johnny, this could be fun." Mark said, "Ah-ha, he was faking. The clue is probably in a tiger's cage." Johnny opened one eye and mumbled, "Are there going to be tigers?" Ed said, "Maybe there will be elephants. Hey, you were sleeping." Sue said, "That hotel I booked is close by and a half hour from the circus." She handed Mark her phone.

He programmed the GPS and they were off.

Intel got to the Wizard Quest. Boris said, "The clue is in a cell with fog." Gloria said, "Another stupid clue. This is the sixth one, it should be a monument." Boris said, "Oh, I am sorry. Look for the top of the monument sticking out of the fog." Scott said, "It should be a thousand-dollar payout." Jeremy said, "Let's do this. It closes in two hours."

They went in, There were a bunch of kids in there. It was taking forever to get through. They had to find the clue. Randy asked, "Is the top of a monument like a pyramid?" Boris said, "Yes, did you find it?" Randy took them all over to a small pit. He blew down there to move the fog and there it was, sticking out of the fog. Randy said, "It's like an eight-foot drop. The problem is not how to get down there, it is how to get out." Scott said, "Well we could boost you up. The thing is what are you landing on when you drop in? There must be a fog machine down there and you can't see the bottom." Jeremy said, "Okay, there must be a ladder or something. Why don't you ask one of the assistants. They are here to help us."

Boris walked around looking for someone to give them a hand. He asked a girl, "How would I get to the bottom of the cell over here?" She smiled and said, "You can't. That is not for players." Boris took a hundred out of his wallet and said, "We need to get a clue from the cell." Scott said, "We are on a quest. We seek the monument you hold." Jeremy said from behind her, "It's a treasure hunt. There are clues hidden and one is in the cell." She said, "Okay then, I could get someone that might know how to get down there."

She took the hundred and walked away. Five minutes later she showed up with the guy who showed Team Three. He said, "Ah, I hear another team is here to get a payday." Boris asked, "So how do you get down there?" The man said, "The last team paid two hundred dollars." Boris got a little ticked off. Gloria said, "We paid a hundred already, here is another hundred." The man stepped over to the fake rock. He opened it, showing the ladder. He said, "Here you go. It has been nice doing business with you." He asked, "How many teams are there?" Jeremy said, "There are three. By the way, when was the last team here?" The guy said, "Around one o'clock, so you guys are a few hours behind." Jeremy was the last one down the ladder. They met down in the fog, which was about four feet thick. They waved to move the fog and find the key holes. Once they all had their keys in, Randy did the countdown, "Three, two, one turn." Gloria said, "This is more like it." She took out the bundles of cash and handed them out. Boris said, "Let's get out of here. Too bad we couldn't get this fog higher to cover

the monument."

They got out of the Wizard Quest. Randy said, "The longest and deepest. Now what could that be?" Boris said, "It's on top of a cliff at the Lost Canyon." Scott asked, "Can we go there tonight?" Boris said, "We could try." Jeremy said, "It's dark and we know nothing about where this canyon is." Gloria said as she read her phone, "It is very deep. One slip you could fall into a crevasse, falling hundreds of feet." Randy said, "That's cool. And by the way, rattlesnakes come out at night, so we should find ourselves a hotel."

Team Odin got to the Wizard Quest at ten o'clock. The admission said, "Sorry, you will have to come back tomorrow. It takes more than an hour to go through." Robert held up a fifty and said, "How about a guided tour?" The admission guy said, "It still is going to be $13.50 apiece." Jack said, "Fine, we are on a treasure hunt." The guy said, "Hey, I have heard about that. You're looking for a clue." Jack said, "Okay, so do you know where the clue is." The man smiled and said, "Now what fun would that be?" Robert held up another fifty. The man smiled and said, "Okay, let me get someone up here and we can get started."

Dawn said, "I wish we had time. This looks like it could be a good time." The man said, "Okay, so we don't need tablets. We can cut right through to the pit it is in. Follow me and watch your step." He led them through the place, right to the pit. They had to wait until a group found a clue to a secret door to another room. Jack said, "So the tablets help you through the maze." The man said, "Not only that, it helps us keep an eye on you. That way we keep it moving. You only have so much time to solve a clue. Some people would be in here for days if you didn't push them along. Okay, this is the hatch to the access ladder." He lifted the fake rock. He said, "When you are done, I can take you straight out." Joe said, "Let me go first." He quickly went down the hole. Soon they were all down there getting their payout. Twenty minutes later they were in the van.

Cherry said, "This sucks. There is a three on top of the clue. We are in last place." Dawn said. "What sucks is there is only a thousand dollars here. If we were going to win the million, we would have had to be in first place all the time." Robert asked, "So what is the clue? Do we need to get a hotel here?" Jack said, "It has been a long day. I vote we find a hotel and crash." Cherry said, "Longest and deepest, that is our clue." Robert said, "Dawn, Jack is right. Find us a hotel, would you please." Dawn said, "There is a Belmont for a hundred with free breakfast. Here." She handed over her phone. Robert programmed the GPS.

Jack said, "'Longest and deepest' sounds like the river." Cherry said, "If you Google it, there is a canyon tour that goes through the longest and deepest canyon in the state." Joe said, "What the hell would we have done without the internet?" Jack said, "That would have sucked, go to the library and flip through books." Robert said, "It really wasn't that bad."

They got to the hotel. Everyone got their rooms. A half hour later Dawn was banging on Jack's door. Jack let her in. She said, "This fucking place is haunted." Jack said, "You're not staying. Here go back to your own room." She said, "No way in hell. I was lying there and a voice said, 'I got you now. I am going to eat you.' I thought I was imagining it, but then I heard it again." Jack said, "Just give me your key, you sleep here."

He went to her room and just started to get to sleep when he heard a voice, "I got you now. I am going to eat you." He got up and opened the bathroom door and saw an old man picking his nose. Jack asked, "How the hell did you get in there?" The old man said, "This is my room." Jack said, "No, it's not. Come on, let's go and find your room. You scared the shit out of the girl that was staying in this room."

They walked out into the hall and found a room with the door opened. Jack asked, "Is this your room?" The old man said, "Well that is my wife." She sat up and said, "Where is the extra pillow?" Jack said, "Let me order you one. They will bring it right up to your room." He walked in, picked up the phone and asked for an extra pillow, and went back to bed.

CHAPTER NINETEEN

Circus World

Team Three got up and went down for breakfast. Ed was back from an early morning jog. Everybody was sitting, eating when little Johnny came downstairs. You could see he was crying. Ed asked, "Hey, little camper, who pissed in your cereal this morning?" Johnny looked at him like he was nuts. He slid in the booth with him. Ed asked, "What's wrong? Are you bleeding?" Johnny said, "No, my mom. She hit her toe really bad this morning." Ed said, "Why the hell are you crying over that? She will be okay." Mark said, "I would have laughed." Johnny said, "Yeah, that's what I did. Boy, did that piss her off." Ed said, "Go get yourself some breakfast."

Johnny came back with a plate heaping with food. Ed said, "You take it, you eat it. You know there are children starving in Ethiopia." Johnny picked up a piece of bacon and said, "Knock, knock." Ed raised his coffee and said, "Fine, who is there?" Johnny said, "Bacon." Ed replied, "Bacon who?" Johnny smiled, "I'm bacon you a cake for your birthday." Mark turned and said, "What is green and smells like bacon? You give up? It is Kermit the Frog's finger." Jane said, "Why would you say that?" Mark said, "I thought it was funny." Johnny looked up at him and mouthed, "What?"

Sue asked, "Well, are you excited to go to the circus? There will be elephants and clowns." Johnny asked, "What did the cannibal say when he was eating a clown? He said, 'This tastes funny.'" Mark said, "That was a good one."

Johnny asked Ed, "Why don't you have sex with my mom?" Ed said quietly, "What?" Mark laughed, "Oh my god. Yes, please tell us why." Ed asked Johnny, "Why would you ask that?" Johnny said, "She is always happier after she has a sleepover." Mark asked, "And how many men have had a sleepover at your place?" The table got quiet.

Mary stepped over to the table with a plate of food and she noticed everyone had stopped talking. She asked, "So what are we talking about?" Nobody said a word. Johnny said, "We were just talking about how many guys you had sex with. I asked Ed why he hasn't laid you yet." Mark damn near died. He literally laughed so hard he started to choke. He got out of the booth and tried to walk it off. Mary turned bright red. Ed said, "I really like to get to know someone before spending the night with her that way." Everyone looked at Mark. He was on his hands and knees. He came back to the table. You could see where tears had run down his face. He said, "That damn near killed me. So why hasn't Ed here slipped Mary the bone?" Ed shot him a look and said, "That conversation is dead. Now we need to focus of the task at hand."

Mary said, "The circus opens at nine." Ed said, "There will be elephants there. Pretty soon they will have to get rid of the elephants because of animal rights, then they will have no use for them and they will go extinct. There will only be elephants in the zoos. In the big picture they are expensive. You have to feed them, have special veterinarians, not to mention the insurance. I say kill them all." Jane said, "That's terrible." Ed said, "No, that is business. How far is it?" Mark said, "Half hour. We could finish up here and get on the road."

Mary caught Ed's eye and mouthed, "I am sorry." Ed looked at Johnny and said, "Why did you ask me to screw your mother?" Johnny knew he did wrong. He turned red and hid his face. Sue asked, "Where are the other two vans?" Mark said, "They are still in the Dells here." Ed said, "Keep an eye on them please. It would be nice to see what clue they are on." Mark said, "Intel seems to be flying through the clues. They caught up to the Odins." Ed said, "Insider's information." Jane said, "We should call it in." Ed said,

"There is no proof. You have to have something to nail them on." Mark said, "Okay, twenty minutes, at the van."

Ed stepped up to Mary and said, "Sorry about Johnny, he doesn't know." She said in a pissed-off tone, "The hell he doesn't." Ed said, "Twenty minutes." He sat back down. Sue said, "What are you doing?" Ed said, "I am going to talk with Marcus here, then maybe take a shit. Why do you ask?" She said, "You have to pack." Mark said, "We both checked our bags at the concierge. Now run along now." Jane said, "He can be an ass at times."

Mark said, "That Johnny comes up with the craziest things. You have to admit that was funnier than shit. Did you see Mary's face?" Ed was sitting there chuckling. He couldn't even take a sip of his coffee. He finally put it down, wiped a tear from his eye, and said more to himself, "Oh my god, that was funny. Then I thought you were going to need mouth-to-mouth. Lucky you didn't piss your pants." Mark said, "I have not laughed like that ever. You just can't make this shit up." Ed said, "Well, I am going to go up to my room and take a dump. I will be ready." Mark said, "Meet you outside at the van."

Ed did his business and met Mary in the elevator. A couple of old women got in. They could feel the tension between Ed and Mary. Ed leaned over to Mary and asked, "Do you think your husband knows about the two of us?" The two ladies looked at each other. Mary asked after they got off the elevator, "Why did you say that?" Ed said, "Those two will talk about it for weeks, cheap entertainment."

They got to the van. As soon as they were in, Mark said, "Well, did you do it? If you did, she doesn't seem happier." Ed said with a commanding voice, "Drop it." Mark said, "Okay, let's just get to work." Jane said, "This isn't that big of a place but it could be hidden anywhere. They have a huge collection of circus wagons. We have to cross a bridge to get to the circus."

Johnny was excited. Ed handed Johnny a small camera and asked, "Do you want to take some pictures?" Johnny started to review what was on the camera. He was showing his mother they were mostly of him and his mom. Mary said, "That is cute. You'll have to send those to me." Ed said, "Wait until we are done and I will send the whole thing to you." Mark pulled into the parking lot at

Circus World. He said, "We have six minutes. Shall we look around? I will get the tickets. By the way, everyone is going to have to kick in a couple of hundred. Gas and hotels and food, we are burning a lot of cash."

They walked around the building. The only way you could get on the bridge was through the building. Ed took small binoculars out of his breast pocket and started to scan the bridge and the circus on the other side of the river. Johnny wanted to look. Ed handed him the binoculars and said, "These are a thousand dollars, be careful with them." Mary said, "You didn't just give him a thousand-dollar set of binoculars, did you?" Ed smiled and said, "You have to have a little faith."

Johnny was looking up in the trees, at the parking lot, in the river. Mark waved everyone inside. They walked through all kinds of old circus posters. Ed said, "Now, Johnny, these are really old. Do not touch." He dropped to one knee, looked him in the eye, and said one word, "Understand?" Johnny just nodded. There were a couple of circus wagons, a calliope. Ed was explaining everything to Johnny.

Mark said, "Jane, you and Sue go and check out the big building. I think that is where the circus wagons are held. Mary, you come with me. We are going to do a walk around the outside of the grounds. Ed, take Johnny to the tent."

Everyone split up. Jane and Sue walked around looking under and around the circus wagons. Jane called Mark and said, "That clue could be in any of these wagons. Some of them are huge, and there are so many." Mark said, "Just keep looking. And keep your eye out for cameras, they are filming us." Jane said to Sue, "He brought up a good idea. Keep an eye out for cameras, something that has just been installed."

Ed and Johnny were questioning the workers and having fun. They did the "want to be a clown" thing, watched a magic act. Ed left Johnny sitting in the stands as he explored. He questioned a mime about the clue. The mime just acted out. Ed pulled out a fifty. The mime said in a deep voice, "Follow me."

They went in the back where the animals were kept. Sure as shit the question mark was in the big cat's cage. It was a big cage. Ed said, "I need a lion tamer." The mime rubbed his finger and thumb together. Ed pulled out a twenty. The mime frowned. Ed pulled another twenty and said, "A hundred to the lion tamer." The mime puckered his lips, nodded, and then pulled a cell phone out and texted. He looked at Ed and held up three fingers. Ed said, "Ya know, I think I can just go in there and get the clue. The cat is just a big house cat." The mime shook his finger, then made an invisible hang man's noose and hung himself.

A muscular man came in and said, "You know he is right. Old Sinbad here, if he doesn't know you, he is not a happy camper." Ed handed the man the hundred-dollar bill and said, "Let's hurry. I have a kid out there watching the magic act." The man entered the cage with a whip. He pushed the big cat with the handle, then put him into a head lock and kissed him on the top of his head. Ed walked in. The big cat snapped his head to watch him, and Ed turned and looked him in the eye and held up one finger. He kept facing him as he went to the clue, put the key in it, and took the clue. He put it right in his pocket and headed for the door, facing the tiger. Ed got out and asked the trainer, "So why is he alone? The other cats are all together." The trainer said, "He is antisocial and could really damage the other cats. He is getting old."

Ed read the clue on the way to the tent. All it said was "spies." Ed called in the team. He went and told Johnny, "It's time to go." Johnny said, "Ah, can't we stay for just a little longer?"

The team met just a few feet from the grandstands and discussed the clue. Mark walked up and Ed said, "You were right on the nose. The clue was in with one of the big cats. And let me tell you, that is one big kitty cat." Mark said, "And the clue is?" Ed said, "Spies, that's all." Jane said, "There is a lot of spy stuff in Wisconsin, but I would put my money on the Safe House. It is a restaurant in Milwaukee."

Team Intel was up early. They were out of the hotel by seven and were on the top of the canyon, hiking the trails, looking for the clue. Gloria asked Boris, "So where the fuck is the clue?" Boris said, "All I know is it is on top of the canyon, under a tree. Now Team Three has been here yesterday, so look for footprints." Scott said,

"That's going to be hard to find. We are in the woods." Jeremy asked, "Hey, Boris, are you a good tracker?" Boris said, "I have tracked people from time to time." Jeremy said "so are we on the right side of the canyon." Boris said "I think so. The picture of the clue had a shadow on it, so it should have been this side." Jeremy pointed out where the leaves were moved and said, "Two bicycles have been through here. We are on the right track."

They hiked along. Scott said, "Let's be quiet, we are trespassing." The team moved through the woods without saying a word. They moved quickly over a narrow bridge to a spot where you could see where someone got off their bike. Jeremy pointed and stepped off the trail and walked to the side of the canyon wall. He held up a hand and said, "Let me do this. Come on, Scott."

They climbed down to the clue then back up again. Boris said, "Let's go, we are wasting time." Gloria said, "Well what is the clue?" Randy whispered, "Shut your pie hole. Your voice echoes through the canyon." Boris said, "Devil's Lake, not far." They turned and walked back down the trail. It was a good half mile. Jeremy waited until they got into the van. He read the clue out loud, "Lucifer. Okay, Devil's Lake sounds good."

Team Odin got to the Lost Canyon at eight o'clock. It didn't open till eight thirty. They passed the Intels' van on the road as they were leaving. Cherry said, "Now how the hell did they get in before us?" There was nobody in the parking lot. They parked and everyone got out and went to the ticket window. The guy said, "We don't open for another half hour." Cherry said, "We just seen a van." Robert interrupted and said, "Good morning, sir. We are on a treasure hunt. There is a question mark here that we need a clue out of." The man said, "I know that question mark is right under a tree." Joe said, "Could you show us?" The man said, "The last crew that was here paid two hundred bucks." Joe said, "Fine, we will match that." The man said, "We have to hurry then. Who can ride a bike?" Jack said, "I can ride; I have done a couple of hundred mile races " The man said, "We have a half hour, let's move."

Jack jogged behind the guy and soon they were riding up the hill. Jack stayed right on his ass. They got to the spot. Jack quickly climbed down rocks to the tree where the clue was and he climbed back up. He said, "Let's go. You have to get your ass back to work. Do you know anything about a Lucifer around here?" The man said, "Now it's all downhill. Be careful. The leaves are slippery."

They flew down the hill to the road, then around to the parking lot. The guy said, "With five minutes to spare. And Lucifer, the only thing I can think of is Devil's Lake. It isn't far from here." Jack pulled two hundred-dollar bills from his pocket and handed them to him and said, "Thanks for the ride. That was great."

He jogged over to the van. Robert asked, "What is the clue?" Jack said, "Lucifer. I think it is Devil's Lake." Dawn Googled it and said, "It has five-hundred-foot bluffs overlooking a 360-acre lake, and has twenty-nine miles of hiking trails. This could take a week." Robert said, "Let's move. I have it programmed, but it shows the shortest way. We will take the highway."

Team Intel pulled into the parking lot at the Devil's Lake state park. Gloria said, "This place is huge. There are over four hundred campsites." Boris said, "It is on the trail near the water. Come, this shouldn't take long. There are huge boulders." They all followed him down the trail. Randy said, "This place is the bomb, coolest shit I have ever seen." Scott said, "You could hide a clue anywhere here." Boris said, "Team Three found it. Look for cameras." Jeremy said, "They must have solar panels. There is no juice out here." Boris said, "They could be way up on the cliff, looking down into the rocks." Gloria said, "Rocks? These things are boulders."

They weaved through the maze on a trail. They got to the other end. Boris said, "Back through. We missed it." Scott said, "Are you sure this is where the clue is? There are miles of trails." Boris said, "I have seen it. The clue is in a small cave in the rocks, just like these." Randy said, "Let's just take it easy and slowly go back though. This time really look."

The team slowly walked through, checking out all the small trails, walking around the rocks. Gloria said excitedly, "Over here, it is over here." Boris shouted, "Where are you?" They wandered through the rocks until they found her. She said, "Squeeze through the rocks back here. I can see it in the cave right there." She pointed.

Jeremy followed her through the rocks and went inside and got the clue. Boris said, "Let's go, Circus World." Team Odin pulled into the park. Robert walked up to Team Intels' van and stuck a screwdriver though their radiator. He walked back to their van and said, "We should park somewhere else. Remember the flat tires?" He got into the van and parked it behind a truck. They got out and headed for the trails. Dawn said, "We will take the high road. You take the lakeside. Call if you find anything."

They started on their hike. Robert said, "I am going to jog through the park, you two take the trail." Jack and Joe were starting to weave through the rocks when they heard Team Intel. They slowed and listened. They got close to where they could see where Intel was. Jack said quietly to Joe, "Step back in here and let them pass." They hid and let them go by. Team Intel went right to their van and left.

Joe called Cherry and Robert. Jack went in and got the clue. When they got back to the van, Dawn asked, "So what is the clue?" Jack said, "R-B-B-B. I haven't the foggiest." Dawn said, "Ringling Bros. and Barnum & Bailey circus. It must be Circus World." Robert asked, "How far?" Cherry handed over her phone. Robert said as he programmed the GPS, "Not too far, let's roll." Cherry said, "We have to come back here, what a beautiful view."

They got down the road about ten miles and there was a green van parked alongside the road with its hood up. Robert said, "Looks like someone has a leak in their radiator." Joe said, "Well, it's not as bad as four flat tires. Thanks again for replacing them." Robert said, "That was over a grand. The petty cash is almost gone. I still am amazed that Fix-a-Flat worked."

CHAPTER TWENTY

The Safe house

Team Three got to the Safe House. Mark dropped off the team and went out to find a parking spot. They walked in to find a girl behind a desk asking for the password. Mary said, "What do you mean a password? Let's try 'let us in, bitch.'" Sue smiled and asked, "So if we don't know the password, how do we get it?" The girl said, "Cluck like a chicken." Ed bent over, stuck out his elbows, and started to cluck and scratch with his feet. Johnny did the same. Then Jane looked up to the ceiling and started to cluck. The bookcase opened and they went inside. Johnny laughed and said, "That was fun." Mary said, "That was stupid."

A waitress came up and brought them to a table. There was spy stuff all over. Pieces of the wall were moving, the wait staff called them agents. Ed said, "Hey, look on the TV. Here comes Mark." Mark stepped in front of the girl at the desk at the entrance. She asked him for the password. He looked at her and started to do some jumping jacks then came in the restaurant. Ed ordered a vodka martini, shaken not stirred. Jane asked a waitress, "You know what? We are looking for a question mark. We are on a treasure hunt. Has anything changed in the last few weeks?" The waitress said, "Oh that. If you watch the wall move, you will see it just for a second. Go in the other room and go in the telephone box. Pick up the receiver, the phone box will turn and let you into this room."

Ed said, "Come on, Johnny, we have a case to crack." The two of them walked into the other room and went into the phone booth. Ed said, "Okay, Johnny make the call." Johnny asked, "Why did they put this phone in a box?" Ed said, "This was how you could make a call. They had them on street corners. You put money in them to make a phone call." Johnny asked, "How do I do it?" Ed took the receiver off the phone and handed it to him. The booth turned in the wall. Ed took Johnny by the arm and said, "Come on, we need Jane for this one."

They walked over to the table. To his surprise, his martini was there already. Ed said, "Jane, you're going to have to get it. I am too fat and you have to step into the wall. Time it just right or you could get crushed." Sue said, "I'm coming with. How do you work it?" Johnny said, "Just lift the thingy and it turns." Mark said, "You can see it when the wall moves. This is a cool place. I would like to come here at night. They have spy movies, all different stuff."

Jane and Sue got into the phone booth. In a few seconds they were gone. Mark said, "You should take Johnny to the men's room, have him wash his hands. Food should be here soon."

Jane watched as the booth turned and there was a space between both walls. The clue was sitting about three feet in. Sue said, "I can do it." Jane said, "With your big tits? I will do it. Just when it comes for me to get out you are going to have to help pull me out quickly." They lifted the receiver again and it slowly turned and Jane stepped into the wall. She was sideways trying to get the key from around her neck into the question mark. Johnny asked, "Where is Jane?" Mark pointed as he said, "There in the wall. Did you see her?"

Sue picked up the receiver and the booth turned. She asked, "Are you okay?" Jane turned her head, the clue in her hand, and said, "Next turn pull me out." Sue put the receiver back in its cradle then lifted it. When it turned, she reached out and grabbed Jane and pulled. They both fell in the booth.

Jane walked to the table followed by Sue. She said, "Damn, that was a tight squeeze." Ed looked at Mary and said, "See, I didn't put Johnny in there." Mark said, "That would have been the best idea. We don't want to lose Jane." Mary shot him a dirty look. Mark said,

"I was kidding. That clue was too high for him to reach." Jane looked at the clue and said, "Blu, spelled B-L-U." Johnny said, "I have to lance the lizard." Ed said, "You have been hanging around Mark too much. Come on."

Mark held up his finger and said, "Watch." Ed walked to a door that said "men." Johnny grabbed it with both hands, opened it, and almost walked into a brick wall. Mark said, "I did the same thing coming in. If Ed hadn't grabbed him, he would have walled right face-first into the wall." Mary said, "And that would have been funny how?" Mark said, "Lighten up. What crawled up your ass and died?" Sue said, "You have been a bit edgy today." Mary said, "Ah, it's just that time of the month." Mark said, "To get laid maybe. Johnny might be right." Jane said, "You can take care of that." Mark said "I don't think so. If I want kids, I will make my own." Mary asked, "Are we done here? We should get going."

Mark held up a credit card and the waitress came right over to the table. Mark said, "The tip will be bigger if you hurry with the check." The girl pulled out their bill and handed it to him. Mark said, "That's fine. Just this is a bill, not a check. And I did ask for a check. And it would be nice if it was made out to cash." Jane said, "That is so lame, she probably hears that ten times a day." The waitress smiled and said, "Actually, that is kind of funny. First time someone has said that to me, and I have been waitressing part time for three years." A smart-ass smile slid onto Mark's face as he said, "See, that's the way to get a good tip, suck up to the agent." Sue said, "Agent my ass. Now Ed, he could be a spy. Have you noticed he went to a bigger gun." Mary said, "You noticed that too?" Mark said, "And he picked up a wooden crate somewhere and two ammo boxes." Mary said, "Ever since you said he is well off, I have noticed he has been picking up some of the bills and not asking to get reimbursed."

Ed and Johnny came back to the table the same time the wait-ress started to clear off the table. Mark handed her a fifty, winked, and said, "Thanks." Ed asked, "Okay, where is the next clue? And did you see that? A door that opens to a brick wall." Jane said, "First we would like to know why you are doing this. It seems like you have money." Ed said, "I told you I am on vacation and this is fun." Sue said, "Blu is a bar and lounge up on the twenty-third floor of the Pfister Hotel, just blocks from here." Mark said, "Parking is a premium here. Maybe we should just leave the van where it is." Sue said, "They have valet parking. And if you look, there are parking ramps around. You just have to know where to look."

Mary asked, "Where is Johnny?" Ed said, "He is looking around. This place has so many different spy things." Mary said, "That's nice. We have to get moving. Mark, where are the other teams?" Mark took out his phone and then said, "One is at Circus World and the other is in a small town." Sue asked, "Driving through." Mark said, "No, they're parked I think. Someone must have had to use the restroom."

Ed said, "I think this is the way to the exit. One person at a time." Jane asked, "What is up with that?" Ed said, "Spy stuff. Let's just get that next clue. That will be number five, it could be a monument." Mary said, "Payday, let's move." Ed said, "If it is a payout, I have to get to a bank. I have been carrying a lot of cash." Mark said, "About that, what is that crate you picked up?" Ed said, "That's my business, and it will be gone soon. I have a buyer that is going to meet up with us one of these days when we head south."

Ed opened the door, stepped in, and lifted the phone receiver. The door opened to a staircase. He turned and said outside the door, "Just answer the phone." When they got to the street, Sue said as she dug out some hand sanitizer, "There must be other ways out. Just think, every person touched that phone." Mark said, "I'm sure there is fire exits and other ways of getting out."

Everyone followed Mark down the street. Jane slid her arm around Sue and said, "Isn't this nice?" Mary stepped to Ed's side and said, "So this is what you do on vacation?" Ed said, "Well so far it has been a nice vacation, met some nice people, made some money, and played a game." Sue handed her phone to Mark and said, "This is the address." Ed said, "We're not staying. Should we park and walk there?" Mark said, "Valet is just so much easier." Jane said, "We just go up for a drink and dessert, chocolate lava cake. You want to split one?" Sue leaned over and kissed her lightly on the lips. Jane blushed. Mary said, "Get a room." Sue said, "This is a nice place. I bet the rooms are nice at over three hundred a night." Ed said, "Nothing that special. Food is great. And yes, I have been to the Blu. Come to think of it, great jazz and the view over the city." Mary said, "And who were you with?" Ed closed one eye as he thought, then you could see he remembered and smiled as he said, "Oh, nobody special." Johnny kept looking up at the tall buildings. Mary said, "This is the heart of the city, you stay close." Johnny said, "Yes, Mommy." Mark said, "Mommy? When did you start calling her Mommy?" Johnny's face blushed.

Mark pulled into the valet parking. He gave the key to a young man and said as he handed him a ten, "Keep it close. We don't plan on staying long." Everyone went into the hotel. Ed said, "I am going to ask about the clue. It could be anywhere in this place." Sue said, "Or you can see it from the Blu." Jane said, "You're right. It could be anywhere. Let's head up."

Ed walked up to the front desk and asked the woman, "Miss, you wouldn't have seen a question mark? It is metal and can be six inches to six feet. We are on a treasure hunt." She said, "Really? A treasure hunt? What fun. Let's see, a question mark . . . No, I can't say I have." Ed said, "Well thank you anyway. Is the Blu open?" She said, "Yes, the second elevator will take you to the top." Mark came jogging in. He asked, "So does anyone know where it is?" Mary said, "If you are not looking for it, you wouldn't notice it is there." Ed said, "To the Blu. I say we get a bottle of champagne and chill for a minute." Sue said, "I think we should split up. There are some beautiful ballrooms in this place." Johnny tugged on Ed's pants and said, "This is something. They put pictures on the ceiling." Ed said, "Well, they are paintings and it is really neat. You have to go to Vegas. There you will see acres of polished marble floors, ceilings painted beautifully, gold and statues." Mary looked at him and said, "Sounds like you like Vegas." Ed said, "Oh, the architecture is great. Some of those hotels are just beautiful." Jane said, "I love the Venetian." Sue said, "I would love to see it with you." Jane said, "It's a date. We can take in a few shows. 'Beatles Love' is fantastic." Mark said, "Okay, let's get back to business." The doors of the elevator opened and Johnny said, "Mom, can I go to the pool?" Mary asked, "Who the hell would put a pool on the top floor?" Ed said, "Isn't it a great view? Swim around and look at the city. And no, Johnny, you need a room key to get into the pool area." Johnny said, depressed, "Man, that sucks." Mark said, "I will order the champagne and get some dessert menus."

Johnny went straight to the window and looked out. He asked, "What is that?" Ed said, "That is the Gas Light Building, it tells the weather." Johnny asked, "How does it do that?" Ed said, "I don't know, you will have to look it up. Ah shit, there is something on the building." Sue said, "The flame on the top of the building sits 250 feet high. It has twenty floors, and it opened in 1930. When the light is blue it means no change in the weather. When it is gold, it is going to be cold out. When it is red, it is going to be hot. And when it flickers, it is going to rain."

Ed had his small binoculars out and he said, "This is going to be a bitch. See the corner of the Gas Light Building? There is your clue." Jane handed Sue and Ed a glass of champagne. She asked, "Did you find it?" Ed said, "It is a clue. I will go get it." Johnny begged, "Can I come? You are going on top of that building. I want to go." Ed said, "No, this is a job for me. It will be much faster if I go myself." Jane said, "I think you should take someone with." Ed polished off his glass and handed it to Mary and said, "I will be back within the hour."

Mark handed out dessert menus. He asked, "What is going on?" Mary said, "See that light on that building over there? Look to the corner of the building. There is our question mark." Mark said, "Holy fuck, how can you even see that?" Mary said, "Ed is going over to get it. He said he doesn't need any help, it would be faster if he does it by himself." Sue said, "That flame is twenty-one feet tall and weighs four tons. They just upgraded it to LED. That is why the clue looks so small." Mary said, "Well he had better be able to do it." Mark said, "If he can't, I don't know who can." Jane handed Johnny a kiddie cocktail and said, "You watch for Ed." Johnny said, "Four cherries, yes. Okay, I will watch for him."

A man started to play light jazz. Mary asked Mark, "Where are the other teams?" Mark pulled out his phone and said, "That's a good question. Team Odin is at the Circus Museum, and team Intel is still at that small town. Maybe they had a breakdown."

Team Odin was just pulling into the Circus museum. Cherry said, "Okay, this is what we are going to do. Dawn and I will go and interview some of the helpers." Robert said, "Okay, the three of us will spread out and search the place."

They bought their tickets and went in, quickly walking through all the posters and the few circus wagons. They started to cross the bridge over to the circus. You could hear all the chatter. Someone was talking into a microphone, introducing a clown act. Dawn said. "Oh god, I hate clowns." Joe said, "How could you hate clowns? They are funny. They make balloon animals. They have big feet."

Cherry said, "What a beautiful day. Hey, Robert, maybe you can find yourself a leprechaun." Robert shot her a look and said, "Okay, this is how we are going to do this. Jack, you take the circus wagon building. That is one big fricken building. Joe, you go over and check out the carousel. Girls, do the circus tent. I will do a perimeter check, ask everyone you see."

They got to the other side and split up. Jack walked over to the circus wagon building. It was huge. There were wagons with dragons, ones with statues all around them. There were wagons that caged animals. Some were small, others were thirty feet long, fifteen feet high. Jack called Robert and said, "I am just going to do a walk-through. That clue could be anywhere in here."

Joe headed for the carousel. He looked in the train cars. There were so many small buildings and wagons, trucks, exhibits. He finally got to the carousel and watched it. He asked the man who ran it if he had seen a question mark. The young man said, "Not over here, I just run the ride sometimes. I work the concession stand." Joe watched the carousel, making sure the clue wasn't there. He called Robert and said, "It is not on the carousel. There are a few buildings. I will make my way back to the big top."

Robert was checking out everything he found, train cars, carriages, and random stuff under roof. There were small buildings. Cherry and Dawn went to the big top and started to watch a clown show. It was good. They talked with a guy selling toys, balloons, and stuff. Cherry said, "Sir, we are on a treasure hunt. You wouldn't have seen a question mark?" He smiled and said, "Maybe and maybe not. Did this question mark have to be about two feet tall and made of metal?" Cherry's eyes popped open and she said excitedly, "Yes, yes. Where is it?" The man said, "I didn't say I know where it is." Dawn pulled out a twenty, waved it in the air. The man reached out and took it and said, "Yes, I know where it is." Cherry asked, "Well, where is it?" He cocked his head and hummed. Dawn pulled another twenty out. He took that one too and said, "The tiger cage." Cherry said, "What the fuck? In a tiger's cage? Where?" He looked at her. Dawn said, "Jesus Christ, give him another twenty." The man took the twenty and pointed to the back of the tent. Cherry said, "You're a dick."

Dawn called Robert and said, "We know where it is, in a tiger's cage." Robert said, "You have to be shitting me. A real tiger?" Dawn said, "Meet us at the big top and we can go over there." Robert called Joe and Jack. They all met over at the big top. The clowns were out there doing their act. It was impressive. A balancing act. The dog act was great. A dog that would walk across the tight wire, poodles hopping around, jumping six dogs lined up. They had two huge pigs doing an act.

Cherry said, "Follow me, the guy pointed to this building." Robert said, "Let's wait a minute, let the elephants through." Four elephants walked by following four showgirls. Joe said, "How the hell do those little girls handle those big elephants?" Jack said, "I would follow those girls anywhere. They must be like pets. Elephants are supposed to be smart." A man with a shovel walked behind them. Robert said, "Sir, we are looking for a question mark." Dawn pulled out a twenty and waved it. The guy stopped and took the bill and asked, "What about it?" Dawn pulled out another twenty and asked, "Can you show it to us?" He said, "Sure, why not. We have to be quick about it." He turned and watched the elephants enter the tent. He said, "Follow me."

He quickly walked to a building that smelled like manure. He said, "Right there, strapped to the cage. They put it up two weeks ago." He turned to leave. Robert said, "How do we get in there?" The man said, "You wait until tomorrow. Bruno is off today. He is the lion tamer." Joe asked, "Why is he alone?" The man said, "Oh, that is Shere Khan. He has a temper. Don't put your hands in the cage. In fact, I stay at least four feet from the cage." Robert said, "Is there anybody here that will go in the cage?" The man rubbed his fingers together. Dawn handed him a twenty and said, "That's it, I am out of cash." The man took it and said, "No, he is the only one that works with the old cat." He turned and walked to the big top.

Jack said, "I can reach it if I stand on a bucket. Just get the cat away from that side." Dawn said, "Look at the claw marks on that clue. Lucky it is steel." Joe said, "I know, let's play a little ball out here, Cats love moving things." Jack said, "Where you going to find a ball?" Cherry said, "I will be right back." She ran to the big top and found the vendor that was walking around selling things and bought a bright orange ball. She ran back. Robert said, "Look into his eyes. That is a wild beast." Joe said, "It's just tiger's eyes." Robert said, "Look into the other tigers' eyes. There is something different."

Joe walked over to the large enclosure holding a half dozen big cats. One walked right up and looked at him. Joe walked back and said, "You're right, Shere Khan here wants to eat your ass. Just look at him." Cherry said, "I got the ball." Jack said, "Great, I will get into position. You start playing catch in front of the cage." Robert walked to the other end of the cage and rolled the ball. It was about sixteen feet. The big cat watched the two of them play catch. He started to walk back and forth from one end of the cage to the other end. Jack put the five-gallon bucket against the cage and stepped up on it. He put his key in the slot. The clue came out. He got his key out of it and reached in for the clue.

The big cat took two leaps and was across the twelve feet to the other side of the cage. It stuck his paw through the bars and grabbed Jack, pinning him to the bars. Jack yelled, "Oh fuck." He fell off the pail and the cat had its claws in his back, holding him a foot off the ground. Joe was in a full run around the cage. Jack pushed away from the bars with his arms and feet and fell to the ground, still holding the clue. Joe got to him and asked, "Are you alright?" Jack said, "I just didn't see him." Dawn walked over and said, "What the hell? You took your eyes off of him." Jack asked, "Am I bleeding?" Robert held his hand out to him. Jack sat up. Dawn said, "Oh yeah, sliced right through your shirt." Jack asked, "Is it going to need stitches?" Cherry said, "You're going to have to go and see a doctor and get that cleaned right." Jack said, "Just help me to my feet, hurts like hell." Robert looked at the big cat and said, "You almost got a free lunch." Dawn said, "Look at him licking the blood from his paws. Jack, you need to get that cleaned. There is such a thing as cat scratch fever." Robert said, "That's a Ted Nugent song."

Cherry asked, "So what is the clue?" Jack handed it to Joe. He read it, "It says 'spies.' That's it, just spies." Dawn said, "We had better look at your back. You're bleeding pretty good." Jack said, "There is a first aid kit in the van." Robert said, "Well, we should put something over it so it isn't so noticeable." Joe said, "I will walk right behind you. Let's go." Jack said, "Not too fast." Cherry said, "No, really. Let's move if you want to wait until we get to the van. The faster we get there, the faster we get you patched up."

Dawn said, "Spies, there is something going on with the public radio, some painting services. Ah, here we go. The Safe House in Milwaukee, that has to be it." Cherry said, "Just follow the exit signs. It takes you right around the place to the parking lot." Jack asked, "How bad do you think it is?" Joe said, "Well your shirt is soaked. And it is past your butt cheeks, so your pants are shot." Robert said, "Let's get your shirt off." Jack started to pull off his shirt and stopped and said, "I can't raise my arm up any farther." Cherry said, "Oh wow, that's gross. You need stitches, and a lot of them." Joe said, "Here is the first aid kit. I will put all the Band-Aids on, then to keep them closed, we have tape and gauze. Let's get him to lie down face-first and get this patch job done till we get him to a hospital."

Cherry wet a towel and held his arm back. She said, "Now stay this way. It holds the skin tight together." Joe said, "Someone open the Band-Aids and I will put them on like butterfly stitches. Then we will tape the gauze over that." Cherry said, "What the hell are we doing? There is a hospital like a mile from here." Joe said, "Just let me get a few more to hold this together." Robert said, "Okay, we need to get our story straight. He fell on a rake." Jack said, "Sounds good to me." Jack said, "This better not take long." Cherry said, "It has to be done. Let's go." Robert asked, "Do we have a bag or something to put over the chair? Blood smells terrible. Once it gets into the seat you will never get it out." Dawn said, "Do you want him to walk?" Cherry took the bag out of a trash can and put it over the seat. Joe said, "Okay, let's get you into the van."

Robert grabbed an arm and Joe grabbed the other and helped him to his knees then lifted him to his feet. Robert said, "Okay, girls, get in. We will put him on the outside." Soon they were in the emergency room. They got him right in and three hours later they were in the van. Jack started to cry. He sobbed, "I am sorry, guys. I should have watched the tiger. We have lost so much time." Robert said, "You big fucking pussy. Lucky that tiger didn't kill your ass." Cherry said, "Sixty-four stitches. He isn't going to be climbing anything soon." Joe asked, "Do we dump him? He isn't going to be much help." Joe said, "This Safe House you are talking about, does it serve food?" Dawn said, "It is a restaurant. Can we just leave him in the van?" Cherry said, "The doctor said he is going to be out of it until morning. They got some heavy-duty painkillers." Joe pulled out the bottle and said, "Oxycodone, this should put him to sleep."

Team Intel finally made it to the Baraboo. Boris said, "We stop at grocery store, buy a couple of steaks, yeah?" Randy said, "Could we get some munchies and a few Cokes?" Boris said, "We need meat. I will run in, get this." Gloria said as soon as Boris left, "I don't know about this guy. If they find out we have insider's information, shit is going to hit the fan." Randy asked, "What do you think he needs raw meat for?" Scott said, "It must be to feed it to something. I bet the clue is in the lion's cage." Jeremy said, "It's a circus, lions, tigers, and bears. Oh my." Randy said, "They all suck, Cincinnati Bengals, Detroit Lions, and the Chicago Bears."

Boris got to the van and said, holding a receipt, "You owe me thirty-two dollars." Scott said, "Gloria, don't forget to give him thirty-two dollars." Boris said, "I thought you were the captain." Scott said, "I think you are the captain now. You have the inside scoop. So what are we feeding this to?" Boris said, "One big mean tiger. Tore up one of the Odins a couple of hours ago." Randy said, "So we are not that far behind." Scott said as they parked, "So do you know where this tiger is?" Boris said, "That I do not know. I do know the clue is strapped inside the cage with him." Randy said, "Well, it shouldn't be hard to find. This place isn't that big." Gloria said, "We just have to ask." Boris smiled and said, "Let's get in there and back out."

Gloria went and paid for the tickets and paid Boris for the meat. They went inside, over the bridge, and stopped the first circus worker they found and asked, "Where do you keep the tigers?" The man said, "In the back. They are off limits to guests." Boris said as he held out a hundred, "Could you show us?" The man looked around and said, "Right this way." He quickly walked through the grounds to the building the animals were kept in. He said, "These are the big cats." Randy said, "We are looking for a question mark." The man said, "That is over by Shere Khan. Do not get close to this old cat. He has issues." Boris said, "Jeremy, you are the tallest. Get around to the back. I will distract him, you get the clue."

Jeremy walked around and righted the pail that was there. He watched the big cat. Boris pulled out one of the steaks and slid it though the bars. The cat took one swipe at it and pulled it from his hands. Jeremy stood on the pail and got the key into the question mark and the clue popped out. He quickly got the clue. The cat sat there eating his big steak. Jeremy got to the team. He said, "Spies, that is what the clue is." Boris said, "We go to Milwaukee, to a place called the Safe House." Jeremy said, "You were right. There is a pool of blood back there. The tiger must have got a hold of one of the other team. It is still red, so we can't be far behind."

CHAPTER TWENTY-ONE

Cruise

Team Three waited up in the bar at Blu. Johnny ran over to the table. They were eating desserts and chatting while a man played light jazz on a saxophone. Johnny said, "He is there." Everyone stood and looked out the window. Mark said, "Boy, he looks small from here." Jane said, "That is farther than you think. The building is so big it looks closer. Go to Vegas. It looks like the casinos are close by but they're so big it takes forever to walk to one." Sue slid her arm around Jane's waist, nuzzled her neck, and said lightly, "You have to take me there." Jane turned to her, looked in her eyes, and said, "I will take you wherever you want to go." Johnny was looking out, staring at Ed.

Mary got a call. She said, "Cruise. That is what the clue is, cruise." Sue said, looking at her phone, "There are three different boats touring the river." Mark stepped close to her. She showed him her phone. He said, "Book the open-top one. It is a beautiful day and we have to look for that clue. Mary, tell Ed we will meet him in front of the hotel. Drink up, everyone." Johnny said, "I wonder how he got up there." Mark said, "He walked ding-ding. Now let's go."

Johnny started to shovel ice cream in his mouth. Sue said, "Leave it, we are going downstairs." You could see the brain freeze kicking in as Johnny's face scrunched up. He put his hands on his head. Mark chuckled and handed Johnny his kiddie cocktail and said, "Drink, and let's go."

They got into the elevator and walked outside to see Ed jogging up the sidewalk. He got to them and asked, "Where are we going?" Sue said, "We have a van on the way for a taxi, then we are going on a riverboat. God, I hope this is the right boat." Ed said, half out of breath, "It is probably on one of the bridges when they open up. We have to look at every one." He reached down and rubbed Johnny's head and said, "This one should be a marker. Remember what they look like?" Johnny looked up and said, "Da."

They got into the van and were on their way to the river boat. It was two stories tall. Jane said, "I would have thought you would have picked the other one." Sue said, "This one is more open, and it is a beautiful day." Sue walked onboard the ship and showed them her phone. Mark said, "Please start a tab under Hunt."

Johnny said, "This is the biggest boat I have ever been on." Ed said, "This is a ship." Johnny asked, "What's the difference? It's a big boat." Ed looked at Mary and asked, "How old is he again and what grade?" She said, "He is eight years old and is in third grade." Ed said, "They don't teach you this in school." Jane said to Sue, "He doesn't know." Ed's eyes shifted to look at her. He said, "When a boat displaces more than five hundred tons, it is considered a ship. A yacht is a boat that is thirty-three feet or longer. And a submarine is always a boat, it doesn't matter how long it is." Jane said, "Okay, that will never come up in school."

They went to the upper deck. Mark asked, "How much is this setting us back?" Sue said, "It is eighteen apiece and nine for the child." Mark smiled and said, "Not bad. How long of a cruise?" Sue said, "It's a two-hour narrated cruise." Johnny asked, "Where are we going?" Sue said, "Out to the harbor. That would be Lake Michigan."

Johnny asked a mate, "Do ships sink often?" She looked at him and said, "Just once. May I get you something from the bar?" Johnny said, "A kiddie cocktail please."

The captain walked through saying his speech about the life jackets and the ship. He stared at a guy with purple, green, and blue hair just a little too long. The guy asked, "What are you looking at, old man?" The captain said, "You know, I was young and foolish once. I married a parrot. I just thought maybe you were my son."

The ship filled with laughter. Johnny looked up, confused. Ed said, "Don't worry. That one just went over your head." Mark said, "It just means the captain fucked a parrot and—" Mary shot him a look that shut him right up. Johnny looked at Ed. He said, "It was a joke."

The ship started to cruise through the river. They kept their eye out looking for the clue. The bridges opened differently. Some went straight up on hydraulics; others, just one end would lift. Most of them were drawbridges.

The waitress came over by Johnny and asked, "So how much does it cost a pirate to pierce his ears?" Johnny said, "They do it with their hook." She said, "No, it is a buck an ear. Get it? A buccaneer. Okay, try this one. What did the lake say to the boat? Nothing, it just waved." Mark moaned, "Ah, that one sucked. How about this one? What is the difference between a girlfriend and a wife? About fifty pounds. Did you hear about the passenger and the waitress having sex all night? I will tell you in the morning." She blushed. Ed said, "You don't have that kind of money."

A bridge went up and they drove through. Jane asked, "Why do you think the marker will be under a bridge?" Ed said, "Don't you think that would be a great place for it? That's where I would put it." Mark said, "I think it is going to be on a balcony." Jane said, "It might be on the river; a boat dock, a marker, or island." Sue said, "How about a boat? We might have just got on the wrong one."

They pulled out into the harbor. Ed took out his binoculars and looked at the art museum. Johnny said, "It looks like a ship with great big sails." Sue said, "They can open and close the sails. Pretty cool, hey?" Jane said, "I would have put it on the lighthouse. My goodness it is just wonderful out here."

Ed went to the bar and got a manhattan. Johnny was bored and started to walk around the boat, acting like a pirate.

Mark said as he hopped out of his seat, "There it is, against the wall, under the bridge." Mary said, "No shit, that's an easy one." Sue said, "Not really. That is a ten-foot drop to it, and we only have a few minutes to get all five of us in there then back out." Ed stood there looking at it, then said, "Charter us a pontoon boat. We need it now." Sue sat down at the table and started to play with her phone.

Ed stepped up to her and said, "Tell them we need a six-foot ladder. Boy, this should be interesting." Mark said, "Dammit, I wish I would have timed it." Sue said, "We can get wave runners. There's a nineteen-foot fishing boat." Ed said, "A pontoon would be the jam. We need to run up there and get the cash and back down within two minutes." Mark said, "Here you go. Type in 'pontoon boats for rent in Milwaukee.'" Sue said, "What the hell do you think I was doing? I got one. We meet him where the boat docks. He does diving out in the lake." Mark asked, "How much?" Sue said, "Six hundred. He has a gang plank. That will work."

Their tour came to an end and a pontoon boat pulled up. The guy powered it up to the dock wall. Ed said, "This should do fine. Ahoy there." The pontoon captain called out, "You looking to rent a boat?" Sue said, "Let's board this thing. We want the big bucks." Jane said, "This could be interesting. The damn boat is moving, so is the plank." Ed stood at the top and said, "Take your time. The captain will give you a hand."

Johnny ran right down the plank. Mary followed slowly. Soon everyone was on the boat. Sue stepped over to the captain and said, "St. Paul Bridge, and here is the six hundred." Ed said, "If you get this done quickly there is another hundred in it for you." The captain said, "Okay, then give me a hand with the gang plank and we will shove off, me hearties." Jane asked, "You do know the bridge?" The captain said, "The St. Paul Avenue Bridge is a vertical lift bridge. I believe it is fifty-two feet."

Fifteen minutes later they were pulling up to the bridge. The captain said, "Now we wait till a big boat comes and they lift the bridge and you can scurry up there." Jane asked, "Can we drop anchor and tie off on the side?" A tour boat was coming. Mark said, "Let's get this done. Pull her up tight." The captain flopped rubber bumpers over the side and butted it up against the concrete wall and said, "I will keep the motor running, holding it tight to the wall. You guys slide the plank up. Remember, you have about three to four minutes." Mark said, "Jane, you first. Hold the plank once you are up there."

The bridge rose and everything went like clockwork. Ed and Mark slid the plank in place. Jane ran up, held the plank for everyone. They stepped to the marker. They put in their keys and got the payout and were back on the boat before the bridge even started to drop. Ed walked over to the captain and handed him a hundred and said, "You did good. Now you can put us ashore anywhere." Mark asked the captain, "Do you know of something to do with dome?" The captain said, "There are the three domes up on Twenty-seventh. They have been there forever." The captain said, "I will put you ashore by the brewery Rock Bottom. If you have the time, they have great food."

Ed said, "Sue, could you get us a cab at the Rock Bottom?" She said, "Will do, and the three domes are Mitchell Park Horticultural Conservatory. The domes must be fifty feet tall. One is Jungle and the other is Desert, then the third is Show." Ed ordered a round of beers. He said, "You go to a brewery you sample the beer."

The van got there and in a half hour they were at the three domes. They walked around for a good hour. Ed asked, "That clue, did it say dome or domes?" Mary pulled the clue from her pocket and said, "Just dome. What are you thinking?" Ed asked an older woman, "If I said to you a popular dome in Milwaukee, you would say . . . ?" She said, "Let me see. I would say the Basilica of St. Josaphat. I think that is the third largest dome east of the Mississippi. Or maybe the Brewers' stadium. Their roof opens and closes." Ed smiled and said, "But that's a roof. We are in the wrong place. Sue, call a cab." Mark said, "Hey, I am the leader of this team. Sue, call a cab." Mary said, "I think you are right. If it meant here it would have said domes, not dome." Sue said, "Oh boy, you're not going to like this. It is a big one. I do mean huge. There are three churches in it. They built it in 1907. There is sixty-five thousand square feet." Mary said, "I hope to God this is the place." Ed said, "Well, if you are going to pray to God, this will be the place. How far?" Mark said, "Let's go back to the hotel, get the van, then a half hour." Sue smiled and said, "And here comes the taxi. You do know I am keeping track of everything I spend?" Mark said, "Just write a note what you spent and take it out of the spending money."

Team Odin got to the Safe House. Cherry whispered something to Dawn before they walked in the door. There was a guy at the door. Cherry leaned in and whispered in his ear. The bookcase opened and she walked through. Dawn did the same thing; she walked in. Robert walked up to the man. He asked, "What is the password?" Robert said, "Password? What the hell do you need a password for?" The man said, "Ah, you don't know it. Stand on one leg for thirty seconds and I will let you in." Jack stood on one leg, looking at his watch. Joe stepped in and the man asked for the password. Joe said, "Open sesame, abracadabra." The man said, "That's magic words. Give up?" Joe said, "I guess." The doorman said, "Walk around like a chicken for ten seconds." Joe hunched over, stuck out his elbow, and nodded his head. The bookcase opened and he went inside. Jack walked in. The doorman asked for the password. Jack pulled a twenty off his money clip and said, "Jackson." The doorman said, "Close enough." The bookcase opened and he went inside.

Jack walked straight to the bar, ordered a vodka gimlet, and took two pain pills. He then went to the table with the rest of the team. Cherry said, "So where the hell would you hide a question mark?" Dawn said, "Why don't you ask the waitress?" Robert said, "That's the reason we keep you around." He held up his arm and waved to a waitress with a twenty in his hand. The waitress came over and Robert asked, "Do you know of a question mark around here? It is steel and can be any color." She said as she took the bill, "Watch the wall. When it moves to one end, there it is." She asked, "Are you ready to order?" Cherry said, "Well I will be a monkey's uncle, it was right in front of us." Jack laughed, "You an uncle? You have tits, you can't be an uncle." Robert said, "Let's order. The painkillers are getting to him." Jack said, "And a manhattan, make it Crown." Joe said, "Make that a Coke. Better yet, make it two."

Dawn asked, "How do you get to the clue?" The waitress said, "Step into the phone booth and it will turn and you can get out the other side." Jack had his head against the wall. He was out for the count, drool hung from his mouth. Cherry said, "I am going to check it out." Dawn said, "I am coming, might just as well powder my nose." Jack's eyes opened. He smiled and said, "She is going to take a big shit, smell up the whole place. We will have to call the fire department and repaint the walls. It will strip the flesh right off your bones. Don't do it." Robert said, "She is going next door. Don't worry, just take a nap."

Cherry said, "Wow, those drugs must be a good batch." She stepped into the phone booth, lifted the receiver, and the booth turned around, leaving a blank wall. A minute went by and she was back. Cherry said, "Okay, come with me and stand in the back. I am going to step out between the walls and get the clue. Give me two minutes, then come back through and I will hop back in." Dawn stepped in, squeezed by her, and stood against the side of the phone booth. Cherry lifted the receiver and the booth turned. She popped out in between the walls. She got the clue and stood waiting for Dawn to turn the booth around. Dawn watched her phone. As soon as two minutes passed, she picked up the receiver and the booth turned back. Cherry stepped into the booth without a second to spare. They walked to the table.

Robert had Jack's arm wrapped around his shoulders. He said, "We will be right back. He has to piss." He took him down to the men's room. He opened the door and Jack walked face-first into the brick wall. Robert caught him and shouted, "What the fuck? Are you okay?" A man said, "Men's room is around the corner." Jack's face was covered in blood. His nose was streaming blood down his face. Robert dragged him to the men's room, stood him in front of the sink, and said, "Hold your head over the sink." Jack held his head over the sink and the blood slowed to a drip. Robert handed him a handful of paper towels and said, "Hold this against your nose and pinch it closed. For fuck's sakes, didn't you see the wall?" Jack said, "I really have to piss." Robert said, "Jesus Christ, you need a new shirt. Hell, your shoes are covered with blood." Jack said, with one hand on the wall, the other holding his dick, "I'm getting dizzy." Robert stepped to his side and put his hand on his shoulder and said, "Just finish."

Robert took him back to the sink and said, "They sell shirts here.

Take yours off and I will buy you a new one." Jack took off his shirt. Robert wet some toweling and wiped him down. He said, "Come on, let's go buy you a shirt." He took Jack's arm, slung it around his neck, and practically dragged him to the counter and said, "I need a shirt. Extra large, I think." The girl said, "What happened?" Robert said, "He walked into the brick wall that was supposed to be the men's room." She smiled and asked, "What color?" Robert said, "Whatever, green, blue, whatever is close."

Robert had Jack lean against the wall. You could see the four gash marks across his back that were all stitched up. The girl gave him the shirt and asked, "What happened to him?" Robert smiled and said, "Tiger." He helped Jack put on his shirt. It was a chore because he couldn't lift one arm because of all the stitches. The girl asked again, "Really, what happened to him?" Jack went, "Big kitty. Don't ever take your eyes off of big kitty. He will eat you." "Come on, Jack, we need to get some food in you. How many painkillers did you take?" Jack said, holding up his fingers, "Two."

Robert said as they got to the table, "We need two doggy bags. Box up mine and Jack's. We will meet you at the car." Joe got up and said as he took Jack's other arm, "What did you do to him?" Cherry said, "He is going to have two black eyes." Robert said, "He walked face-first into a brick wall. So what was the clue?" Cherry said, "Blu, it is a bar on top of a historic hotel a few blocks from here." Robert said, "This one is not a marker, we can leave him in the van." Joe said, "I think we should just leave him, put him on a street corner somewhere." Dawn said, "We can't do that, give him some time." Robert said, "At the van in ten minutes." Joe said, "How did he get so messed up?" Robert said, "Well the doc had him on some heavy meds when they were sewing him up. He took a couple more when he got into the van and two more washed down with some whiskey." Joe said, "We have to get some food into him. How do you get out of this place?" Robert pointed to someone on their hands and knees spraying bleach on the blood and wiping it up. "That's where he walked into the wall." Joe said, "This way."

They got him to where it narrowed. Joe took him to the exit. You had to walk in and pick up the phone, and the door would open to the staircase. Robert said, "Now take your time. You fall, you are going to take me with you. Screw it." Robert ran down the stairs just in case Jack fell. They got to the street. Robert jogged around the building across the bridge to the restaurant Rock Bottom. He picked everyone up. Dawn said, "There is valet service at the Pfister." Robert said, "Shit, will they let us leave Jack in the van?" Dawn said, "He can stay downstairs, in the hotel lobby." Cherry said, "He is pretty wasted." Robert said, "Get some water in him and food." Joe asked, "Will he throw up?" Cherry pointed, "There it is. I wonder where the hell they put this clue. I could have got crushed getting the last one." Joe said, "See, it's nice not having big tits."

Odin left the van with the valet. As they expected, they couldn't leave Jack in the van. Robert asked, "Who is going to babysit Jack?" Cherry said, "Just put him in a chair somewhere with a glass of water." Joe took Jack by the arm and led him into the hotel. Jack said, "I am fine. I can walk—whoa, the building is moving." Dawn said, "No more pain pills for you." Cherry said, "We should have left him in Baraboo. He is going to be an anchor slowing us down."

Jack stood there with drool hanging from his mouth. Robert looked at him and said, "Maybe you're right. It has been what, four hours since they stitched him up." He took Jack by the hand and said, "Follow me," and took him to a chair. Cherry went to the front desk and found out how to get to the Blu. They all went into the elevator.

When they got up to the top floor they started to look for the question mark. Dawn asked, "Why can't we get into the pool?" Joe said, "That is for guests of the hotel. You need a room key." Robert said, "I could use a drink. Wish I wasn't driving." Joe said to the bartender, "Give me a Singapore sling. No wait, change that to a mai tai." Cherry said, "Oh, that sounds good. Make that two." Dawn said, "A house Pinot noir and a Coke for this guy."

Cherry asked the bartender, "Hey, what is the building with the flame on top?" The bartender said, "That's the Gas Light Building." She then asked, "Did a team of five people come in here within a couple of hours?" The bartender said, "No, we were having high tea up to fifteen minutes ago and I was getting the bar ready, so no group of five came in." Cherry said, "They are getting insider's info. That's how come they are catching us." Robert asked, "What the hell are you babbling about?" Cherry said, "Look at the top of that building. See the clue? They are up there. They had to come here first." Joe said, "She is right you know. I bet they are going right to the next clue. Drink up, me hearties." Robert said as he dialed the phone, "You're right. We have to call that Lance guy." Cherry said from the back of the elevator, "We are only supposed to call him if we need a clue." Robert said, "We are calling him. You're right, I think they are cheating." Joe said, "That would be nice if they were disqualified."

As they got down to the lobby they saw Jack crying in his chair. Cherry said, "Now what the hell is going on?" Robert said, "I will get the van, you deal with the drama queen over there." Joe walked over with Dawn and Cherry. Dawn got down on one knee and asked, "What's wrong?" Jack looked up and said, "A little girl called me a duck." Dawn said, "Really, a duck? Why would she call you a duck?" Jack said, "She said I was a quack head." Joe said, "That's a crack-head, you dumb shit. Come on, let's get you to the van."

Joe took Jack to the van. He had one foot on the curb, the other on street. Jack said, "My god, I think I am crippled." Joe pulled him up on the sidewalk and said, "Come on, Jack, snap out of it." Jack mumbled, "Did you find the clue?" Joe said, "Yes, we found the clue. Now let's walk to the van." Jack said, "The building is moving again." Dawn said, "Maybe you are right." Joe looked at her and nodded. Cherry said, "Let him sleep it off. We will see in the morning."

They got to the van. Robert was talking to himself. He said, "Lance knows about it. There is something going on. They are reviewing the conversations that were going on in the van. So they can hear whatever we say in here." Jack said, "Cherry, sit on my face. I love you." Robert said, "Well, he is getting better. Do we go after the clue or the van?" Joe said, "The clue, we need the clue." Cherry said, "The van. They will take us right to the next clue. We already know where this one is. If we have to come back, so be it." Joe said, "How are you going to find the van?" Robert pointed, "It is sitting at the stop light." Dawn said, "They are going to see us." Robert pulled out and said, "Let's try it."

They followed the Intels' van. It stopped at the bridge and two of them got out and ran up and looked as the bridge was in the raised position. Cherry said, "It must be under the bridge." Robert said, "Well I don't think it is a clue. It must be a marker." Jack was fast asleep. Dawn said, "If we drop in, grab the cash, then hop into the river he can't do it." Joe said, "We can work it with four of us." Dawn said, "It takes five, and there are cameras."

The Intels were discussing how to do the marker. Boris said, "We do it quick. Drop a ladder to get out, down and back out in two minutes." Scott said, "First we have to time how long the bridge is up when a boat is going through." Boris said, "Nine. We do this next boat." Jeremy said, "Okay, we find a parking spot and then a ladder." Gloria said, "This is stupid. You are putting all our lives at risk. We could get squashed." Boris said, "If time runs out, jump into the river. No problem." Randy said, "How much are we talking about?" Jeremy said, "A grand." Randy said, "I'm in. Hop down there and back out, no problem." Gloria said, "Well you're tall. How am I going to get out of there?" Randy said, "I will give you a boost, you know you want me to handle you." Gloria rolled her eyes and said, "In your wildest dreams." Randy said, "Not even close, unless you like rollerblading in the nude." Scott said, "Really, having sex on rollerblades?" Randy said, "Always wanted to try it."

Boris said, "Drive around the block. Park there." Scott said, "Well it might be there after we circle the block." To everyone's surprise, it was still there. They parked and Boris said, "Okay, we hang around until a boat comes." Randy said, "A big boat, something slow." They stood around for about twenty minutes not knowing the Odin team was watching. A tour boat came down the river. Boris said, "Now, let's walk up to the bridge." As soon as the bridge lifted they dropped in and got the money and were back out in less than a minute. They walked away from the bridge like nothing happened. Boris said, "We go to the basilica. We will catch the team in the lead."

Team Odin was watching team Intel. Cherry said, "There is no way Jack can drop down there and back out." Joe said, "Let me ask that black kid. Looks a little stoned but I think he will do." He walked over and talked with the boy. Both of them came back to the building. Cherry said, "Jack, you have to stay right here. I am going to need your key." Robert said, "Okay, but if we keep the black guy we have to have proof of insurance." The black guy looked and said, "What's you talking about, honky? You had better be able to get yo white cracker ass out of there." Joe said, "Okay, here comes a boat. Let's do this."

They walked up to the bridge. As soon as it was raised, Robert and Joe dropped down six feet and helped the girls down. They all put their keys in. Joe said to the black guy, "Now turn it clockwise all at the same time. Three, two, one, turn." The door opened up. Cherry grabbed the money, stuck it in her bra, and shouted, "Let's get out of here." Joe grabbed Dawn and boosted her up. Robert took Cherry, who already was pulling herself up. He put his hand on her ass and gave her a shove and soon they were on the street. Joe said, "Let's move. That had to be illegal," The black guy said, "So where is my hundred?" Joe said as he peeled off five twenties, "You give me the key and I will give you five twenties." Robert said, "Give him another hundred. Sure do appreciate your help. Would you like to travel with us?" Cherry said, "That's fine. You got two hundred bucks, now piss off." Robert looked at her. She said, "Did you see the tracks on his arm? He is a user."

They got back in the van. Joe asked, "What should I do with Jack's key?" Robert looked at him and said, "We give him a couple of days. That tiger did a lot of damage, but I think he will be able to move around as soon as those stitches heal." Jane said, "He knows. Don't worry about him, he is a team player." Dawn said, "There is no way he could have pulled himself up six feet." Robert said, "Let's get back to solving this clue. The other team is cheating and I think we should call it in again." Joe said, "We only call in if we need a clue." Jane said, "Screw that. They came right to this bridge. They knew where the clue was. What do they call that?" Robert said, "Insider trading. That's illegal. We should call again."

They got to the van. Jack was out. Joe said, "Painkillers and whiskey will make you sleepy." Jane said, "Let's solve this clue and get on the road. Tonight we stay at a dive hotel." Dawn asked, "Why? I like nice hotels." Jane said, "Today was payday. We only made a grand." Robert said, "That's one thousand apiece. A nice hotel with a bar. It doesn't have to be a four-star." Cherry pulled out the money. She took two hundred out of one and set it on Jack. She then gave Joe one stack and the two hundred. She said, "Jack paid for the guy to stand in for him." She handed out the rest of the money. Robert said, "So what is the clue so we can get on the road?" Cherry pulled the clue off the ten hundred-dollar bills. She said, "Dome. That's it, just dome." Everyone pulled out their phones and searched domes in Milwaukee, Wisconsin. Jane said, "It must be the Mitchell Park domes. These things are huge. It is just off Twenty-seventh, 524 South Layton Boulevard." Robert said, "There is no Layton Boulevard, just avenue." Dawn said, "Whoa there, that is on the south side of town. Use my phone, it is only a few miles away."

Jane said, "Push the button. I want to talk to this Lance guy." Joe said, "St. Josaphat Basilica is the sixth largest dome in the world." Jane said, "Hold on to that thought. Lance, is that you?" A voice through the speaker in the van said, "Yes. I am talking to the Odin team, right?" Jane said, "Yes, we would like to report Team Intel is cheating. They must have insider's information." Lance said, "We are looking into it. We have tracked some of the phone messages. It does seem there is someone feeding information to them." Robert asked, "So what are we supposed to do? We can't compete. They know right where the clues are." Lance said, "Just chill. Like I told you before, we think we know who it is. We are checking phone records. There is a lot of cash riding on this." Robert said, "There are the three domes. Let me pull into the parking lot. The Intel van is not here, it should be here." Lance said, "Don't fall too far behind. Team Three already went to the church." Cherry said, "Plug in the basilica. He gave us the clue." Joe said, "But I wanted to walk through the domes."

CHAPTER TWENTY-TWO

St. Josaphat

Team Three retrieved the van from the Pfister Hotel and made it to the basilica. Jane said to Sue, "I want to kiss you right in front of the altar." Sue said, "By the way, I am Catholic." Jane said, "Hey, so am I, and I believe God loves us all. The church needs an upgrade. Their operating system is getting obsolete Still believe that Christ was sent down here to prove we are worthy of going to heaven." Mark said, "I believe in the Big Bang. Once you die, you no longer exist. It is science. They can prove dinosaurs roamed this land a million years ago." Ed said, "This is true. And when God made Eden and Adam that was millions of years after the earth was created. He started human life on the planet. Then when Eve went against God he sent them out into a new cruel world, with the cavemen and the dinosaurs. The Bible just has their timeline screwed up." Mark said, "So where does God get the stuff to make worlds?" Ed said, "And where does the stuff come from to make the Big Bang? And is that God's doing? It is an ever-expanding universe."

Johnny asked, "Why are there so many gods?" Mary said, "There is only one God." Ed said, "He just has many names. Buddha, Yahweh, Allah, they are all one God but different religions. Everyone thinks a little different. If you are Christian you believe God has many names and is a peace-loving God." Jane said, "Nowadays people worship money." Sue ran her hand up Jane's leg to her upper thigh and said, "Some worship love."

Ed asked Mary, "So what religion are you?" Johnny looked up at her. She said, "Lutheran." Ed said with a gasp, "Oh, a fucking Lutheran." Mary's jaw dropped. Ed laughed, "Just shitting you. That's fine. Are you a practicing Lutheran?" He looked at Johnny and asked, "Do you go to church?" Mary blushed and said, "Well, it has been a while." Sue asked, "So what are you?" Ed said, "I am a man. Haven't you seen me go into the men's room? Okay, I am a Catholic born and raised. I don't belong to a church. Maybe I do, but I do go to church. Not every week but at least once a month."

Johnny stared at the church and said, "That is the biggest church I have ever seen." Mark said, "Yup, that's a big one. I hope we can find the clue." Jane said, "Okay, we need to go around the outside and see if it is just stuck on the building." Ed said as they walked up the stairs, "I don't think it will be in the main church. It's just a very big church." Jane said, "It's a major basilica. And you are right, there is more to this place than meets the eye." Sue said, "Look here at the door handles, the old post office handles." Ed asked, "Why would they have doorknobs from the post office?" Jane said, "Back in the late 1800s they were going to demolish a post office in Chicago. The church bought it, had it dismantled, and put it on five hundred train cars and shipped up here. You can still see some of the post office in the building." Johnny said, "Wow, this is beautiful."

Ed stepped into the main church, dipped his fingers in holy water, and made the sign of the cross. He said quietly, "Come on, Johnny, let's light a candle." Jane took Sue by the arm and walked her down the aisle. Sue said, "This is just amazing." Mark said loud enough that everyone heard him, "I am going to find someone to ask."

Ed took Johnny to where the candles were lit. He put a few dollars in the coffer and said, "This is what people do, they pray and light a candle, and that holds your prayer." Johnny said, "It's like throwing a penny in a fountain and making a wish." Ed said, "Something like that. This way you concentrate on your wish and ask God to help make it come true." Johnny asked, "So if you tell someone your prayer it won't come true?" Ed got down on his knees and said, "No. This is what I am praying for: oh God, please help us on our treasure hunt. Help us find the clues and watch over us so we stay safe. And help Mary and Johnny find a new home."

Jane and Sue stood in the main aisle, right in front of the altar. Jane leaned in and gave her a small kiss. Sue hugged her tight and started to kiss her passionately. Ed quietly ran over to them two and told them, "Mark is back."

Ed started toward the back of the church to where Mark and Mary stood with a little old lady. Everyone met and followed the woman upstairs into the bell tower. There was the question mark. Mark said, "See, if you ask someone it saves a hell of a lot of time." Jane grabbed Sue by the ass and said, "Go ahead, get the clue." Sue gave her a sly look, took her key from around her neck and put it in the clue. Then she read it and said, "Paintball, that is the clue." Mark handed the lady a fifty and thanked her. She said, "Well I have a tour to do, so you kids have fun."

Mark said, "Let's roll. What does that clue mean?" Mary said, "Now don't be looking at your phones while you are walking. Remember that story about that Charlie guy." Mark said, "Yeah, I wonder if he lost his leg." Sue asked, "I wonder if he lived. He lost a lot of blood." Mark said, "Let's look at this in the van."

They went down, out to the van, and the Intels' van pulled up. Mark said, "There is something wrong. We should be at least a day ahead of them." Ed said, "Let's get into the van, don't show them our faces. Mary, walk with me and Johnny. We are going to swing around and come to the van from the rear." Jane said, "Good idea, they don't know the three of you."

Once they got into the van, everyone had their phones out looking up paintball. Sue said, "There are two in the city." Mark said, "There are a few around, some of them are huge. Here is one that is a hundred acres." Jane asked, "How do we do this? Just start at the nearest one? And I heard those paintballs really hurt." Ed said, "There is one right downtown. It is a three-story factory. It won't be on the web. Well maybe. It's an army and cop thing. I helped design it back in the day." Mary said, "So you're an engineer too?" Ed smiled and said, "I have done a lot of things. Jack of all trades and master of none. Some guys will pay a huge price for paintball guns." He pulled out his phone and gave Mark the address.

The Intels went inside the basilica. As soon as they walked through the doors Randy put his hand over his mouth and said, "Oh my lord, this is beautiful." Jeremy dipped his finger in the holy water, which was in a large shell held by an angel, and did the sign of the cross. Boris said, "We need someone that works here. The clue is in the bell tower." Scott said, "Let's get that clue. We are one step from the lead." Gloria came with a janitor following right behind her. She said, "This is Juan. He is going to take us up to the question mark."

They followed Juan up the stairs to the bell tower, got the clue, and were back in the van. Boris got back in the van and made a call. He asked for Shelia, then programmed in the address to the paintball course. Gloria asked, "Where is this place?" Boris said, "Right down-town, over by the third ward. Old factory. It should be fun."

Team Odin got to St. Josaphat just before evening mass. People were coming and started filling the church. Jack could hardly move. The scars on his back were stiffening up. Joe took him by the arm and helped him up the stairs, then sat him in the last pew. He asked, "Jack, are you going to make it?" Jack put his head in his hands and leaned forward with a groan. An older lady said, "Is he alright? There is blood seeping through his shirt." Joe said, "He was scratched by a lion." Jack looked up and said, "Tiger." Joe said, "Hey, miss, do you know of a question mark? We are on a treasure hunt and one of the clues led us here." Cherry came up to him and said, "Joe, come with me. We found the clue. Leave Jack. It is in the bell tower." Joe said, "Hang tight, we will get you on the way out."

Cherry said as they walked, "He is getting to be a liability. He is going to slow us down." Joe said, "Yeah, everyone knows that. I just don't know what to do with him. We can't just kick him to the curb." Cherry stopped, she asked, "Why not?" Joe said, "Because he is our teammate." Dawn said, "This is Juan. He is a caretaker of this beautiful place. He will take us up to the bell tower. And he said Ermma took a team up about three hours ago." Juan said, "They paid her fifty bucks." They followed Juan up the stairs and discussed what they should do with Jack. Juan asked, "Is Jack a United States citizen?

If so, my sister could put him up in the back bedroom for a couple days and we could get the paperwork going and have him put into a home until he is better. As long as he has paid taxes, the government should pay for his stay. It

is all in the paperwork. It is the right thing to do."

They got to the tower and Dawn took out her key and got the clue she read it and said, "Paintball. Oh, this going to suck." Cherry looked Juan in the eye and asked, "Are you serious? Do you think your sister would take in Jack?" Juan asked, "Is he a nice guy that is in pain, in need of help? Then yes, she would take him in. What does he do for a living?" Robert said, "He is a high school teacher and coach. In Colorado, I think." Joe said, "Colorado Springs. He teaches history, skiing, and whitewater rafting." Juan asked, "Is he married?" Dawn said, "That one you have to ask him. He just had a bad breakup." Robert asked, "When can we find out if your sister will take him?" Juan said, "After mass. She is singing in the choir." They headed downstairs to catch the last of the mass. Robert and Cherry went for communion.

After the last song Juan caught up to his sister and had her come to the back of the church. The team was talking and looking up paintball places. Dawn asked a young man, "You wouldn't know of a paintball place around here?" He smiled and said, "My uncle is big into paintball. Stay right here, I will get him." He jogged down the aisle and came back with a rather large man in a suit. He asked, "You were asking about paintball? I might be able to help you." The team stopped talking and looked at him. Cherry asked, "Yes, we are looking for paintball. That was our clue." The man said, "One of the best courses is kind of a secret, right downtown in an old factory. They run a high-tech course. This is an advanced game. We have teams of cops and military." Robert said, "That has to be the one. Could we get the address?"

They got the address and Juan walked down the aisle with his sister. She was a looker, dressed to impress. Joe said to Jack, "Jack, I hate to say this but you are going to slow us down. And it isn't the best thing for you to be moving around so much. This is Juan." Juan said to his sister, "This is the man in need. This is Maria." Cherry said, "He has sixty-some stitches across his back." Jack asked, "What is going on here?" Dawn said "Maria might take care of you until you get back on your feet." Robert said, "We have a grand to help. We think he should be ready to travel in a week or two." Maria asked, "Jack, would you like me to help you?" Jack grabbed onto the pew in front of him and pulled himself to his feet. Joe reached over and took his arm and helped him into the aisle. Jack said, "Well, I knew something was going to happen. I am stiffening up, and not in a good way." Maria said, "Let me see the stitches." Juan said, "She is a nurse at the old folks' home."

Dawn helped Jack take his shirt off. He was a very fit man. Maria looked closely at his back and said, "Sixty? It's more like a hundred and sixty. My god, this is a tiger scratch. That must have been a big cat." Joe said, "It was a big kitty. He took his eyes off him for a second and that was enough." Cherry handed Juan ten hundred-dollar bills and said, "This should help. Thank you so much." Joe said, "I will get his luggage." He went out to the parking lot.

The team said their goodbyes. Joe came in with Jack's luggage in tow. He parked it next to Juan. Maria said, "I am taking Jack home with me. He seems like a nice guy. I will get him on his feet." Jack smiled and said, "If it isn't too much trouble. When I outstay my visit, just stick me on a plane and I will go home." Cherry said, "Sitting on a plane for five hours would hurt. Is there someone there to take care of you?" Jack said, "Not really, just my job. My family is in California." Juan slid his arm around Jack's waist. Jack said, "I can walk, just not so fast." Maria said, "We will take him from here out." Dawn said, "If you get better, call. We need a fifth man." Robert said, "Let's roll. It's time to get shot." Cherry asked, "Does it hurt when you get shot?" Joe smiled and said, "No, of course not." Dawn said, "He is lying. It hurts like hell."

Team Three got to the paintball place. It was a large old factory. Mark said, "Well, Ed, come on." Ed said, "It's a clue, you don't need me. I am going to help Johnny with his multiplication worksheets and do some spelling. What else was there? He is reading a book to me. The third grade is a big one." Dawn said, "I will help him study."

Ed smiled and said, "No, that is fine. Just watch out for the strobes. They will flash you then shoot you while your eyes are dilated."

The team went inside, rented their equipment, and started in the maze. A shooter stood up and shot Jane. She screamed. Then he shot Sue. She yelled, "Fuck you, you bastard." She unloaded her gun on the guy. Mark said as he dove for cover, "Watch out." Mary ducked. She ran forward and got shot. She yelled, "Jesus Christ, that hurts." Mark looked around for the shooter. He saw him and tried to get a shot. There were three quick shots blasting orange paint spots on his back. He raised his arms, holding his paint gun up. He said, "Guys, this is going to be a hard one." Mary said, "We need Edward."

Team Odin arrived. Boris asked, "So who here has done paintballing?" Nobody raised their hand. He then asked, "Has anyone shot a gun?" Gloria and Randy raised their hands. Randy said, "I shot trap and went deer hunting with the old man." Gloria said, "I took a shooting class and bought myself a 9mm handgun." Boris said, "This should be fun."

They got their equipment and headed in. They were about twenty yards in when the first guy shot, hitting Scott. He yelled, "He shot me." Boris turned and returned fire. He was shot in the back. He yelled, "Dammit all to hell." Randy said, "This is some scary shit." Jeremy said, "You take the lead. Gloria, you follow me."

They turned the corner, only to get hammered on by a sniper shooting all three. Gloria said, "Oh my god, I got shot in the tit, does it hurt." Boris said, "Again. This time Randy leads." They went out to the beginning. Jeremy said, "We didn't even get off the first floor." Boris said, "You can't be afraid of shooting. How many rounds did you fire?" Jeremy said, "None, it all happened so fast." Gloria said, "There is no fricken way you are getting me back in there." Boris said, "We have a job to do, and we are going to keep at it until we get that clue." Scott asked, "Don't you know where the next clue is? Can't we skip it." Boris said, "We have to get the clue. Now let's get back to the start and get back in there."

They went in and paid for another round. They were given paper suits to wear so they didn't look like they were shot. Randy whined, "I don't want to go first. Boris, you are the one that knows how to do this." Boris said, "I will back you up. Someone has to make it through." Randy took off running in the course, firing at everything. Scott ran in after him. They both made it about fifty yards, then they came under fire. Both were hit. Boris pointed at where the shots came from and he took one of the shooters out. Jeremy took his time sneaking through. He sat up for a shot and was hit right square in the chest. He yelled, "Jesus, does that hurt." Boris took that guy out. Gloria followed him closely. He stepped through a door and was hit three times from different angles. He said, "Fuck, this isn't working." They went through the first check and all but Gloria was sent back to the beginning. She snuck up the trail and watched, then she crawled in behind some stuff

for cover and hid.

Team Three started back at the beginning. Jane said, "I think I bruised my ribs." Sue said, "I was hit in the shoulder and the hip, but I got him." Mark said, "That you did, hit him about ten times. That was crazy." They got to the beginning. Mark said, "Mary, go and get Ed. We need him." Mary took off her gear and went out to the van.

Ed had Johnny doing spelling. She said, "We failed. We need your help." Ed said to Johnny, "See, I told you." Johnny said, "Alright, can I come? I want to shoot someone." Ed asked, "So, Mary, does it hurt to be shot?" She said, "It's unbelievable. My thigh is on fire." Ed said, "Well let's go. Team Intel came in about twenty minutes ago." Johnny said, "They're going to need . . . what is that again?" Ed smiled and said, "Triple-A, it seems they lost their distributor cap." Mary said, "Come on, everyone is waiting." Ed said, "Fine." He took a small case with him into the old factory."

Mark said, "We need someone to take point. None of us have done much of this." Ed asked, "Did you see the other team?" Jane got up. Johnny laughed. "You got shot twice." Jane said, "You should have seen Sue. She shot a guy like ten times."

Ed said, "This is the way it works. I will take the lead. You guys will just get in the way." Mark said, "Are you sure? It's crazy in there." Ed smiled and he opened his case, taking out a flat black pistol and a mask. Then he took out a holster from inside the mask. Johnny begged, "Can I come?" Ed walked up to the counter and said, "Okay, this is what I need. A RAP4, three twenty-ounce CO_2 and a 300bar/4500psi. Now let's get high-velocity paint."

The man went in back and came out with the gun. Johnny said, "A machinegun, cool." Ed said, "This is a very nice gun. It is over two thousand dollars, a straight shooter. And with good ammunition, we can do something." A man came from the back, held out his hand, and said "Frank, it has been a long time." Ed said, "Marty, it has been a long time. So where is the question mark?" Marty said, "Up on the third floor. They paid five hundred bucks to put it there for a month." Ed asked, "You wouldn't have any grenades, would you?" Marty pulled a box out from under the counter, set it on the counter and opened it. The salesman looked over his shoulder and said, "I didn't know we even had these." Marty said, "We don't. Take four, they're on the house." Ed said, "It's a treasure hunt. This shouldn't take long. I need a strobe too."

Marty unlocked the safe. He handed Ed a small box and said, "Let's be safe in there. If you like, I can walk you though." Ed smiled and said, "No, that will be fine. If I get hit maybe. Time will tell. Just going to take a run-through." Marty said, "Well if you need anything, just call. Don't hurt anyone." Ed smiled as he popped off a side panel on the rifle and adjusted the pressure.

Marty looked over Ed's shoulder and said, "So who is the broad with the kid?" Ed smiled and said, "Just players in the game, don't ask." Marty said, "Have a good time. We are making money. The one in New York is a gold mine." Ed smiled and headed for the door. Jane stepped up and asked, "Are you sure you want to try this alone?" Ed said, "Oh yeah, you'll just get in the way." She leaned over and kissed him full on the lips, which surprised everyone. She said, "For luck." Ed said, "Half hour, forty-five minutes."

He went inside, put on his mask. It was high-tech. He could see heat signatures, there were movement alerts, flash protection. He started to fire, the paintballs splattering as they hit their mark. There were snipers hiding, waiting for him in the dark corners. To their surprise, he could see them. He went through a doorway and the lights went out. It was completely dark. He hit his strobe. A bright light flashed and he opened fire, hammering two assailants.

He quickly went through the room, up the stairs. One man stood in the rafters. Ed took two shots, hitting him both times. He looked over. In a small corner was a girl. She was hiding. He could see her heat glowing. He whispered, "Are you okay?" She said, "Holy fuck, this is insane. I am okay, just trying to sneak through without getting shot." Ed smiled and said, "Well, good luck with that."

He headed up the stairs, firing as he went. She came out from under her hiding spot and followed him. Ed reached the third floor. He was taking out people on the second floor from his advantage point. One guy stood and fired on him after he was hit. Ed shot him right in the balls. The man howled in pain as he grabbed his crotch and went to the floor. Ed said, "When you're hit, stay down." He shot him one more time.

There was a red sign saying "safe room." You had to go through it. He stepped into the white room. A man was standing there. He said, "Very good, you haven't been hit once. Would you like a soda? A bathroom break? So you are Frank, one of the owners." Ed asked, "Where is that question mark that is hidden here?" The girl said from the doorway, "You're with the game." Ed took three quick steps, stuck her with a paint knife, and said, "You're dead. This is as far as you go." Gloria said, "Fuck you, you bastard. How could you do this?" The man said, "That is the rules. Any fatal wounds, you go Back to start." Ed said, "How about this. Give me your key. I will get you the clue. Meet me at the Pfister in the bar. Here is my card with phone number Come alone." Gloria asked, "Why are you doing this?" Ed said, "Your team is cheating, I want to know how." The man said, "Miss, if you would step over here. Go right through this door. There is a slide down to the beginning." Ed said, "Could I use that after I find the clue?" The man said, "You don't want to finish?" Ed said, "Well not really, I have things to do." The guy smiled and said, "Like that gal that just went down the slide." Ed smiled and said, "Well maybe. Is there a check before the question mark?" The man said, "Actually, the question mark is right outside, about fifty feet. So even if you get shot you still can make it." Ed smiled and said, "You have an ambush right outside the door, don't you?" The man shrugged his shoulders. Ed said, "Well, nice talking to you."

He took one of the grenades, threw it out the door, and a loud *pop* came. Ed jumped through the door and ran five yards, shooting any heat source. There was a huge paint splatter glowing from the grenade. There was the question mark. He walked over and scanned the area. There was nobody there. He got the clue for his team and the Intels. He walked back to the safe room and went down the slide to the beginning.

His team sat there waiting. When he slid out, there was a groan, "Ah, you didn't make it." Ed stood and said, "Of course, I did. What did you expect?" Johnny ran up and hugged him. Mary blushed and said, "He really likes you." Mark asked, "Did you get it?" Ed said, "Yes, of course. Let me turn this stuff in and we can discuss it in the van." Ed looked over at Gloria and pointed to the counter. Johnny asked, "Can I carry the gun?" Ed said as he handed him the gun, "Just be careful, it is loaded and is heavy. Point it to the ground."

As they got to the counter, Johnny asked, "Can I shoot it?" Ed said with a sigh, "Oh my god. Fine. There is a shooting range somewhere." Gloria met him at the counter. Ed asked, "Where is the shooting range? The boy wants to shoot the gun. Can I have a piece of paper?" The man said, "The range is down the hall to the right. And here is your paper." Ed wrote his cell number on it and said as he passed Gloria, "In an hour, come alone." She stepped over and leaned on the counter, picking up the paper.

Johnny followed Ed to the shooting range. They shot a few rounds. Ed was giving Johnny some pointers. Of course, Johnny knew everything. He couldn't even hit the paper. Ed said, "Slow down, pick your shot. Slowly breathe out and squeeze. This is a fine instrument. You're jerking the trigger." Mark said from behind him, "We should get going. And that gun shoots straight, mine threw them all over." Ed said, "It's your paint. The cheap ones aren't balanced. They go anywhere. There you go, Johnny, that's better." Johnny hit the target. Ed said, "Here, let me show you how it is done." He took the gun, rested it on the table, and took three quick shots, covering the bull's-eye. Then he said, "Let's go." Johnny said, "But you didn't let me shoot your pistol." Ed said, "Oh for Christ's sakes, here." He pulled his pistol out of his holster, a long CO_2 cartridge stuck out of it. He handed it to Johnny, who of course pointed it at him. Ed said, "Watch what you're doing. It's a loaded weapon, you don't point it at people." Johnny blushed and said, "Sorry." He turned and shot, hitting the wall with blue paint. Ed said, "Oh, you're done. Let's go, everyone is waiting for us." Johnny handed him the gun. Ed winked, turned, and shot three times, almost covering the yellow that was on the bull's-eye." Mark leaned to him and said quietly, "Nice shooting."

Ed handed in the rifle and the gas cartridges, then set two grenades on the counter with the strobe. They got to the team. Sue said, "Are you guys ready?" Ed said, "King Tut, that's the clue." Mary said, "The museums will be closed by now." Jane had out her phone, "There is an exhibit of the King Tut." Ed said, "Well let's get back to the hotel and we can start from there."

Team Odin pulled into the parking lot. Ed said, "Shit, the gang is all here. I thought this place was kind of private." Jane said, "It isn't on the web, not in any area business reports." Team Intel got to their van. Johnny said, "Can we watch?" Ed said, "Just drive." Sue asked, "What's going on?" Johnny picked up a distributor cap and said, "They're not going nowhere for a while." Mark said as he looked under the hood, "They must have got the clue."

Team Odin went into the big old building. Robert went up to the counter and said, "We are going to need gear for four." Cherry said, "No, let's do this. Here is five hundred dollars if you bring me to that question mark." The young man said, "Five hundred, I could do that. Here, take this white hat and follow me." Joe said, "What the hell, I wanted to shoot something." Dawn said, "Both the teams are here. They have the clue, we are catching up." Robert said, "We can't keep spending money like that. We are going to go broke."

The young man took Cherry right to the clue. There was paint splattered everywhere. It looked really cool. She got back to the beginning and the team was nowhere to be found. The young man said, "Try the shooting range down the hall." She found them shooting. She said, "King Tut, that is the clue." Joe said, "Well, that should be at a museum or a statue." Dawn said. "Let's just do a little research. There is a King Tut at the museum. It just seems too easy." Joe said, "It opens at nine, so all three teams will be there."

Ed got a call. It was Gloria. She said, "Nice job killing the van. How am I going to make our rendezvous?" Ed said, "Get a cab," and he ended the call. Mark said, "Would you like to fill us in?" Ed said, "I am working on something."

They dropped off the van at the valet and went into the hotel. Ed went to the front desk and got a key to his room. Mary asked, "Did you lose your key?" Ed said with a huge smile on his face, "Something like that." Mary said, "Johnny and I are going to get a bite to eat. It's a bit pricey in here." Ed stepped up to Mark and said, "I have a job for you. Your room is next to mine, so I need you to listen in on a conversation or put a phone next to the speaker."

They stepped into the elevator and went up to Ed's room. He took out a pin and a phone. He said, "This is a dummy phone, like a walkie-talkie. It is good for a mile." He pulled a piece of paper out of the pin and set it on the TV stand. Then he took out a quarter from his pocket and put it on top of the paper. He smiled and said, "It keeps it from draining the battery. Now this is linked with this phone. See the app? Now I am going to question this chick Gloria from the Intels. I have her key and their clue." Mark said, "And what do you want me to do?" Ed said, "Just take notes. I will interview her. It shouldn't take long."

They went up to the Blu and had a drink. Ed ordered a bottle of champagne and two glasses and had them delivered to his room. He got a call. He looked over at Mark and said, "Showtime. Okay, here is the phone. Can you hear me?" Mark put the phone to his ear. Ed said, "So is it working?" Mark said, "Works fine. Where do you find this stuff?" Ed said, "You can buy anything on Amazon or Spies R Us. Now she is coming up here." Mark said, "She can't get off in the hotel, you need a key." Ed said, "She is coming up here then I will take her to mine room and we can get this started."

Ed saw Gloria walk in the bar. He got up from the table and walked over and said, "Okay, let's take this to my room. This won't take long." Gloria said, "I would rather just sit at a table. It is a wonderful view." Ed said, "This is business. Let's just get this done and you can be on your merry way."

The ride in the elevator was silent. They went into Ed's room. He walked over to the bottle of champagne and poured both glasses. He started with, "Okay, we know your team is cheating. We have contacted Vegas and they are not happy." She took a drink and asked, "Do you have my key and clue?" Ed said, "All in due time. I would like a few answers." She smiled and held out her glass for a refill. She said, "I will tell you what I can." Ed said, "That is all I ask." He handed her the glass, stepped behind her, and started to massage her shoulders as he talked. He asked, "Now, do the clues mean anything or are they just random?" Gloria said, "Oh god, that is nice. You have a great touch." Ed said, "I was a masseur in a different life." She asked, "So what do you do know?" Ed smiled as he worked down her spine. She bent over so he could go from her neck to her butt. He said, "I am retired, this is just a hobby. I have never played a game like this before." Gloria asked, "What did you do before?" Ed said, "Let's not focus on me. The clues, what do they mean?" She groaned, "I was hit in the ribs with a paintball." Ed said, "If you would like, I could give you a proper massage on the bed. Just stop me when you would like. Now the clues . . ." Gloria had another glass of champagne and said, "Sure, I could us a massage." Ed said, "Okay, this will be fine. Now we are both adults, and I am old enough to be your father, so leave on your panties and bra. Have another glass of champagne. In fact, this is good stuff. I will order another bottle."

Gloria blushed and said, "Maybe this is a bad idea." Ed stepped behind her, ran both hands down her back, and firmly gabbed her ass. He said, "You are stressed. So what have you thought about this game?" Gloria dropped her jeans. She wasn't wearing underwear. Ed said, "Okay, so we are doing this. Take off your shirt. Let me turn up the heat a few degrees and order that bottle. I think I have some apricot oil. Yes, I do." Gloria asked, "Do you do this often?" Ed chuckled, "No, no. I can't remember the last time I gave a massage. Wait a minute. Hawaii . . . no, St. Lucia. That's right. I was doing a job down there. Their massage therapist treas out on maternity leave. I stayed for two weeks. That must have been ten years now."

She slid into the bed and asked, "Have you ever been married?" Ed said as he opened the door and flipped over the security latch to leave it unlocked. He said, "No, wish I had. I was in search of the almighty dollar. Now I have nobody." He stepped over to her with the small bottle of oil in a glass of hot water. He asked, "So do you have someone waiting for you at home?" She smiled, held up her glass, and said, "Not at this time. Men are jerks."

Ed took the oil out of the glass. He poured some oil into his hands and started to work on her back. He said, "That paintball hit is going to bruise. Mind if I unhitched your bra?" She said, "Oh, that was a nasty. Thank god you came around. When you did, I was shitting bricks hiding and I froze, couldn't move at all." Ed said, "They tell me your team has a new player." Gloria moaned, "Oh, this feels good. Yeah, one died falling down a ski jump. Who would believe that? And another— oh, that feels so good. He got hit by a goat up in Door County, knocked him off the roof. You just can't make this shit up."

Ed worked on her toes and feet. He slid his hand up her thighs, over her buttocks, up to the base of her neck, concentrating on the massage. He asked, "Who took their place?" Gloria said, "There is Randy, the black guy. He is funny. And Boris. He pretty much is in charge now." There was a knock on the door and a light, "Room service." Ed said, commanding, "Get in here. There is a twenty by the TV. Uncork the thing. Okay, where were we? Oh yes, a guy named Boris that took over your team." She looked up at him and said, "Now what are you trying to do here?" Ed said, "Oh, nothing. I am just giving you a massage. Anytime you want to leave just ask." She said, "No, you want me to rat on Boris." Ed said, "Let me get you a glass of champagne and we can discuss this." She said, "Oh, do my other arm first."

Ed took off his shirt and climbed on the bed. He massaged her arm then straddled her back, working on her backbone, working every vertebra. She moaned when he got to her butt. She rolled over and said, "Do my front." Ed asked, "Who is giving you the clues?" She said, "I want your hands on me. Touch my boobies." Ed said, "Here, have another glass of champagne." She said, "No, I want you to rub me." Ed oiled up his hands and ran them from her neck down to her toes in one motion. She moaned. "Oh, that feels so good."

He worked one leg at a time up her thighs. She said, "Make me cum, do it." He lifted one leg, laid it on his shoulder, and put his lips to her clit and sucked lightly. She moaned. He looked up and asked, "Who is giving Boris the information?" Gloria arched her back and said, "Don't stop." Ed gently worked on her until he felt her legs start to spasm with the oncoming orgasm. He looked up and asked, "Who is telling Boris the clues?" She moaned loudly, "Don't stop, you fucking dick. He said Sheila. What are you doing?" She said excitedly, "Yes, lick my asshole. Yes, stick your tongue in it. You're a fucking animal."

Ed worked his way back to her clit and sent her over the edge. She left out a huge moan and said, "Oh my god, it feels like my ass is having an orgasm. I want your dick inside of me." Ed said. "Oh, what the hell." He slid off his pants to show a large cock fully erect. She slid to the side of the bed and said, "That's a big one." He rolled on a condom with one stroke and worked in the tip. She said, "Stop playing around. I want it all." Ed dove deep inside her. He said, "Right to the balls." Gloria moaned loudly and said, "I can't stop cumming, don't stop." Ed lifted her from the bed and leaned her against the wall. He asked, "What do the clues mean?" Gloria said, "Shut up and fuck me." Ed roared, "Oh god, here we go."

A minute later they were done. Ed said, "Well, why don't you lie back and I will give you a quick rub down? And you can take a shower. In fact, I will come with you and scrub your back, then you can get out of here."

Mark was in the other room listening with Mary, Jane, and Sue. Mary got up and you could see the wet spot between her legs. She asked, "Why didn't he just ask her? He had her key and the clue." Mark said, "He did before you came in. She didn't tell him anything, but in the heat of passion she did. She just wanted to get off." Jane said, "Still, he only got a first name." Sue smiled and said, "See, that's a start. If they look at this Sheila's phone records, they will find this Boris guy." Mark said, "I will see if he can get Boris' number." Mary said, "No, let me call him."

Ed answered the phone and said, "I am just about to get into the shower. Can I call you back?" Mary said, "I am here with Mark.

We were wondering if this slut Gloria has Boris' number." Ed said sheepishly, "Oh, I see. Have you been there long?" She said, "Long enough. How could you?" Ed just said, "Okay then, I will see. Tell Mark drinks at the Blu in twenty."

Gloria turned, fully nude, and asked, "Are you coming?" Ed asked as he stepped up to her close, wrapping his arm around her, pulling her close, "Do you have Boris' number? They're going to want to check this Sheila's phone records. Didn't you guys think you were going to get caught?" She reached down, took his manhood in her hand, and kissed him on the neck then whispered in his ear, "That was a good one. I will give you his number when you give me the key and clue." His manhood started to swell in her hand. She said, "Someone is getting excited." Ed said, "Let's do it in the shower." Gloria said, "No, this time I get on top. I am going to ride you like there is no tomorrow."

She pushed him onto the bed and straddled him. He reached around her, grabbed her by the butt checks, and pulled her up onto his chest then onto his face. She leaned on the wall and just started to moan, begging him to lick her pussy. She started to cum. She begged him to stop. She slid down to his fully erect member and slid it right inside of her. Then she started to ride him just like a horse. Within five minutes they were done.

Mark called and said, "If you get that number now, I can call it in before going upstairs. That was a good one by the way. I think Mary is masturbating in the bathroom." Ed said, "No, she hasn't left yet. These things take some time. I will ask her." He pushed end call, then said to Gloria, "They would like to have that number so they can call it in. So here is your key and clue. You are a very beautiful girl, one hell of a nice ride." She smiled and took her phone out of her purse and read off the number. He wrote it on a notepad.

She said, "Aren't you going to call it in?" Ed said, "We can do that later, just didn't want to forget. Let's get in the shower. Looks like I am having bar food for dinner." She put on a shower cap and they soaped each other up. The water beaded on Gloria with that massage oil on her. Ed washed her from foot to neck, stopping to kiss her pussy and breasts. Ed asked, "You're not going to tell your team about this, are you?" She smiled and kissed him on the neck and said, "About the amazing sex? No, I wouldn't do that. And I do say that is the best sex I have had in a long time. About the clue, yes. I will tell them everything, that you know about us getting information from Vegas. I won't tell them about Shelia. I just heard him use that name once."

They got dressed and Ed said, "This has been nice. We should do it again some time." Gloria kissed him passionately and gently grabbed him by the balls and whispered, "I would like that." They got dressed. Ed walked her out into the hallway, patted her on the rear end, and said, "This has been great. Good luck." She turned and walked toward the elevator. Ed watched her ass as she walked. She stopped and looked back as she waited for the doors to open, and waved to him. He smiled and waved back.

Ed walked next door to Mark's room. He knocked and Sue answered the door. Ed looked inside to see the whole team in there. He said, "Shit, I am going to the bar to get a bite. Mark, meet me up there." Sue smiled and said, "You have been a bad boy, and you're good at it."

He got up to the bar and ordered a martini, a manhattan, a large water, and some bar bites. Mary came in and asked, "So what the hell?" Ed said, "No, the question is why were you listening in? That was private." She blushed and said, "Well that doesn't matter, does it? You still did that. You had sex with that girl, and she is half your age." Ed had a huge smile on his face. He lifted his martini and said, "Yes, she was. And she was really good in bed. But that has nothing to do with it. We are playing a game. She wouldn't have given up that information. Would you like a drink? And where is Master Johnny?" Mary said, "He is fine. He is eating a kid's pizza and watching TV."

Jane said as she walked up, "Good one, sounds like you had fun." Sue said, "He's not the only one." She grabbed Jane lightly by the ass. Jane asked, "Where is Mark?" Mary said, "He is down in the van, calling in the name and Boris' number." Ed said, "Vegas should be able to break into his phone and prove who was sharing clues. I wouldn't want to be in Boris' shoes. He is a plant a rich guy put into the game. The Intels were falling behind. Shit is going to hit the fan."

Mary said, "Did you use a condom?" Ed said, "This isn't my first rodeo, of course I used a condom. You know how expensive kids are. Now why don't you guys piss off, let me have a drink in peace and a snack. I have a lot to do tonight." Jane said, "After a good romp in the hay, a snack and good nap is always nice." Sue said, "Let's go for a walk. We can catch a cab and go down to the river walk and find some chocolate." Jane said, "That sounds good. If we find Mark we will send him up." Mary shot Ed an evil look. She turned and headed to the door.

CHAPTER TWENTY-THREE

The Gold Pyramid

Gloria caught a cab to her hotel and went to Scott and Jeremy's room. Everyone was there waiting for her. They were watching *Tarzan*. He looked like Frankenstein. The doctor asked him, "So, Tarzan, how was that eagle eye we transplanted after the accident?" Tarzan said, "Doc, I swear I can see for miles. This eye is great." The doc asked, "How about those antelope legs?" Tarzan said, "I am almost as fast as a cheetah. And that gorilla arm, I can swing through the trees like never before." The doc asked, "How about that baby elephant's trunk I put on for your penis?" Tarzan said, "Well Jane really likes it, but every time I walk through the grass it picks it and shoves it up my ass."

Scott said, "Now that's funny, didn't see that one coming. So, Gloria, did you get the clue?" Boris said, "As long as it was taken out of the question mark we are good. The morning we head to Illinois, Onan's Gold Pyramid. We have a tour at ten." Gloria said, "They're on to us. He questioned me about who was giving us the information." Boris asked, "Are you sure?" Gloria said, "Vegas has GPS on the van. We have been going straight to the clue. It must not look good." Boris asked, "Okay, what did you tell him?" Gloria said, "I told him the truth. I don't know who is feeding you the information." Boris said, "Shit, why the fuck did you do that? What to do? Well we have a couple of days. I have to make a call."

Randy said, "Dude, did you see this place? It is a pyramid that is set in a lake, It is 17,000 square feet, six stories, with huge statues and pyramid garages. This is just whacked out. It is 24-karat gold leaf, the largest gold-plated object in North America." Scott said, "It kind of looks like the largest thing ever plated in gold. They have a replica of King Tut's tomb, and they have dogs. We might have to call for a tour." Jeremy asked, "So who was this guy from the other team?" Gloria said, "He's a nice-looking guy from Team Three. He asked a few times what the clues meant. I still think they are just random clues, right?" Scott said, "They have nothing in common. They are just places for clues for the game."

The morning came. Seven o'clock, Mark was calling rooms. He said, "Get up. The Intels are on the move. They left ten minutes ago and are heading south." Ed said, "Meet out in the hall in five minutes." Ed was out in three. He went to Mary and Johnny's room. Mary was in the bathroom putting on her makeup. Johnny was excited. He asked, "Are we going to the museum? There is a butterfly house there." Ed said, "No, we are headed down south somewhere. It's an adventure. Now help pack your luggage." He spoke loudly, "Mary, we have to leave. Let's go." Ed tried the bathroom door. It opened. She was standing in front of the mirror in her bra and pant-ies. Ed said, "Jesus, you're not even dressed. You can do your makeup in the van. Put something on,

let's go."

Mary came out of the bathroom to find everyone in her room. She stood in her bra and panties. Ed held out some clothes and said, "Here, we are waiting." Jane said, "Mark is downstairs. He is checking out. And he called the valet, so we are good to go." Ed asked Johnny, "Did you go pee?" Johnny said, "Yeah." Ed asked, "Brushed your teeth?" Johnny said, "Fine." Ed said, "Nope, don't have time. Let's go." Sue said, "We have time." Mary said, "Nope, if we are in that much of a hurry, let's go." Ed rubbed Johnny's head and said, "We will stop for breakfast, some greasy truck stop. You can get grits." Johnny said, "Is that a real thing?" Jane said as they got in the ele-vator, "I like grits, just not all the time." Sue smiled and said, "After this we should go to Disney World." Jane asked, "And take Johnny?"

Sue said, "Oh hell no, just the two of us. It would be so much fun." Jane said, "I really am not into rides." Sue said, "Would you like to drink around the world in an afternoon and watch fireworks? Disney knows how to take care of you." Jane said, "That does sound nice." Johnny looked up at Ed and said, "Those fuckers are going to Disney without me." Mary's eyes popped open. She said, "Language. And they can do whatever they want." Ed smiled and said, "I haven't been there in a long time. And yes, it is much better without kids." Johnny pulled on his shirt and asked, "You have been to Disney World?" Ed said, "Disney World I think five times, Disney Land I think three, Tokyo two or three, Paris once, Shanghai twice, and Hawaii once. That is just a resort but I recommend it."

Sue said, "I think we are going to Wadsworth, Illinois. There is this golden pyramid. It is called Onan's Gold Pyramid House. Onan was the family that built it." Johnny asked, "You mean like the ones in the desert?" Sue said, "Yes, but this one is gold leaf. It has a replica of King Tut's tomb. It is 17,000 square feet and six stories high. And we can tour the first two floors." Ed asked, "So it's not like the pyramids of Giza. The big one there is like fifty stories, huge blocks." Mary asked, "Have you been there?" Ed said, "Well yes, I have been around. That is really the only thing to see out there. It's a fricken desert. Hey, Johnny, what is the most important day in Egypt? Mummy's day." Johnny said, "Really?" Ed smiled and asked, "What kind of music do mummies like? Wrap music. Get it, wrap, because they are wrapped up."

Mark said, "Come on, the van is here. And why are kids confused in Egypt? Because their daddies are mummies." Jane said, "Stick to driving. That was so lame." Ed asked, "Do you still have the Intels on your phone?" Mark said, "Yes, sir. They are headed down 43 toward Chicago." Sue said, "That has to be outside of the 200-mile limit." Mark smiled and said, "That is what I thought. It is just inside, so we don't have to go into Chicago. That would be a shit fest to drive in." Ed said, "It really isn't that bad. You just have to watch rush hour."

Johnny said quietly, "I have to go pee." Jane said, "Oh for fuck's sake, you didn't go at the hotel?" Johnny said, "I didn't have to go then." Mark said, "Fine, we need to stop and get a quick bite." Sue said, "Mickey D's two miles, a ten-minute stop." Ed said, "They are going to beat us there anyway. And it is just the third clue, not like it is a pay day." Johnny said, "I really have to go." Mary turned from up front and said, "Just hold it. We will be there in five minutes." Jane said, "A nice big glass of water. You're not going to make it. Do you feel it start running down your leg? You're going to pee." Mary turned and said, "You're not helping. Do you want this place to smell like piss?"

Team Odin got to the museum and sat in the parking lot waiting for it to open. Joe said, "Something is wrong. The other two teams should be here." Cherry said, "I think you are right. Something is off. We must have screwed up the clue. It was just King Tut, right?" Robert took out the clue and said, "That is all it says. Nothing weird about it, no punctuations, just 'King Tut.'" Dawn said, "This is King Tut's chariot. There is a King Tut's tomb down near Chicago, in a golden pyramid." Robert asked, "A replica, right?" Dawn said, "Yeah, what the hell were you thinking, they would move a pyramid from Egypt? It says here a rich guy built a huge pyramid and plated it with gold. This might be it." Cherry said, "We are here. We go in and take a look. If not, we head to this other place." Robert said, "I still think this has to be the place. You would have thought the clue would have had something do with gold." Dawn said, "I hope we get to see this pyramid thing. It looks wild." Joe said, "Someone is at the door. There, it is open."

They went into the museum. It was quiet. They went right to the King Tut exhibit. Joe said, "There is nothing here." Robert said, "Chill, let's just take a second. Everyone look closely, is there a question mark?" Cherry said loudly, "Screw this, I am going to ask the security guard." Two minutes later she was back and said, "Nope, there is no question mark here. How the hell did the other teams know?" Dawn said, "That is weird, isn't it?" They walked out to the van. Cherry hit the call button. Robert asked, "What the hell are you doing? That is to be used only for a clue." Cherry said, "I got your fucking clue for you. Something is wrong, and that rat bastard Lance better have some answers." Someone spoke on the radio, "Ah, this is team Odin, right?" Cherry said, "Okay, what is going on? We got a clue, King Tut, and the other teams aren't here. There is no way they could have figured out the museum wasn't the place." Lance said, "Yes, we have a leak. It will be fixed today. Other than that, how is it going? I see you only have four of you on your team." Dawn said, "Jack was stiffing up. He could hardly move." Lance said, "Boy, that tiger moved fast, didn't he? I thought he was going to pull him right into the cage." Robert said, "Cameras. I would like to see that again." Joe asked, "I suppose you couldn't tell us if Onan's Pyramid house is the clue?" Lance said, "Well I suppose I can't tell you that is where the clue is. So what is up with this leprechaun?" Dawn laughed, "Robert got fucked in the ass by a really short guy, thought he was going to get a big dick for a wish." Lance asked, "What? Wait, he did what?" Robert said, "That's enough of that. We have to get on the road." He turned off the intercom and asked, "Why did you have to tell him about that?" Cherry said, "Now that's something I would have liked to see."

Joe asked, "Isn't Chicago out of the 200-mile radius?" Dawn said, "I checked on that. It looks like it is 231 miles, so it would be just out of the 200 mark." Robert said, "What other options do we have?" Sue smiled and said, "You heard Lance, he said he couldn't tell us Onan is where the clue is. It is how he said it." Cherry said into her phone, "Hello there, I was wondering if we could get a tour today? That's great. You wouldn't have seen a green van there, would you? I see, question mark. We will be there in a couple of hours, thank you." Joe said, "So what the fuck?" Cherry said, "The other team is there now. And yes, there is a question mark." Dawn said, "It is north of Chi-town, so it is just inside the 200-mile mark."

Team Two, the Intels, pulled into the Gold Pyramid. Boris said, "Holy shit, look at this place." Gloria said, "Well the gate is open, they are expecting us. Look at all the fine details. The walls are full of murals with sand script." Boris said, "What kind of crazy bastard built this?" Gloria said, "Well he had to be rich and a dreamer. This place is wild. Could you see living here?" Scott asked, "You said he raised his family here. I wonder if they had jet skis in the moat and ice skating in the winter. This would be a great place to bring up kids." Jeremy asked, "I wonder if they have fish planted in the moat." Randy said, "Fish, probably alligators. This place creeps me out." Boris said, "Let's get moving. Something is wrong, I can just feel it." Scott said, "Why, don't you know the next clue?" Boris said quietly, "Not yet. That is what is bothering me." Randy said, "Dude, if they find out you have been cheating, what are they going to do, break your legs?" Boris' eyes opened wide and he started to walk faster and said, "Let's get this done."

They reached the front door. A woman in her forties answered the door. Boris said, "We are the Intels, we called. Here is the money for the tour and an extra couple hundred if you take us straight to the King Tut exhibit." The gal said, "If you would follow me." She turned and walked quickly to a separate building, skipping everything.

Gloria talked nonstop, pointing out beautiful décor. She asked the woman, "Hey, I have seen this one before, the one with the head of a dog." The woman said, "That is Anubis. He has the head of a jackal. He watches over the dead." Randy said, "This is some serious collecting. Where did they get all this stuff? And isn't there a curse if you move a mummy?" The gal stopped at a doorway and said, "Most of the stuff are reproductions. There is a lot that is original. And the curse is just a fairy tale. Now this is King Tutankhamen's tomb, just like it was over three thousand years ago. He was laid to rest in a golden coffin." Boris said, "I feel like we are being watched." The guide said, "A lot of people say that. Kind of weird, isn't it? What did you say your name was." Scott said, "Let me introduce ourselves. I am Scott, this is Jeremy, Randy, Boris over there, and Gloria." The guide said loudly, "Boris, the question mark is right inside. If you would follow me."

Boris turned to follow her and shot Scott an "I could kill you" look. Scott asked quietly, "What?" Boris asked, "Why did you give her our names?" The guide said, "This is how the sarcophagus held three coffins, the golden one held the boy king." Randy said, "This is fucking weird. The clue is right over there. Let's get out of here."

Jeremy examined the coffins and all the statues. There were old statues everywhere. He asked, "Was there that much gold?" The guide said, "These are reproductions. The real stuff was pure gold and there were four chambers full." Randy put his key in the question mark and took the slip of paper, read it aloud. "Sexy bunny. What the fuck does that mean? The only sexy rabbit I know is Jessica Rabbit." Scott said, "All I come up with is bunny costumes and some kind of vibrator." Jeremy said, "It's the ears. I had a girlfriend that had one of those." Gloria said, "Google 'Playboy bunny in Wisconsin.' They used to have a mansion at Lake Geneva." Randy said, "Let's go, that has to be the place." Gloria asked, "What the hell would we do without computers?" Jeremy asked, "Can we take the tour? This place is amazing." Boris said, "On your own time, we have to move."

Scott said as they got into the van, "Did you notice someone was watching us?" Boris said, "I have a bad feeling about this. No call, now this." Gloria said, "Ah, that is why she wanted to know our names. They wanted to know which one is Boris." Scott said, "The van has a tracker on it, so we can't lose them." Boris said, "No shit, Sherlock. I will just pay them off. Who knows, maybe it's nothing." Gloria asked, "Can we take a lunch break soon? I have to pee." Boris said, "Fine, we stop at the gas station with a restaurant."

They pulled into a gas station with a McDonalds. Gloria gave Scott her order and went to the bathroom. Randy said, "I have to wash my hands. That place was creepy."

They ate. Boris went to the restroom and a couple of guys followed. One shot him with a stun gun, the other held the door. The guy holding the stun gun kicked him right in the ribs and said, "Boris, you are going to leave this game right now." He knelt on his back, grabbed him by the back of his hair, and slammed his face into the floor, then said, "You will not get into the van. You will not meet up with them later. Do you understand? You are done." The guy holding the door said, "Hey, what is the difference between a dead hooker and your job? Your job still sucks." The goon that was kneeling on Boris looked up and asked, "What the fuck has that to do with anything?" The guy at the door said, "Oh, it just popped into my mind. Are you going to break his leg? If not, let's get the hell out of here." Boris pleaded, "No, don't. I am done. Please, I quit." The guy got off his back walked out the door with the other guy.

Jeremy walked in and helped Boris get to his feet. Blood was running out of his nose. Boris said, "Get me to the sink." He hung his head over the sink and pinched his nose. Jeremy said as he balled up toilet paper, "I take it Vegas figured out what is going on." Boris turned, still pinching his nose together, and asked, "Do you think?" Jeremy put the wad of paper on the floor, covering the pool of blood. The paper sucked it up right away. He asked, "So you are done?" Boris said, "Yes, I am. I am going to get on an airplane and get back to Vegas—oh, a dead hooker, I get it." Jeremy asked as he wiped up the blood, "What?"

Boris let go of his nose. It stopped bleeding. He washed his face, then took a step toward the door, grimaced, and grabbed his ribs. Jeremy asked, "Are you going to be okay?" Boris said, "I am getting too old for this shit. Just hold the door." Jeremy stepped around him and held the door so he could limp through to the table. Gloria asked, "What the fuck happened to you? Your face is swollen." Jeremy said, "He got a message from Vegas, this is his last clue."

He stood holding two hundred-dollar bills and said loudly, "Is anybody here going to Chicago? Two hundred bucks if you take me with." Scott said, "I will get your luggage. And I need the key." Boris held out the key. Scott took it and headed outside. A young couple stopped him and asked, "Is he dangerous? Why does he need a ride?" Scott said, "No, he isn't dangerous. He just got kicked off a team. He needs to get to the airport." The man said, "Fuck that, that's a madhouse." Scott said, "I think he just needs a ride into the city. He can take a cab to the airport." The young man got up and walked over to the table and said, "Three hundred, you got yourself a ride." Scott came in with Boris' bag and they said their goodbyes.

Team Three reached Onan's Gold Pyramid. Johnny was amazed, "Look at the huge statue. Can we get out and look at it?" Ed said, "Let's stop. Quick, Mary, you stand with him and I will take your picture." Jane said, "Sue, come with me. Ed can take our picture too." Sue smiled and said, "This is Ramses, an Egyptian Pharaoh It is fifty feet tall." They all had their picture taken. Mark didn't get out of the van.

They drove up to the house. A woman met them at the pyramid. Everyone got out of the van. She said, "Hello, I am Maria. I shall be your guide." Mark said, "We have a Groupon, so that would be two hundred, right?" She smiled and said, "Works for me. Now I see you are in a green van. So you are here to see the tomb of Tutankhamen, the young king. That is where your clue is." Mark said, "Yes, but we would like the full tour. This is a beautiful place you have here."

Ed bent down and said sternly too little Johnny, "This is like a museum. Touch nothing unless she says you can." Maria said, "This is true. There are a lot of artifacts that are irreplaceable. The tomb was discovered November 4, 1922. It was opened the next year. This is a replica of the tomb just as it was. Come, we can start there. The pyramid is—" Johnny interrupted, "Are there fish in the moat? Can we catch some?" Maria said, "Yes, there fish in the moat, small mouth bass, crappie, bluegill, perch, carp, and northern pike. And no, you can't fish them." Johnny said, "Boy, that is the longest fence I have ever seen." Mary turned and gave him a look. He said, "Sorry."

Maria said, "The tomb is a building that looks like a pile of dirt. It is as close to being the one in Egypt as they could make it." Jane said, "This is an amazing place. Do they use the garages?" Maria said, "They are full of old cars. We take the cars out and put them on display in peak tourist times. The boy in the family . . . well, he isn't a boy anymore, but he does most of the tours. He has been in the Middle East lately, doing tours over there. Now watch your step. We can show you King Tutankhamen's tomb, everything is exactly like is in Egypt." Mark asked, "Could we do a quick tour? I know everyone wants to see the place, but could we do a quick walk-through?" Maria smiled and said, "Not a problem, just the highlights. So if you look to the right there is one of the four rooms. It is called the antechamber and the one behind it is the annex. Shall we move on?" Jane said, "Look at all the gold, it is amazing." Johnny asked, "What is with the dog heads?" Maria said, "That is Anubis, he has a jackal's head. He is the god of rebirth, the god of the afterlife. The one with the gray dog's head is Wepwawet, a war god from Upper Egypt." Johnny said, "Cool. What are those gold people?" Ed said, "That's a mummy case. They put your mummy in there." Maria said, "Yes, you are right. Follow me and we will go into the burial chamber. Please don't touch the walls." Johnny looked up at Ed and said, "No touchy." Ed smiled and said, "This place is great, it's like you stepped right into Tut's tomb." Sue asked, "Have you been to Egypt?" Ed smiled and said, "Maybe." Johnny asked, "What's in the box?" Maria said, "It is a sarcophagi. It is where they put the mummy case in. This is King Tut's mummy case. He wasn't much older than you when he became Pharaoh. They figure he was eight or nine years old. Now King Tut ruled Egypt for ten years, from 1333 BC to 1324 BC. His dad died when he was seven years old. He became Pharaoh two years later and married his sister." Johnny said, "You can't do that. And how could he rule from 1333 to 1324?" Ed said, "Back then they wanted to keep their blood pure, and BC means before Christ, they count backwards." Johnny said, "Oh."

Jane asked, "The pictures on the walls, do they tell a story?" Maria said, "Yes, but they are told in a few ways. I don't know the real story." Mark asked, "Who would like to get the clue?" Sue said, "I will get it. She walked up to the question mark, put in her key, and took out the clue, then said, "Sexy bunny." Maria said, "The group before thought it means the old Playboy club in Geneva." Jane had her phone out and said, "I think they are right."

Mark said, "Shall we continue the tour?" Maria said, "Okay then, let's give you a look at the treasury room. Now you might think this is weird but there were fourteen boats in here. They were here to help the Pharaoh float to the other side. Take a quick look, then I shall run you through the house. Then you can be on your merry way." Johnny pointed to some beautiful jars. He asked, "What are those?" Maria said, "Those? They kind of look out of place, don't they? And they are guarded. They call them canopic jars. They hold the organs of the young king." Johnny eyes popped open. He asked, "You mean his guts are put in jars?" Ed smiled and said, "That's what they did in the old days. Come on, let's get moving."

They went through the house. The first two floors were beautiful. When they got up to the van, Mark asked Johnny, "Okay, what was the highlight of the tour?" Johnny said, "That was the coolest pool I have ever seen, and the tomb was neat. What was your favorite part?" Mark said, "When Maria bent over and I saw her thong. Damn, near made wood." Ed said, "You caught that too? She was sweet." Mary looked at him and shook her head. Mark asked, "Sue, do you have that address to the Playboy club." She said, "They call it the Grand Geneva. There are 350 rooms. This could be a hard find, and the thong was a light green." Jane asked, "You were looking too. She wasn't that pretty."

Team One, the Odins, pulled into the Gold Pyramid. Robert said, "Look at that huge statue." Dawn said, "That is Ramses II. There is the moat. This place is amazing. It was built in 1977 and it has six stories and is 17,000 square feet." Joe said, "Whoa, that's a good size. How are we going to find the clue?" Robert said as he parked, "It should be in the tomb room with King Tut." Robert said, "We are just going in and getting the clue." Cherry said, "The guide knows where it is." Dawn said as they walked across the bridge to the Pyramid, "This sucks. We need to get a big payday. The other teams are ahead of us." Cherry said, "Okay, let's do a selfie. I want to send it to Jack." Joe asked, "How is he doing anyway?" Cherry said, "I don't know, but one thing is for certain, we have to keep an eye out for his replacement."

The guide, Maria, met them at the door. Robert said, "There are sensors on the driveway and on the bridge." Maria said, "Yes. We are going to upgrade one day. Those are old-school." Dawn said. "I didn't see them." Joe smiled and said, "They are the old electronic eyes. Miss, I would like to introduce the crew. I am Joe, he is Robert, and Dawn. Last but not least, Cherry. We are in a bit of a hurry. Could you bring us right to the clue?" She smiled and said, "That will be four hundred dollars." Cherry said, "That is a little steep, but here is the four hundred." She handed Maria the four bills. Robert asked, "When was the last team here?" Maria said, "About three hours ago." Joe said, "We are not that far behind."

Cherry asked, "Did they go right to the clue or did they take the tour?" Maria said as they got to the tomb, "The first team this morning went straight to the clue, they were the Intels. It means something weird. The second team was nice. They took the full tour. Now here is the passage room. The young King Tutankhamen. He died at the age of nineteen. He ruled Egypt for ten years as their Pharaoh." Dawn said, "The child king. What was he? Nine? When he became king?" Maria said, "The tomb was discovered in 1922 by a British archaeologist, and it was opened a year later. Now King Tutankhamen got his name from the sun god Aten they worshiped. Later he abandoned her and worshiped the king of the gods, Amun, and he changed his name. This is the antechamber. We will walk right through to the burial chamber, where the young king's sarcophagus held his mummy case, which was like a Russian doll. There were three cases. The two outer cases were made of wood and gold overlay. The last one he was laid in was solid gold. Now these are just reproductions."

Joe said, "And there is our question mark. Who wants to get the clue?" Cherry said, "I will get it." She walked over and put the key in it and took the slip. She said, "Sexy bunny. That's our clue, sexy bunny." Maria said, "The other teams are headed for an old Playboy mansion in Lake Geneva." Robert asked, "Why are the toes cut off of that mummy case and left at the end of the stone box?" Maria said, "Well King Tut's is one of the smallest burial sites in the Valley of the Kings. When they placed him in the mummy cases, the last one was too big for them to shut the lid, so they cut off the toes of the case to get it to close."

Joe said, "Playboy mansion, this could be fun." Dawn said, "It is a resort called the Grand Geneva. It has a golf course, pool, water park, the whole nine yards." Robert said, "Too bad we don't have time for a round of golf."

Cherry said, "Okay, this has been nice. I would really like to go through the pyramid but we are short on time. If you could lead us out?" Maria said, "Okay, follow me please. Let me see, does anyone have any questions?" Joe asked, "What did the guy do to afford this?" Maria said, "Oh, I usually start with that. Jim Onan, he owned a concrete business and built it for his family. He had five kids. He was always interested in pyramids. His tests claimed plants grow thirty times faster in a pyramid. Fun fact, the water we sell here is pure spring water. There was no spring until he started building. It came up from the middle of the pyramid. He had it run over to the moat.

Now the pyramid is one-ninth the size of the pyramids of Giza. It is the largest thing ever to be gold plated in the northern hemisphere, some say the world. So this ends our tour. Is there anything else?" Dawn slipped her a twenty and said, "Thanks, we must get going."

Joe said on the way to the van, "She was hot, something about her." Robert said, "I think it was the all the gold, the history. Damn near gave me a woody. Something about the tomb or the pyramid's power." Cherry said, "Come on, you don't believe that, do you?" Cherry said as she got into the van, "We need a big payout. The money is getting low." Robert said, "This is the fourth clue. One or two more will be the payout, and we need a fifth person."

CHAPTER TWENTY-FOUR

To the Old Playboy Mansion

Team Two, the Intels, pulled into the Grand Geneva. Randy said, "Holy shit, this is where the white people get their groove on." Gloria said, "Now why would you say that?" Randy said, "Now watch, I will be the only brother here. It will be wall to wall old white people." Scott said, "Now this is the only AAA four-diamond resort in Wisconsin." Jeremy asked, "Wasn't that Kohler place a five-star resort?" Gloria looked up from her phone and said, "You're right. I think it is just who is rating it."

Scott pulled up to the valet parking. A young black dude came up. Jeremy said, "Don't do it. He is going to take the van." Randy said, "I will be the only black guy that isn't working." The valet asked, "Are you staying at the hotel?" Gloria said, "We are just visiting and are going to grab a bite." The valet said, "There are six places you can eat at. The Chophouse has great steaks and seafood. The Brissago is Italian. The bar and grill is quick, but the Grand Café, I would say, is your best bargain and has a nice menu." Scott said, "This place must be huge. Have you seen a metal question mark?" The valet said, "No, I don't think so. There are maps of the place just inside the doors. Here is your ticket. Please don't lose it." Scott took the ticket and everyone went inside. Jeremy said to Randy, "There's a black dude with a white girl checking in. I don't think he works here." Scott smiled, "Oh, he is going to be working it." Gloria said, "There are the maps. The only way we are going to find the clue here is to question the staff." Jeremy said, "Let's go to the café and grab a bite." They heard a young lady on the phone saying, "Sir, even if the door has a sign hanging from it saying 'do not disturb' you can open it. Yes, it is your exit door to the hall. Now if you don't want anyone to bother you, hang the sign on the outside doorknob."

Randy said, "Did you hear that shit? Must be an old white guy." Gloria said, "Come on, follow me. The café is this way." Randy said, "Where I lived our hotel slogan was 'we put the *ho* in hotel.' You rented it by the hour when the backseat just wasn't enough." Scott said, "I remember the first time I went to the hotel with my parents. Dad asked if they have disabled the porn. The man said, 'No, we only have regular porn, you sick fuck.' I damn near pissed my pants."

Gloria said, "Would you guys knock it off? They have pizza. It is a cheap meal." Scott said, "I could use a beer." Randy said, "That sounds great. You had better ask to be seated. If they see me, we will be here all day." Jeremy said, "Now look over there. It is a family of black people. I don't think they work here."

A waitress grabbed four menus and said, "If you would follow me." Randy said, "A table with a view, if you can." The waitress smiled and said, "Okay, let's go this way. Let me put you somewhere else." She erased a check on a table and checked another. They followed her to a table against the window overlooking the pool and the lake. She said, "This is a nice view. May I take your drink order?" Gloria asked, "Don't you have a hostess?" The waitress said, "This is a bit weird but we get profit share from the restaurant, so we run it lean. It is like a Christmas gift." Gloria said, "We would like a pizza for four with the works and a pitcher of beer." Scott asked, "What do you have on tap? Do you have some pretzels?" The waitress told him the selection of beers and said, "A bowl of pretzels coming up." Randy asked, "You got some collard greens?" Jeremy said, "Don't mind him. You wouldn't know where there is a metal question mark, would you?" She asked, "A metal question mark? Not that I can remember." Jeremy held out a twenty and asked, "If you could ask maintenance or anyone. We are on a treasure hunt. There is another twenty if you find out."

She took the twenty and headed toward the entrance. She seated another table. The waitress from the bar brought out a pitcher of beer and bowl of pretzels. Scott said, "Hey, Randy, there are a couple of black girls down at the pool tanning. I don't think they work here." Gloria said, "There is another black dude running a wave runner on the lake. He might be a mechanic." Jeremy asked, "Do blacks get skin cancer from the sun?" Randy said, "Cancer isn't picky, but white folks are more likely to get it."

The waitress came with the pizza and said, "I did a little digging. The question mark you are looking for is not here. It is at Moose Mountain Falls, a water park on the grounds. And they say it is on top of one of the slides." Jeremy held out a twenty and said, "I thank you so very much." Gloria asked, "So who has their swimming trunks handy?" Scott said, "Let's take a vote." Gloria said, "The fuck we will." Randy said, "Come on, you want to show us your booty." Jeremy said, "Fine, I can run up and get a clue . . . if it is a clue." Scott said, "It's a question mark, not a monument. Let's finish eating and get over there."

They headed to the water park. It was a mile or so away. They went inside. It was a twenty-five-dollar admission. Jeremy said, "Let me get dressed and investigate." He came out in his swimming trunks. Randy gave a wolf whistle. Gloria said, "Nice, do you shave your legs?" Jeremy said, "I am a man, not a monkey." Randy said, "I have more hair on my balls than you have on your chest." Jeremy blushed and said, "Now that's something to be proud of." Scott said, "Now this is going to be tricky. On top of the yellow slide, like fifty feet from the top of the slide. The clue is hanging from the rafters. We are thinking you could climb onto the edge of the slide up the tree, into the rafters to the clue, and come back the same way." Gloria said, "It's not that big of a slide." Scott said, "It is thirty-five feet from the floor. The clue is another ten feet, so a fall to the cement below could be deadly. Let me run and get my suit." Randy said, "You fuckers are crazy. There has to be another way." Gloria said, "We just lost Boris. We are short one guy, let's not make it two." Jeremy said, "Let me do a quick run-through. It might look a lot different from up there." Scott said, "Well, you're the math whiz. Give it a shot and don't fall." Scott jogged down the hall toward the parking lot.

Jeremy went in the water park and up the stairs to the slide. There were kids all over the place. He stood on top studying the question mark. Finally he slid down the slide. Scott showed up in a swimsuit. Jeremy met them and said, "Okay, there are like four lifeguards on duty. We are going to have to pay them off. The easiest way to get this clue is to crawl up onto the roof and work our way to the clue and pull it up. It is hanging on a small cable." Scott asked, "How much do we pay the guard? I need a pair of gloves." Randy said, "No way, you're going to fall." Jeremy said, "This is the easiest way." Randy said, "Get a high lift or a scissor lift jack. They have to change the lights." Gloria said, "Okay, I will pay them off. Let's start with fifty." Scott and Jeremy went into the water park followed by Gloria. Scott stopped and paid to get in. They went up the stairs to the slide, discussed what they were going to do, then slid down.

Jeremy said, "The roof window is opened for ventilation. We need a six-foot broom to catch the cable, and then we pull it up to the window and get the clue." Scott said, "By god, that will work. Let's get our tennis shoes on and find a ladder."

They went outside and found they could climb onto the roof over by the air conditioners. There was an old snow shovel sitting in the corner. They took that up on the roof. Quickly they went up and peered through the window on top and moved over to where the clue was. Scott said, "It might be too far to reach with this shovel." Jeremy said, "It should be six feet. Try it, I will hold your feet." Scott said, "Don't drop me." Jeremy said, "Don't drop the shovel. You hit a kid and there will be hell to pay."

Scott bent over the open window and hooked the cable and pulled it closer to the window. He struggled to get out of the open window. Jeremy reached over him and took the shovel and pulled it up to the window. He said, "Quick, get the clue." Scott took the key from around his neck and got the clue. He said, "Let it down slowly." Jeremy let the question mark down to a point where he had to get down on his hands and knees. He jerked the snow shovel off the cable and the question mark swung there. Scott said, "This is an interesting clue. It says 'Oprah angel.' Now what the bloody hell is that?"

Jeremy smiled and said, "Let's get off this roof before we are arrested." Scott said, "Good idea." The two quickly got off the roof. Randy said, "That was some cool shit, smooth." Gloria said, "You know, we didn't have to pay anyone off. I don't think they even seen you do it." Scott said, "The clue is 'Oprah angel.'" Everyone got on their phone. Randy said, "Wow, Oprah's charities are worth 200 million dollars." Gloria said, "I just don't understand what this has to do with the game. Her Angel Network is huge." Randy said, "She is a billionaire. It's a big tax write-off. Nothing is coming out of her pocket, and she is just getting richer." Jeremy said, "You're such a fun sucker. Look what good she is doing. She could keep it all and still not pay much in taxes. That's what they have lawyers for."

Scott said, "Got it, go in a few pages. It's not her Angel Network. She donated 600 angels to an Angel Museum in Beloit, world's largest in fact. It is in an old church." Gloria rolled her eyes and said, "Another church." Randy said, "Let's get something to eat. Maybe they have some fried chicken and watermelon." Gloria looked at him and said, "You're such a dick." Scott said, "I don't know about you but I am up for it. Some good fried chicken, mashed potatoes, and gravy." Gloria said, "There is a Smokey's Bar-B-Que right here at the water park. That way we don't have to stop somewhere." Randy said, "Yeah, that sounds good. I am going to have the chicken mac. It's grilled chicken, bacon baked with cheese sauces." Jeremy said, "This has to be quick. Beloit is only a few miles away." Scott said, "How the hell could you guys be hungry? We ate two hours ago. Let's get on the road." Gloria said, "He is right you know. Let's go."

Team Three was on their way to Lake Geneva. Johnny said, "Look, there is a van just like ours." Ed said, "That would be the Intels. They must still be getting insider's information." Mary said, "They aren't that far ahead of us." Robert asked, "Okay, what clue is this? Is it a payday?" Sue said, "It is the eighth payday, clue number four. So there are only two more paydays and the game is done." Jane asked, "What are you going to do after the game?" Sue blushed as she said, "I am going to do you and take you to Disney World." Jane kissed her lightly and said, "That's right."

Johnny said, "That is just not fair." Ed said, "Yeah, I know. I should be getting the girl." Johnny said, "You know my mom is a girl." Mary turned and shot him a look. Ed said, "Yes, I know your mom is a girl. She has to get her shit in one bag. She doesn't need a boyfriend right now." Mary turned around and said in a bitchy voice, "How the hell do you know what I need? Just stay out of my business." Johnny said quietly, "Now you're in trouble." Mark said from the driver's seat, "She is just jealous. He got laid by that gal in Odin's team. And laid well, may I add."

Ed said, "Hit that button. Let's talk to Lance." Mary said, "Okay, but don't be getting us in trouble." Lance came on the speaker. He asked, "Okay, this is Team Three, right?" Ed asked, "Did you seal that leak?" Lance said, "The man has been fired and will not be participating in the game, and the lady that was feeding the information lost half of her entrance fee." Mark gave a whistle and said, "A half million, serves her right." Ed said, "Okay then, so now it is a fair game. But they gained ground. They should be three clues behind." Lance said, "I know, you will just have to work harder. Have a safe game."

Sue said, "Pull up to the front entrance. They have a valet." Jane said, "This is a big fricken place. I say we split up and fan out." Sue said, "We should pair up. Jane and I will find a map and we can figure out a plan." Ed said, "It has to do with the Playboy bunnies. Let's see if there is an exhibit." Mark said, "First we find a map, second a drink." Mary said, "I sure the hell could use a drink." Ed pushed Johnny and said, "See, she is a drinker. Do I need that in my life?" Mary turned quickly. You could tell she was pissed. She never said a word, just glared at Ed. Johnny said, "Whoa, it's okay, Mom. He was just kidding." Sue turned and said, "I think you struck a nerve."

Mark got out, talking to the valet. Mary hopped out too. Ed said with a chuckle, "So do you think she is mad at me?" Jane said, "I wouldn't turn your back on her. She looked pissed." Ed said, "Well, Johnny, let's get going. It's an adventure." Johnny said, "You can't be teasing my mom like that." Ed said, "Don't worry, she is just wrapped a bit tight. She will loosen up." Sue said, "You are right, she does drink a bit." Jane said, "Cut her some slack. Christ, she has a dead-beat husband, a kid, no job, nowhere to live. It must be stressful as shit." Sue said, "She has done this all to herself. Every decision she made has brought her to this very spot." Jane said, "You're right, booze and bad decisions. I am glad where I am right now." Sue slid her arm around Jane's waist and said, "So am I, but we need this ten grand." Jane said, "As a waitress, I have seen a lot of people make bad decisions and screw up their lives, especially cocktailing. The drink really devastates some people."

Ed looked down to Johnny and said, "Don't worry, your mom will come off this just fine. She is a good, strong woman, and not bad looking." Sue turned and said, "Damn, I am sorry. Johnny, every-thing will be just fine." Ed said, "They are right, every decision you make is going to shape your life. Like if you didn't pay attention and took a good spill, broke your leg, there you go. You would take you and your mom out of the game. Or if you called Jane a two-bit flea-ridden whore, she would never think the same about you, would you, Jane?" Johnny asked, "What's a bit?" Ed put his hand on Johnny's head and asked, "So that's what you got out of it? A bit is like seven dollars, I think, just means she is cheap." Sue said, "She might be easy but not cheap." Jane smiled and said, "You got that one right."

They walked into the place. Mary took a few maps and handed them out. She gave one to Ed and said, "I am sorry, it's just . . ." Ed said, "You just have to lighten up and make better choices. Have faith, things are turning around." Johnny wrapped his arms around her and hugged her, saying, "Yeah, Mom. You're not a two-bit whore. Two bits are like fourteen dollars." Mary's eyes opened wide and tears started to flow down her cheek. Ed said, "Why the hell did you say that?" Sue's mouth dropped open. Jane burst out laughing and said, "Oh my god, I can't believe you said that. Holy shit." She grabbed on to her stomach and bent over laughing. Sue chuckled and said, "You have a sick sense of humor. I think I love you." Jane stopped laughing, tears were streaming down her face. She looked up at Sue and asked, "Really? I love you too." Ed said, "Isn't that cute? Give me your phone." Jane looked at him and handed him her phone. He took it and said, "Let's see a hug, and turn a bit. This is a moment in time. You both said I love you." He took a few pictures. Mary said to Johnny, "He is kind of a sentimental guy." Johnny said, "He is a nice guy, but he can be scary." Mary said, "Don't you ever call me a whore again." She grabbed him by the back of the hair and gave a nice tug. Johnny winced and said, "Ouch. No, I will never do it again. It was a joke." Mary said, "We are going to talk about this later." Ed handed back the phone and said, "I will be right back. I am going to talk to these golfers here and see if they have seen our clue." Jane looked into Sues eyes and said, "I want to be with you forever." Sue blushed and said, "That would be nice. I would like that."

Ed walked over to a couple of older guys dressed for golf. He asked, "So how is the course?" One guy said, "Well, they are beautiful courses. The Brute, I think, is the better, but most people like the Highlands." The other man said, "Very nicely kept, but they are a bit pricey. The drink cart comes around enough. Do you play?" Ed said, "One day I might show you how it is done. I was wondering, is there a question mark on the course? We are on a treasure hunt." The older man said, "Oh, you're on one of those. They don't call it treasure hunt, they are scavenger hunts. My wife has done a few of them. I think you can register for them at the front desk." Ed asked, "Really? They have them set up?" The golfer said, "You need one of those smart phones. You take a picture of the clue, send it in, and they give you the next clue." Ed said, "Nice talking to you guys. Good luck on the course."

Ed went into the bar and found the team. Mark said, "Here we go, you are partnered with me. Mary and Johnny are going to the Timber Ridge, it has a water park in it. Jane and Sue are going to check out the spa area. We are going to search the old Playboy club." Ed asked, "You can't be drinking, you're our driver." Mark said, "One manhattan. We will be here a couple hours." Ed said, "Okay, this is what I learned. The clue isn't on the golf course. Well, at least those two guys didn't see it. They have a scavenger hunt set up through the city. This might not be that easy, and I thought this was the old Playboy mansion." Mark said, "Oh, it is, just they have a couple of exhibits. I would like to check them out." Ed said, "This just doesn't sound right. The kid is going to play at a water park, the girls are going to a spa, and we don't have time for this." Sue said, "You're right, we will change our facial to a pedicure. That will take half the time." Jane said, "No, we will go and question some of the help. It shouldn't take long."

A waitress came up and asked Ed if he would like something to drink. Ed said, "I am looking for a metal question mark." She smiled and said, "The last group paid forty bucks for that information." Ed said, "I will pay a hundred. A vodka martini please. No, scrap that. I will have a Coke." He pulled a hundred-dollar bill out of his wallet and held it up to her. She said, "It is at Moose Mountain water park, hanging from the ceiling." She took the bill and left.

Ed looked at the table and said, "You guys didn't even ask our waitress, come on." Mary said, "Okay, that was a mistake. I would have found it." Ed said, "That's not the point. Let's get the bill and find that clue." Jane said, "Damn, this is a nice place. I bet the spa is great." Mark said, "Well, you're going to have to come back." Sue smiled and said, "As soon as we are done here, we are going to Disney. I bet their spas are wonderful." Jane said, "Drink up, here she comes." Mark asked, "May we have our bill please? In fact, here is a fifty. Keep the change. Shall we go people?" Everyone filed out to the van. The water park was like a mile away.

Ed asked, "Does everyone have a swimsuit?" They went to the front desk and paid an entrance fee. Ed paid extra for a locker with a key. Jane asked, "Do you always carry a gun?" Ed smiled and answered, "Not always, but I always have a wallet." She said, "You have a point. Can I put my purse in your locker?" Mark said, "And my wallet."

They went in and got changed. Mark came out with trunks that came down to his knees. Ed had tight trunks that had like four-inch legs. Johnny had a yellow Sponge Bob pair on. Mary had a one-piece. Jane and Sue had bikinis. Jane said, "Ed, you have a nice ass." Jane said, "And a nice body. I don't see any tan lines." Ed pulled down his trunks just a bit to show his white butt cheek. Mark said, "Well, it's not hard to find. There is the clue, just above the slide." Jane blurted, "Fuck, that's going to be a bitch." Mark asked, "So why did they invent the bikini? It is to separate the dairy from the hairy. Oh, I have another one. You do know you can't swim on a full stomach, you have to swim in the water." Mary said, "Oh my god, that is so lame." Ed said, "Johnny, now there is a scratch-and-sniff sticker at the bottom of the pool. Don't try it, you will drown." Johnny said, "I know a few jokes. Where do zombies swim?" Sue said, "The Dead Sea." Johnny said, "What do you call a guy with no arms and no legs in the pool?" Jane said, "Bob." Johnny said, "Okay, what kind of fish can't swim?" Nobody answered. Johnny said proudly, "A dead one." Mark said, "Why do squirrels swim on their backs?" He smiled and said, "Because they want to keep their nuts dry."

Ed asked, "Are we done yet? Has anyone figured out how to get the clue?" Jane said, "Let's go down the slide. Mary is the only smart one to bring the key with." They went up the steps to the slide. Johnny was excited. Ed said, "It is about ten feet above the slide, so if I held Jane up she could reach it." Sue said, "And you both fall from standing on slippery plastic, thirty feet to the cement below. I don't think so." Johnny asked, "Mom, can we go?" Mary set the tube down and said, "We will be back. I will ask one of the lifeguards. Come on, Johnny." They sat on the tube and they were gone in a minute. Mary asked one of the lifeguards, "May I ask how do you get to that question mark hanging from the ceiling?" The guard said, "This morning a couple of guys went up on the roof and pulled it to the window. They paid us not to say anything." Mary asked, "How much?" The lifeguard said, "Fifty bucks, there are four of us on duty." Mary said, "Oh for Christ's sakes, we will pay. Come on, Johnny."

They ran up the slide without the tube. The team was still looking at the clue. Mary said, "They hooked the wire with something and pulled it to the open skylight." Ed said, "That's a great idea." Mary said, "The Intels paid the lifeguards fifty bucks apiece not to say anything." Sue said, "Okay, let's do this." Johnny whined, "Can't I play?" Ed said, "Here, take my tube. Meet you at the bottom." He lay down on the slide and he was gone.

Mark put his tube down and said, "I am going on the roof with Ed. Someone has to pay off the lifeguards," and he was gone. Sue said, "Well, here we go. Mary, take Johnny around the water park. You have a half hour." Jane said, "Come on, girl." Sue lay on the tube. Jane gave her a light kiss and they were gone.

Mark walked up to Ed and Ed put his finger in the air. He walked over to a woman in a bikini and said, "Miss . . . ah . . . your boob is hanging out." She looked up, shocked. She said as she lifted her baby, "Damn, must have fallen asleep. I have five other kids here. This is no vacation." Mark asked, "Where is your husband?" She said, "Golf course, this was his idea."

Ed said, "Let's get dressed and get that clue. We could be out of here within the hour." Jane came up and said, "Have you been shot twice?" Ed smiled, "No, that is just a scar from a bike accident." Sue said, "It really looks like a nine millimeter. We need to get into the locker to grab some cash to pay off these guys. If they call the cops we will be here all day." Ed said, "Right, let's do that first." Jane said, "He has a nice bulge, doesn't he?" Ed rolled his eyes and walked toward the lockers. He took out a key and opened it. Sue looked at Mark and said, "I am going to get reimbursed for this, right?" Mark said, "Well yeah, just be quick about it. We will be on the roof in fifteen minutes."

Ed and Mark went to get changed. They were out of the changing room in a couple of minutes and went to find Jane or Sue. They found them and waved them over. Mark asked, "Is it a go? Did you pay them all off?" Sue said, "Yeah, hurry up. Be careful." Ed asked, "Have I told you the two of you look ravishing in those bikinis?" Sue blushed and said, "Doesn't she? I have to start working out." Mark said, "Find Mary and the child. We are out of here in ten."

The two started to walk away. Ed said, "Come on." Mark said loud enough so the girls could hear, "Let's just watch them walk away for a minute." Jane looked over her shoulder and said, "I heard that." Mark smiled and said to Ed, "I would like to throw a baby into her." Ed said, "Let's take a quick walk around and see if we can find a ladder." They got to the AC unit and said, "This is it. This is where they went up, and there is a snow shovel laying in the bushes." Mark asked, "Now what window was it? Shit, we should have measured it." Ed said, "We will just stick our head in the window and find it. I will go up first. You hand me the shovel." In five minutes they were up looking through the skylight. They worked their way down to where the clue was, stuck the snow shovel in, hooked the clue, and pulled it to the window. Mark got the clue and Ed lowered the question mark. Mark said, "Mary is watching you. I think she likes you." Ed said, "She sure doesn't show it. Let's get the hell off this roof." Mark held up the clue and said, "Oh, she just doesn't want to get involved with someone right now, especially someone who knows her past. Speaking of that, are you ever going to show me the video of her and the police chief? Now the clue is 'Oprah Angel.' What kind of clue is that?"

Ed got to the edge of the roof and chucked the snow shovel off of it and slowly got down. He said, "Those women aren't going to be ready." Mark took his sweet time getting off the roof. He said, "That's Johnny. He really likes the water park." Ed said, "He is a good kid. If I remember correctly, Oprah has a large charity named angel something."

They walked inside and Jane and Sue were waiting for them. Sue said, "Johnny and Mary will be right out. So what is the clue?" Mark said, "Oprah Angels, that's it." Everyone started to search it on their phones. Ed said, "It was the Oprah network, donated more than 80 million to charities. It built fifty-five schools." Mark said, "Found it, angel museum. Some broad named Joyce Burg started to collect angels. She must have really got into it. Oprah said there were no black angels, so her viewers sent over 600 of them to her and she donated them to the Angel Museum. That is what ties them together." Sue said, "It is less than an hour away. Let's blow this pop stand." Jane looked at her and said, "Where did that come from? A pop stand?" Sue blushed and said, "It is just something my dad would say." They got into the van and headed to Beloit.

Team Odin got to Lake Geneva a few hours after Team Three. Robert pulled up to the front door to the valet. He asked the driver, "Hey, you wouldn't know about a metal question mark that was added to the resort lately?" The driver said, "Well yes, I have. It is hanging in the water park, some kind of scavenger hunt." Robert asked, "And which way would the water park be?" The valet gave him directions. Dawn handed a twenty up to Robert and said, "Thank you very much." They pulled out and went to the water park.

Robert pulled up and said, "I will drop you guys off here and find a parking spot. Go in and ask about the clue." The team got out and walked into the park. There was a huge wall of glass showing the park. Sure enough, there was the clue hanging from the ceiling. Joe said, "Okay, girls, get your suits on." Cherry said, "You just want to look at my ass." Joe smiled and said, "You know, I never thought of that. You do have a nice ass. I never want to see you naked. You want to know why? Because it would never be as good as I imagined." Dawn said, "You are a perverted man, I like that." Joe said, "I will ask about the clue." He walked up to the desk and asked, "Miss, I would like to know about that question mark that is hanging from the ceiling." She smiled and said, "That is a clue to some scavenger hunt." He asked, "How do they get the clue? That looks danger-ous, standing on top of that slide." She smiled and said, "They go up on the roof and hook the cable and pull it to the skylight." Joe said, "Well that is neat. Thank you so much." She said as he turned around, "They pay us two hundred apiece to look the other way or we would call the cops." Dawn said, "How many of you are there?" The girl said, "There are four of us." Dawn walked back to the team and they headed for the door to meet Robert. Cherry said, "That is eight hundred dollars. Let's take a walk around and see how easy it would be to get on the roof."

Joe said to Robert, "Get the van and keep it running." Robert asked, "What is going on?" Dawn said, "We just need a quick get-away. We found the clue and are going to get it. Hurry." Joe said, "Let's move. There is the way onto the roof, over the air condition-ing unit." Cherry said, "There is a shovel on top of the bushes." Joe asked, "Who is going up?" Cherry said, "We all are. Let's make this quick."

Joe reached into the bushes and took the shovel. Dawn and Cherry were already on the roof. Cherry ran up to the skylight and peeked in, looking for the clue. Joe handed Dawn the shovel and climbed on. Dawn waved them up. Joe reached in and pulled the clue with the shovel. They were off the roof in two minutes and were at the front door as Robert pulled up. They jumped in and Cherry shouted, "Drive, they probably called the cops. A thousand dollars to look the other way my ass." Dawn said, "That was fun." Joe said, "Okay, this is the clue, Oprah Angels."

Everyone got out their phones. Robert, who was driving, said, "I know this. Oprah said there were no black angels and hundreds of people sent her black angels. She donated them to some museum in Wisconsin." Jane said, "You're right, Beloit. Let's see. It is less than an hour away. Let's do this." Joe said, "Now that is the way to get a clue, less than an hour." Joe said, "This is going to be the fifth clue. It could be a payout and we need one more person." Dawn blurted out, "Fuck." A pause, then, "You're right. We can get someone who works there." Robert said, "I doubt it would be a monument just for that reason." Dawn said, "Okay, smartass, what should we do, put a job offer in the paper?" Joe said, "Good idea. I will put one on the web. We just take anyone that is near. All we need is a body." Robert said, "That will do, but we have to register them and need a proof of insurance." Cherry said, "That's right. We can just get some kid that has nothing holding him there." Joe said, "Or someone with a week's vacation. It shouldn't take more than a week. There are only two pay-days left." Robert said, "Well, we will be there in less than an hour."

Team Intel was still in the lead but not by much. They pulled into the church parking lot where the Angel Museum was. Scott said, "Damn, a busload of old folks are here." Gloria said, "This shouldn't be too hard. It's not as big as that church in Milwaukee." Randy said, "Old people freak me out. Let's take a walk around the building and make sure it isn't attached to the building." Jeremy said, "At least there is no bell tower on this one."

They got out and walked around the building. The clue was nowhere to be seen. Randy said, "Well, it was worth a try. Now watch, there are going to be a shitload of old saggy, stinky white people in walkers."

They paid their seven dollars to get in. The busload of people were from Chicago, 80 percent black. Jeremy said, "Randy, see that old fuck over there? That is you in ten years." Randy said, "Ten years my ass, that old coot is got to be eighty years old." Jeremy said, "No, forty. Your people age quickly." Gloria said, "Let's just find that clue and get out of here." A little old lady wearing a silver gown and wings came up and said, "Welcome, I am Joyce. Come on in and see my angels." Scott asked, "Do you have a question mark? We are doing this treasure hunt and one of the clues led us here." Joyce said, "Now, if I told you that wouldn't be fair, would it?" Gloria said, "I am going to hit the choir loft, Jeremy the gift shop. Randy, you question the old farts down here. And don't pick up any of those older women." Scott said, "I am going to walk around the grounds one more time." They walked around for an hour. Scott said, "It's not here, we have looked everywhere."

Team Three showed up in Beloit. Johnny screeched, "Oh my god, look at the bulldog." Ed said, "That's a big one. I would say twenty feet long, eight feet high. Probably made out of fiberglass." Johnny asked, "Why do they have that?" Ed said, "It is to promote the restaurant. It is called Road Dawg Family Restaurant." Mark chuckled, "Could you see the size of the pooper scooper you would need? He would drop a twenty-pound shit." Sue said, "Mark, why would you say that?" Jane smiled and said, "You would need a garbage bag and a shovel." Ed said, "You would have to feed him fifty pounds of dog food a day." Johnny said, "Just think, you would need a really big ball to play fetch." Mary said, "We should eat soon." Mark said, "We are close to the museum. Let's do that first." Ed said, "Yeah, and then we should find a hotel for the night." Jane said, "It all depends on the next clue."

They were a block down the road and Mark said, "We have company. There is a lime-green van in the parking lot." Ed asked, "Don't you still have the GPS tracker on the vans?" Mark said, "Well yeah, it's not like I use it all the time. Oh, you want to see Gloria. Whoot, whoot, booty call." Ed said, "Really, what the hell are you thinking?" Mary said, "This just means the clue is hard to find or it is not here." Jane said, "Oh, it is here. It has to be." Sue said, "Someone is tight lipped. Vegas must know we are just bribing people to find the clues." Ed said, "Everyone has a price, and it is not against the rules." Mary said sarcastically, "Why don't you text your little whore and find out what is going on?" Ed smiled and said, "Hey, that's a great idea. Maybe I can find out what hotel they are staying at." Mary grit her teeth and her face turned three shades redder. Johnny pulled on Ed's shirt and said quietly, "Why is Mom getting so mad?" Sue said, "I think she likes Edward here." Mark said, "We need a plan. I am going to take the grounds." Sue said, "Jane and I will take the gift shop." Mark said, "That figures." Mary said, "Johnny and I will take the choir loft."

Ed said, "Now, Johnny, this is a museum. No touching unless it has a sign saying you can. I will take the main floor. Now if you find the clue or monument text everyone. We want to slip out without whoever this is knowing." Mark said, "It has to be Intel. Let's see." He took out his phone and looked at it and said, "Yes, it is. And Odin is still in Geneva." Ed said, "They will not be far behind. That clue was pretty easy." Jane said, "That's because they told us where the clue was. It wasn't even in the Playboy mansion." Sue said, "We have to go back and spend a couple days there." Jane looked into her eyes and said, "You know, that would be great."

Mary hopped out of the van as soon as they parked. Ed said, "Johnny, you listen to your mother. And if you find the clue, be quiet." Johnny said as he crawled over Ed, "Okay, I will." Sue said, "And don't touch anything. I swear that kid drops more shit." Ed said, "He just doesn't pay attention." Mark said, "Let's do this as tourists. They might not even catch on that we are here." Ed said, "Different plan. Jane, you are with me. Sue, you're with Mark, act like you're on holiday." Sue said, "Holiday? Where the fuck are we, Europe?" Ed said, "Sorry, vacation, my dear." Mark said, "Give her a kiss when Mary is looking. That will get her going." Ed asked, "Do you really think she likes me? She doesn't show it." Jane asked, "We are taking the main floor and they are taking the basement?" Mark said, "I guess so. It is such a nice day. I was going to wander around out here." Ed said, "That's fine. Take a quick walk around the joint. We will go in, and it will look better this way." Mark took Sue by the hand and said, "Let's take a walk around the building. I sure hope the clue is chartreuse." Sue said, "I doubt it. I have a feeling the clues are going to be harder now."

Ed and Jane went in and paid the entrance fee. A lovely old gal came over in a silver robe and with angel wings on. Ed introduced them, "Good day, miss. I am Ed and this is my girlfriend Jane. How are we today." The older lady said, "HI, I am Joyce. This place is crazy today. Every time they bring a bus in more people show up, and well this is half of my angel collection." Jane said, "Half, really? Where is the other half?" Joyce said, "Oh, at home. I don't like to duplicate the angels." Ed said quietly, "We are on a treasure hunt. Another team is here looking for the clue, which is a question mark. Do you know where it is?" Joyce smiled a sly smile and said, "I can't tell you." Ed said, "Would a hundred-dollar bill help you to remember?" Joyce said, "Now don't be doing that." Ed said, "Two hundred." He pulled out his money clip and pulled two hundred out. Joyce said, "You just put that back. You're not playing fair." Ed took out five bills and said, "Five hundred dollars." Her eyes darted from side to side. She reached out and took the money and said, "Down in the gift shop, there is a side door that leads to a garden. Behind the peace lily there is a question mark." Ed leaned in and gave her a light kiss on the cheek.

Ed's phone chirped. He pulled it out and looked at it and smiled. Jane looked at it and said, "How's it hanging? Really?" Ed typed in, "Like a lollipop. Want a lick?" Jane said, "Oh, you're sick." Ed said, "This is kind of private. Go look at something." Jane said, "Mary is going to be pissed." She turned to look right into Gloria's eyes. She said, "Damn," and walked away. Gloria texted back, "I see you paid off the old lady. What did you find out?" Ed looked at her and winked and then texted back, "I can't tell you. You are looking very nice. I hear you lost a teammate." Gloria typed, "How did you know?" Ed texted, "I have to go. Good luck, and thank you." He looked up and stared at her for just a moment, and a huge smile formed on his face as he blushed and quickly caught up to Jane.

He asked, "Did Sue get the clue?" She said, "They are entering the garden now. I hope they know what a peace lily is." Ed said, "She has a phone and Mary and the boy." Jane said, "She seen you looking at Gloria, by the way. She is cute." Ed said, "Really, it was just a second. I meant are they on their way to the van?" Jane held up one finger and said, "They got it, let's move."

They got to the van and Mark said, "A whale. That is it, a whale." Sue said, "There are a few whales around here." Ed said, "It is the House on the Rock. It has a full-sized whale in it. This place is huge. The last time I was through it was a three-and-a-half-mile tour under roof." Johnny asked, "It is a house that is on a rock?" Ed said, "It's a lot more than that. It is like the eighth wonder of the world. You will see dragons. And the infinity room . . . my god, it has been awhile." Mark said, "It is about a hundred miles. Let's get on the road."

They got into the van and Mary asked, "Was that Gloria you were talking to?" Ed said, "I didn't say one word to her." Jane said to Sue, "She texted him and asked how is it hanging. He text back 'you want a lick.'" Ed said, "Oh my god, I said like a lollipop. Just forget it." Johnny asked, "You wanted her to lick your—" Ed said, "Don't go there, it was a joke. We have a clue. This one is going to be a bitch." Mark said, "Team Odin will not be far behind." Ed said, "This is going to tighten up the race. Joyce is going to tell them where the clue is. If she doesn't, that would not be fair. By the way, Mary, you owe me five hundred. That was her price." Mark said, "Really, the old bag held out for that much?" Jane said, "She moved at three, but when he pulled out the five she took it." Sue said, "We would have never found it. The question mark was only six inches high and covered by a plant."

Gloria went to Scott and said, "The old lady knows where it is. We just have to find out her price." Scott asked, "Do you really think so?" They walked up to Joyce, who was explaining where she found this one angel. Scott cleared his throat and asked, "About this question mark, how much would it cost to find out where it is?" Joyce held up a finger to him and motioned him away from the old couple. She said, "That all depends." Gloria said, "I seen you take money from the other team and now they are gone." She said, "They paid five hundred." Scott said, "Bullshit, what did they pay?" Joyce looked at him and asked, "Are you calling me a liar?" Gloria said, "No, we are going to pay you the same. Here are five one-hundred-dollar bills." Joyce said, "Okay, go down into the gift shop and go out the side door. It leads to a garden, and in the garden is a large peace lily. Behind it you will find your question mark."

Scott motioned to Jeremy and they headed down to the gift shop. Soon they were outside in the garden. Scott said, "There is the peace lily against the building." He stepped in the garden and pulled back the plant to reveal a six-inch question mark staked to the ground. He carefully got down on his hands and knees and put his key in and the clue came out the backside of it. Scott stood and read the clue, "A whale, that's what it says. A whale, all in lower case."

The team started searching on their phones for a whale in Wisconsin. Randy said, "These white folks are just weird. They had a whale on their state flag. What is up with that?" Jeremy said, "No way, there are no whales in Wisconsin. It is all fresh water." Randy said, "I shit you not, dude, their very first flag had a whaler with a lasso on it with a whale." Gloria said, "There are a few whales around here, but the House on the Rock keeps coming up." Scott said, "It is a two-hundred-foot sperm whale, and it has its own room. There is a collection of ships." Jeremy said, "This place sounds huge. They have the world's largest carousel. Oh, this is going to be something. That last question mark was small." Gloria said, "The clues are so vague." Randy said, "Well, when we get there, we search the whale room. It's like three stories. Bet you ten bucks the clue is in the whale's mouth. There is a full-sized boat in it." Scott said, "Then we agree, to the House on the Rock." Gloria said, "I would say, it is over an hour away."

Team Odin pulled up as Team Intel was leaving. Dawn said, "There are only four in the van. They lost a couple of people. The black guy is new and kind of cute." Cherry said, "Don't believe everything people say. They aren't all well endowed." Joe asked, "What is so special about black guys? Some of the cutest white girls are having kids with black guys." Robert said, "All I know, they must have found the clue. We need a big payout." Dawn said, "Let's do this and be quick about it."

They piled out of the van and went inside, Robert said, "I will pay your admission, but you all owe me seven dollars." Joe walked up to Joyce. She was still wearing her angel costume. He asked her, "Good day, we are looking for a question mark." She turned and said, "Hello, I am Joyce. This is my collection of angels. And how many are in this treasure hunt?" Joe said, "Okay, you know about the hunt. There are three teams. How many have come through so far?" Joyce said, "Two, you must be the last ones." Joe asked, "Do you know where the question mark is?" Joyce smiled and said, "The other teams gave five hundred dollars for the clue." Joe said, "We don't have that kind of money. How much would it take?" Joyce smiled and said, "Go downstairs and out the door to the right. In the garden there is a large peace lily. Behind that you will find the clue." Joe smiled and said, "Oh, thank you so much." He ran over to Robert and said, "I know where the clue is, follow me." Robert asked, "Did you text the girls?" Joe said, "Let's get the clue. You text them. Okay, it should be right behind the peace lily. See the footprints? Someone was just here. And there is the question mark. And the clue is whale, as in Moby Dick." Joyce, who followed them down, said, "The first team said something about the House on the Rock. It is in Spring Green." Robert said, "Thank you so very much." Cherry asked, "Did you find it?" Joe said, "Let's move. They are ten minutes ahead of us. And that is one nice lady. The two other teams paid five hundred apiece to get the clue, and it just cost us a smile." Robert said,

"You're such a suck ass."

CHAPTER TWENTY-FIVE

The House on the Rock

Team Three pulled into the parking lot. Johnny was excited, "Look at all the cars. There are dragons on the planters." Jane said, "I booked three rooms at the hotel." Ed said, "Three rooms? What the hell, I am not sleeping with Mark." Jane said, "That is all they have, two with queen beds and one with a king." Mark said, "I get the king." Jane said with a sly smile, "No, that is mine and Sue's." Ed said, "Johnny, now look at all the different license plates. This is a destination." Mark said, "No way, there is one from Hawaii. That is odd." Jane said, "What do you think? We have an hour. It's thirty bucks apiece." Mary gave a light whistle. "That's a bit steep; it's just a museum. How much for Johnny?" Sue said, "It's $16 for four to seventeen, and I don't think they will let us in. They are open from nine to four and it is three now." Mark said, "Most people spend three and a half hours here. That is a bit of time. So would you like me to drive to the hotel?" Ed said, "Why don't we just go inside and see what is up? Maybe we can ask someone where the question mark is." Mary said, "It should be a marker. And I think we are the first here, it could be ten grand." Sue asked, "Oh, driver, could you pull up to the front door and drop us off?" Mark said, "Yes, I could do that. It's a fucking Wednesday and there are a thousand cars here. I wonder what is going on."

Ed said, "Keep your eyes peeled. That marker could be any-where." Johnny said, "That is weird, nobody says that. And what does it mean peel your eyes? That's gross." Sue said, "It means be on alert, watch carefully or vigilantly for something." Mary said, "Don't you just love the internet? Drop us off here, or there is a spot over there."

Mark pulled into the spot and they got out. Jane said, "Let's hope someone knows where the marker is. This is over a three-and-a-half-mile walk under roof." Mark said, "No shit, it doesn't look that big." Johnny said, "Is there really a house on the rock, like a real house?" Mary pulled him close and said, "Yes, that is what it says." Johnny said, "Chipmunk," and hopped into the wooded area. Ed said, "None of that. You stick close. They might be tame but if you get bit you will end up getting rabies shots. In the Grand Canyon, the squirrels carry the plague." Mark asked, "Really, the plague?" Ed said, "That's what the signs say. Those damn things would come right up to you and people still feed them." Mark said to Mary, "If I was a squirrel, I would bust a nut in your hole." She rolled her eyes and said, "For Christ's sakes, that's lame." Ed said, "Johnny, how do you catch a squirrel? You climb up a tree and act like a nut." Jane said, "What do you call a squirrel that doesn't have any nuts?" She paused and said, "A girl. Get it? No nuts." Mary said, "He is only eight years old." Johnny said, "I get it, boys have a penis and girls have pussy. But why do they call a vagina a pussy? It doesn't look like a cat." Mary blushed and said, "How the hell do you know what it looks like?" Mark said, "Hey, you let him play on the internet. There is everything you want to know and more. Let's get into this place." Sue said, "The flowers are beautiful."

Ed said quietly to Johnny, "You're in trouble. Think before you speak." Mark held the door and everyone went in. He rubbed Johnny's head and said, "You're going to turn your mom's hair gray." Johnny looked up at him and said, "You started it." Mark smiled and said, "Never say 'dumb cunt.' That is rude." Mary turned, her face was beet red. Mark said quietly, "Wow." Johnny's face blushed. He looked at Ed and Ed said, "Come on, that's your mother." Johnny's jaw dropped. Mark burst out laughing. Jane said, "You fuckers should be ashamed of yourselves." Sue said, "You're going to hell."

Ed said, "Did you see their faces? God, that was funny." Mary shot him a look.

Sue went to the desk and asked if they could get a tour. The girl said, "It's too close to closing." Jane said, "Well, that is that. To the resort then." Ed said, "If we tipped you a hundred bucks, could we do the tour? We are looking for a question mark or a marker that looks like a small skyscraper. It should be around five feet." The gal said, "I am sorry. The tour will take at least three hours, and some people take damn near the whole day." Mark said, "We just want to see the whale." The gal said, "It is in a long way. I am telling you, there is about three and a half miles of tour under roof, and it takes a while."

Ed asked Johnny, "So, boy, have you ever been golfing?" Johnny looked up and said, "No, but it looks boring." Ed smiled and said, "Maybe they have a driving range." Mark said, "That little girl behind the desk, I would like to drive her." Jane said, "Really, she is half your age?" Ed said, "It would be a good time, but the drama, oh my god." Mary asked, "What would you know about that?" Ed just smiled and said, "I know some guys that have young wives. I mean look at that gal, what the hell was her name? She started the sugar daddy thing in San Francisco." Sue said, "Here it is, her name was Alma. She married Adolph Spreckels, a sugar baron. She was twenty-four years his junior. There is a statue of her in the Union Square." Mark said, "She is not my type anyway. It is a thirteen-mile drive to the resort. Have we figured out the sleeping arrangements?" Ed said, "We will see when we get there. If there are no other rooms, I can sleep in Mary's room." Johnny said, "That will be great." Mary shot Sue a look. Sue said, "Hey, those were the only rooms left." Johnny said, "Look at that dragon on the planter. It has a guy's head in its claw. I can't wait to go inside."

Ed said, "Tomorrow we do a quick run-though, find the damn monument, and get some room between us." Mark said, "Tomorrow we will all be waiting for this place to open." Jane asked, "All three teams. Shit, why wouldn't she let us in?" Sue said, "A job is a job. She probably needs this one." Mark said, "She is probably a heroin addict and needs the money for her next fix." Johnny said, "She might have a couple of kids." Mark said, "That little girl? She might. Everyone needs money. That is why we should have offered her more." Ed said, "You're right, everyone has a price." Johnny asked, "What do you mean?" Mark asked, "Would you stick your finger in a light socket for a penny?" Johnny said, "No way." Mark said, "How about a hundred dollars?" Johnny asked, "A hundred dollars?" Mark said, "I will give you two hundred dollars if you would stick your finger in a light socket and let me turn it on for a second." Johnny asked, "Really, two hundred dollars? You will give me two hundred dollars?" Mark said, "There we go. Your price is two hundred dollars. Now if we offered that gal five hundred she might have taken us right to the whale room." Johnny chuckled, "Sperm whale." They got to the hotel and Ed asked at the desk if there were any rooms available and there weren't.

Team Odin got to the House on the Rock. Joe said, "This should be a monument. We need another player." Cherry said, "We can just pay someone a hundred bucks to turn Jack's key." Robert asked, "How is he anyway?" Dawn said, "He is on antibiotics. Other than that, he is doing well. I think he is going to try to fly home next week." Cherry said, "I thought he was going to get a major infection. Those were some deep scratches." Robert said, "Well, let's go in. I doubt we can take the tour it is late." Joe said, "Have you been looking at these crazy planters? There must be a hundred of them." Cherry said, "The flowers are beautiful." Dawn said, "There is a chance we can get a personal tour." Joe said, "It doesn't hurt to try. Now this whale room is a three-story museum exhibit of ships." Robert said, "That is what I have read, and they're not little ships. Some are like sixteen feet long. But is that where the clue is?" Cherry said, "It should be a payday. It is the sixth clue and the eighth monument, and we need this ten grand." Dawn said, "Just two more after this."

They went inside and up to the desk. Dawn said, "Thirty bucks a ticket for a museum. That's a bit much." The girl behind the desk said, "This is one of a kind. We solely run on admissions. And you are too late. In fact, I have to lock the doors." Joe said, "You lock people in?" She looked over her glasses at him and said, "You can go out but you can't come in." Robert said quietly, "People are coming out. We will slip in, just hold the door." The girl said from across the room, "People have tried that. It is a five-hundred-dollar fine and you spend the night in the jail and pay court costs." Cherry said, "Well, maybe not." Dawn said, "Well, it is off to Don Q inn. It sounds like they have a good restaurant." Robert said, "It's like eight miles away. Let's go and have a good meal and get back here for the opening."

They went back out to the van and to the hotel. When they got there the cheap rooms were taken. Joe said, "A hundred bucks more for the themed rooms." Cherry said, "For a hundred bucks, Dawn, would you like to bunk with me?" Joe looked at Robert and said, "Girls can do that, I am not." The guy behind the counter pointed out that the restaurant burned down and what rooms were left. Robert said, "I will take the Sherwood Forest room." Cherry said, "Why don't we take the Northern Lights? That looks cool." Joe said, "Good, nobody took the Casino Royal, a Vegas-themed room."

The man handed out the keys and did the paperwork. Cherry said, "There was a tunnel connecting the hotel to the restaurant. That's kind of cool." The man behind the counter pointed to a screen and said, "There are cameras in the tunnel. People do weird shit down there, and I mean a guy actually took a shit. We saved it and someone put it on the net. It got like two million views." Robert said, "To our rooms. In a half hour we meet here and we can go to a bar. There is one just a couple of miles from here."

Cherry asked the guy, "So when did the restaurant burn down?" The guy said, "That was February 2017. They still are thinking of a rebuild. It was in a hundred-year-old barn, so when it went up, it burnt quick." Joe asked, "So what is up with the plane?" The guy said, "Well it is an ex-military Boeing C-97G. It was the biggest thing in the air back in the forties. They bought it back in the seventies and they were going to use it for a coffee shop or something. Farrah Fawcett did a couple of commercials with it. Now it's just a lawn ornament. The landing strip was long enough to land it but not long enough for takeoff."

They met at the lobby. Cherry said, "Our room is a fucking igloo, so cool. We are going into the hot tub tonight with a bottle of wine." Joe asked, "Naked? Can I come?" Dawn said, "God, you're creepy." Robert said, "Well the forest is cool. It has a tree in the middle of the room." Joe said, "Well mine, the Vegas-themed one, has a red velvet bed, red carpeting, marble tub, kind of cool." Robert asked, "Shall we go to the bar?"

They got into the van and headed to the nearest bar and grill, got a table, and a Scottish guy walked in with a kilt on. Robert asked, "Now why do the Scots wear skirts." Joe said, "I know this one. It is because sheep can hear a zipper a mile away." Everyone burst out laughing. The guy came over to the table and asked, "What's so funny?" Cherry asked, "What do you have under you kilt?" The man said, "If you play your cards right, missy, it could be your lipstick." Joe said, "Good one. What are ya, a bagpiper?" He said, "Yes, I am with the Clan. We had a parade today." Robert said, "Well nice to meet you. We have stuff to discuss. And put on some pants, man." Dawn said, "I like the pipes." Joe said, "Only if they are played right, like underwater." Dawn looked up at him and reached under his kilt. She said, "Don't listen to him. That's gruesome." He said, "Feel again, it grew some more." She smiled and said, "It's a wee bit too small for my liking." His face turned red and he turned and walked away. Cherry said, "You had better wash your hands twice." Dawn said, "Yeah, it was sticky and gross."

Team Intel's Jeremy called and asked if they could get a private tour of the house. They were declined. Scott said, "Shit, I just hope the other teams didn't get here in time to go through." Gloria said, "Anyone have problems with hotel 8?" Randy said, "I don't think they have a bar." Gloria said, "It's eight miles away." Scott said, "Book it, find a restaurant close by." Jeremy said, "Italian would be nice." Gloria said, "Yes, and so would a million dollars, then I wouldn't be stuck in here with you clowns." Randy said, "That's right, lady, I have big feet and you're wondering what else is big." Gloria said, "Not even if you were the last man on earth. I would turn gay first." Jeremy said, "I thought you were."

Scott said, "Let's check in then figure out the dining situation." Gloria said, "Stop at that gas station. We can get a bottle of wine and have Pizza Hut deliver." Scott asked, "Are we down to that? Eating pizza in our rooms, drinking gas station wine." Gloria said, "This will be a twenty-five-dollar meal. We go to a restaurant and the bar bill will be sixty bucks." Randy asked Gloria, "Pizza . . . hey, what does pizza and your father have in common?" Gloria said, "You just knock it off." Scott said, "How about they're filled with shit?" Randy said, "They both came in a greasy box." Jeremy said, "Good one. Try this. What is the difference between a pizza and a Jew?" Scott said, "What the fuck, a pizza and a Jew?" Gloria said, "One is spicy and the other bland." Jeremy said, "The pizza doesn't scream when you put it in the oven." Randy said, "Nazi humor is pretty sick. Hitler was the most famous Jewish cook." Scott said, "And he did invent the high-five. Well everyone put up their hand." Gloria said, "You guys are sick. One thing he did do is ruin a mustache style." Jeremy said, "You are right there. So pizza and we meet down here at 7:00. The house opens at 9:00."

The pizza came. Scott said to the delivery guy, "Dude, what are you doing tomorrow?" The guy said, "I start delivering at 4:00." Scott said, "You live around here, have you seen a question mark or a monument— it has a pyramid on the top—in the House on the Rock?" The guy said, "Nope, never took the tour." Scott said, "We need a fifth person to open the monument. It would be a hundred bucks." The man reached out his hand and said, "A hundred bucks, hey? Sounds good to me. I am Darwin." Jeremy handed him a slip of paper and said, "You have to fill this out quick, a short form to show we are not liable for anything." Darwin filled out the form and handed it back to him. Jeremy took out a triangular stick and scanned the form and handed it back to Darwin. Scott said, "This is a treasure hunt. We are looking for clues. We don't need the application, it's just a formality." Jeremy said, "Everything is good. See you at 7:00 tomorrow morning." They shut the door to the hotel room.

Gloria said, "I thought we were going to find someone there." Randy said, "It is easier this way, and you're only paying a hundred bucks to the dude, sweet." Jeremy said, "Darwin Hornick, he is thirty-two years old. Oh, would you look at that. He has a warrant for his arrest." Gloria said, "Oh what kind of sick fuck did you hire?" Jeremy said, "Looks like he stole a Ming vase worth $12,000. The vase was recovered but the owner is pressing charges. This is interesting, Mr. Hornick had the same address as the owner." Scott said, "Tell us more. Where did he go to school? What was his profession?" Jeremy said, "His application said high school grad. He has worked in several places, fast food delivery, if you dig a little deeper." His computer dinged. "Oh, there we go, just broke into his social media account. Oh, that gal he was living with is pissed. He stole a Rolex and some jewelry, a gold Buddha. Oh hell, she said there is footage of him fucking the pool boy." The computer dinged again. Jeremy said, "Oh boy, someone is looking for him. Let me spike them. Here we go, it is an insurance agent." Gloria asked, "Why would an insurance agent be looking for him?" Scott said, "That Buddha might be worth a lot of money." Jeremy said, "Let's go deeper in his account. It looks like he lived off of women. This one he lived with for a year and a half, then there is this old broad, six months, and another before that." Scott said, "We really don't care; he just has a high school diploma." Jeremy said, "That is all I see." Randy said, "That dog, I have to get a gig like his. And did you say he was screwing the pool boy?" Jeremy said, "I will see if I can hack into her security and get that footage." Gloria asked, "Can he do that?" Jeremy said, "If have the date that makes it a lot easier."

That morning Team Intel met Darwin. Gloria said, "You are one sick fuck, taking advantage of old women." Darwin said, "What do you mean?" Jeremy said, "Don't listen to her. We just need you to turn a key when we find the monument." Randy said, "Oh, by the way, the cops are looking for you." Darwin's eyes darted from side to side. Randy smiled and said, "We didn't rat you out. Looks like you stole something from your last lover and she must have hired someone to retrieve it." Darwin said, "Fuck, how did she find me?" Jeremy said, "I hacked into your account, which must have rung a few bells." Gloria asked, "Do you have the Buddha with you? I see you're wearing the Rolex." Darwin said, "These things are hard to pawn. Would you like to buy it cheap? Five grand, that is a quarter of what it is worth."

They were the first team in the parking lot. They got in line waiting for the doors to open. Team Odin sat in the van waiting for the line to move. Team Three pulled into the parking lot and Ed said, "Whoa, let's hold back here. They don't need to know who all is in the team. Let's park way back here and we go in as couples. That way we will blend in." Mary said, "There are five people in the van. They must have picked up a player to open the monument." Sue said, "Hey, there is Team Intel. They are standing in line." Mark said, "Okay, I see them. Scott, I think, the guy behind him." Ed said, "And there is Gloria." Mary's face blushed as she said, "You would have noticed her." Sue said, "That's right, good old Gloria. Ed, maybe you could hook up with her and find out what's shakin'."

Sue said, "Well we might as well get going. I am going in with Jane." Mark said, "You're not sticking me with the boy." Mary said, "Fine, you and Edward go together. Me and Johnny will go." Ed asked, "Johnny, would you rather go with me or your mom?" Johnny looked up at his mom and asked, "Would it be okay if I went with Ed?" Mary's eyes watered and she said. "No, that would be fine. Ed, don't get him hurt." Mark stepped to Ed's side and said, "You do know if you meet up with that Gloria chick Johnny will squeal on you?"

Ed started to jog toward the door. He said, "Come on, Johnny, check out all the dragons." Gloria saw him and gave a small wave with a confused look on her face. Johnny stopped running. Ed said, "You have to keep up." Johnny, holding his chest, said, out of breath, "That girl, she waved to you." Ed smiled and said, "Pay no attention to her. She sees me with you, that should throw her off. She thinks it is me, but she is not sure. She thinks I am your dad." Johnny said, "You could be my dad, just saying. Boy, are we going to be running a lot?" Ed picked Johnny up, put him on his shoulders, and quickly walked to the door.

Mark said, "Johnny and Ed get along. You know, if you would wear a little makeup, dressed a little more sexy—you know, get your bait pile in shape—you could have a shot at him." Mary looked at him and said, "If I wanted any shit from you I would squeeze your head." Jane said from behind them, "You know, he is right. I think Ed likes you." Sue said, "And what the fuck is up with you, Mark? You haven't made a move on any of us. Are you queer?" Mark smiled, "I have swung both ways. Women are downright cruel. I have had my heart ripped out of my chest, stomped on, and kicked to the curb. One hell of a lesson." Jane said, "How long ago was that?" Mark said, "Going on three years now. I think I am ready for my next relationship. I went to Thailand last year and got laid, beautiful country." Sue asked, "You flew all the way to Thailand to get your rocks off?" Mark said, "It was a vacation. A guy from the army got divorced and said the best time he had in the army was in Thailand. We went there for two weeks, had a great time. Just too long of a flight." Sue said, "How was the sex? Did you fuck some young little girl? You're going to catch some weird-ass disease." Mark said, "No bodily fluids were exchanged, and they were checked by the government. They were very nice and knew what they were doing. Would I go back? It's just such a long flight. My friend said if he doesn't find anyone in a year we are going to Vegas. It's more expensive but not a long flight."

Mary said, "The lines are gone, let's go. I can't believe you have a problem picking up women, you are cute." Sue said, "That's not it, is it? You don't want to be fucked over like the last one." Mark said, "How do you know who is the one? You stick your neck out for someone and they chop it off." Sue said, "Let's pair up and separate. Is that Cherry from Odin?" Mary said, "I saw Gloria. She walked in right before Edward." Mark said, "Yes, they are all here. That is why we split up, cover more ground." Jane said, "They know the two of us, but Mary is new. Mark, get in close and do a little eavesdropping." Sue slid her arm around Jane and pulled her close and said, "Okay then, let's get moving." Jane wrapped her arms around her and gave her a big kiss and slipped her the tongue.

Mark said, "Come on, Mary. We are going to catch up to Ed and your son." Mary asked, "Aren't we supposed to be a couple? And how long were you with this girl that crushed your heart?" Mark smiled and said, "Three years. I saved up eight grand to buy her a wedding ring. One day out of the blue she left, said she needed a change. And you're right. You pay." Mary shot him a look and then said, "That sucks." Mark said, "Look at these beautiful flowers. We are tourists, right? Let's enjoy the day." Mary said, "We find the clue. I could use ten grand."

Mark smiled and put his arm on her shoulders and pulled her to him and said, "Don't worry, you'll get your shit together. It just takes time. And little Johnny is going to be just fine. I told Ed he should buy him off of you or get a dog." Mary pulled away from him and asked, "What?" Mark chuckled and said, "Well a dog would be easier to train." Mary asked, "Whatever happened to your ex-girlfriend?" Mark said, "She changed everything, where she lived, her religion, her job, and her man." Mary said, "Well you are probably better without her." Mark said, "But all the time and energy, all the memories. You build a life with someone and they just flush it down the toilet."

Mary said, "If we are going to catch the boys, we have to move a lot quicker." Jane said, "They are inside and walking through the house." Mary turned and said, "No shit, that is where we are." Jane said, "What I mean is they got to the house and are walking through it."

Ed pulled Johnny though the house, pointing out stuff. He texted Gloria, "Hey, you are looking very nice today." Gloria looked around. Johnny waved. She texted back, "Who is the kid?" Ed texted, "Some kid. I am using him as cover." Gloria texted, "Where are you staying? We could hook up." Ed texted back, "At the resort. Do you know where the clue is?" Gloria looked at him, rubbed her boobies, and texted, "You want some of this? And I couldn't tell you if I knew."

Johnny said, "Did you see that?" Ed said, "Come on, we have to make some time." Johnny stood and said, "Look, all the instruments are playing all by themselves." Ed said, "That clue could be anywhere. Johnny, if you look closely, there are small tubes running to each instrument. See the drums and the violins?" Johnny stood and watched. Ed took out his phone and called Mary. He said, "Johnny and I are going to rush though this place to the whale. You guys carefully look for that monument or clue. This could be a bitch. It could be anywhere." Mary said, "Okay, just keep an eye on Johnny. He can disappear in a second."

Darwin from the Intels asked, "So tell me about this treasure hunt." Gloria said in a pissed-off tone, "We just need your ass to turn a key." Darwin asked, "What is she all pissed off about?" Jeremy said, "You're just lucky she hasn't called the cops on you, she isn't too keen on you taking advantage of those women." Darwin said, "Women? What women? So I took a girl's Buddha." Scott said, "That is grand theft. And you have been living off of old women for years." Darwin asked, "Did you ever take your hot grilled cheese and pull the bread apart? The cheese is stringy. That's what an old bag's pussy looks like." Randy said, "Now that is just disgusting. I was on your side until you said that. All women need some loving." Darwin said, "They knew what they were buying. We vacationed, I did whatever they wanted, I brought life back into their old, boring lives. So I spent a little money."

Gloria smiled and put a token in a music room and it came alive all the instruments started to play. She turned to Randy and said, "That is sweet." Randy smiled and gave Scott the thumbs-up. Scott shook his head and said, "It will never happen." Darwin asked, "What will never happen?" Jeremy said, "Randy has been trying to bang Gloria, and there is no way you're going to." Darwin said, "I bet you a hundred bucks I can slip her the weasel." Gloria turned and said, "I will take that bet." Scott said, "The clue could be anywhere." Jeremy said, "It should be a monument, could be a clue. Hell, the whole treasure hunt could have been in this place."

Mark and Mary stood right behind them watching the music show.

Mark pulled her close and whispered in her ear, "They don't have a clue.

Let's get ahead of them."

Team Odin got to the infinity room. Cherry said, "This place is amazing. Do you think it will hold us?" Joe said, "You're funny. Whole busloads of kids will get to the very end and get this baby to sway. I was here for a sixth-grade class trip." Robert said, "So you can be our guide." Joe said, "That was a long time ago. This place keeps changing. Like those gardens we went through, I don't remember them. That whole design building wasn't there. I do remember going through a bar with a lot of stuffed animals and a gun in a fake leg."

Cherry asked as they walked to the end of the infinity room, "You walked through a bar?" Joe said, "Yeah, it was weird. You walked right through it like it was part of the tour. We stopped and had a soda and chips." They got to the end and looked through a window, looking straight down to the ground. Robert started to rock back and forth. You could feel the whole room move. Dawn said, "Knock it off." Joe said, "Look at the construction. All huge steel beams coming out of a solid rock foundation." Ed and Johnny got to the room to see Odin at the end. Johnny said, "Whoa, this is cool, it goes on forever." Ed said, "It is an optical illusion. Let's quickly walk out to the end and I will show you. Don't say anything about the hunt or our team." Johnny asked, "Is that the other team?" Ed said, "They are all the way to the end, looking down, there must be a window."

Johnny looked through the windows and Ed said, "Don't do it. Don't you be touching the windows. There must be five thousand of them. You get them dirty, they will have you clean them all." Johnny said, "They would not, would they?" Ed started to walk down toward the point of the room. Johnny said, "There is no end, it keeps going forever."

Team Odin walked by. Cherry was talking. She said, "That would have been something to build this thing." Robert said, "Just think every twenty years or so some roofing company has to put a layer of shingles on here. That would be a rush."

Johnny asked Ed, "How did they build this? It sticks way out with nothing holding it up." Ed chuckled as he said, "Engineering, me boy. Okay now, do you see the room keeps getting smaller? That makes it look like it goes on forever, and you can't see anything but leaves though the window." Johnny said excitedly, "We are really high." Ed said, "We can't stay in one spot. We have to keep moving. We are going to get ahead of Odin." Johnny said, "I will race you," and he took off running.

Ed jogged to keep up. They got to the door. Ed said, "That's it, no more running in this place. Too many people and too many things to break." He took out his phone and called Sue. He asked, "Where are you?" Sue said, "We are in the house. This is so cool. I love how they carpeted the ceiling and the whole living with nature thing. Jane said you would freeze your ass off in the winter, this huge Japanese window and the Tiffany stained glass." Ed said, "Oh for Christ's sakes, remember why we are here. We just seen Odin. We are at the infinity room. Keep an eye out. The clue could be anywhere."

Johnny said, "I have to go to the bathroom." Ed said, "Fine, let's move." They started to move quickly in search of a bathroom. They found one. It was filled with trains. Johnny was just amazed. Ed said, "Wash your hands. Odin is in the gun room." Johnny said, "Guns? Real guns?"

Ed led him into the gun room close to Odin and listened. Well, tried to listen. He had to answer three hundred questions from Johnny. Cherry asked, "How did they weld all those pistols together?" Joe said, "These are old, single shot, so if you wanted more shots you just blacksmith them together. That was way before electricity." Johnny said, "These are before electricity? Wow, look at this one." Ed said, "That, my boy, is a Gatling gun, the first truly automatic weapon back in 1861. You can read, can't you?" Johnny looked up at him and said, "Really? Do you want me to read it to you?" Ed said, "That would take forever."

Ed's phone chirped. He looked at the text, it was Gloria. Johnny said, "Was it my mom? I wish she was with us." Ed said, "Faster. Oh look, something you would like. Hundreds of dollhouses from around the world." Johnny said, "Dolls, Let's go." Ed said, "Now take your time. Quickly glance over all the houses. Is one like a monument?" Johnny started to pull Ed along. Ed said, "You're right. Let's quickly walk through them. This should slow down Odin."

They came to a room with small saving banks, all kinds of banks, clown banks, which led into storefronts, small buildings. It wound through the place. Ed said, "Here we go, there is the whale." Johnny said, "Oh my god, it is huge." Ed said, "Let's look closely but quickly. Look at every ship but not more than ten seconds. There are a lot of ships." Johnny said, "There, big. Let's go up and look at the whale." Ed called Mary and said, "We made it to the whale. There is a big sheet of glass in front of it. I don't think you can jump into its mouth. Where are you?" Mary said, "We are in front of the blue room, watching the orchestra. You know everything moves. The monument could be behind a bass or anything." Ed said, "Yeah, this is going to be something. These ships are behind the glass. Some of them are fifteen to twenty feet long." Johnny asked, "Can I spit over the railing?" Ed was surprised. "No, what the hell are you thinking?"

They went to the third floor where they could see into the whale's mouth. There was just a guy in a boat. "I don't think it is in this room." Mary said, "Shit, we need to find it. It could be anywhere in this place." Ed smiled and said, "Keep looking. I will call you if we find it. Oh, here is the boy." Johnny took the phone and said, "Did you get to the circus? They have a miniature circus set up and all the weird banks. In the bathroom there are all kinds of trains. You should see the *Titanic*, it is huge." Ed took the phone and said, "Let's move. I think we have to find someone who works here. It's like finding a needle in a haystack."

They looked at the *Titanic*. Johnny said, "It hit an iceberg in 1912 and 1,517 people drowned." Ed said, "Come on, we want to find that monument. Your mom could really use the money." His phone rang. He answered it. "Mary said, "We found Intel. They are watching a full orchestra of mannequins." Ed said, "You had me going when you said you found it. Yes, we have been through there. So do you think the monument is there?" Mary said, "Well, it could be." Ed said, "Call me when you find it." He looked down at Johnny and said, "You mother is weird. Nice girl, but weird." Johnny asked, "Do you like my mom?" Ed smiled and said, "Well let's put it this way. I don't dislike her. Do I want to date her? Well not really. Just think of the drama." Johnny looked up at him, his eyes were brimming with tears. Ed said, "Don't give me that shit. I enjoy my life the way it is. I am doing this because I want to, not for the money. If you're going to act like a baby, I am not teaming up with you again." Johnny looked sad. He slowly followed Ed.

Intel was slowly catching up to Odin. Randy was pointing out the way black people were portrayed and he said, "Look at this. They have a brother with his head chopped of." Jeremy said, "That's an Indian. Look at his hair, it is straight. Might be a white guy. And it is preserved in some kind of liquid." Scott said, "These are historic circus props, just put in different setting." Gloria said, "Dickhead—I mean, Darwin, we are looking for a monument, a tall building-looking thing with a pyramid on the top." Darwin asked, "Do I get a kiss if I find it?" Gloria said, "Sure, you can kiss Randy. Just find it and you get a hundred bucks."

Jeremy exclaimed, "Holy fuck, there are dollhouses up the ass. I mean a thousand of the cock-sucking things." Scott said, "Language please. There are kids in here." Jeremy said, "How are we going to find that stupid thing?" Gloria said, "Just take your time. Look over every one. I think the monument is too tall, it would stick out." Randy said, "None of the monuments were the same, were they? Who says it can't be six feet long and look like a house?" Scott rolled his eyes and said, "Okay, let's take it slow, but quickly."

Gloria said, "There are so many different kinds of houses. This is really cool." Darwin asked, "So if this monument can be any shape, how do we find it?" Randy said, "Haven't you been listening, fool? It has five keyholes and the keys have to be turned at the same time." Darwin said, "Okay, now I get it. What do the keys look like?" Gloria pulled out her key that was hanging around her neck. Darwin asked, "Can I feel it, smell it, and maybe taste it?" Gloria said, "There is something wrong with you." Darwin said, "The only thing wrong with me is the feelings I have for you." Scott said, "The warrant for your arrest is kind of working against you, isn't it?" Jeremy said, "The way you have swindled those old ladies out of the money is kind of wrong."

Randy said, "I think we should just plow through this place and see if it is right out in the open." Scott said, "But then if we miss it, we have to start again from the beginning." Gloria said, "Okay, let's walk through this exhibit. I think you are right, just keep an eye out for something that is out of place." Randy chuckled and said, "Girl, everything is out of place here." Jeremy said, "This place is amazing. You could hide an elephant in here easily." Scott said, "The clue is 'whale.' Let's just run to the whale and see if it is in that room." Jeremy said, "I am up for that." Gloria said, "Just let's keep an eye out. It is somewhere here. I can feel we are at the right place."

Odin got to the whale room. Cherry said, "Wow, I knew it was going to be big, but holy smokes." Dawn said, "I like the music,

'Octopus's Garden' by the Beatles." Joe said, "Well, Robert, let's see if you are right and the monument is in its mouth. We can walk right up and look." Dawn said, "They must have bought a whole museum of ships. Look at the old sailing ships." Robert said, "Let's get moving. Look at every one. I don't know what we would do if we find it. They are behind glass." Cherry said, "There must be a walkway behind them." Dawn asked, "Is this Moby Dick? If so, where is his . . . you know?" Joe asked, "What is on the bottom of the ocean? Moby's dick." Robert said, "Let's get a move on. We are still in the lead."

They quickly looked at the three stories of ships. Cherry looked into the whale's mouth and said, "Boy, this thing is huge. There is a guy in a rain jacket sitting in a boat, but no monument." Robert caught up to her and said, "That boat he is sitting in looks like a twenty-footer. This thing is huge. Let's just keep moving." Dawn walked over by the *Titanic* and asked, "Has anyone seen a picture of the *Titanic* next to a new cruise ship? It is tiny in comparison."

Ed called Mary and asked, "Where are you? We are coming into a pizza restaurant. We are going to catch a quick bite and a soda." Mary said, "We are in a room with a half dozen hot air balloons. This place is huge." Ed asked, "Do you still see the Intels?" Mary said, "Yes, sir. We are following them, and they are starting to move a bit quicker." Ed said to the person behind the counter, "Two Cokes and two slices of pepperoni." Mary said, "He doesn't like pepperoni." Ed said, "Yeah. So have you talked to Sue?" Mary said, "Yes, they are going to catch up. You do know he is not going to eat that." Ed said, "More for me. You keep an eye on the Intels, tell me if you catch up to the Odins." Mary hung up and said, "I bet he is talking to that whore Gloria." Mark said, "Someone is getting a bit jealous, aren't they?" Mary said, "The tour goes through a pizza place."

Johnny took his soda and said, "I don't like pepperoni." Ed said, "Well when you buy you can order." Johnny said, "That's not fair, I don't have any money." Ed said, "Just pick the pepperoni off then. Are you hungry? If not, you don't have to eat." They sat down. Johnny said quietly, "Fine, whatever." Ed said, "See the clock on the wall? Five minutes we leave."

Five minutes went by. Jonny had half his pizza gone and almost all of his Coke. Ed said, "Time is up. We are going to the bathroom and get moving." Johnny said, "I don't have to go." Ed asked, "Was I asking? I don't think so. Your mom could use ten grand." Johnny shrugged his shoulders and said, "Fine." He took a big bite of pizza and dropped it on his plate. They went into the bathroom. Johnny said, "Wow, look at the bear." There was a full mount of a grizzly bear. Ed said, "That is a grizzly, and over there is a coyote, geese hanging from the ceiling. This is kind of cool. The urinals are built right in the rocks." Johnny said as he pointed, "What is that?" Ed said, "That is a full mount of a mountain lion or cougar. They have them in the woods around here; not many, but a few." Johnny said, "And those are big deer." Ed said, "Watch what you are doing? Those are ether caribou or reindeer, I really don't know the difference. Wash your hands. Let's go."

Mary called and asked, "How are we going to find the monument? Mark and I are on the Streets of Yesteryear, it just keeps going on." Ed asked, "Are you still shadowing the Intels?" Mary said, "They are starting to move faster."

Ed led Johnny to the carousel. Johnny's jaw dropped and he said, "Wow, look at all the horses and the angels." Ed said, "Now, you are looking for the monument. Let's step closer to the carousel. That would be a great place to hide it." Johnny said, "It feels like the room is moving." Ed said, "Now don't be doing that. It is just because the carousel is so big and it is moving. Now there isn't a single horse on it. There are 269 animals, 20,000 lights, and 182 chandeliers. That makes it the largest in the world." Johnny said, "Ha, they lied. There is a horse." Ed said, "That's a unicorn. There are hundreds of horses hanging on the wall. We watch the carousel go around one more time then we move on. I have this feeling we are going to go through this again."

Johnny took Ed's hand and started to walk. He said, "We have to find this clue. My mom really needs the money." Ed said, "Your mom is going to have to go bankrupt. She is so far in debt. But don't you worry, I have people working on it." Johnny looked up and asked, "Really? Are we going to get our house back?" Ed smiled and said, "No, but you should be able to buy a new one. You're never going to live in that town again." Johnny asked, "Where do you live?" Ed smiled as he said, "Now that all depends. In the summer I have a cabin in Colorado, one in Maine, and one in Oregon. And in the winter I have cabins in Texas, California, and Florida. Oh yes, one in Hawaii." Johnny said, "Wow, you must be rich." Ed said, "They are investment properties and it is somewhere to hang my hat." Johnny said, "That's seven houses." Ed said, "And you know I am always traveling, so I am never there." Ed said, "Now this is interesting. Look at the size of this steam engine. It is huge, must weigh forty tons. Now look for the monument and let's keep moving. We want to stay ahead of everyone."

Mary called Ed and asked, "Where are you?" He said, "We just walked through Satan's mouth. That was weird. Keep looking and watch the Intels. I have no idea how far the Odins are. You should be coming up to the restaurant area. If the Intels stop, you stop." Mary said, "Mark is in charge, remember?"

Ed rolled his eyes and said, "The organ room. Oh my god, look at the size of that organ." Johnny said, "There are so many. That one has five sets of keys." Ed said, "Look at that one. The pipes are over ten feet in diameter. And some are like thirty feet tall. Whoa, there's our monument." Johnny asked, "Where? I don't see it." Ed said as he pointed, "Let's see, one, two, three, four, then go down like five feet. It is stuck between those two." Johnny said excitedly, "I see it, I see it." Ed said, "Now how do we get to it?" Johnny said, "Call my mom."

Ed called and said, "Okay, we found it. Slowly get by the Intels without alerting them and call Jane. Let's do this." Mark and Mary slowly walked by the Intels. Mark didn't look at them, and they had never seen Mary before. They quickly walked through not looking at anything. Jane and Sue chatted, not even looking at the people. Mark and Mary walked right by them. Mark leaned in close to Mary and said, "You did call them, didn't you?" Jane and Sue slowly followed them through the museum, taking in the exhibits.

Odin was sitting at a table having pizza and a beer when Joe said to Robert, "Hey, that is Team Three. Remember that cute little redhead?" Robert said, "You're right. The blonde is with them. I never forget a nice ass." Cherry said, "You're right. The tall guy is Mark. Let's let them move and shadow them." Dawn said, "There are plenty of people moving through here, they won't notice us."

Team Three quickly moved through the place, weaving through till they caught up to Ed and Johnny. Johnny ran to them and said excitedly to his mother, "We found it, it is right over here." They followed Johnny to a point where you could just see the monument. Johnny said proudly as he pointed, "Right there, up against the wall." Mark said, "Wow." Jane said, "Holy fuck, how are we going to get that?" Johnny grabbed his mom's hand and said, "We have to do this quickly, there are cameras. Ed has figured out a way, and I get to help." Sue said, "Oh god, this is not going to be pretty." Mark asked as they reached Ed, "You have to be kidding me, right? You're going to climb freehand up and over those pipes, walking on the lip of the pipes, and you're talking thirty feet off the ground." Ed said, "Yeah, that's what I was thinking. I don't see any other way." Sue said, "We could get some planking, a few ladders, safety harnesses." Jane said, "Okay, I am in. How are we doing this?"

Ed said, "Okay, are we doing this? There are cameras. We have to do this quickly. Mary, we need to use the boy." Mary said, "Damn, it's ten grand. Let's do it." Ed said, "Mark, you are our first lift. I go first then everyone get up and follow me. There is no stopping. We have to do this quickly. Mary, you carry Mark's key and give it to Johnny when he needs it." Jane said, "Good idea, that kid drops everything and it falls into one of those pipes." Ed said, "Okay, let's do this. Up over the railing. Mark, to the shortest pipe. Give me a boost."

Mark put his back to a pipe that was ten feet tall. He cupped his hands. Ed grabbed Johnny and put him on his shoulders and said, "I will boost you up to the rim of the pipe, don't fall in." Johnny's face drained of color. He asked, "Don't what?" Ed said, "Trust me, buddy." He stepped into Mark's hands. Ed stepped onto his shoulder and told Johnny to stand, then Ed reached up and grabbed onto the pipe and pulled himself up. Jane came up next, then Mary and Sue.

They all followed Ed. He kept on lifting Johnny and the girls to the next pipe. Soon they were at the monument.

The Odins stood out of sight and watched.

Ed said, "Okay, this is how it is going to work. Sue, you are going first. You squeeze in there. Jane, you get on my shoulders. And, Johnny, you need to get on hers. Now, Mary, you need to get on my back. Jane, you need to find the keyhole. It has to be on the side somewhere." Mary asked, "Are you kidding me? This is crazy." Jane said, "And we are standing on a three-inch edge of a thirty-foot pipe." Ed said, "Johnny, this is important. Do not drop anything. The money is going to come out of the top. You put it in your shirt, got it?" Johnny said, "I won't drop it, Mommy."

Sue leaned onto a pipe as she slid around it squeezed between two pipes. Ed crouched down and Jane got on his shoulders, Johnny climbed onto hers, and Ed stood, holding on to the monument. Mary climbed on his back. Ed said, "Okay, everyone, put in your key." Mary reached around the monument and found the keyhole. Sue took the bottom one. Jane stretched to find the one on the other side, and Johnny stood on Jane's shoulders. Johnny said, "I have it in." Ed said, "Okay, wait. I will count down, three, two, one, turn." Johnny said, "It opened." Jane said, "Okay, carefully take out the money and put it down your shirt." Ed said, "Do not let go of the monument, do it one-handed." Mary said, "And hurry up, I am slipping." Johnny said, "I have it, now what?" Ed took out his key and the door closed. He said, "Carefully take out your key. Has everyone done that? Now, Sue, climb back in your corner and help Mary get down, then I will squat down and get Jane down."

They were all down, standing on top of the pipe. Ed said, "Johnny, before we get going, give me the money one stack at a time." Johnny protested, "I got it." Ed said, "Do as you are told. I don't need you falling." They all filed down, skirting the tubes and dropping from one to the other. Mary hugged Ed when they got down. She said, "If one of us fell, they would have died." Ed said, "Well, everything went to plan." Mark said, "Let's get the hell out of here before anyone sees us." Ed said, "Good idea. Johnny, my boy, got all five bundles of cash. We are doing well. We will look at the clue when we get to the van."

Odin stood looking at the pipes. Then Cherry said, "We have to find someone." Robert said, "I think we can do this. I can reach the first two. It is a stretch. Then, Joe, you stand on my shoulders and get the one to the left. Cherry, the one on the right. And, Dawn, you stand on her and get the one on the top." Joe said, "Really? This isn't going to work." Robert said, "Let's do this. I will boost you all up. Joe, you just hang there. I will pull you up." Joe sarcastically said, "This sounds like a damn good plan." In ten minutes they were up at the monument. Robert said, "Damn it all to hell, I think you are right. We need to get someone." Dawn said, "No, you are right. Just get into position, put both of your keys into the keyholes. Now, Joe, you need to stand on his shoulders. I will climb on your back. And, Dawn, baby, stand on my shoulder." Robert said, "We are all going to die."

Robert put both keys in their holes then stretched out, holding them. Joe stepped on his knee, then one foot on his shoulder, balancing, then put his other on a pipe to steady himself. Cherry said, "Don't move. Joe, you got your key in?" Joe said, "Just hurry up." Cherry climbed up onto his back. She held on to the monument with one hand and put her key into the slot. She said, "Okay, Dawn, let's hurry up."

A crowd started to build in the room as they watched the team assemble. Dawn got on top of Joe and asked Cherry, "Is this going to work?" Cherry said, "I have a hold on this, just hurry up." Dawn held on to the monument and climbed up Robert then Joe and Cherry, standing one foot on her shoulder. She put her key in the slot and said, "Okay, on the count of one, three, two, one." They turned their keys and Dawn reached up and took out the money. She pulled out her key and worked her way back down to Robert. Cherry said, "This isn't good, I can't move." Joe reached out and pushed her up. Cherry got hold of the edge of the monument and pulled herself upright. Joe said, "You owe me one." Cherry crawled down him and Joe got both keys out of the slots. They made it down.

Ten minutes later, they were on the ground. Dawn handed out the bundles of cash. Joe said, "'Some have nuts, some don't.' What the fuck kind of clue is that?" Dawn said, "Some are girls and some are guys." An old guy behind them said, "Sometimes you feel like a nut, sometimes you don't. Almond Joy has nuts, Mounds don't. That was a nice bit of climbing." Robert said, "Thanks, we have to get out of here before the cops get here."

Odin headed out quickly. They found Team Three sitting in the van looking at their smart phones. Cherry Googled Almond Joy then Mounds near Spring Green. She smiled and said, "Let's sneak out of the parking lot. We are going to the Cave of the Mounds, it is twenty-seven miles and it will take a half hour."

Ed asked, "Johnny, did you see that?" Johnny looked up from his game and asked, "What, did I miss something?" Ed said, "Look out the window. Think what did you miss." Mark said, "The van, it's gone." Ed asked, "Was I asking you? How is Johnny going to learn if you give him the answers?" Jane said, "Where are they going?" Mark pulled up their GPS tracker and started the engine. He said, "We will find out."

They were on the road for a few minutes when Mary said, "Cave of the Mounds, that's it." Ed said, "Caves are nasty things. Watch for cave spiders." Johnny asked, "Do they have spiders in caves?" Ed said, "Sometimes, and they leave a nasty infection." Ed's phone chirped. He looked at it and quickly texted back, "Organ room." Sue asked, "Is that your wife?" Ed said, "Oh hell no. Did that once, not doing it again. Just some business." Johnny said, "It's guns, isn't it?"

The Intels started to backtrack to the organ room. The room was huge, there were all kinds of organs. Randy asked, "Now why the hell do you think it is in here?" Gloria said, "I know it is here. Can't you feel it?" Randy said, "This bitch is off her rocker. We have been through here." Scott said as he pointed, "My god, she is right. It is in plain view. If you stand here, up on top of those pipes." Randy said, "You're fucking crazy if you're thinking about climbing up there." Jeremy asked, "Okay, smarty-pants, how do you figure we get up there without climbing?" Darwin said, "A hundred bucks to climb up there? No thanks." Gloria said, "Five hundred." Darwin said,

"Oh, that will do. So tell me, how does this work again?" Scott said, "Oh for Christ's sakes, we put in our keys and turn at once and get our payday." Jeremy said, "Okay, let's look around and see if we can find a ladder or some planking." Gloria said, "There is a ladder over there." Scott said, "Wait a minute until the coast is clear and we sneak over there."

Randy said, "There is a shitload of people here. What is going to happen when they see us?" Darwin said, "We go downtown to the cop shop, get a free meal, and answer a bunch of questions." Scott said quietly, "Fuck. Dar, do you have health insurance?" Darwin smiled and said, "Yes, I have health care. Not good stuff, my deductible is fifteen grand. It is through the state." Randy said, "Come on, you white fucks, let's get going." Darwin asked, "Did you hear what he called you?" Jeremy said, "Yeah, let's go, cracker."

They climbed over the railing and snuck into the exhibit. The room was huge. Randy led them to the pipes. Gloria said, "This way. Around the back side of this one, see? It is a rung of a ladder. We go up behind the pipes and just have to walk around one." Darwin said, "I really don't like heights." Randy said, "Suck it up, buttercup, it is five big ones." Gloria said, "Scott, you're our leader. You first." Scott said, more to himself, "This captain shit sucks." He went up the ladder about thirty feet. Gloria was right behind him. She said, "Okay, step off on the pipe and shimmy around and see if you can see the clue." Jeremy stepped off and said, "Shit, this is high, and there is nothing to hold on to." Gloria said, "Just don't look down. Everything will be fine." Scott said, "We need a short ladder and a five-foot plank to put it on."

Gloria texted Randy, "We need a short ladder and a five-foot plank." Randy texted her back asking if he was a hardware store. Randy said to Darwin, "Look around and see if there is a ladder and a five-foot plank." A couple of minutes later Darwin said, "I found the ladder and plank, and a rope to pull it up with." Jeremy said, "Good job. Randy, you climb up with the rope and we will tie the plank on." Randy said, "Why the fuck should I pull the stuff up?" Darwin said, "You fucking monkey, get your ass up there or we are going to get caught." Randy pointed at him and said, "Don't you be calling me no monkey."

As soon as Randy got ten feet up the ladder, Darwin said to Jeremy, "He talks a lot of shit but he can't take it, can he?" Jeremy said, "Oh, he is a dick, thinks the world owes him something just because he is black." Darwin said, "Are all your clues this hard?" Randy got up the ladder and dropped the rope. Darwin tied on the plank and Randy pulled the plank up and handed it to Gloria, who slid it to Scott, who stood on it, saying, "This is a pain in the ass. One false move and you fall thirty feet to your death." Randy dropped the rope again and Darwin tied on the rope and up it went. Randy slid the ladder to Gloria. She slid the ladder out, then crept out and stood next to him. Soon everyone was standing on the plank shoulder to shoulder. Jeremy said, "Okay, Gloria is the lightest. She can go up the ladder and I will go up with her. Darwin, here is your key. Do not drop this. Put it in the side keyhole and turn it when I say *one*." Everyone got into place and got their keys in the holes and turned, opening the door on top for Gloria to grab the money. She put it in her bra. Once they got down to the ground, she handed the money out. Randy put the bundle of cash to his cheek and said, "Still warm, gets my junk growing." Gloria rolled her eyes. She took five hundred-dollar bills and gave them to Darwin. Scott said, "You can ride with us. If we are the first ones to the monument, it is five grand." Randy said, "It's ten grand." Scott, Jeremy, and Gloria turned and gave him a look. He said, "Oh, my bad. Yeah, it is five grand." Darwin said, "No, it is ten grand. And for ten grand I will help you."

Scott said, "The clue is 'some have nuts, some don't.'" Randy said, "Now that could be anything, and nowadays you can add nuts to anyone." Gloria said, "That is sick. If you Google it, all that comes up is allergies, mostly peanut." Scott said, "Well that is a big thing nowadays." Jeremy said, "It's a huge business. That is why they don't give you peanuts on a plane anymore. Some people are so allergic just the peanut odor can cause an attack." Darwin said, "It's all a bunch of shit. People are a bunch crybabies." Randy said, "I was in college and a girl ate something at a party that had nuts in it. She went into ana-phylactic shock, her whole head swelled up. Someone hit her with an epinephrine they had for bee stings. We rushed her to the hospital. I mean her head swelled to twice the size, she couldn't breathe." Jeremy said, "So what happened?" Randy said, "Hell, I don't know. We partied until some broad dragged me to her place." Gloria said, "In your wildest dreams."

They got to the van. Gloria said, "It smells like shit in here." Scott said, "Everyone, check your shoes." Randy said, "Darwin, it is you. You smell like shit." Darwin said, "Well I did take a shit." Scott asked, "Did you wash your hands?" Dar said, "We were in a hurry. I wiped them on my pants." Randy said, "That's fucking gross, dude." Gloria asked, "When is the last time you washed your jeans?" Darwin said, "You don't wash jeans. Who the hell washes jeans?" Jeremy said, "Everyone, who doesn't wash jeans?" Scott said, "Okay, Darwin, we will stop. You can buy a pair of jeans and burn those."

Darwin whispered to Randy, "Hey, what's up with Gloria? Is she banging anyone? I would eat a quarter mile of her shit just to lick her asshole." Gloria turned and said, "Never in a million years." Jeremy said, "Now that is pretty sick. I had a teacher once, she was super hot. I was doing terrible in her class. All I could think about was her, so I imagined her taking a dump. That did it." Darwin said, "Have you ever had a girl squat on a glass table and take a shit? That's cool." Randy asked, "Are you some kind of sicko?" Jeremy said, "That is a thing. I hit a search and over twenty-four million hits. What is this world coming to?" Randy said, "Women are sick. Why would you do that?" Scott said, "Let's get back to the task at hand. Some have nuts, some don't. Almond Joy has nuts, Mounds don't." Gloria said, "That's it. The Cave of the Mounds. It is close by." She picked up the GPS and programmed it.

CHAPTER TWENTY-SIX

Cave of the Mounds

Team Three was the first to get to the cave. There were signs all over, you couldn't miss it. Mark said, "Okay, I will drop you guys at the door and find a place to park." Ed said, "Mary, take the cash out of the glove box and pay the admission. I will walk with Mark." They stopped and Johnny said, "I will walk with you guys." Ed said flatly, "No, you will do as you are told. We could be on a five-mile hike. You keep your eye out for the clue." Mary said, "He is right you know, that was a long walk through the House on the Rock."

Sue said, "Let's hurry up and get the tickets. I think this is a guided tour, so they will only take so many people at a time." Jane slid her arm around Sue's waist and said, "I want you forever, let's get married." Sue turned and kissed her full on the lips and said, "Now is not the time to discuss this. And yes, I would love to spend the rest of my life with you." Mary had tears streaming down her face. Johnny asked, "Mom, what is wrong?" Mary choked out, "That was so beautiful." Jane and Sue turned their heads to look at Mary. Johnny said, "Come on, the guys are already on their way."

They went inside and up to the counter, got the tickets, and got in line for the next tour. Ed was carrying a small backpack. They cut the line to get up to the girls. Ed said, "Okay, are we ready? Johnny, did you go to the bathroom." Johnny said, "I don't have to go." Ed gave him a stern look. Mark said, "Come on, Johnny, I have to lance the lizard myself. You can't pee down in the cave. In fact, you aren't supposed to touch anything. In a virgin cave you have to disinfect everything." Johnny asked, "Why?" Mark said, "Because the spores—you know what spores are? They're like little eggs from plants. You can pick them up with your shoes or brushing against a plant, whatever. They want to keep the caves in pure, natural condition. Now let's move. We have to catch the next tour."

Ed asked as he stood in line, "So have you questioned the tour guide about the question mark?" Mary said, "The girls got engaged. Jane asked Sue if she would marry her." Ed said, "In line at the Cave of the Mounds? What the hell were you thinking?" Sue said, "It was a spontaneous thing, and I don't know anyone I would rather spend my life with." Jane said, "That is so cute, I love you too." Sue blushed.

Mark crawled under the ropes to get in line with Johnny in tow. He asked, "So did we find out where the clue is?" Mary said, "We were just talking about Jane and Sue getting married." Mark said, "Really now? Johnny didn't say anything about that." Johnny looked up and said, "Sorry." Ed said, "This is a big step. When is the wedding?" Jane smiled and said, "This is all new, so we haven't set a date." Sue said, "This is just a promise that we are to be as one, nobody will stand between us." Jane said, "That is heavy. I too will have nobody but you, and we shall be together forever." Johnny asked, "What the hell is going on?" Ed said, "That is what I would like to know. We have a job to do."

Mark said, "Johnny, let's just focus. Ed, you're in charge of the child. If the tour guide is a guy, Jane, you suck up to him. If it is a girl, I will handle it." Ed said, "Slip them a fifty, these are probably college students." Mary leaned into Ed and said, "It was so beautiful. Jane just asked her out on the sidewalk." Mark asked, "Jane, did you get down on one knee? I did and she ended up ripping my heart out of my chest, leaving a big gaping hole." Johnny said, "Really?" Mark said, "No, not really. I gave her everything. I loved her more than myself, and she kicked me to the curb. She said her life had no meaning. She wanted a change." ED asked, "When was that?" Mark said, "Three years ago. Let's not talk about it." Ed said, "How much did that cost?" Mark said, "Seventy-eight thousand dollars. Lost my house, my car. Sold my cabin, fishing boat. The only thing I got was a timeshare that makes me think of her. Damn near had to give that away." Sue said, "Three years, move on, dude. Find love, get married, have kids." Mark said, "Still too soon. Don't know what is going to happen in life, but I am never going down that road again." Johnny pulled on his mom's pants leg and said, "He needs a girlfriend." Mark said, "Oh hell no, you're not doing that." Ed chuckled and said, "And Johnny here needs a daddy." Mark smiled and said, "Fuck you and the horse you rode in on." Ed said, "Jane, I need your phone. Now the two of you stand together. A light kiss. This is a milestone, a moment to remember."

They went into a room and watched a short film on how the cave was found, then the tour guide started her speech. "Back in 1939, they were blasting limestone in a quarry and they found an opening to this cave. There were so many souvenir hunters that the cave was closed for a few years. Now if you will follow me." Johnny looked up at Ed and asked, "Was that before you were born?" Ed said as he put his finger to his lips, "Yes, a long time before I was born." Mary said, "Would you two be quiet? Johnny, this is a national nature landmark, so it is a federal crime to break anything."

Ed worked his way to the front of the tour. He cleared his throat loud enough to make an echo. The tour guide looked at him and asked, "Do you have a question?" Ed looked her right in the eye and slowly down to his hand where he was palming a fifty-dollar bill. He asked as he shook her hand, "Good day, miss. I am Edward, and I would like to know about a question mark. They are steel and can be from six inches to six feet. Have you seen one?" She said, "In the cave? A question mark, like the punctuation?" Ed said, "Yes. We are on a treasure hunt and they hold the clues." She said, "Not that I know of. And if you get off the trail you would leave foot marks that would last for a hundred years." Johnny said, "Cool." Mary slapped him on the back of the head and said, "No, don't even think about it." Ed worked his way back to the team. Jane said, "Let's just take the tour. Keep our eye out and watch for anything out of the ordinary." Mark said as he flashed a small flashlight into the corners of the cave as they were walking through. "Glad I brought this flashlight, but she is right you know. If you step off the path you would leave footprints." The guide said, "Yes, if you look over to your right, there is a set of footprints up the flow stone and to where that stalagmite that was cut off. That was done in 1939, so stay on the path." Jane said, "Well then, look on the path, under the staircases."

Mark said, "We should have spent time in the gift shop. Wouldn't that have been something?" Johnny said, "They have cool rocks and fossilized dinosaur poop." Sue said, "They do not." Johnny said, "They do. Really, they do, don't they?" Mark said, "Nope, didn't see a thing." Johnny whined, "But you showed it to me." Ed said, "The baby is getting tired. Time for his nap." Mary gave him a look and said one word, "Really."

Mark said quietly "it has to be here" he shined his flashlight into corners. Every time they went down a staircase he looked under it. Sue asked, "Are there spiders in this cave?" The guide said, "Because the cave was completely enclosed, there are no bats or fish and no spiders. The only thing that is living in here are small spring-tailed insects that seep in with the rain. You might be able to see one in one of the pools."

Johnny was looking in every puddle to find one of the cave insects. Mark was the last one on the tour. He looked under every staircase that wasn't stone. Ed noticed Mark fall behind. He snuck off and found Mark crawling under a staircase. Ed asked, "Did you find it?" Mark said, "Yeah, it's a tight squeeze. I should have had one of the girls do it, but we want to keep this a secret. I have the key in it. There we go, I got it." Mark crawled out and read the clue as they caught up to the others. "Penicillin, that's it, that is the clue." Ed pulled Mary close and said into her ear, "The clue is penicillin." Mary told Jane what the clue was. She automatically pulled out her cell phone and said, "Shit," which echoed through the huge room they were going through. Everyone stopped to look at her. She sheepishly said, "No bars down here." The tour guide chuckled and said, "No, there is no cell service down here." Mark handed Johnny the flashlight. This just thrilled him. He looked at every nook and corner. Mark bent down and said, "Look for the clue." Johnny looked everywhere they went. Sue whispered, "That is cruel." Mark smiled and said, "But funny, right?" Mary said quietly, "It's fricken freezing in here." Ed said, "We are almost done. Johnny is having a good time." Mary said, "I seen you slip him a candy bar." Ed said, "It's just a little sugar. The little bastard is going to freeze down here." Mary said, "I did bring him a sweatshirt, but the men aren't wearing any, so he isn't going to."

They got back to the surface. Johnny asked, "Can we go to the gift shop?" He grabbed Jane by the hand and pulled. He said, "I will show you the dinosaur poop." Jane complained, "Johnny, we have to figure out this clue." Mark said, "Spread out everyone. Ah nuts, they must have seen our van." Mary said, "There's your little whore Gloria. I bet you would like to do her." Sue smiled and said, "Someone is a little jealous." Ed blushed. He walked over by Gloria and gave her a wink. She pushed her tongue against her cheek, then reached down and grabbed her crotch. Ed turned to see Mary's reaction. You could see she was pissed. Ed walked by her and said, "You should have never listened." She took out her phone and started to research penicillin in Wisconsin.

Ed took out his phone and texted Gloria, "Hey there, you're looking good today." She texted back, "It looks like your girlfriend is pissed. So did you find the clue?" Ed texted back, "Not my girlfriend, and you know I can't tell you." Mark came up and said, "Ed, penicillin is made from mold, right? There is a mold graveyard a few miles from here." Ed said, "Okay, there is a connection. I really don't see how they go together. Let's ask the girls. Oh, do you get your flashlight back from Johnny before he loses it."

Ed and Mark walked into the gift shop. Mary said, "What the hell was that? Are you planning a date?" Mark asked as he looked around, "Let's go into the van. There may be ears out here." The team loaded into the van. Mark said, "Okay, what have you found?" Sue said, "The UW sent penicillin over to the D-Day invasion at Normandy." Mark said, "This is what I have found, there is a mold graveyard not far from here and they have huge molds of all kinds of stuff." Jane said, "What has that to do with penicillin?" Mary said, "Penicillin is made of bread mold, so it does have something to do with it." Ed said, "Let's go there. Everyone, keep on researching, and it really isn't a mold it is a fungus penicillin is made from." Sue said,

"This is interesting. They show you how to make penicillin at home." Ed said don't believe everything you read on the internet.

Johnny asked as he ate jelly out of one of those packets he took from the table at breakfast, "What is the difference between jelly and jam?" Ed said, "The difference is jelly is made from fruit juice and jam is made of crushed fruit." Johnny said, "I like the jam better." Mark leaned over and said to Mary, "I can't jelly my dick up your ass, but I sure could jam it." Mary asked, "Have I told you, you are one sick puppy?" Mark said with a smile, "Not today."

Johnny asked Ed, "Do you think Mark likes my mom?" Ed said loud enough so everyone would hear, "Yes, I think Mark likes your mom. We all like your mom." Johnny gave Ed the puppy eyes and asked, "Do you like my mom?" Ed asked, "Why do you keep asking me? Yes, I think your mom is a very nice person. Now Mark, on the other hand, is a dick, aren't you, Mark?" Mark said, "I am trying. So this mold thing yard, are we trespassing?" Jane said, "Nope, it is open to the public. We just have to watch out for wasps." Ed said, "FAST stands for Fiberglass Animals, Shapes, and Trademarks." Sue said, "Can't really see anything on Google Earth, but YouTube shows it has elephants, lumberjacks, all kinds of weird stuff."

Scott said, "Dammit all to hell, Team Three figured it out. We shouldn't have stopped to eat." Gloria said, "It is just a clue. Let's go and see if we can find it." Jeremy said, "Now this is an environment that leaves foot marks for decades, so if someone steps outside the tour lines we will be able to see. So bring flashlights." Scott asked, "Are you into spelunking? That is, cave exploration?" Jeremy said, "I have been in some huge caves. Carlsbad is enormous." Gloria said, "I did the Ruby Falls one, the waterfalls was beautiful." Randy said, "Caves freak me out, it's just weird." Gloria said, "This is a tourist thing. It has stairs, walkways, it should be better than that mine we did in Michigan." Scott said, "That was before him. We had a clue across a lake, underground. That was something."

Darwin cut the cheese. Scott ran all the windows down and said, "What the fuck? Couldn't you wait until you were outside the van?" Randy said, "Whoa, that brings tears to your eyes." Gloria said, "Let's just get in there and get that clue before Team Three finds the next one. We are falling behind." They got in line and were in the small theater watching the short film on the history of the cave. Gloria said, "Next stop we get Darwin here some new clothes and some deodorant." They went through the cave shining their light into every little nook and cranny looking for a footprint or any clue to the clue.

They went through twice. Gloria texted Edward, "Where in the hell is that clue? Is it in the cave?" Ed texted back, "This is going to cost you." She texted back, "Will you take it out in trade?" Ed texted back, "Sure, text me where you are staying. Maybe we can hook up. You walked right over it."

Johnny asked, "Are you buying guns?" Ed said, "No, but I am working on something."

Scott said, "Okay, the clue isn't in the cave. Let's look around the grounds. Gloria, check the ladies room." Gloria said, "No, it is in the cave. Can't you feel it? We just aren't looking right." Jeremy said, "It is not in the cave. There is no evidence someone stepped off the path." Gloria said, "Did you ever think it is on the path? Just think of all the stairs we climbed, did you once look under one?" Darwin said, "She is a smart one. I bet she is going to make a great mother to some ungrateful kid." Scott said, "That makes sense. You could be right. Let's go through one more time." Gloria said, "This race is really close. There are only a few monuments left."

They got in line again and this time they checked under every staircase. Randy said, "I will be damned. There are scuff marks where someone crawled under the staircase." They walked over and Randy shined his flashlight under the staircase to just get a glimpse of the question mark. Gloria said, "I will go in and get it." She climbed through the wooden structure and got the clue. The tour was waiting for them. Gloria read the clue. "Penicillin, that is it." Scott asked, "So what do we know about penicillin? It is made of mold." Jeremy said, "I did some work with molds and fungi at NASA. The penicillin mold is penicillium. It is a naturally produced antibiotic. It was Alex Fleming in 1928. He was Scottish, I think." Darwin asked, "You worked for NASA?" Jeremy said, "Yeah, I kind of still do." Randy said, "What does that have anything to do with the treasure hunt?"

Darwin said quietly, "I bet her cunt would be the treasure." Scott asked, "Do you always think with your penis?" Darwin smiled and said, "It's funnier that way." Randy said, "That could be treasure booty."

They got out of the cave and stood in the warm sunshine to warm up. Gloria said, "You're right, it was Alex Fleming, a Scottish scientist. He discovered penicillin the morning of September 3 in 1928." Randy said, "That's all nice and dandy, but what does it have to do with the game?" Scott said, "There is a fiberglass manufacturer a half hour away that you can tour their mold scrap yard. It looks like twenty acres of old molds." Jeremy said, "Let's go, we need to take the lead, and I need a ten-grand paycheck." They got into the van. Gloria said, "Darwin, tonight you have to get cleaned up. My god, you stink." They started to pull out and Team Odin pulled in.

Team Odin jumped out of the van and ran to the door to get into the tour. Robert said, "First thing we find out who was the last tour guide and question them, see if they seen anything out of the ordinary." Cherry said, "Fifty bucks. I will go and ask." She went to the counter and bought tickets for the team and asked who the last tour guide was and if she could talk to her. She went to her team and said, "The tour guide is Lori. She will be out to talk to us in a minute. The next tour is in fifteen minutes." A young college girl came out and asked, "You wanted to talk to me?" Cherry held up a fifty. Dawn smiled and said, "We are on a treasure hunt. A team was right ahead of us. They must have been on your tour." Lori said, "Oh, that's why. They took three tours back to back, and the last one they stopped at a staircase halfway through the tour, just after the big room." Cherry stretched out her arm, giving her the fifty. Joe gave Dawn a wink and said, "You do good work. Let's get in line." Soon they were in the cave taking the tour. About forty-five minutes into it Robert said as he walked down the stairs, "She was right, there are footprints on the floor." The tour guide stopped and talked, telling about the cave. Cherry asked, "Does anyone have a flashlight?" Joe held out his phone with the light on. He said, "Hurry up now." Two minutes later, Cherry was back listening to the tour guide. As soon as she was done, Cherry said, "The clue is penicillin."

Once they got out of the cave, Cherry walked up to the counter at the gift shop and asked the gal behind the counter if she knew anything about penicillin around here. The girl shrugged her shoulders. Robert said, "How about molds?" She said, "Oh, there is a fiberglass factory. It's about a half-hour's drive. You can walk through the old molds. It is kind of neat." Cherry handed her a twenty. The girl said, "Oh no, that's fine." Cherry said forcefully, "Take it." Joe said, "We have a heading. It is FAST Fiberglass Mold in Sparta."

CHAPTER TWENTY-SEVEN

To FAST Mold Graveyard

Team Three got to the fiberglass place. Mark asked, "Should we stop and get some wasp spray?" Ed said, "They just placed the clues not long ago, so that should not be a problem." Mary said, "But we are going to have to look at a lot of old molds, there is a ton of them." Jane leaned over and kissed Sue on the neck and said, "After this is done, we should go on a vacation in the islands, an all-inclusive." Sue turned and kissed her lightly on the lips and said, "I would like that."

Johnny said, "That is just gross." Ed chuckled and sang, "Young love, first love . . . don't worry, it is just a phase." Mark said, "You can say that again. It is the best part of the relationship. Next it will be nitpicking, 'You left the toilet seat up.' 'You didn't take off your shoes at the door.' 'Get that thing away from me.'" Mary said, "Oh, you're exaggerating." Mark asked, "Am I? Think about it." Mary said, "It was more like, 'You're drunk again.' 'You have lipstick on your cock.' And, 'What do you mean you spent the house payment?'" Jane said, "Sounds like you married a dick." Mary said, "Don't get me started." Sue said, "Mine just made excuses not to be home, off on business, until I checked. It was monkey business with his coworker." Jane said, "I loved my boyfriend. We just drifted apart." Sue said, "I like this relationship. I really like you. I have never had feelings like this for a girl." Jane blushed and said, "I know what you mean."

Mark said, "We are here. So what are we looking for?" Ed said, "Look for something that has been moved, tire tracks, footprints, anything out of the ordinary." Mary asked, "Should we pair up or all split up? What is the plan?" Jane said, "It is a huge field. I say we spread apart and walk through it like a deer drive. Johnny, who do you want to go with?" Johnny said, "I want to go with Edward. He carries a gun." Ed said, "Whatever, we have to get moving. Man, there are some big molds here, look at the dinosaur." Mark asked Johnny, "Did you know there are gay dinosaurs?" Johnny said, "Yeah, it's a megasoreass and lickalotopuss. You told me before." Mary said, "You know, you aren't the best role model." Ed said, "He is just having a little fun. Okay, I am going to jog to the end of the field. Are we going to take it in one sweep or would you like to do it in two?" Sue said, "Let's take half. That way we shouldn't miss anything."

Johnny said, "Look, there is a giant cow." Ed rubbed Johnny's head and said, "This is a factory that makes big stuff out of fiberglass. Remember that huge dog? That was probably made here." Johnny asked, "What is fiberglass." Ed said, "You come with me and I will tell you." Ed started to jog across the field. Johnny was at a full run to keep up.

Jane said to Mary, "Johnny sure looks up to him." Mary said quietly as she watched them, "He sure does." Mark was at full stride to get in position. Everyone lined up and started to walk through the yard, looking in and around the molds. Jane yelled to Sue, "There are footprints all over the place." She yelled back, "There are a lot of big ones you can't see in."

Ed and Johnny started to walk across the field, bypassing everything. They were following tire tracks. They came to a large T-Rex. Ed said, "I think this is it. You can see where they picked it up and laid it down." He pulled out his phone and said, "I think we found it, over by the big T-Rex. This is going to be a pain in the ass." Johnny said, "What kind of dinosaur is this?" Ed said, "It is a tyrannosaurus. They were around 20,000 pounds. Not the biggest, but one of biggest carnivores." Johnny said, "They eat meat?" Ed said as he went through his backpack, "Keep an eye out. We are going to have to dig under the mold to get inside of it. This is going to be something."

Mark asked, "Why do you think this is it?" Johnny said, "The tire tracks. You can see where they laid it down in the grass and stood it back up." He was proud to be showing them. Mary said, "You can't dig with that little shovel." Ed looked up at her and asked, "Did you bring a shovel?" Mark said, "Cut the sod first, then I can help." Jane asked, "Do you have a plastic garbage bag?" Ed, holding the shovel so Mark could step on it, said, "In the backpack there is one, why?" Jane said, "All the dirt goes on the bag. If we leave a big pile of dirt the other teams will find it." Ed said, "Look at the tracks. They are going to find it. We just have to make time. You figure out how we are going to climb the thing. It is a waxed mold."

They took out a section of grass four feet long and three feet wide, then went down about eight inches under the mold. Mark said, "Send in the kid with a flashlight." Jane said, "I will do it." She crawled on her belly and squeezed under the mold and looked up. There it was, hanging from the top. The sides of the mold were slick orange. She turned, stuck her head back out of the mold, and said, "This is the one. Now how can we reach it?"

Johnny crawled under and Ed started to dig again so he could fit through. He pushed his backpack through first then went in. Jane was inspecting the seam between the two halves of the mold. She said to Ed, "They are too tight to get your climbing gear in." Mary said, "It looks about twenty feet. We could get a couple of ladders." Mark asked, "How would you get an extension ladder in here?" Sue said, "Let's do a human ladder. Mark, you stand on Ed's shoulders and I will stand on his." Mary said, "That's not going to work, it's twenty feet." Sue said, "If we can get a board across his arms, then it would be only six feet." Mark said, "Okay, how are you going to get a board in here that is at least ten feet long?"

Ed said, "Crap, this is going to be a bigger project than I thought." Mary said, "We could bring in blocks and make a staircase." Johnny said, "Why don't we get a stick and knock it down to us?" Mark said, "Rules of the game." Jane said, "Speaking of that, there is a red light. Turn off your flashlights." They turned off their flashlights and a small red light came from one side under the tail. Ed snapped on his light, shining it right on the small camera. It was the size of a dime, maybe smaller. He said, "Now why haven't we seen these before?" He walked up to it and pushed the small piece of black tape back over the light and said, "Okay, everyone look at this. Where there is a clue, these are the cameras they are using."

Mary said, "There is a hole in the eye of the beast. Look, you can see light peeking through." Mark said, "It's an air hole. They blow air in between the mold and the part to help it release." Ed asked, "How big of a hole is it?" Mark said, "Hell if I know. I watched it on YouTube. They put clay or something in it so it doesn't leave a mark in the finished product." Jane said, "Sue, come on. We will see if we can climb this thing." Ed asked, "Hey, Mark, you still have that small rope?" Mark took a small roll from his fanny pack and said, "Sure, it is a quarter-inch utility cord good for up to 250 pounds. But it is too small to climb." Mary said, "But we could pull up one of the girls." Ed said, "they aren't much lighter than you." Mary said, "Oh bullshit, Jane has to be thirty pounds lighter." Johnny said, "I will do it, let me." Ed said, "You don't have the wing span." Mark said, "He can do it. The clue is close to the side. Let's go now. We drop the cord and tie a loop in the end so the little bastard can stand in it." Mary said sharply, "Don't call him that." Mark said, "Okay, the little fucktard can stand in it."

Jane said, "Let's get moving. Sue, you stay here, keep thinking this might not work. Ed, you are with me." Ed followed her squirming out of the hole. He dug just enough to get through. He pushed his backpack through first. Jane said, "This could be a bitch. There is nothing to grab on to." Ed said, "The seam has bolts in it. Start from the tail and work your way up. Let me go first. You are going to have to call Sue on the phone so we know what to do."

Ed quickly made it to the top of the mold. It was a good twenty feet. He sat with his legs wrapped around the neck and leaned over and dug into the eye with his pocket knife. Sure enough, it was a blowhole. He lowered the cord, pushing it through the hole. Jane said, "Stop, they have enough."

Mark quickly ran the cord through Johnny's shirt, through his belt loop, and tied a loop in the end. He picked up Johnny's foot and slid his foot into it. Mary said, "You know, I think I should do it." Mark said, "We can do it later at the hotel. Sue, tell Ed to bring him up. Now, Johnny, always keep one hand on the rope."

Ed wrapped the cord around his arm and started to lift Johnny three feet at a pull. Jane kept talking to Sue, keeping him informed on the progress. Mark, holding a light on Johnny, said, "Okay, tell him to slow up, take it easy another five feet." Mary talked to Johnny and told him to stop moving. Johnny took the key from his neck. Mark said to Sue, "Twenty bucks he drops it." Johnny yelled down, "I am not going to drop it." He reached out and got the key into the slot, turned it, and the clue came out. He stopped the clue from swinging and took the clue and pulled the key from the slot and dropped it. Mark let out a, "Yes, I knew he could do it." Sue said, "You are such a jerk." Mark smiled and said, "I could take it out in trade, five bucks an hour." Sue said, "Let him down nice and slow."

Mary said, "You did a great job, Johnny, now stay still." Mark caught the boy, slipped his foot out of the loop, cut off the knot, and said, "Have him pull out the cord and fill in that blowhole." Sue asked, "Johnny, you do have the clue?" Johnny reached in his pocket and pulled out a crumpled-up paper. Sue took it and said, "We have to move. If the next team sees us they will know where the clue is." Mark said, "Everyone out. I will start filling the hole."

Everyone crawled out and Mark started to fill the hole. He threw as much inside the mold as he could. Ed carried the sod over and they placed it on top of the dirt. You could still see fresh dirt. Mary said, "Well, it is better than leaving a hole. You wouldn't notice unless you walked right by it."

Sue said, "The clue is big abs." Ed asked, "What did you say? Big abs?" Sue said, "That's what is written here, all in lower case, B-I-G A-B-S. That would be your stomach muscles, right? Mary said, "How do you get strong abs? Sit-ups, crunches?" Jane said, "Running, any exercise." Mark said, "Lose weight, you fatass." Jane lifted her shirt to show a tight tummy. She said, "You lose some weight." Mary said, "Tight abs are called a six-pack, and the world's largest six-pack is in La Crosse, just an hour from here." Ed grabbed Johnny by the shoulder and pulled him into a hug against his thigh and said, "See, that's why we have your mommy around." Mary said, "The longer we stay, the more likely the other team will see us." Sue said, "And we are all covered in dirt. That would give them a hint to where the clue is." They quickly went to the van.

Mary took Johnny and started to knock the dirt off his shirt. Mark smiled and asked, "Can I do that for you?" Jane said, "What is going on with you today? Are you horny or what?" Johnny looked up at his mom and asked, "What is horny?" Ed smiled and said, "This should be interesting." Mark said, "Wait until we are inside. Sue, I need that address." He programmed the GPS. Mary said, "How do I say this? When a guy likes a girl and wants to be her girlfriend, he gets a feeling of wanting to be with them. That's what it means." Johnny said, "Oh, that's what that means. So when I miss you, I am horny. I want to be with you." Mark laughed and said, "Yeah, that's it. You miss someone, you are horny." Ed said, "Anyone can get horny. It is sexually excited, when a person wants to have sex. You're too young for that right now. We don't want to complicate things." Mark said, "God has given everyone feelings of reproducing to keep the species going. Some animals will fight for the right to mate, and some will travel many miles to get the chance to mate." Ed said, "I know a guy that goes to Thailand twice a year to get his bean snapped." Mary asked, "Really? That must cost thousands of dollars." Ed said, "He thinks it is cheaper than getting married, and he says it's like playing a different golf course every time." Mark said, "But, Johnny, people carry diseases, herpes, gonorrhea, syphilis. So you don't want to be kissing too many girls they are dirty." Jane said, "You forgot AIDS, HIV, that will kill you and you would never know who has it." Sue said, "How did we get into this conversation? Oh, that's right, Mark is horny. Why don't you rub one out tonight in the shower?" Ed said, "That's getting a little personal, don't you think?"

Team Intel got to the mold graveyard. Scott pulled into the parking lot. Jeremy said, "This is a lot bigger than I thought. How should we do this? Should we do a grid search?" Gloria said, "I think a zone search would work in this situation." Randy said, "I don't know about you white folks do but a spiral search would work better here." Darwin said, "You eggheads are all the same. Let's just line up and walk through." Scott said, "We could do that. Let's take half at a time. We walk down then back."

Darwin turned from the team and started to take a piss. Gloria asked, "Darwin, are you doing what I think you are?" Dar looked over his shoulder and asked, "Do you want to watch?" Scott shook his head and said, "Let's line up."

They walked to the end of the field looking in all the molds. There were so many large ones, gorillas, cows, clowns. They lined up and started back. Jeremy said, "Hey, we have tire tracks." Scott said, "Let's just complete the sweep, and we will compile the information at the end." Gloria said, "I think this is it, this *Tyrannosaurus rex* has fresh dirt by it, and you can see all the grass was flattened when they laid it down. The clue must be inside."

Everyone gathered at the large mold. Jeremy said, "This must have been a life-sized mold. It is twenty feet high, one of the largest theropods. They have hollow bones and are three-toed. They are generally classed as a group of Saurischian dinosaurs." Darwin said, "Who really gives a shit? Are we going to dig under and look inside?" Gloria said, "Let's analyze this first. It is a huge mold weighing about two tons, twenty feet high and around fifty feet long." Scott said, "It has many parts bolted together. The head is bolted on, and they must make this in pieces then bolt them together." Darwin said, "They make the two sides then bolt them together. We could go up there and unbolt the head and look down inside, or we could just crawl under like the other team has done." Jeremy said, "Now why do you think another team beat us here?" Darwin stood, picking up a piece of sod, and said, "Look, dumbass. The tracks led here. This is where the truck stood and picked up the mold. It laid it down on its side, and they went inside and put the clue in there, then stood it back up. The fresh dirt shows that someone has been here." He got down on all fours and lifted another piece of sod. He looked up and said, "This was done today. It is still loose." Scott said, "Jeremy and Randy, go back to the van and get some tools. We might have to take a panel off this thing." Darwin said, "Maybe we should come back at night, We are going to get caught, and I am sure this isn't legal." Gloria said, "I will give them a call to bring flashlights. What if there is a wild animal in there?" Darwin said, "Just do me a favor and shut up."

Scott kept pushing the dirt away from where Darwin dug bare-handed. In less than five minutes he broke through and climbed in. He called out, "Hey, get in here and bring a light." Scott looked at Gloria and said, "Oh, what the hell." He crawled through the dirt and into the mold. He had his cell phone light on. Darwin said, "There are a few holes that must be air holes for mold release." Scott crawled in and shined his light around the mold then up. He said, "It had to be up at the top." Darwin took a pinch of chew and put it in his lip and said, "Of course, now how did the other team do it?" Scott said, "We can take the side of the head off. All we have to do is unbolt it." Darwin spit and said, "Sounds good to me. We will get the monkey to do it. Them people have good balance." Scott smiled and said, "He doesn't like to be called a monkey." Darwin said, "How about a burr head, spear chucker, jungle bunny, cotton picker, or just plain old nigger?" Scott said, "Wow, now that is racist. Let's just get out of here."

Scott crawled out, brushing the dirt off. He said, "Glo, did you know Darwin here is a racist? What the hell is your problem with blacks?" Darwin looked at him then to Randy and said, "There is nothing wrong with blacks, I think everyone should own one." Gloria said, "That is just wrong in so many ways." Darwin said, "There is nothing wrong with the black race. Hell, Obama was one of our best presidents. Football wouldn't be the same without them." Randy said, "You're just an ass. I suppose you think a woman's place is in the home, barefoot and pregnant." Dar smiled and said, "What's wrong with that? You can't live with them, and can't do most positions without them."

Randy said, "These are good-sized bolts. We have a twenty-volt driver. If the other team took off a side, then they should be loose. It will be a piece of cake." Jeremy started to pull sockets out of the case and find one that fit. Scott said, "We are going to need a safety harness." Jeremy said, "Got it, who wants to run the driver? This piece of mold might weigh a few pounds." Randy loosened a bolt on the tail just to try it out. He said, "Okay, Jeremy, let's do this." Gloria said, "You know, I thought it would have been in one of the elephants." Darwin chuckled and said, "What do you get when you cross an elephant and a poodle? You get a dead poodle with an eight-inch asshole." Randy said, "You are one sick puppy. Now, Jeremy, when we are up there, tie me off to one of the bolts."

The two climbed the mold. Randy yelled down and said, "We are right, someone was just up here. They stuck some stuff in the eye." Randy took all the bolts out except one. He lifted the section of the mold. Jeremy grabbed on to the cable it was hanging from and pulled the question mark to him and got the clue. Randy slowly set the mold back into place and put one bolts back into it. They walked down the dinosaur's back. Jeremy said, "The clue is big abs." Gloria asked, "Abs? As in abdominal muscles? Now what has that anything to do with the game?" Jeremy said, "The *rectus abdominis* muscle runs from your pelvis to your sternum." Scott said as he played with his phone, "They are also called a six-pack and the world's largest six-pack is an hour away." Gloria said, "Let's move." She turned and headed back to the van, which was quite the hike.

Darwin said, "I just don't believe not one of you are tapping that beautiful ass of hers." Scott said, "I wish you would keep your comments to yourself." Gloria turned and said, "That would be nice." Darwin said, "What would be nice, if someone would slip you the bone every once and a while. Maybe you would loosen up." Gloria stared right into his eyes and said, "My sex life is none of your business. We need to have a meeting."

Team Odin saw the Intels pull out of the parking lot. Cherry said, "Dammit, why can't we ever be the first to the clue? We need ten grand." Joe said, "What we need is another player. We're going to get to a monument and not be able to open it." Robert said, "Let's just get in here and find the clue. Now that we know the other team has been here, we should be able to find their tracks in the grass." They parked and Dawn said, "Look, Robert, a leprechaun. Think he can give you a big wang?" Robert blushed. Cherry asked, "Are you ever going to let that go?" Dawn said, "Come on, it's funny." Joe said, "That it is, and I still can't believe it." Robert said, "Okay, let's get back down to business." Dawn chuckled and said, "That's what he said in the bathroom stall."

Joe walked over to where the grass was flattened and said, "Let's go this way. It looks like a lot of people walked here." Robert said, "This is amazing. All the different molds, they have made everything." Cherry said, "I think it is going to be in Paul Bunyan down there." Joe said, "We should be able to follow the tracks right to it."

Fifteen minutes later they came to the T-Rex. Dawn said, "Look, they took out the bolts holding the side of his head." Joe said, "I will crawl under and look at the clue, but I think you are right." Joe crawled through the hole Team Intel had left open. In a minute he was out and said, "It is the clue hanging from the top. That does look the easiest way." Dawn said, "I need some muscle. Robert, are you up to it?" He set his backpack down and pulled out a crescent wrench, slid it into his back pocket. Cherry said, "Be careful, we don't need to be looking for two players."

Dawn went up first, followed by Robert. Dawn said, "Okay, we take out the bolt, you stand on the other side and hold the mold open, and I will get the clue." Robert got the bolt out and lifted the half of the dinosaur's face and said, "Okay, be quick about it." Dawn stood and looked him in the eye and winked and said, "I bet that's what you said to your little leprechaun." She reached in and grabbed the wire and pulled the question mark over to the side where she could get the key in and get the clue. She said, "Clear, you can let it down now." Robert said as he put the bolt back in, "Okay, so I made a mistake. Let it go." Dawn smiled and asked sensually, "But did you like it?"

They headed down. Cherry said, "Let's get the hell out of here. What is the clue?" Dawn said, "Big abs, that's it." Robert lifted his shirt to show a lean stomach and tightened his muscles. Cherry said, "Wow, that's a nice six-pack." Dawn said, "An hour away, the world's largest six-pack in La Crosse. It is at a brewery." Joe said, "Did you see that Santa Claus? It's huge. Man, they have a lot of stuff here." Cherry asked, "What number is on the top of the clue?" Dawn frowned and said, "Three, we are in last place again." Joe said, "Well, we are at least an hour behind. The race is tightening up. And if we can get this clue, we will be tied." Robert said, "Tomorrow is a brand-new day, and we will be the first out of the gate."

CHAPTER TWENTY-EIGHT

World's Largest Six-Pack

Team Three pulled into La Crosse. Mary said, "This is a nice town." Ed asked, "Are you looking for a place to settle down?" Mark said, "It is an easy place to get around. I don't know what there is here. We know there is a brewery." Ed said, "It's a nice little city, 52,000 people. There seems to be a few things to do." Johnny pointed as he asked, "What is that?" Sue said, "That, my boy, is Grandad Bluff. It is a park overlooking the city, and there are a few parks here." Jane said, "There are 367 job openings right now. What kind of job would you like?" Mary, stuttered, "D-d-don't you like me?" Jane said, "Oh, that's not what I meant. After the game." Mark said, "Yeah, we don't need to lose anyone. We are coming up to the big payout." Ed said, "It is not going to be a million dollars, if you think that. Every clue is worth around seventy grand and times that by ten that comes out to seven hundred grand. So the last one will be three hundred grand." Mark said, "You are a fun sucker, but you are right. Still, a cool million would be nice." Jane said, "Where else can you make a hundred grand in three weeks?" Mary asked, "Do you have to claim it?" Ed said, "I am. People are watching. That means the government is watching, even though it is cash." Mark said, "Now if you would look up ahead you will see the world's largest six-pack." Sue said, "Here is a little trivia. The cans were painted old style. Now they are wrapped in vinyl. They hold 688,200 gallons of beer. If you drank a six-pack a day, it would take you 3,351 years to drink all the beer."

Mark said, "Now there is a challenge. Okay, let's just do a drive-by. Keep a look out, maybe we can get lucky." Jane looked at Sue and ran her tongue across her lips and whispered, "Get lucky."

Mary said, "Okay, it says on the side of the building, ER Eusening Cellars and ten million gallons of beer." Jane said, "It also says private property. We will be trespassing." Mark said, "Keep an eye out. The clue might be nearby and not at the brewery." Johnny said, "That is a big house." Mary said, "That is an old historical mansion. I wonder if they have tours." Ed said, "Okay, this place is big. I wonder if they have a tasting room. I could go for a cold one." Sue said, "Pull over in front of that statue." Johnny said, "He looks like a king." Ed smiled and said, "We will find out, won't we?"

They filed out of the van and stood in front of the statue. Ed said to Johnny, "This is a new fiberglass statue." Sue said, "You are correct. The old one was vandalized." Mark said, "So, Johnny, you were right. He is a king." Mary said, "He is King Gambrinus. In the fifteenth century, he invented beer." Ed said, "It is a nice day. Why don't we walk and talk to some of the employees, see if they know where this stupid clue is?" Jane said, "I bet it is on the top of one of the six-packs." Mark said, "Too easy, and we would get caught trespassing." Ed said, "It is a clue. We only need one person to get to it." Mark said, "So what are you are saying is we just walk in at shift change, put on one of their uniforms, and act like we are maintenance." Ed said, "Let's take a closer look. Do you need a badge to get in the plant?" Mary said, "Let's take a walk around it and see if we can see the clue." Sue said, "I will be dammed. There it is on a railing up on top of the third silo." Ed said, "Okay, let's cross the street and read the sign. I am going to slip into the silos and pop up there and get the clue." Jane said, "It's not that easy, and the bottom of the ladders are locked." They crossed the street and Ed said, "Hey, you are right. I thought maybe one would be unlocked." Johnny said, "I have to take a leak." Ed slipped around the silo and got inside where he wouldn't be noticed and climbed on the outside of the cage around the ladder. In three minutes he was on top, heading across the catwalks to the clue. Johnny said, "I wish I could do that." Mary pulled him close and said, "That is dangerous." Mark said, "And you are an accident waiting to happen."

Ed got the clue and climbed back down slowly. Mary asked when he got back, "What is the clue?" Mark asked, "What number is the clue?" Ed said, "We are in the lead. It is number one, and the clue is God." Johnny said excitedly, "Another big church." Jane said, "Not just a big church, a shrine, Our Lady of Guadalupe. I was hoping we would be going there."

The Intels pulled into La Crosse and drove over to the brewery. Randy said, "Leave me off here, let me go and talk to one of my brothers." He hopped out of the van and went up to a picnic table where a few black guys were having a break. Randy asked, "Yo, what's up? I am looking for a question mark. It could be six inches or six feet." An older guy said, "What is up with that? They installed one about three weeks ago." Randy said, "Great, where is it?" A younger fellow said, "What is it to you?" Randy said, "It holds a clue, we are on a treasure hunt." The black guy said, "So what does that have to do with us?" Jeremy said, holding a fifty between his fingers, "We need someone to put a key in the thing and bring us the clue. And there is another fifty when we get the clue." The old man stood and said, "Fuck it. Ramone, you just had a kid. You need the hundred bucks." A younger, thin guy jumped up and said "were cutting it close but I think I can make it," as he looked at his watch. The old guy said, "Bolted to the railing, above silo four."

Ramone took the fifty and the key then jogged to the door. The older black guy said, "He will be back in seven minutes. That is when break is done. So what do you get if you win this treasure hunt?" Scott said, "If we got the first place every time, we would each get a hundred grand." Gloria said as she walked up, "We got first place once, that was ten grand. Other than that, we really aren't making any money." Randy asked, "You did say the clue was up on top of one of the cans in the six pack, why did he go inside?" One of the guys said, "It's faster to use the stairs instead of using the ladder. Anyway, safety says we have to." A younger guy asked Gloria, "Hey, did you grow up on a farm? Because you sure know how to raise a cock." A different guy said, "Hey, sweetie, my dick just died. Would you mind if I buried it in your ass?" Randy said, "That was a good one. I have been working on tagging this little white ass for a week now." Jeremy asked, "How is the beer business? Can you drink on the job?" The old man smiled and said, "Don't mind those guys, sugar. We are making it as fast as we can. Where the hell it all goes, beats me. And no, we can't drink on the job. These guys are so damn safety conscious it slows the whole process down. And here comes Ramone with a minute to spare. We are maintenance, so it really doesn't matter. But they are watching our breaks, the fucking bastards." Jeremy handed Ramone the other fifty, and Ramone handed him the clue and the key. Jeremy read it and said, "Well, we are in second place. The clue is God. That's it, just God." The old black guy said, "That would probably be the shrine. It's a few miles out of town." A guy asked Gloria, "hey, girl, what is long, black, and hard?" Gloria chuckled and said, "It's first grade, right? What do you and apples have in common? You both would look good hanging from a tree." Scott said, "Now let's not be pissing off the workers here. They have to get back to work, just like us." Jeremy said, "That was a good one."

Scott asked, "To the Shrine of Our Lady of Guadalupe?" Jeremy said, "Let's have a discussion about that. It seems too easy." Gloria said, "The clues are not that hard, come on." Jeremy asked, "This shrine it is dedicated to the Blessed Virgin Mary. Do we see God in there?" Gloria said, "You might have a point there. Let's see what other church is around here." Randy said, "There is this huge motherhouse, it is right here in town, Franciscan Sister of Perpetual Adoration Motherhouse." Scott said, "Okay, we start there."

Darwin sat up in the seat of the van and said, "Are we going to eat?" Scott said, "No, we are going to Walmart and getting you new clothes." Jeremy said, "And we are getting a can of Glade air freshener." Darwin said, "I don't smell that bad." Gloria said, "We can do a test. You get in the checkout line and see if people smell you." Randy said, "I don't need to go in." Scott said, "Come on, brother, let's just take a lap around the place and look at women." A big smile formed on his face and he said, "That I can do. I could use some deodorant." Gloria said, "Get some industrial shit for Dar Boy." Randy said, "Okay, Gloria, you take Darwin. Meet us back in front by the registers in a half hour." Gloria said, "Fine, anything to get this guy to smell better." Scott said, "Let's go and look at the TVs."

Once they got to the entertainment section, Jeremy said, "Okay, this is the deal. Darwin is one sick puppy. I don't trust him. Should we leave him here?" Randy said, "Yeah, he is a poor excuse for a white guy." Scott said, "Let's give him a chance. We need that fifth person." Jeremy said, "I am sure we can find someone better than that." Randy said, "He is just such a sick fuck. I don't trust him as far as I can throw him."

Odin pulled up to the City Brewery and Robert asked, "How in the hell are we going to find a clue in this place? It's two blocks long and on both sides of the street." Cherry said, "Let's get out and question as many people as we can." Joe said, "Hey look, a king holding a beer." Dawn said, "That would be King Gambrinus. He invented beer back in the 1500s." Joe said, "We could fly a drone around the place." Robert said, "Let's do what Cherry suggested. If there is something different, the workers would have probably seen it." Dawn said, "This is private property. We don't need a ride downtown to the cop shop, so be casual." Joe said, "Drop me off here. I am going to walk around the six-pack. That was the clue." Robert said, "That's too easy."

Joe walked up to the six-pack, read the sign, walked around to the corner, and saw the question mark bolted to the railing. He pulled out his phone and said, "Get everyone back into the van. Pick me up in five minutes. I have found the clue." He slipped around the silo and climbed up the outside of the ladder up to the catwalk and to the question mark, then back down to the ground. Joe stood on the sidewalk waiting for the van. As soon as it got there he read off the address to the Shrine of Our Lady of Guadalupe. He said, "Like a ninja, the clue is number three, so we are in the last place. And the clue is God." Cherry said, "This is weird. It is a new shrine, and it sits on seventy acres." Joe said, "We just went to a brewery and never had a beer." Dawn asked "Did you know the City Brewery has three locations? The one here in La Crosse, one in Latrobe, and one in Memphis. This one produces 50 million cases a year and the one in Memphis 60 million cases. And they do more than just beer." Cherry said, "Not to sound stupid, but where is Latrobe?" Dawn said, "Give me one second. There, it is a town in Pennsylvania." Robert said, "I will get you a beer at the hotel. Let's focus on the shrine." Cherry said, "It is only open till four, it's past five." Joe said, "Let's do a drive-by." Dawn said, "We are not breaking into a shrine, bad juju." Robert said, "Okay, find a hotel, one with a bar."

They pulled up to a hotel. It had a big "$69.95" on the sign and it said "Cheap and easy, just like your mother." Cherry said, "No fucking way." Joe said, "You know, you are right. I doubt they would have a bar or food." Dawn pulled out her phone and said, "You know, you guys could look this shit up. I am almost out of data."

Robert said "well it looks like a nice hotel," as he pulled into a Hilton Garden. They checked in and Dawn said, "Okay, let's just dump our baggage in the room and meet down here at the bar. And then we will do the drive-by." Cherry said, "And find a place to eat."

Robert did just that. He tossed his luggage on the other bed and headed down to the bar. He got a local beer. He asked the guy next to him, "Hey, are you alright?" The man looked up and said, "I am just depressed, I found my wife dead a couple of days ago." Robert said, "Wow, that sucks. How did she die?" The man took a long pull off his whiskey and said, "She died in her sleep. I didn't notice right away. The sex was the same, but the dishes started to pile up." Robert got up and said, "Well my friends are here. You just hold in there."

Joe asked, "Are you ready? Let's do that drive-by. Maybe we can get lucky." Dawn said, "Tonight I think I will get lucky. I will just grab some random guy and fuck his brains out." Cherry said, "I just don't know how you can do that." Joe said, "She is a cute woman, and you know guys." Robert said, "Yeah, guys will beg for a roll in the hay even after they are married." Joe said, "Especially after they are married. Women have half the money and all the pussy, and they don't share." Dawn said, "You poor little bastard. When was the last time you got laid?"

CHAPTER TWENTY-NINE

The Motherhouse

Team Three's Ed was up early and out for a jog. He stopped and talked with some older women and questioned them about the shrine. He jogged back to the hotel, showered, and called the team and said, "We don't have to wait until 9:00 for the tour. They open a half hour before." Johnny came running down the hall to Ed's room. He said, "Mom is on the way. We are supposed to order for her." Ed said, "Who dressed you?" Johnny said, "Mom's in the bathroom getting ready and I have to drain the dragon." Ed said, "Well, come on in." Johnny said, "You're not ready." Ed said, "I just took a three-mile run, it is a beautiful day." Johnny said, "I love hotels. I wish I could live in one." Ed said as he carried his suitcase to the door, "No, you don't. It gets old after a while."

Johnny came out of the bathroom and said, "Thank you so very much. I am having a real good time." Ed asked, "Did you wash your hands?" Johnny did a dramatic head roll and headed back to the bathroom. Ed asked, "Did your mother say anything about moving to La Crosse? She seems to like the city." Johnny said as he wiped his hands on his pants, "Nope, she doesn't include me in those decisions." Ed said, "Come on, they will be waiting for us. And remember, always try to make good decisions. Your mom has made a couple bad ones, now she has to live with them. Even small ones can affect your life. Like telling your teacher she is a whore. Even if she is one, you should think before you speak. Now she will never treat you the same. She could fail you, and that could affect your life." Johnny said, "I only did that once. I do know if you're mean to your waitress she will spit in your food." Ed said, "Yeah, like that. And people carry a lot of diseases. You could get herpes and have them for life." Johnny said, "I really like you." Ed rubbed Johnny's head and said, "You're not as much of a pain in the ass as I thought you would be."

Ed and Johnny went down to the restaurant. Mark was sitting at a table all by himself. Mark said, "Right on time. So, Johnny, where is your mother?" Johnny said, "Oh, she is in the shower. We are supposed to order for her." Ed said, "I will do that." Mark said, "No, let me. This should be fun."

Jane and Sue came down. Mark raised his hand and a waiter came over. Mark looked at everyone and said, "Coffee for everyone. I will have the western omelet, and I am ordering for the girl that is not here. Let's start her off with a bloody Mary medium, make it a double, and a bowl of oatmeal." Johnny said, "My mom doesn't like oatmeal." Mark said, "That doesn't matter, now does it?" Ed said, "And a plate of bacon. Everyone likes bacon."

Mary came down. Everyone was eating. She asked, "Who ordered the oatmeal?" Mark raised his fork and said with a mouth full, "That would be me. The ice in your bloody Mary is melting, so drink it quick." Mary whispered to Johnny, "You know I don't like oatmeal." Johnny blushed and said quietly, "I told him." Ed said, "Okay, let's get this party started. We get to the shrine a half hour before it opens and hopefully get a guided tour to the clue."

Mary looked at Mark and said, "At least you could have ordered brown sugar. This has no flavor at all." Mark smiled and said, "Eat up. You have fifteen minutes. I hope you are packed." She looked up and said, "For Christ's sakes." She reached over and took a piece of toast from Ed's plate and a couple of pieces of bacon and left. Sue said so she could hear, "You snooze, you lose." Ed said to Johnny, "You're done. Run and help your mother. And I mean help, not get in the way." Mark said, "I wasn't kidding. Fifteen minutes, we leave. This is the fourth clue on the ninth payday, and I need this ten grand." Jane said, "No shit, Sherlock. Meet you at the van."

Ed asked, "Who is paying for this?" Mark said, "You had better get packing." Ed lifted his coffee and said, "Done, just have to grab my bag. Have you looked into this shrine?" Mark said, "I have Google Earthed it. I think it could be in two places. There are a few buildings." Ed said, "It is just such a vague clue. There are so many churches. What else does 'God' mean around here?" Mark said as he played with his phone, "There are at least a dozen churches around here, but this is different. God's Country, Grandad Bluff. We seen that on the way in." Ed raised his hand and the waitress came with the bills. Ed asked as he lifted Mary's bloody Mary, "A hundred bucks should cover it, right?" He set a hundred on the table and said, "If it doesn't cover it, take care of it." He took the bloody Mary up with him to his room to get his suitcase. Mark smiled and said, "I will pull up the van."

They got to the shrine a half hour before the tour. Johnny said, "This isn't as big as the last church." Mark said, "That is because this isn't the church, numb nuts. The shrine is a half-mile walk." Sue said, "You have to be shitting me." Jane smiled and said, "It's a beautiful day, let's enjoy it." Mary said, "And let's be quick about it. I don't think we have much of a lead." Ed smiled and said, "Let's keep an eye out, something doesn't feel right."

They got out of the van and started toward a building. Johnny ran up to a statue and asked, "Who is this Juan Diego?" Jane said, "He was just a guy who the Mother Mary showed herself to down in Mexico, I think." Johnny said, "They have a gift shop here, come on." Ed smiled at Mary and said, "He is going to be disappointed."

They went through the building and onto the trail to the shrine. Johnny read every statue. He grabbed Ed's hand and pulled him to an Indian girl. He asked, "How do you pronounce her name?" Ed said, "Just the way it is spelled, Tekawitha. She is a saint. She is the lily of the Mohawks. There must be a good story with her." Mary asked, "Did you give him that Coke?" Ed said, "That wasn't me. Don't worry, his sugar rush will burn out. We're not going to mass, so he doesn't have to sit still."

Jane slipped her arm around Sue's waist and whispered in her ear. Mark looked back and said, "Hey, you're in the eyes of the Lord.

They don't allow that here." Sue stopped and kissed Jane lightly on the lips and said, "Sure they do. Our God is a loving God. And by the way, this is a shrine to Mother Mary. We might be in the wrong place." Ed said, "See, that's what I said. What does Mary have to do with God? Jesus I could see." Mark said, "We are here. Look everywhere. When we get to this church we take the tour. And if we can't find it we search somewhere else." Ed said, "Ask everyone. Caretakers would know if someone placed a clue here."

Mark went up to the doors. They were locked. Ed said, "We walk around it and see if they have it on the outside."

Team Odin got together in the gym at the hotel. Robert said, "It's a beautiful day. Joe and I went for a four-mile run." Cherry asked Dawn, "Did you have a fun night?" Joe asked, "Did you pick up some strange?" Dawn said, "It was nice. He was a nice guy, up here working in sales or something." Cherry said, "She just walked up to him at the bar and asked, 'Do you want to get laid?'" Robert said, "Did he have a big dick?" Dawn said, "Just average, six inches or so. But he really put everything he had into it." Joe asked, "So did he go down on you?" Dawn said, "No, we didn't swap any bodily fluids. You never know where they have been. Men are sick." Robert said, "This is true. We work out for another fifteen minutes then shower, pack, and meet in the restaurant. We want to make the first tour of the shrine." Cherry gave Dawn a look. Dawn said, "Hey, it's a lot better than a vibrator."

Joe started to pump iron. You could see him looking at Dawn and thinking about her doing the guy the night before. He started to get a chubby. Cherry asked him, "What are you thinking about? Looks like it is something nasty." Joe blushed and said, "Aren't you going to work out?" Cherry smiled and said, "You wish, you pervert." Robert asked, "What's her problem?"

They did breakfast and were at the shrine five minutes before the first tour. They met Team Three as they came around the back of the church. Dawn said, "Aren't you Team Three?" Mark said, "Team Odin, I presume. There are only four of you." Cherry said, "Jack got a little too close to the tiger cage at the Circus Museum." Mark said, "That must have hurt. Did it kill him?" Cherry smiled, "No, he just got like sixty stitches. A tee shirt didn't stop those claws." Dawn said, "Your team has changed a bit." Ed took Mary by the hand and led her off with Johnny. Mark said, "We lost a couple. Charlie snapped off his leg at some waterfalls, and Sam got his face ripped off by a dog in Meteor. We're still getting by." Robert said, "The rules say you must have five in a team." Jane said, "So you only have three." "Who says we don't have two more just not here right now?" Cherry said, "Well, I guess you haven't found the clue yet." Mark said, "Now why would we be here if we found it already?"

Mary asked Ed, "Why aren't we going on the tour?" Ed smiled and said, "Act like you are my wife. And, Johnny, call me Dad." Johnny beamed as he said, "Okay, Dad." Mary slid her arm around Ed and pulled him toward the growing crowd of people for the tour. Johnny said, "Kiss her, make it look like you're married." Ed said loud enough for everyone to hear, "Johnny, this is like a museum. Don't touch anything." Johnny said, "Yes, Dad."

Mark chuckled and said, "Well, it looks like I am here with two good-looking girls that are in love with each other." Johnny kept asking questions about everything. Ed said, "Just wait when you are older. You can go to Vegas and see great architecture. This is great, but when you get in Caesar's Palace you will see acres of polished marble floors." Mary said, "This is the most beautiful church I have ever seen." She held Ed tight. Ed said, "You're looking wrong, seek the question mark." Mary said, "Oh, I am sorry. I forgot." Ed bent down and kissed her forehead.

They went through the whole tour and found nothing. Mark stepped close to Ed and said quietly, "I don't think it is here. Maybe we should try that bluff." Ed looked into Mary's eyes and asked her, "What do you think?" She licked her lips seductively and said, "I don't know, whatever you think." Ed said, "Slowly retreat. We will go first. Don't let Odin know that we left." Mark stepped over to the two girls and told them to drift off down the trail toward the van. Ed got to the gift shop and asked Johnny, "Do you have to go pee?" Johnny said, "No, I am good." Ed said, "Well I have to, come along." They went and took a pee. Johnny kept on looking over trying to see Ed's dick. Ed asked, "Now what the hell are you doing? Go wash your hands."

Everyone met at the van. Sue said, "I just don't know what a bluff has to do with God. The clue should be here." Ed said, "We asked people that work here, nobody knows about a question mark." Jane said, "Guys, take a look at this church. It also has tours." Mark said, "That is a big one." Johnny said, looking at his mom, "Speaking of big ones, Ed has a big ding dong." Ed looked down at him and said, "What?" Mary said, "Johnny, that's rude." Johnny pouted and said, "Well he has. I just thought . . . well . . ." Mark said, "He wants Ed to slip you the pork sausage. He looked prouder than hell when you guys were playing a family back there." Sue said, "You do make a good-looking family." Mary's face got beet red.

Ed changed the subject and said, "Where is this church?" Jane said, "It's right here in town. It is Franciscan Sisters of Perpetual Adoration Motherhouse. That's a mouthful." Mark said with a chuckle, "Speaking of a mouthful . . . okay, let's blow this pop stand before the Odin team catches us." Sue said, "I hope it's not here and we missed it." Mark said, "Those fuckers, the Intels are there." Mary asked, "How do you know?" Mark said, "The GPS on their van. Dammit, I should have checked it." Ed asked, "They're at the church?" Mark said, "No, they are on the move." Ed asked, "Are they headed this way?" Mary said, "Give me that thing, just drive. No, they are headed out of town."

The Intels got up early and went down for breakfast. Gloria said to Randy, "That Darwin is one sick puppy. I helped him cut his hair, just a straight cut across the shoulder blades. He wanted me to watch him jack off." Scott said, "We are going to have to do something about him. I just can't stand the smell." Jeremy said, "I emptied a can of spray in the van and left all the windows open last night."

Darwin walked up to the table. Nobody gave him a thought until he pulled out the chair and sat down. Randy said, "Oh my god, is that you? Wow, you clean up nice." Gloria said, "Hey, you have lips." Scott said, "This might just work. You're looking good." Darwin smiled, the first time they could see his teeth through his mustache. He said, "A twenty-minute shower does wonders." Jeremy said, "Hey, you're a white guy, and you don't stink." Darwin squared up his shoulders and asked, "Are you surprised? The homeless are people." Scott said, "Most are mentally ill or just don't give a rat's ass." Gloria said, "Some have just fallen on hard times and slipped through the cracks."

Randy looked hard at Darwin and said, "Some are running from the law. Are you in some kind of trouble?" Darwin shifted his eyes to Randy and then picked up a menu. Randy asked again, "So what is it? Did you kill someone?" Darwin said, "It's nothing like that. I owe someone a shitload of cash. If I don't use my social security number, I can't be tracked." Gloria asked, "Student loans?" Darwin said, "Oh fuck, that too. Christ, there must be a quarter million in student loans. The interest just keeps building." Jeremy asked, "Where did you go?" Darwin said, "Chicago, it was about fifty-five thousand a year. I took out twenty more to live on. I got a bachelor's degree in business, got a job as marketing manager. I was pulling down sixty-four K a year." Scott said, "So what happened?" Darwin leaned onto the table and said, "Okay, this is just between us, you got that?" Everyone agreed that it would not leave the table. Darwin said, "My wife was sleeping with my best friend. She divorced me, took my house, my three kids, my car, my 401K, my boat, and left me with the motor home and all the bills. So I said fuck it, I am not paying for anything, and just walked away." Jeremy said, "Wow, who would have thought?"

Randy asked, "So do you miss it?" Darwin stared at the ceiling and said, "Yeah, I really miss my best friend. We had some great times." Gloria asked, "Marketing manager, that's a four-year degree, right?" Darwin said, "Yeah, that is why I don't cut my hair, go to an airport or any government buildings. They have facial recognition software, and those damn computers will pick you out of a crowd." Gloria said, "They sure will. I have a doctorate in computer science, so if they have you in the search, your face will throw a flag." Darwin said, "Not this face. This is the first time I have ever had a beard or long hair." Randy said, "That's a good story. So you are on the run from the law. This fucking cracker could be a serial killer. If a brother gave you a story like that would you believe him?" Gloria said, "Well, we believe you are a civil engineer. You never did tell us what happened at your job." Randy said, "Those racist mothers, they downsized and who was the first to go? The black guy, that's who." Scott asked, "Who had the most seniority?" Randy said, "That doesn't matter. I was the only black guy on the team." Jeremy said to Darwin, "Randy here thinks the world owes him something because he is black." Darwin said, "I have noticed. So now that I have told you I am an educated man you're not going to turn me in?" Scott said, "We need you. And god, you smelled bad." Darwin said, "Life is just so much better now, stress free, and just have to work on my next meal and where to sleep."

Team Intel headed to the sisters' motherhouse. Jeremy said, "Now that is one big church. I say we do a walk around and see if they stuck it on the building." Randy said, "I sure the hell hope not. That is one tall building. Someone else can climb that thing." Darwin said, "He is a team player, isn't he? Let's do this, whoever finds the clue first gets to sleep with Gloria." Gloria blushed and said, "I don't think so, not in your lifetime." Dar said, "Well, you had better find it first." Scott said, "Tours start at nine, so a quick walk around. I will take Jeremy and Gloria. Randy and Darwin, you go the other way. Look close. We will meet in the back. Call if you find something." Darwin said, "I would rather go with Glo. We could get to know one another." Randy said, "That's just not going to happen. The ice queen's legs are frozen shut, and I have been working on riding that booty for over week now." Darwin asked, "Have you tried to get her drunk?" Randy said, "You are a sick dude. And yes, I have tried. She just doesn't let her guard down. Now we are looking for a question mark. It doesn't have to be on the building."

Scott and his team walked around the church. On the way, he asked Jeremy, "Do you buy what Darwin said at breakfast?" Jeremy said, "Oh yeah, I have seen it. The more you make, the ex-wife just keeps bringing you back to court for more. And yes, they do take your retirement, your house. Just think the debt he had, student loans, a house, couple of cars, three kids, probably in private school, and a wife he couldn't satisfy. Still, was it the right thing to do?" Gloria said, "It's his kids. He just left her trying to raise them by herself." Scott smiled and said, "Let's just look for the clue and not talk about Darwin's blood-sucking ex-wife. Never did ask him if she worked or just spent his money."

Jeremy said, "This place is huge. It's the whole block." Gloria said, "It is a college, coed, liberal arts. The church just has so many roofs." Scott pulled out his phone and called Randy and said, "We have twenty minutes to catch the tour, so don't lollygag." Randy said, "Lollygag? I will gag you with my lolly. Who the fuck says that?" Darwin said, "To lollygag, back in the 1800s it was to fool around sexually. Now it is just to fool around, be lazy." Randy said, "Well that motherfucker can gag on my lolly. Just keep looking. We have to be out in front in less than twenty minutes." Darwin said, "You know, a drone would do this better." Randy clapped his hands and said, "See, you get it. We have one in the van, but those sacks of shit won't use it." Darwin said, "Well, you have to look up local laws. And you have that invasion of privacy, you know, looking in people's windows. And if you are trying to keep a low profile, you would draw attention." Randy said, "Fine, you made your point. Let's just pick up some speed here."

The team met at the back of the buildings. Scott said, "Let's just take the tour and question some people. This might be a hard find." Jeremy asked Darwin, "Hey, did your ex work?" Darwin said, "No, she was a stay-at-home mom. Three kids under the age of seven, she had her hands full." Scott said, "You didn't say what kind of house." Darwin said, "It was an old three-story Victorian, $396,000. And she talked me into a $40,000 pool, that's with all the fence and crap. Oh yeah, she had me so far in debt, I would have had to work until I was ninety. And what sucked is I didn't like my job, it was like going from purgatory to hell every day."

They met in front of the church, waiting for the tour to begin. A van pulled up, it was Team Three. Mark said, "Well, there they are. They have five on their team." Mary said, "No shit, Sherlock. It takes five to turn the keys." Ed said, "Well, I guess they are going to see us, so they will know who the team is." Sue said, "Well not really. Drive around the place. Drop me and Jane off here. We will hide behind that truck for a minute and get in line for the tour. Ed and

Johnny, you get out on the side of the church. And, Mark and Mary, park the van, and hurry." The side door slid open and Jane and Sue slipped out. Mark pulled out of the parking lot and around the side of the church. Ed and Johnny got out. Ed grabbed Johnny and put him on his shoulders and said, "Now you are higher, look for that question mark." Johnny said, "This is a big freakin' place. What's up with the girls in the black robes?" Ed said, "They are nuns. Let's see, if I remember, they have been here since 1849. We will learn more on the tour." Johnny said, "Man, is this place big? And those nuns have been here for over a hundred years." Ed smiled and said, "You know what I mean. Their order of nuns have been here. Just keep looking. And don't talk about my junk. Your mother doesn't need to know what size it is." Johnny said, "Sorry, I just thought—" Ed said, "There you go thinking again. It's not that I don't like you guys. I have this thing called a life, and I don't know if you would fit in. See,

I travel a lot." Johnny said, "I like to travel, this is fun."

They caught up to Jane and Sue in front of the church. Johnny said, "Hey, Daddy, who is that statue up there?" Ed said, "Johnny, me boy, that would be an archangel. I think Michael. I believe he is the defender of the church." Randy asked, "Dude, you wouldn't have seen a question mark, would you?" Ed asked, "Like the Riddler wears on his suit?" Randy said, "Yeah, just like that. It can be a small one or one as tall as I am." Ed said, "That's a weird thing to be looking for, but I haven't seen one."

Jane stepped close to Ed and said, "Beautiful church, isn't it? There is a lot of buildings close to it also." Ed nodded and started to look at the other buildings. It was a college campus. A nun opened the front door and stepped out on the steps and said, "Okay, this is a quiet tour. We are praying. If you would step this way." Johnny said, "What does that mean?" Mary started to speak and Ed put his hand on Johnny's shoulder, turned him, and said, "That means be quiet and respectful. She is going to tell us about the sisters and the building."

They went in and the place was huge. Marble everywhere. Huge arches, and the altar was just beautiful. Gold leaf shined bright. They all huddled together to hear the sister talk. Gloria stepped close to the nun and asked, "Is there a question mark, like punctuation, in here?" The nun said, "Now that you ask, they put one up like three weeks ago. What does it mean?" Gloria asked, "Where, may I ask?" The nun said, "Turn around; it is on top of the pipes for the organ." Scott said, "We are on a treasure hunt and that holds a clue to the next clue. How can we get to it?" The nun said, "After the tour we will take a walk up there and see."

Jane stepped in close to Mark and said, "Sue and I are going to sneak up there and see if we can get the clue before the Intels." Mark said, "Just be careful." He nodded to Ed. Ed looked back to see the two girls walking down the aisle. He said to Johnny, "Stay close to your mom and keep asking questions. Stall them, keep them looking anywhere but back."

The tour continued. Scott and Jeremy slipped away from the group and headed to the back of the church. The pipes stood twenty feet tall, sitting in the choir loft. Jane said, "We need a ladder or a sky lift." Sue asked, "Did the nun say how they got it up there?" Jane smiled and said, "I think I can climb the tubes." Sue said, "You fall and you are going to splat on the floor. That is pretty frickin' high." Jane took off her shoes and said, "We both have to go up. You're going to have to give me a boost." Sue said, "We should wait for the men. How are we going to get up the first ten feet just to get to the tubes?" Jane said, "Faith. Come on. There has to be something here."

Ed said from behind them, "We have to hurry. The Intels are right behind me." He picked up Jane, put her on his shoulders just like he did with Johnny, and whispered, "Stand on my shoulders and I will give you a boost." Jane stood leaning against the back of the organ pipes. They were ten feet up on a huge wooden case. Sue said, "This isn't going to work. There isn't enough room for me to give her a boost up on the top." Ed picked her up and said, "See? Jane made it to the first level. She needs you."

Sue stood on Ed's shoulders and he put his hands under her feet and lifted her up. She climbed up to Jane and got down on her hands and knees, then climbed up to the kneeling position, then stood, giving Jane the height to reach the top.

Johnny kept asking questions about the dome and how Christ was the bread, and if it was real gold, if anyone drowned getting baptized, why she wore those robes, did she have any kids, what she was wearing under her habit, has she ever met Mother Mary.

Jane stood on top of the organ tubes case and walked over to the question mark. She put in her key and got the clue. She was back down in two minutes.

Scott and Jeremy stepped in right after Ed helped the girls down. Scott said, "Team Three, I presume." Jane said, "We were just up here admiring the view. What a beautiful church." Ed said, "Come on, girls. Let's catch back up to the to the tour. Your mother is going to be pissed." Jeremy stood looking at the organ and asked, "What do you think?" Scott said, "We need at least two ladders. The first on is a twelve-footer and the second a ten. And I suppose there aren't any around here." Jeremy said, "Well I guess we talk to the old nun." Scott said, "Old? I think she is around thirty. It's hard to tell, but if you put some makeup on her she would be a cutie." Jeremy said, "Now don't be talking about a woman of the cloth. I think you would burn in hell if you fooled around with her."

Scott said, "That folding ladder in the van will fold out to sixteen feet. And once you get up there, you pull the ladder up to get to the top." Jeremy said, "You're right, let's go." The two ran down the stairs and out to the van. They snuck back in with a five-foot ladder. Once they got into the choir loft, they folded it out. Every noise echoed in the church, so they did it very slowly. Scott said, "Hold the ladder, I will go up," and up he went. He pulled the ladder up trying to be as quiet as he could. Everyone looked up at him.

The nun took three steps into the small tour and said, "Now what are they doing up there? They should have safety harnesses on." Darwin asked her now that she was just feet from him, "Hey, when was the last time you got laid?" She cracked a smile and said, "Now if I wanted any shit from you, sir, I would squeeze your head." Scott got the clue and he said in amazement, "Fuck." It echoed through the church. Johnny said, "Somebody is in trouble." Ed asked the team, "Do we have to stay for the whole tour?" Mark said, "It is very interesting, but we got the clue. And now we know so does Intel. Let's go."

Mary asked, "What is the clue?" Jane pulled it out of her pocket and read, "Honeymoon falls, all in lower case."

They walked out of the church. Ed dipped his finger in the holy water and made the sign of the cross on his forehead. Johnny asked, "Why did you do that?" Ed said, "It reminds us of our baptism. The water has been blessed by a priest. It is not just water." Johnny asked his mother, "Have I ever been baptized?" Mary blushed and said, "No, your father wasn't a religious man, and we never had the time." Ed asked, "Is that something you would like to do? You would be a hoot in religion class."

They got into the van. Mark handed Johnny his iPad and said, "This is what baptism is about." Johnny took it and hit play. It was an old drunk man staggering down a dirt road. He plowed into a priest. The priest asked, "Sir, what religion are you?" The man slurs, "I don't have a religion." The priest then asked, "Do you believe in God?" The drunk burped and said, "Of course I do." The priest asked, "Have you been baptized?" The drunk grabbed onto the priest to keep his balance and said, "No, Father, I haven't." The priest said, "We could do it right now. Follow me to the river." The two went to the riverbank. The priest had the drunkard kneel next to the water. He grabbed him by the back of the head and pushed his head underwater, asking God to wash away his sins. There was a clock in the corner of the iPad, counted off fifteen seconds. He let him up and asked the drunk, "Have you seen the Lord?" The drunk gasped, "No, I haven't." The priest shoved his head under the water again, this time the clock ticked off thirteen seconds as he prayed to God to release this man's demons. He let him up and asked, "Did you see your Lord Jesus Christ?" The drunkard said, "Holy shit, man. No, I didn't see him." The priest shoved his head under. This time a minute ticked by as the priest asked God to help this poor soul, to lead him to the righteous path to give up the drink, to start bathing. He let him up and asked again, "Have you seen the Lord?" The drunk looked up and asked, "Are you sure this is where he fell in?"

Ed said, "Mark, what the hell did I just watch?" Mark said as he was driving, "I just Googled funny baptism. Was it funny?" Ed said, "Boy, it is hard to get good help nowadays. Johnny, let me tell you what baptism is. Most people are baptized when they are young. It is to wash away their original sin when Adam and Eve ate the fruit from the forbidden tree, and a promise to God that you will be brought up with the faith and start a new life with Christ." Johnny asked, "Can I get baptized any time?" Ed said, "Well yes, a lot of older people get baptized." Johnny said, "Good, I want to wait until I am old. I have a lot of sinning to do yet."

Jane reached into Sue's shirt and said, "The boy has a point." Mary said, "So where are we going?" Mark said, "We're going to the Niagara Cave, right? Where do you go for your honeymoon? To Niagara Falls, right? There is a cave like twenty-five miles from here." Johnny was excited, "I love caves. They're always different." Sue said, "They're the same, just a hole in the ground." Mark said, "This one has a sixty-foot waterfalls. Over 400 weddings have been performed there."

The Intels were outside the church. Gloria asked, "What the hell did you say 'fuck' for in the church?" Scott said, "I was just surprised we were not the first to get the clue." Randy asked as he took out his phone, "So what is the clue?" Scott read the clue, "Honeymoon falls." Gloria said, "That would be Niagara Falls but that must be 500 miles from here." Jeremy said, "There is a city on the border of Michigan, remember driving through it. It had the high cliff right next to the river. Let's see, there is the Niagara Escarpment that was created by the glaciers, follows Door County to Niagara Falls." Randy said, "How about the Niagara Cave? That is like thirty miles from here. It has a waterfalls inside it."

Darwin wandered away from the team and went up to a nun. He pushed her into a dark corner and said, "I always wanted to do a nun." She couldn't get away from him. She said, "Okay, if we are going to do this, I will raise my habit, you drop you drawers." The nun lifted her habit. Darwin dropped his pants and the nun took off running. A nun could outrun a guy with his pants down. Darwin reached down and pulled up his pants and continued the chase. The nun ran up to another nun. She yelled, "He tried to rape me." The nun said, "What? Who?" Randy, Scott, and Jeremy took off at a full run. They saw Darwin chasing a nun across the lawn. Darwin reached out for the nun. She grabbed his arm and gave him a judo flip. She gave him a kick to the ribs. He got up. She stepped in close to him and elbowed him in the throat, head slapped his ears. Darwin's hands went to his head. The sister used his ribs as a punching bag, giving him a good twenty hits. She then stepped back and gave him a roundhouse kick to the face. The three men stood there with their mouths hanging open. Gloria was the first to speak, "We are so sorry. I don't know what he did, but I am sure he deserved what he got." The old nun said, "That son of a

dog tried to rape me."

Darwin gat to his hands and knees. The old nun walked up behind him and kicked him in the balls. Darwin went face-first into the lawn and curled up, moaning. A priest showed up from nowhere. He asked, "Is this true, Sister Angela?" The old nun said, "He grabbed me and pushed me up against the church." The priest said, "How did you get away?" The nun said, "Come on, Father, a woman in a dress can run faster than a guy with his pants around his ankles." The priest said, "Sister Joyce, are you okay? And, Sister Angela, do you want to press charges?" The young nun said, "I am just fine, I am glad the Lord put me here to help." The older nun said, "I don't want to press charges. What good would it do? I am too old for that."

Darwin got to his hands and knees. The old nun grabbed him by the ear and lifted as she said, "You had better change your evil ways. Now go." She started to drag him by the ear. He couldn't get up. He was crawling behind her toward the van. The young nun apologized, "I am sorry about your friend. He has problems, and he might need help." Randy said, "Hell, girl, you have some moves, kicked the shit right out of him." The priest said, "Sister Joyce here does boxing for charities. She has raised a lot of money for the poor. Now leave and get some help for your friend." Scott said, "He is no friend of mine."

They got into the van. Scott said, "Okay, what the hell was that about?" Darwin mumbled as his lip swelled, "Didn't you ever wonder what is under those habits? Just gets you hard." Jeremy said, "You are one sick motherfucker and your ass should be in jail. Just think what the boys would do if they knew you tried to rape a nun." Randy said, "We have to get rid of this piece of white trash." Gloria said, "We need him. I don't care what kind of slimeball he is, we need five people, and this could be a payday." Scott said, "There is something seriously wrong with him."

Team Odin showed up at the Franciscan church a few hours later. Cherry said, "They have tours. This is going to be a beautiful church." Joe said, "I am going to light a candle for Jack. How is he anyway?" Dawn said, "Last time I checked he was hoping to go home. It is just sitting that long in a plane, he either stands or lies on his stomach. His stitches have stopped weeping, and I think they are to come out this week."

Robert said, "Shall we do a walk around and see if the clue is on the building?" Cherry said, "Let's just do the tour, we can ask the guide." They went inside. There was a couple of nuns praying up front and four other people in the church. Joe walked up to the steps before the altar and kneeled as he prayed. Cherry whispered to Dawn, "I will walk down this side, you take the other." When they got to the front and started back, Dawn lifted her arm and pointed to the choir loft. Cherry put her arm on Joe's shoulder and whispered, "We found it." Joe smiled and got up.

They went up the stairs to the choir loft. Robert said, "I will hoist up Joe, then Cherry." In less than two minutes they were down with the clue. Dawn was excited. She stood looking at her phone. She asked, "What is the clue?" Cherry said as she pulled the clue out of her back pocket, "Honeymoon falls." Dawn Googled it and said, "There are a lot of places to have honeymoons here. Oh, and there are a ton of waterfalls." Robert said, "The falls you go to for you honeymoon is Niagara Falls." Dawn said, "You're right. It's a cave, Niagara Cave, and it has a ninety-foot waterfall inside." Robert said, "Let's do this. I can't believe we are still in last place."

CHARTER THIRTY

To the Niagara Cave

Ed was teaching Johnny about words. He said, "Okay, Johnny, multi-syllable words like Mon-day, that is two. Sa-tur-day is a three-syllable word. Can you tell me a four-syllable word?" Johnny smiled and said, "Mas-tur-ba-tion." Jane said, "Wow, that's a mouth-ful." Johnny said, "You're thinking of a blow job. That's a two-syl-lable word." Mark couldn't hold it. He burst out laughing. Ed said, "Very good, Johnny. You are right, and good shock value. But that was two one-syllable words."

They reached the Niagara Cave. Johnny was excited. There was an eighteen-hole mini golf. Kids were panning for gem stones. Ed said, "I would give you a twenty to go and play but you wouldn't bring back the change." Johnny frowned and said, "Yeah I would. Please?" Mark said, "We don't have time for that. Let's do this as quickly as possible. This should be a payday." Mary said, "It's going to be cold, slippery, and a bitch. I can see it already." Jane said, "Have faith. Come on, Sue, let's go to the gift shop. We will ask about the monument there."

Johnny's face lit up as a smile came across it. "There's a gift shop? Can I come?" Sue asked Johnny, "Why do you have TGIF, thank god it's Friday, on your shoes?" Johnny said, "That was Mark being an ass. It stands for 'toes go in first.'" Sue chuckled and said, "He does have a dry humor, doesn't he?" Jane said, "We could have a threesome with him." Sue said, "He is our driver. We don't need him having a heart attack." Johnny asked, "Should I tell him?" Jane said, "You don't know what we are talking about." Johnny said, "My dad did a threesome at the bar. It's having sex with three people. That's why Mom went crazy." Mary said, "We will be there in a minute." Ed said, "Tours leave every fifteen to twenty minutes, so we don't have much time to look around here. you get the kid a sweatshirt. It's going to be in the low fifties underground." Mary said, "Oh shit, you're right." She went to the back of the van and asked, "What's in the wooden crate? It says it is a semiautomatic grenade launcher and a box of grenades." Ed said, "Now that is none of your business." Mark said, "It's a fucking grenade launcher? What happened to the mini gun?" Ed smiled and asked, "You

knew about that? I traded it for this. Well, it wasn't an even trade." Mark said, "Let's move. We don't want to miss the tour. The Intels are not far behind." Ed asked, "What about the Odins?" Mark pulled out his phone and said, "Let's see here where they are. Still at the church. So they figured out the clue. Let's see if they figure out this one." Mary asked, "Can you see the Intels?" Mark said, "Oh hell, they're on their way, maybe an hour behind us." Ed said, "We don't want to miss this tour and have to find the clue in one shot." Mark said, "I will get the tickets. Ed, get the kid and the girls." Ed jogged into the gift shop. He said loudly, "Johnny, Jane, and Sue, we are leaving." Jane came up with Sue. Ed said, "What did you do with the child?" Sue said, "He was just here." Ed said, "Go, I will find him. Stall if you have to. Son of a bitch. I will check the bathroom."

Ed took a quick walk around the gift shop and to the bathroom. He stepped outside. There was Johnny watching three women eating ice cream. He jogged up to him and said, "Come on, Johnny, we have to go." Johnny said, "Look at those three women. They all eat their ice cream differently. The first one lightly licks it, the second one is taking small bites out of it, and the third one sticks the whole thing in her mouth. Which one do you think is married?" Ed said, "We don't have time for this. Okay, the one that deep-throats it." Johnny said, "Nope, the one with the wedding ring, but I like the way you think." Ed said as he grabbed Johnny's hand and started to jog to the tour, "For Christ's sakes, Johnny, you have to stay with the person that is watching you. We can't miss this tour."

They were the last to get into the line. Ed yelled as he came in the door, "Hold the tour, we are here." Mary handed the young man the tickets. She shot Johnny an "I could kill you" look. Johnny said, "What, I stepped outside just for a minute." As they started the tour, Johnny kept asking Ed questions. Ed finally said, "Listen to the tour guide. His job is to tell you about the cave."

Johnny stopped talking and didn't say a word as he was going through the tour. Johnny was just amazed. There was a ninety-foot waterfall and a river running through it. Ed said, "Look closely, we don't want to miss it." He was shining his flashlight in every little crack up on all the ceilings. Johnny said, "There is a monument thing in the golf course." Mark turned and said loudly, "What? Are you sure?" The tour stopped, the sound of water running filled the cave, but Mark's sharp voice got everyone to stop in their tracks. Johnny looked scared and said shyly, "There is one of those things you put your key in at the golf course." Mary asked, "Are you sure?" Johnny nodded. Sue rubbed his head and said, "Thank you, Johnny. Now let's enjoy the tour and go and get our payday when we get up there." Mark pulled out his phone and said, "Dammit, no bars down here." Mary said, "What did you expect? You're a hundred feet underground." Mark said, "I just hope team Intel doesn't notice the monument. Shit, we must have walked right by it. Why didn't Johnny say anything?" Ed said, "Because he is a little boy. And don't touch that, it took thousands of years for the water to make it."

They finished their tour and went up and paid for a round of mini golf. Mark said, "We have to shake our ass, Team Intel is almost here." They went out on the mini golf and Mary said, "Johnny, we're not playing. We are going to the monument." Jane said, "Why did we even pay?" Ed said, "Because it is the right thing to do." Sue said, "Run ahead, Johnny, you can play the hole next to the monument." Johnny ran ahead and started to play the hole.

The monument was a good six foot high, they all put in their keys in. Ed said, "Mary, if you would please." Mary said, "Four, three, two, one, turn." The door on top opened and Mark took out the pile of cash. Jane said, "The next one is a million dollars." Ed said "I don't think so. It probably pays out a million altogether."

Mark walked around and handed out eight grand apiece. Mary asked, "Why did you short me two grand?" Mark said, "We are running short on cash for operations, fuel, food, and lodging. In the beginning of the game we all pitched in two grand apiece." Mary said, "At the end of the game that had better be split between us." Mark said, "I will consult the team captain." Jane said, "Team captain my ass. Sue has all the receipts if you would like to see them." Sue said, "Speaking of your ass, it's a nice one." Jane blushed and asked, "So who has the clue." Mark held it up and said, "This is the first clue of the last race. Speaking of that, let's get out of here before Team Intel catches us by the monument."

Ed stepped close to little Johnny. He dropped a ball and said, "Johnny, my boy, I bet you if I make this shot you do what you are told for the day. And if I miss, I will buy you an ice cream." Johnny smiled and said, "You're on, sucker. This is a par five hole." Ed gave it a light hit. It bounced off a lighthouse, up a small hill, rolled across the bridge, into the cup on the other side. Ed said, "Just like that. Now go get the ball and we will get out of here." Johnny protested, "I want to play." Ed said, "You lost the bet, now you have to do what you are told for the whole day."

Mark said on the way to the van, "We have to hurry. The Intels are almost here. The clue is Hawaiian meat. I don't know what they eat over there." Jane said, "They do the luau, that is burying a pig and cooking it underground." Sue asked, "Have you ever been to Hawaii?" Jane said, "It's on my bucket list. So who has been to Hawaii?" Ed said, "Oh come on, everyone has been to Hawaii. Have you guys been living under a rock?" Mary said, "No, everyone wants to visit Hawaii, not everyone gets to." Ed said, "Well I have been there a few times. The seafood is great. They have everything we have and more. What meat have you found on the net?" Mark said, "I don't care, we are going to get on the road so the Intels don't see us." He pulled out and started to drive. Sue said, "They eat poi. It's something like potatoes, beef, chicken, but pork comes up the most." Ed said, "It is SPAM. You can buy SPAM at McDonald's. They love the shit there." Mark said, "No frickin way, you think SPAM is the answer to the clue?" Sue said, "SPAM, you're right. They eat a lot of SPAM." Mary said, "SPAM museum, I shit you not. It's like fifteen miles way. Let me plug it into the GPS." Mark said, "SPAM, who would have guessed that one?"

Johnny pulled on Ed's sleeve and asked, "What is SPAM?" Ed said, "You have to be kidding me. Your mom has never made you SPAM and eggs? Say it's not true." Mary turned and said, "That stuff is so salty." Ed said, "Well that would be hard to make in a car. It is canned meat. Hard to explain. And sometimes it is on the menu." Sue said, "There is low-sodium SPAM. It comes in thirteen different flavors, hickory smoked, roasted turkey, bacon, jalapeno. This is amazing, who would have known?" Mary said, "Anybody that goes to the grocery story. What the hell people?"

The Intels pulled into the Niagara Cave parking lot. The ride there was pretty quiet. Darwin said, "Okay, so I did a bad thing. I shouldn't have chased the nun, but hey, I paid for it." Randy said, "You white piece of trash, you whipped out your dick in front of a nun. You white people are crazy." Scott said, "Your ass should be in jail. What were you thinking raping a nun? There is a special place in hell for people like you." Darwin said, "Haven't you ever wondered what it would be like?" Jeremy said, "No, and I mean hell no. What is wrong with you? We should dump him here." Gloria said, "No, we don't. We need him." Randy said, "What are you saying, woman? I don't trust him as far as I can piss." Scott said, "Let's get inside and find the clue." Randy said, "Clue my black ass, it should be a payday." Gloria said, "It is the fifth clue, and then the last race to the finish."

They went inside. Jeremy leaned into Scott and said, "We leave Darwin here." Scott said, "Yes, something has to be done, but not now." Robert said, "Glo, you stay with me. Dar, you dam well keep your hands off of her." Darwin said, "Okay, I did a booboo. That is in the past. It won't happen again." Jeremy said, "You got your ass kicked by a nun, and kicked good." Randy said, "If a brother would have done that, his ass would have been sent straight to prison." Scott said, "Well the priest measured the odds. He didn't want to have one of his sisters getting sued. She did put a whopping on your ass. And you are right, she must be built like a brick shithouse." Gloria said, "Scott, she is a woman of the cloth. I couldn't believe that nun boxed for charities."

They went for the tour. Gloria said, "This is a beautiful cave, the waterfalls, and the river running through it." Jeremy took off his jacket and gave it to Gloria. He said, "Your headlights are on. Let's not get the pervert going." Gloria took it and asked, "Which one? Thanks, it is colder than I thought it would be." Scott said, "The water is a lot louder than I thought it would be, but it is one hell of a cave." Jeremy said, "Let's make sure we don't fall over the railing while looking for the clue," He looked at Scott then to Darwin and made a motion with his head, like shove him to his death. Scott shook his head and said, "Karma. Have faith, my brother." Randy said, "Something is getting weird in here."

They went through the tour. Darwin said, "I am going out for a smoke." Gloria said, "We have to get rid of him. The van smells like cigarette smoke, which is better than his body odor." Jeremy said, "I am going to the gift shop and ask in there. We could have missed it." Jeremy went in and asked the sales lady, "Miss, we are on a treasure hunt and are looking for a steel question mark or a monument that looks like the Lincoln Memorial but smaller." He held up a twenty. She smiled and reached out and took the bill and said, "They put one of those in the mini golf a couple of weeks ago." Jeremy rolled his eyes back and looked at the ceiling, then back to her and questioned, "Really?" She smiled and said, "I wondered why they put that in there. It doesn't go with the theme."

He walked out to the team and came right out and said, "It is in the mini golf, we walked right by it." Gloria smiled and said, "You're kidding, right? Well I am glad we went through the cave. The pools of water were just beautiful." Randy said, "Almost as beautiful as you." Gloria said, "You're talking with your dick again. It's never going to happen." Darwin put out his cigarette on the sidewalk. Gloria said, "You are such a slob and moron. The fucking monument is right there if you would have looked." Scott said, "You know, it is the largest thing in the mini golf." Randy asked, "Does everyone have their key? Hey, dickhead, you got your key?" Everyone looked at Darwin,

"Yes, I have the key." Scott stepped close to Jeremy, "We need that key." Jeremy said, "I kind of forgot about that." Randy looked at the two and said, "I have seen that look before, it never ends well. Should I get a golf club?" Scott said, "What the hell you talking about? Shall we get some money?"

They went and got the monument and put their key into it and Jeremy said, "Okay, are you ready? Turn." A drawer opened and Gloria took the money from it. She handed out twenty-five hundred a piece. Randy said, "We are still in second place. The clue is Hawaiian meat." Scott said, "They're big into pork. I have been to a couple of luaus. God, I love Hawaii." Gloria said, "A raise of hands, who has been to Hawaii?" Scott, Randy, Gloria, and Darwin raised their hands. Jeremy said, "What the hell? I am the only one that hasn't traveled to Hawaii. It seems like such a long plane ride." Darwin said, "SPAM, I had SPAM at the McDonald's there and had it for breakfast. They like their SPAM." Jeremy said, "Well I went to *Spamalot* in Vegas. It's a spoof on Monty Python."

Gloria said, "I will be damned, the pervert was right. There is a SPAM Museum not far from here." Scott said, "Now that you mention it, they do eat a lot of SPAM." Jeremy asked, "Really? That's hard to believe. A SPAM Museum, so what time do they close?" Gloria said, "At 5:00 we have plenty of time." Scott said, "I beg to differ. We are in second place. We need this next one. It's the last and we don't know how much it will be." Jeremy said, "At least ten grand. Think of it, if we made first place every time it would have been a hundred grand apiece." Gloria said, "The prize is a million dollars." Scott said, "Is it? Or are they paying a million dollars in prize money?" Gloria said, "Hit the button." Randy said, "Who cares? We need to take the lead. Let's get going." Scott said, "You know he is right."

Odin was on the way to the cave. Cherry asked Robert, "So what are you doing after the game, are you going to settle down with your leprechaun?" Robert said, "You're never going to let that go, are you? I will go and find a job, I guess. I could try out for baseball, get in the minor league. I played a couple of seasons." Joe said, "I have some cash saved up now, so I think I am going to climb Mount Rainier. You should come along. It would be an adventure." Robert said, "If we get first prize I am down with that." Dawn said, "First prize my ass, we are lucky to get the grand. I am going to find myself a sugar daddy." Cherry asked, "Are you going to chase that basketball player?" Dawn said, "No, he has way too big of a dick." Joe said, "I thought that's what you liked." Dawn said, "Oh, it's a good time, let me tell you. I could have sworn I heard a rib crack, gets me moist just thinking about it. But that's not something you want to ride all the time."

They got to the cave. Dawn walked up to the front desk for tickets and showed the girl at the desk a picture of a clue and one of a monument. The girl said as she pointed to the phone, "That one. It's in the middle of the mini golf. Some guys put it there a few weeks ago." Dawn said, "Okay, everyone outside." She led the team outside and pointed, "It is hidden right out in the open, right there in the mini golf." Joe said, "Let's get tickets." Cherry said, "No, boys, we are just going over there to get the clue. Who knows, maybe it's ten grand." Robert said, "Cherry, grab a kid. We need five to open this."

Cherry approached a couple that were close to the monument and got the girl to help open it. Joe did the countdown, "Three, two, one, turn. And there it is." Robert took the cash out of the drawer. He peeled off a hundred and gave it to the girl that helped. Cherry said, "Well, that is one good thing about being one short, we get to split the cash." Robert said, "Jack's nine hundred is going in the glove box for gas." Dawn said, "You're a fun sucker. What's the clue?" Robert said, "Hawaiian meat." Joe said, "Well, let's look at this. You would go to Hawaii for your honeymoon or your second anniversary of going together. Lori would have been a great life, fucking bitch. She married my personal trainer. May she rot in hell." Cherry said, "You had a personal trainer?" He said, "I was trying to get into the Olympics program. My marathon time was just over two hours and forty-two minutes, just wasn't good enough. I needed two hours, six minutes, and thirty-two seconds." Dawn asked, "That's a full marathon, twenty-six miles." Robert said, "And 385 yards, people always forget that." Cherry said, "That is one long run, and someone did it in two and a half hours. Wait, your folks must have money." Robert said, "They are well-off, but are tighter than the bark on a tree. I raised the money. I just couldn't get the time down to make the cut."

Joe said, "Hey, dickheads, talk in the van. Let's get moving. We can do this." Dawn said, "Where are we going?" Joe said, "The SPAM Museum." Cherry said, "No way, they have a museum about SPAM? And what has that to do with SPAM?" Robert said, "Spam is the state meat of Hawaii, everyone knows that." Dawn said, "No way."

They got down the road a few miles. Joe said, "Found it, you're right. SPAM, the state meat of Hawaii." Dawn said, "If you look hard enough you can find anything on the net. Look at the state website. Their state animal is a humpback whale."

CHAPTER THIRTY-ONE

The SPAM Museum

Team Three pulled into Austin, Minnesota, and went straight to the SPAM Museum. Johnny asked, "Who is the statue in front of the place and why is he walking two pigs?" Mark said, "That, my dear boy, is the Earl of Spam, and those two pigs are his kids. He is married to a huge pig." Mary turned and said, "Don't listen to him. I am sure there is a plaque telling who it is." Ed said, "I bet you a dollar it is the guy who invented SPAM." Sue asked, "So how did SPAM get its name? Is it crap you get in your e-mail?" Mark said, "Now that is a good question, but we might want to shake a leg. Team Odin is still at the cave but they will be nipping at our heels if we lollygag."

Johnny pulled on Ed's shirt and asked quietly, "What's lollygagging?" Mark said, "Fuck the dog, screw the pooch." Mary rolled her eyes and said, "If we take our time, the other team will catch us." Ed said, "I have no idea. Lollygag is just one of those words. When you get back in the van Google it. He is right, we have to move." Jane said, looking at her phone, "SPAM, there are a couple of definitions, one is special processed American meat, another is something posing as meat, and it could be the abbreviation of spiced meat, spare meat, or shoulder of pork and ham." Mark said, "So nobody really knows for sure." Jane said, "They sent it to World War II to feed the troops, so maybe it was the American meat."

She gently patted Sue's butt and said, "Come on, sweetheart, let's find that thing." Johnny asked, "Are those two going to get married?" Sue turned and smiled. She said, "I don't know. What do you think, Jane?" Jane said "I suppose we can nowadays. Do you want to get married?" Sue blushed and asked, "Did you just propose to me again?" Jane blushed and stuttered, "I-I-I guess I did." Sue smiled, stepped close to her, pulled her close, and said, "Maybe." She kissed her passionately. Mark said, "Get a room." Mary blushed and said, "That was so sweet."

Ed said, "We're burning light, let's do this," and headed toward the door. Mary stepped close to him and said, "Wasn't that nice?" Then yelled, "Johnny, get off that pig." Ed smiled and said, "You just missed a Kodak moment. How many times are you going to see your kid riding a bronze statue of a pig?"

Mark said as he walked through the doors, "Holy SPAM, Batman, there must be a million cans in here." Jane said, "Oh my god, do you think the clue is in a can of SPAM? There is a conveyor running through the place with thousands of cans on it." Johnny pointed up and said, "That's the biggest sandwich I have ever seen." Ed said, "Okay, guys, split up. And, Johnny, don't break anything." Johnny said, "I'm coming with you." Mark said to Mary, "I don't know what the kid sees in him, but he sure likes him." Mary said, "There is a wall of SPAM. There must be 5,000 cans in it." Mark said, "You're not too bad for an old broad. There are 3,390 cans in that wall, says right there." He pointed to a sign. She said, "Who the hell are you calling an old broad?" Mark smiled and said, "Under eighteen protected by law, over thirty-five protected by nature." Mary said, "You're such a dickhead."

Jane sat and watched a never-ending stream of cans flow overhead. She said, "It has to be one of those. That would be a bitch trying to get a key in it." Sue asked, "Why is there a Viking holding cans of SPAM?" Johnny grabbed Ed by the hand and started pulling him to a measuring stick on the wall. He stood with his back to the wall and asked, "How many cans tall am I?" Ed put his hand on top of Johnny's head and said, "You are this tall, ten and a half cans tall." Johnny said, "You try it." Ed stood in front of the measuring stick. Johnny said, "Wow, you are twenty-three cans tall." Ed said, "We can't be fooling around. We have to find that clue and get out of here." Mark walked up and said, "There are a million cans in this place. Hell, there is a grocery store here with all of Hormel's products. Jane thinks it's on the conveyor. That would be a bitch." Johnny said, "Stand over here. Let's see how many cans tall you are."

Mark said, "Why don't you guys go to the kitchen? I am going to check out the war exhibit. You don't think the clue could be as small as a can of SPAM, do you?" Ed said, "I don't see why not. It just spits out a piece of paper. Now, Johnny, you look for a can with a question mark on it." Sue walked by and asked, "Any luck?" Ed smiled and asked, "Would we still be here if we found it? So what do you think?" Sue said, "It could be anywhere. We didn't even look outside." Ed had a sly smile on his face and he asked, "Let's not talk about that. Shall we talk about getting married?" Sue's face blushed and she said, "Let's just worry about that clue." She walked off studying the columns of SPAM.

Ed asked Johnny, "How would you like to go to Hawaii? That was part of the clue." Johnny took off running to Hawaii. Ed jogged right behind him. Johnny got there, breathing hard. Ed asked, "Would you like to surf when you grow up?" Johnny said, "There are more surfboards in the SPAM shack." Ed started to read about Hawaii and SPAM. He looked at the television screen and asked Johnny, "Do you see anything different about the TV?" Johnny looked and said, "No, it's just a TV." Ed said, "Look under the TV." Johnny said, "It's just a bunch of SPAM." Ed asked, "Are you blind, boy? Go down a few rows of SPAM."

Johnny really concentrated. "There is one can on the end. It has a question mark on it." Ed said, "There you go, you found the clue." Ed put both of his hands on the counter and hopped right over, pulled out his key that hung around his neck and put in the can, and out came the clue. He put his hand around Johnny's shoulders and started to walk. Johnny said excitedly, "What's the clue?" Ed said, "Let's just get some distance between us and where the clue is. Someone could be watching us." They walked up to Jane, who was still watching the cans of SPAM flow by. Ed said, "Johnny, go and get everyone discreetly and have them meet us here. So, Jane, have you had any luck?" Jane kept her eye on the cans as they went by. She said, "I don't know where they start and were they stop, but if I was going to hide a clue that is where I would hide it." Ed pulled out the paper and said, "Ho-ho-ho, that is the clue." Jane turned and looked at him, then rubbed her eyes. She said, "Oh thank god, my eyes are killing me. Where was it?" Ed smiled and said, "You were right about it being in a can."

Johnny came with everyone. Ed asked, "Johnny, do you know what discreetly is?" Mark asked, "Do we have a heading captain?" Ed said, "Kind of. We have the clue. Let's get to the van and get away from here." Mary said, "That is a good idea, get a little distance. That van sticks out like a sore thumb." Johnny said, "Can I ride up front? And why does Mark always get to drive."

They got into the van. Ed said, "The clue is ho-ho-ho." Johnny said, "It is Santa Claus." Mark said, "No, it's your mother." Johnny shot him a look and said, "Don't you be calling my mom a hoe." Mark smiled and said, "You're right, who would pay for that?" Mary asked, "What did you say?" Jane said, "There is a ton of stuff about Christmas in Minneapolis." Ed said, "I didn't say Minneapolis, I said ho-ho-ho." Mary said, "There is a Ho Ho Gourmet. In fact, there are a few of those." Jane said, "What the . . . ? You have to be kidding. Ho-ho-ho is something a giant would say, and there is a fifty-five-foot statue of the Green Giant just a few miles from here." Mark said, "Sounds good to me. Give me a heading." Jane said, "It is in Blue Earth on Highway 90."

Mark started to punch in GPS then said to Johnny, "See the woman in black, she makes a living on her back." Then he said, "See the girl in blue, she really knows how to screw." Johnny leaned over and pointed out a lady in pink. Mark said, "See the lady in pink, she can make your fingers stink." Mary yelled from the backseat, "What the hell are you teaching him? He is never sitting up front again." Mark smiled and said, "Your mom is in red, is she great in bed?" Johnny said, "She might give great head." Mary yelled, "Johnny." Johnny said, "Just joking, Mom." Mark said, "That should take care of you riding shotgun." Johnny asked, "Riding shotgun? What do you mean?" Ed said, "Riding shotgun came from back in the horse and carriage days. You sit next to the driver with a shotgun as protection." Johnny said, "Really? What would be after them?" Ed said, "Mountain lions, bears, Indians, and robbers. They called it the Wild West for a reason." Sue turned to look him in the eye and said, "Johnny is a good boy." Ed said, "I don't know. He needs some stability. Mary, you're going to have to find yourself a sugar daddy." Mary said, "Sugar daddy? Some old geezer with money? Where do you find one of those?"

Team Intel just missed Team Three. As soon as the van stopped, Darwin crawled out and lit up a cigarette. Scott said, "We have to get rid of him." Jeremy asked, "But how? Can we just leave him somewhere?" Gloria said, "We need the key. It's around his neck." Randy smiled ear to ear as he said, "Motherfuckers, just fire his ass. No big problem. He has money. I going to get myself some SPAM, I love that shit." Darwin finished his cigarette in like four drags, lit another one off the one he had going, then went into a coughing fit and hacked up a lung cookie. He spit it on the sidewalk. Gloria said, "God, that is gross." Jeremy said excitedly, "Did you see that? It actually bounced. Do it again." Randy said as he headed toward the door, "Sick fucks, we are never going to win this race."

Scott asked Darwin, "Why the hell do you smoke? It is nasty, expensive, and it is going to kill you." Darwin looked at him and said, "Because I like to smoke." Scott said, "Well, it's a reason. And you pay a lot of taxes. Pick up that butt, you shouldn't litter. Gloria, let's do this." Gloria asked, "So who is the farmer with the pigs?" Scott shouted, "Hey, Jeremy, check out the statue, see if there is a clue." Jeremy jogged over to it. He ran his hands over the pig, got down on his hands and knees, checking under the pigs, and then walked around the farmer. He then walked over to meet them. Gloria said, "So no clue. It's not going to be that easy." Jeremy said, "It's a nice bronze. The pigs aren't anatomically correct." Gloria asked, "Did you check their asshole for a key slot?" Jeremy said, "Yes, and there isn't one." "You have been hanging out with Randy to long." Jeremy held the door for Gloria and said, "There's Randy. He found free samples, might as well try some." Scott stepped in and said, "Wow, how the hell are we going to find the clue in this place? there must be a half million cans of SPAM in here." Jeremy walked right over and took a sample and asked Randy, "Dude, did you ask her?" Randy said, "This shit is the bomb. She is bringing out the bacon flavor next." Jeremy took a pretzel stick with a piece of SPAM on it and asked, "You wouldn't have seen a question mark added to the museum within the last month?" She thought and asked, "You are talking about a punctuation mark, right?" Jeremy said, "Yeah, you know, a question mark. It could be on anything. We are on a treasure hunt, and the clues have a question mark on them." She said, "Nope, nothing comes to mind. I asked around, nobody knows about it. There was a few guys looking for it, they were just here."

Randy said as he took another sample, "It could be on something big as a truck. Speaking of that, did you check that old delivery truck outside? Or as small as a can of SPAM." Gloria asked, "Do you really think it is a can of SPAM? I mean really, look at this place. And there is a steady flow of cans going overhead." Scott asked, "Are those cans on the conveyor just riding around or are they in production?" The lady said, "No, sweetheart, this is a museum. We have a gift shop, and those cans are Velcroed to the belt. You always get some smart aleck trying to knock one off."

Gloria said, "Okay, let's spread out. I will go to the kitchen. Scott, you go to that wall of cans. Randy, you go to the education center. Jeremy, go that way, make your way around, watch the time. We meet in the center under the SPAM display in twenty minutes. Look close." Scott said, "Who died and made her boss?" Randy said, "I think her kitty has a bloody nose." Scott asked, "Say what? Brother, you just talkin' shit." Jeremy said, "He thinks she is on the rag; you know, Aunt Flo." Darwin said, "I would still eat that shit. A brave soldier isn't afraid of a little blood, strain the blood clots with your teeth." Randy cringed and said, "That is disgusting, dude, damn." Scott said, "You don't have to picture it in your head, and I don't think anyone has been down there in a while." Randy said, "Darwin, do you want to check outside? That would suck if it was in plain view. Look in the delivery truck." Scott said, "We have to get rid of him. I smelled him twenty feet away." Jeremy said, "Smoking is such a bad habit, and it smells better than his body odor." Scott said,

"I think you need to burn his clothes. It's body odor or something, rotting flesh maybe."

Randy said, "Did you see that look? We better get going or Gloria will have her foot up our ass." Scott said, "I wouldn't mind sticking six inches up hers." Randy said, "You wish. Just find that stupid clue." Jeremy said, "Bet you five bucks it's on that conveyor." Randy said as he headed where some kids were playing, "Now that would just suck."

Twenty minutes later they met in the center of the museum. Gloria said, "So what do you guys think?" Scott said, "I was in the war exhibits. If you look at every can of SPAM this could take a long time." Gloria asked, "Are you reading the exhibits or just looking? It's a hell of a lot faster if you just look." Jeremy said, "I just left the Japan exhibit and am working through the countries." Randy said, "It's not in the learning room. You should try to pack a can of SPAM, takes me like ten times longer than a worker." Gloria said, "We have to step up our game." Scott said, "We have an hour and a half before the place closes, so let's do a quick once-over." Randy said, "I hate to say it but dickhead might be right." Scott asked, "Dickhead? Who you calling dickhead?" Jeremy said, "Ah, so you think it's on the conveyor too." Gloria said, "Let's get back to it and just look at everything. Find that question mark."

Scott asked, "Has anyone seen Darwin?" Randy said, "Once we are done here, we need to get that key and give him the boot." Gloria said, "We get the key and leave him at the hotel." Scott said, "That we can do. Let's find the clue. I have looked at so many cans, and we are talking tens of thousands of cans." Gloria said, "Twenty minutes back here."

She started to look right where they were, looking at all the columns, under chairs, desks. Scott went back to the World War II exhibit. Randy walked around, looking up at a huge sandwich that hung from the ceiling. Jeremy went back to the countries. Twenty minutes went by and they met at the center of the museum. Scott said, "Hey, did you read the jokes about SPAM?" Gloria said, "The place is going to close and you're reading?" Jeremy said, "There are just so many places you could hide a clue here." Randy said, "I spent ten minutes staring at those damn cans flowing overhead." Jeremy said, "Okay, let's do this. What exactly was the clue?" Gloria said, "Hawaiian meat." Scott said, "Well, shouldn't we look in Hawaii?" Randy said, "It can't be that easy."

They walked over to Hawaii. Scott said, "What the hell? It is right there." Jeremy said, "Where? I was here." Scott said, "Second row, at the end, the can of SPAM with the question mark on it." Gloria said, "No shit, there it is." Scott said, "I got it." He crawled over the counter and put in his key, took the clue, and said, "Gloria, Gloria, Gloria. Oh wait, it says ho-ho-ho, just kidding." Gloria said, "Your mother is a whore." Scott said as he crawled over the counter, "At least she got paid for it. So, hoe, what do you think the clue is about?" Jeremy said, "Well, you have the Ho-Chunk Indian casino. There is actually a few of those. A Westward Ho RV park. Tally Ho, there are two of those, they are Irish bars." Darwin said, "Did you ever think of Christmas, you know, Santa? Ho-ho-ho, merry Christmas." Gloria asked, "Were the hell have you been?" Darwin said, "They are serving Portuguese sausage SPAM. That is some good stuff." Randy said, "You don't say. You white motherfuckers figure this out. I am going to track some of that shit down."

Jeremy said, "I will meet you guys at the van. The place is closing." Darwin smiled. Gloria asked, "What was that look for?" Darwin said, "I ate whatever was left, damn near a half a can." Scott said, "I bet those farts are going to smell good." Gloria asked, "How much do you owe in child support?" Darwin chuckled and said, "It must be north of a million dollars now. Fucking bitch had herself a good lawyer. I lost my lake house. God, she was a bitch, could never satisfy her. I am much happier now." Scott asked, "Really? You don't know where your next meal is coming from or where you're going to sleep." Darwin said, "Dude, that is all trivial. I don't care, do you? In the meaning of life, who cares. I don't have the stress of making all the credit card bills, the upkeep of the house, the cars, the kids' schooling, the clubs, taxes. My god, the family spent it faster than I made it. And guess what, they didn't care." Scott said, "It is a juggling act, but you just can't give up." Darwin asked, "Why? Just walk away from the madness. I have found stress-free happiness. I don't need anything."

They reached the van. Gloria said, "Okay, I just Googled Christmas in Wisconsin. There are 125 million results. What the hell?" Jeremy said, "There are 2,850,000 results when you type in 'Santa Claus Wisconsin.'" Randy said, "Darwin, you are such a dickhead. I bought a can of Portuguese sausage SPAM and like four other flavors." Gloria said quietly, "Ho-ho-ho, now what in the bloody hell does that mean?" Scott said, "Ho-ho-ho has four meaning. One is laughter, also a postal code in Canada. Next, well . . . in Australia Santa says ha-ha-ha. That's just weird. And last is Santa, but he is not the only character that says it. There are the Jolly Green Giant, Jabba the Hutt, and King Harkinian." Gloria said, "Got it, Blue Earth, a statue that is fifty-five feet tall on Interstate 90 a few miles from here." Scott asked, "Do you have an address? Let's roll." Gloria said, "It's 1126 Green Giant lane, Blue Earth, Minnesota, 56013."

Team Odin got to the SPAM Museum. Dawn said, "The clue is Hawaiian meat, concentrate on that. We have a half hour till the place closes." Robert said, "I will drop you at the door then park this thing." Joe and the two girls jogged to the front door. Once they got there Cherry said, "You know, I hate this stuff. My mom fried it with eggs all the time." Joe said, "I like it. We don't have much time. Look for something to do with Hawaii and ask anyone you find." Dawn said, "Hawaii, right over there. There are a couple of surfboards over by it."

She walked into the Hawaii exhibit and said, "It is right there, the can with the question mark on it." Cherry asked, "Where? It's in a can?" Dawn put one hand on the counter and swung right over the counter. She pulled her key out of her shirt and put it into the keyhole, and she read the clue and said, "Shit, it has a number three on it. We are in last place." Cherry asked, "What is the clue?" Dawn climbed back over the counter and yelled, "Yo, Joseph." She waved Joe over and told Cherry, "It said ho-ho-ho, that's it."

Robert walked in and met Joe halfway across the floor. All four met in the middle of the museum. Dawn said, "The clue is ho-ho-ho, that's it." Joe said, "First of all, this is crazy. I love this museum."

Robert said, "I will go and ask someone." Cherry said, "My goodness, look up Santa in Minnesota. This might be interesting." Joe was looking at his phone and said, "You are right, that is what Santa says, ho-ho-ho, merry Christmas."

Robert talked with a girl that worked there and asked, "If I said ho-ho-ho, what would come to mind? We are on a treasure hunt and that is our clue." She smiled and said, "There is a canning factory not far from here, B&G Green Giant, but what I think you are looking for is the Jolly Green Giant. It's a statue on Highway 90, like ten miles from here." Robert peeled a twenty off his money clip and handed it to her. She said, "No, that's fine, I am glad I could help." Robert said, "Take it, I really do appreciate this." He jogged back to the team and said, "Let's roll, we are looking for the Jolly Green Giant." Cherry said, "There he is, makes sense. Ho-ho-ho, that is what a giant says." Joe said. "I will be damned, let's roll." Robert asked, "So where was the clue?" Cherry said, "It was in a can. The can had a little question mark on it, and Dawn spotted it right away." Joe said, "Holy shit, there must be a million cans in that place. It could have taken a month." Dawn said, "It has a three on it, we are in last place."

CHAPTER THIRTY-TWO

Jolly Green Giant

Team Three got to the Green Giant statue. Johnny said, "Look, it is a giant." Ed said, "Now the Green Giant, he is a brand of canned vegetables. He had a son, didn't he? Called Sprout or something." Sue said, "I bet he would have been hung." Jane smiled and said, "Wouldn't that make a picture." Mark said as he parked, "Thanks, now I have that picture in my head. Let's get out and find that clue. It has to be easier than the last one." Johnny said, "Well, it was nice sitting up front for a change, don't see that happening again. Do you like my mom?" Mark froze and the van went silent as he picked his words. "I think your mom is a very nice lady and is doing the best she can." Johnny asked, "But would you do her, I mean date her?" Ed said "Mark would do anyone, Johnny. Do you want him as your daddy? Ooh, Daddy Mark." Mary shot him a look. Ed said, "What? I am sure Mark would be a fine father figure for your son." He quickly got out of the van with his hand covering his mouth.

Jane raced Johnny to the statue and she looked up between his legs and said, "There it is the clue, the question mark." Johnny said, "That's really high." Jane said, "Now, you don't worry about your mom. Everything will work out. I think she likes Ed, don't you?" Johnny asked, "Really, do you think so? She doesn't act that way." Jane said, "Ah, that's the way she is playing it. Ed went out of his way to help you guys, he likes her too. The question is, do you like Ed?"

Johnny said with a sly smile, "He likes guns and is really smart. Yeah, I like him a lot."

Johnny said as everyone gathered around, "It is right up there. Jane found it. That is really high, in the crack of his ass." Mark said, "Now who would have thought I would be digging in a giant's ass today? So how are we going to get up there? Can you climb it?" Jane said, "This is not a flagpole, this would be a bitch." Sue asked, "Could we get logger gear and climb it like a tree?" Mark said, "That isn't going to work. They have special spikes on the shoes. And this is fiberglass, so it is smooth."

Jane slid her arm around Sue and lightly grabbed her by the ass. Sue turned and their mouths met. It was a short but passionate kiss. Mark said, "Knock it off. I am growing wood over here." Mary said, "We need a ladder truck." Ed asked, "How tall is that ladder on the van?" Mark said, "I think in the straight position it is around fourteen feet. That has to be damn near thirty." Ed said, "Let's try it, maybe it will reach." Jane said, "We could put it on something." Sue said, "You could stand on his shoulders." Jane asked, "Do you want to get rid of me?" Sue said, "You were a cheerleader once." Jane said, "Fine, barefoot I could do it. He has to be shirtless." Mary asked, "Why is that?" Jane smiled and said, "We used to practice in the pool, and in Mexico . . . But that is a different story. Clothing moves." Sue said, "You were quite the party animal, weren't you?" Jane said, "That was a long time ago."

The men had the ladder, snapped it at the straight position, wrapped towels on the top, and put it between the giants legs. It was way too short. Johnny said, "I can climb up to the top and you can lift the ladder." Ed said, "Smashing idea." Mary said, "Smashing? Where the hell did you come from? And no way in hell is Johnny doing that." Jane said, "She is right, I will do it." She slipped the key off her neck and held it in her mouth, stepped between the two men, and took the key out of her mouth and said, "Don't you drop me." Ed said, "Now we do this slowly. She is what, a buck twenty?" Sue said, "She is 134 pounds naked." Mark said, "Naked? Hey, you get a nice view from down here." Jane said, "Okay, I am at the top." Ed said, "Bend at the knees and slowly lift the ladder, sliding it up his leg." They lifted the ladder, pushing her into the crotch of the giant. Mary held Johnny tight and said, "If she falls, she is going to splat on the concrete." Sue stepped back and said, "Okay, guys, that's high enough, hold it right there."

Jane reached up into his crack under the leaves he was wearing and put in the key, then took the clue and put it into her bra with the key. She gave the thumbs-up sign. Sue said, "Okay, boys, let her down slowly." Mark said, "Nice and slow, keep her straight." Ed said as they got down to the waist level, "Now bend at the knees and set her down softly." Sue said, "Now hold it as she climbs down, good boys." Johnny looked up at his mom and asked, "Do you like Ed?" She looked down at him and said, "What is up with you? He seems to be a nice guy."

Jane climbed down the ladder and said, "Now that is something I thought I would never do." Mark asked, "Does your hand smell like giant ass?" Jane said, "You are so funny." She pulled the clue out of her bra and read it, "Old man." Everyone pulled out their phones. Mark leaned down to Johnny and whispered in his ear. Johnny said, "That is so lame." Then he said to the rest of the crew, "Did you hear about the giant with diarrhea? It's all over town. Get it?" Ed said, "So why did the Jolly Green Giant get kicked out of the garden? It's because he took a pea." Johnny said, "The grass is always greener when you water it with your wiener." Sue said, "Would you guys knock it off? we are trying to find the next clue."

Mark said, "Try this, the Old Man of the Dalles. This natural wonder is one of the many odd rock formations and rocky crags along the St. Croix River. It is located in Interstate State Park." Mary said, "Minnesota. No fricken wonder I couldn't find anything."

Sue said to Johnny, "Why shouldn't you eat Jolly Green Giant vegetables?" Johnny said, "I don't know." Sue smiled and said, "Because he stands over the corn and peas. Ho-ho-ho, get it?" Jane said, "That's a good one. How about if I told you, you have a nice body? Would you hold it against me?" Sue stepped over and hugged her and gave her a kiss. Mark said, "Enough of that. We have a heading. Back into the van." Ed said to Johnny, "We are going rock climbing." Mary said, "No, we are getting a hotel. Let's just get close." Sue said, "She is right. We don't want to be caught in the dark on some rock." Ed said, "Snakes come out at night, and there timber rattlers here." Johnny said, "Can we go and look for one?" Mary said, "No, you can't."

The Intels got to the Blue Earth and looked at the Jolly Green Giant statue. Scott said as he parked, "That's a big one. There isn't much here, so the clue should be easy to find." Randy said, "Why would you white folks build a statue of some canned vegetable giant?" Darwin crawled out of the van and lit a cigarette. Gloria said, "That is just so disgusting." Jeremy asked, "Do you smoke after sex? If you do, maybe you should try some lube. Do you get it?" Gloria said, "My god, how did I get stuck with these people?" Scott said, "Boy, that is a tall one. What did they say? Fifty-five feet tall. Is that with the stand or is the statue fifty-five feet?" Randy said, "Whoa, could you see trying to feed a motherfucker that big?" Scott said, "I will do a perimeter check. It probably is on the statue, way the hell up there." Gloria asked, "How would you get up there?" Jeremy said, "Boom truck or a ladder truck. If the clue is on his head, the base is six feet, that would be over sixty feet." Randy said, "You're right, it is on his head. Well, near it. Look at his crotch, there is a question mark." Jeremy yelled, "Scott, we found it."

Darwin lit a cigarette off of the one he was smoking and said, "Damn, that is a long way up." Gloria said, "Do yeah think? How are we going to get up there?" Randy said, "We call in a boom truck like you just said. Don't you even listen to yourself?" Gloria said, "Can we get a ladder? Man, that must be at least twenty feet." Scott asked, "Where is it?" Randy said, "It's in his asshole, up there between his legs." Jeremy said, "Let's just look at it. His legs are smooth and too big to get your hands around. There is nothing near it." Darwin said, "Climbing stick, like the one you use for hunting. They come in four-foot sections. You need six sections. Five might do, but to be safe." Gloria said, "We will get right on that. What do we do, call Amazon, have it delivered?" Jeremy said, "Hardware store fourteen miles from here. Let's go." Scott asked, "A twenty-foot extension ladder?" Jeremy said, "Whatever it takes. Let's get it done. We need a first place on this one."

Randy said, "You're not getting my ass up on that ladder." Scott said, "Even if Gloria throws you a little sugar?" Randy smiled so big it lit the van. Gloria said, "I would rather climb the damn ladder." Randy said, "You could climb on something else. Once you've gone black, you will never go back." Gloria said, "Been there, done that a couple of times. It's nothing special." Randy said, "Oh, it's something special alright." Darwin said, "You have to wine and dine a girl, then slip her one of those date rape drugs. You people know what those are." Randy said in a pissed-off tone, "We are not all like that. We don't need drugs to rape girls." Darwin said, "No, you can rape them the old-fashioned way, just get them drunk or hit them over the head." Jeremy said, "Dar, stop screwing with Randy. We all know he likes Gloria but it is never going to happen. She might do you though." Gloria shot him a look and said, "Randy, you have a better shot than Darwin." Randy smiled and said, "So I do have a shot. Who would you sleep with in the team?" Scott said, "We are not going there. Let's not put her on the spot."

They pulled into the hardware store and bought a climbing stick. It was a quarter of the price as a ladder. They got back to the statue. It was starting to get dark. They assembled the climbing stick. Jeremy wrapped a blanket around the top so it didn't scratch the fiberglass. Darwin said, "Now jam that son of a bitch right in his ass."

The three men, Scott, Jeremy, and Randy, climbed up onto the base and stuck the stick into the Green Giant's crotch. Randy said, "I am not going up there." Jeremy asked, "Gloria, what do you think?" Scott said, "She doesn't have to sleep with anyone. I will go up there, just hold the ladder." The stick bowed because it wasn't straight up and down. Five minutes he was back on the ground. He read it and said, "Old man. That is it, old man." Gloria said, "Let's find a hotel. I need a shower and a good meal."

They got to a hotel and Scott said, "I have a good idea, we eat, shit, shower, and shave. Meet in our room in two hours. We will figure out the clue and make plans for tomorrow." Gloria was the first one to Scott and Jeremy's room. They were looking at some gay guy doing a dance move on YouTube. Gloria asked, "Are you guys gay?" Scott said, "No, we were made to take a vacation. We are stuck on a project at work. Here, let me pull up our last vacation. We went to Vegas to get laid." Jeremy said, "We had a bet on who could get laid the most." Jeremy said, "Okay, these are the pictures. This is a red-head. She was from Vegas, she was my first. Then I went to a blonde. This is the housekeeper, I did her twice."

Gloria asked, "You paid for these women?" Jeremy said, "Oh yes, I went to the BunnyRanch and did some professionals in the morning. And boy, do they know their stuff. I started to go through the races, started with an Indian girl from India, then a black girl from Florida, a Filipino straight from the Philippines, an Irish girl. This girl was funny. She was a Mexican from California. She could deep throat it right to the balls. Talk about a professional. Now this girl, she is a little heavier, but she really liked her job. Look at the size of her tits. And could she tighten that pussy right up. I thought she was going to rip my dick right off. The next one, she was from . . . damn, where was she from? Anyway, she got on top and rode me like a horse. I am telling you, two minutes I was done. Thought my balls were going to explode. The last one, she looks really young but she was eighteen, legal and one hell of a ride. Look at her, she was beautiful."

Scott said as he turned his laptop toward her, "These are my pictures. I talked to a girl who was watching her girlfriends play blackjack, and she already lost more than she wanted to lose. I asked her about Vegas. We sat and had a drink. I told her what I was there for. She said she wasn't doing anything and would like to get laid. We headed for my room. We stopped at a roulette table and I placed a bet of a hundred dollars on her shoe size, red eight. I won and took half the winnings, then let the rest ride on thirty-two black, her inseam. Took half of that, let it ride. Then guessed her waist at twenty-two and the color of her underwear, red, and won again. We walked away from the table with over twenty grand. Here we go, first picture. I didn't take nudes, just our bare legs every time we did the deed. This is the room at Excalibur. Then we went to her hotel. There we are in the Luxor, did her up against the window overlooking the Sphinx. We went to the Venetian, got a room. I mean look at this room. We did it in the shower, then in the bed. Here we are.

I rented a tux. She rented a wedding gown, then I got Elvis in a gondola to marry us. Here are our vows. 'I, Scott, will do whatever Mary says. I will not say no unless it is illegal until we leave Vegas.' And Mary wrote hers own. 'I, Mary, will do whatever, whenever, however, Scott wants me to do. I will not say no unless it unsafe or illegal until we depart Sunday morning.' We then went to an adult toy shop. Look at the pile of toys. That was interesting. Do you know there is an electroshock sex toy? That was interesting. She always wanted to strap on a dick and do a guy in the ass. That was a first. We went to her hotel room to put a wedding picture on her bed at the Luxor, found one of her friends in there. She was sad. She lost everything, her next car payment, her rent, everything. We all went back to my hotel room. I gave her five grand and we had a threesome. Mary had never kissed a girl, and let me tell you they did more than kiss. So that counted as two. We went back to the casino. I hooked her up with some dude from Texas. Here is his driver's license, never can be too safe. We went to the Stratosphere, bribed a guy to let us be by ourselves on the roof for a few minutes and did it up there. Here we are overlooking the Fremont Street from the Golden Nugget. That girl was kinky. She shoved an icy pop up her ass as we did it, then she gave me a head job with a mouthful of Pop Rocks. Took a sunrise helicopter ride to the canyon, did it in the helicopter and in the canyon watching the sunrise. Did you know they have pink rattlesnakes there? We didn't see any but that is what the pilot said. Here we are as we had sex against the window overlooking the strip. I only had sex with one girl. She said her pussy felt like a petri dish and my dick was sore for a week."

Gloria asked, "So who won?" Scott said, "I won. We want to do it again. Hell, we should have done it this vacation." Jeremy said, "True, we would be back at work by now." Randy said, "How long are you dudes on vacation?" Jeremy said, "As long as it takes. We have a ton of work to do." Scott said, "And we keep adding more. This has been a very productive vacation so far." Gloria asked, "As long as what takes?" Jeremy said, "The game. We started it and we are going to finish. It can't be that much longer."

Randy asked, "So what are we going to do about Darwin? I just can't take that cigarette smell any longer." Scott asked, "Where is he?" Randy said, "Smoking and then to the bar." Gloria said, "We need the key and we need him, the fifth guy. It's too late to look for someone else." Jeremy said, "Okay, game plan. The clue is old man. This is what I think, Old Man of the Dalles. It is in Taylor Falls, Minnesota. It is a rock formation. I say we leave at first light. If the other team didn't make it tonight, we catch them in the morning." Gloria said, "First light my ass. How about 8:00, after breakfast?"

Randy said, "I am up with that. So you got fucked in the ass by some white chick?" Gloria said, "I am impressed. Never thought you guys would do something like that." Scott said, "It was the receptionist's idea. She told Jeremy he should get laid, so what better place than Vegas? No commitments, just sex." Gloria said, "She probably wanted to have sex with you, did you ever think that?" Scott said, "She did look a little depressed when you told her about the trip. I thought she would have been happy we did it." Jeremy said, "Gloria, you might have been right about that. She has treated me different ever since." Scott said, "Now, she told him to get laid, how were we supposed to know she was the one that we were supposed to lay?"

Jeremy said, "I just sent her a text. We will see what she says." Gloria asked, "What? What did you just send her? Did you ask if she wanted have sex with you?" Jeremy said, "No. Well, not in that many words. I just wrote, 'It has been brought to my attention that when you told me to get laid you subconsciously wanted to have sex with me. Is this true?'" Randy said, "Oh my god, how do you people even get laid?" Jeremy's phone dinged. He looked at it and said, "She replied one word, 'YES,' all in capitals." Randy said, "You have to be shitting me." Scott said, "Well that is interesting. Should you respond? Do you want a relationship with Mary?" Jeremy tapped the phone and said, "Let's find out her intentions." Scott said, "Tomorrow, downstairs. Be packed, 8:00, breakfast." Jeremy's phone dinged. He said, "She just wants to have sex and get pregnant. Her husband is dumb as a box of rocks." Gloria said, "So she is married." Scott said, "So I wonder if she will have sex with me too then." Jeremy said, "Well I would suppose she just wants to deepen the gene pool. Do you think she has discussed this with her husband?" Randy said, "Really, do you think she would ask her husband if she could bang the two of you?" Gloria said, "If you guys do her, it has to be a secret."

Jeremy's phone dinged and he said, "Yes, she would like to do you too. And I do remember sending her a gift of cash for a wedding. Remember? She wanted us to come. We were gene splicing that wheat with rice." Scott said, "I remember she was gone. We ran out of coffee. That's right, she did get married. Oh my god, mitochondrial NADH dehydrogenase; mRNAs spliced with mitochondrial Cis group 11 introns, that could be our building block." Gloria asked, "Is that what you are working on?" Jeremy's eyes opened wide, his jaw dropped. You could see he was in deep thought. He texted his lab and said, "We worked on that last year. And yes, I think that will work. Wow, that might just work." Randy said, "Get some sleep. I can't believe your Vegas trip. You go again, I want to come. And I do mean *cum*."

Team Odin got to the statue of the Jolly Green Giant. Robert said, "Holy fuck, that's a big one." Joe said, "Now that doesn't mean the clue is on the statue, but that is where I would put it." Dawn said, "Now why the hell would you make a statue of a green giant?" Robert said, "They have a canning factory around here, and the town wants you to stop." Cherry said, "Well lets go and take a look." Robert said, "It has to be on the thing, there isn't much around here." Joe said, "Christ, that thing is tall." Cherry said, "Fifty-five feet, and I don't think they include the base, so over sixty feet."

Robert stayed back and started to circle the statue. Cherry yelled, "Found it. Take a look up between his legs." Joe smiled and said, "The first place you looked." Dawn said, "Wow, that has to be twenty, maybe thirty feet." Cherry said, "It is to smooth to climb." Robert said, "Even with those plunger things." Joe asked, "Do they make those?" Robert said, "Oh yeah. I don't know where you can buy them, probably on Amazon." Cherry said, "My god, that is a long throw." Dawn asked, "What are you thinking?" Cherry said, "If we can get a rope through his arms, I can climb it. But I need one through both arms, one to get me up there and one to pull me over." Joe said, "Dawn, you threw discs. Can you throw a rope up thirty feet?" Dawn said, "Thirty feet straight up? Are you smoking drugs?" Robert said, "I got this. Do you have a small rope? We can then tie on a larger rope." Dawn said, "That is a long way up." Robert said, "Let's get the equipment. I will show you my idea."

They went back to the van. Cherry took a harness out of her suitcase. She said, "This is a lightweight harness. I wouldn't go rock climbing with it." Robert pulled out a fishing rod. Joe said, "I get it, that you can do."

They carried all the ropes to the statue. Robert cast a sinker through the arm of the giant. They tied on a small rope and he reeled it through the arm, the same with the other arm. They used every foot of rope they had. Cherry said, "This is going to be interesting. When I get to his crotch, pull me over with the rope from his other arm. I hope I can reach in far enough to reach the clue." Joe asked, "Are you sure you can do this? If you fall we will be scraping your ass off the cement." Cherry said, "Thanks for the vote of confidence. The climb is nothing. Getting close enough to get the clue is the trick." She started to climb.

Robert said, "She has such a nice ass." Dawn said, "Yes, she does." Cherry looked down and said, "You do know I can hear you?" Joe asked, "If this doesn't work, what should we do?" Dawn said, "It will work." Joe yelled up, "You're almost there. We are going to gently pull you over. Tell us when it is far enough," They pulled the rope and she swung over between his legs. Cherry said, "That's far enough." She climbed a couple of feet and reached in and got the clue, then rappelled down to the base of the statue. She said, "Piece of cake, went better than I thought it would."

Robert said, "Let's get this shit put away and get out of here. I am sure this is breaking the law." They were putting away the ropes. Dawn asked, "So what is the clue?" Cherry said, "Old man, that's it. All I can think of is the *Old Man and the Sea*." Joe said, "Less chatter, more work. Let's get on the road." Dawn said, "I could use a good drink and a shower." Joe smiled and said, "Sounds good. I could join you." Dawn smiled and said, "If I want to get laid, I will grab some guy from the bar, less drama." Cherry said, "Oh, and she can. Men are such pushovers. Could you turn her down if she walked up to you and said, 'Hey, you want to come to my room and get laid?'"

Robert smiled and said, "It might work for a woman. A guy ever did that, he would be thrown in jail." Joe said, "No way, dude, just for asking?" Robert said, "More than once is considered harassment. And if you try to pay for it, trust me, it's not pretty." Cherry asked, "Did you do that?" Robert said, "Alcohol does strange things to young horny men. There was the girl I wanted to get in bed for the longest time. Let's just say that was the first and last time I had a restraining order put on me." Dawn said, "Aw, isn't that cute. Did you love her?" Robert said, "I really thought so. Whenever I was close to her I felt nauseous. My hands would sweat, my mouth went dry, I couldn't think." Cherry said, "Wow, you really had it for this girl. What did you do?" Robert said, "She was a whore. She slept everyone except me. She finally got married and fat. Now she is divorced. Her husband got the kids and got remarried. I think she is bipolar or some shit." Joe chuckled and said, "It is not like you are keeping track of her." Robert said, "She can rot in hell." Dawn said, "Someone holds a grudge." Robert said, "It could have been something beautiful. Oh well, that is just water over the bridge."

Cherry said as she got in the van, "Old man in Minnesota, there are a few. But I would say the Old Man in the Dalles is the one." Robert asked, "What number is on top of the clue?" Cherry reached in her bra and pulled out the clue and handed it to him. He put it to his cheek and said, "Still warm, and we are in last place. It has a three on it." Dawn said, "Now we should talk about this clue. If you look it up, the best view is from the diving cliffs from across the river. If the other teams go to the rock formation, maybe we can get a jump on them." Joe said, "How do we know they aren't three days ahead of us?" Robert said, "We find a hotel close by and hope for the best. This is the last payout."

CHAPTER THIRTY-THREE

Old Man of The Dalles

Team Three was getting in the van at first light. Johnny looked like he was drunk off his ass, staggering down the hall. Ed said as he picked him up, "Morning, sunshine. You can sleep in the van. This is going to be a rock-climbing thing." Mary asked, "Where is your luggage?" Ed said, "I brought that down a half hour ago. It's going to be a beautiful day." Mark said from behind them, "Jane and Sue are on their way. She was giggling. The shower took longer than they thought it was going to." Ed sang, "Young love, first love." Mark said, "Yep, that will wear off soon. So how is the dead solider?" Mary said, "Sound asleep."

They got to the van. Ed said, "Let's get the ropes out. This is an outcropping, so we will probably climb to the top and lower down to the clue." Mark said, "Here come the girls, I will fire this baby up." Jane said, "Sorry we are late, had a problem getting out of the shower." Sue said, "But let me tell you, we are super clean." Ed asked, "Am I the only one that has rock climbed?" Sue leaned in and kissed Jane full on the lips and asked, "Have you ever rock climbed? I haven't but if you want to . . ." Jane said, "Let's try on a cruise ship and see if we like it."

They got in the van and headed to the interstate park. Mark said, "We are going to go to the Minnesota side. That has the best view of the old man." Mary said, "The clue might be there." They got to the overlook and got out. Ed scanned the rocks across the river with the field glasses and said, "There it is, halfway down the rock face, a lime green spot." Mark said, "Let me see." He looked and said, "Okay, that would be around a fifty-foot climb. We will have to mark the spot right above it." Jane asked, "Do you want us to stay here? I can call you when you are right above it." Mark asked, "Should we leave Johnny here? You know we are going to lose time having to come back and pick you guys up." Ed said, "No, they are right. This way they can get us in the right position. Let's go leave the child with them." Mary said, "Johnny, you stay with the girls. We will be right back." Ed said in a low voice, "Stay down, boy, and don't wander off."

They got to the trailhead and Mark asked, "So it's a quarter of a mile. Do you have climbing gear?" Ed pulled out a large D-ring and said, "This will have to do." Mary said, "These fucking mosquitoes are crazy." Mark jogged back to the van and sprayed her back, then handed her the can. Ed said, "Let's move. I have a feeling the other teams aren't far behind." Mark took out his phone and said, "Both teams are in hotels close by. Team Odin must have got the clue late last night."

Ed was on a mission. He set the pace, leaving Mary behind. Ed stepped out on the dome of the rock overlooking the river. His phone went off. He answered it and said, "Shit, we are a couple of hundred yards too far ahead." Mark said, "Boy, I am glad these are light ropes." They walked back on the top of the rocks until he got another call. Ed said, "We are supposed to be looking for two birch trees. There are trees all over." Mary huffed and said, "From their point, come this way." Mark stood in front of a birch and waved. Ed said, "That's it. Tie a rope. No, let me tie the rope. Not that I don't trust you, but I don't."

He wrapped the rope around himself and through the D-ring and said, "I don't think this is a good idea, but what the hell." Mark threw the rope over the side and said, "I hope there is enough. You want me to tie on another chunk?" Ed headed slowly down the face of the rock. He got down to the clue, wrapped the rope around his arm, and hung there while he put the key in the box. Out came the clue. He read it and started back up. Mark said to Mary, "Better him than me. You would be fishing my ass out of the river." Mary said,

"I couldn't do that in a million years." Mark said, "Look across the river, a team is here." He pulled out his phone and said, "It's Odin. the Intels are still at the hotel." Ed got to the top. Mark knelt, holding his arm over the edge. He asked Mary, "Hold on to my leg so this fat fucker doesn't pull me over." Ed said, "Fat fucker, I will give you fat, you cubby little bastard." Mark said, "Just take my hand, old man." Ed grabbed Mark's hand and came over the edge. Ed said, "I am getting too old for this shit." Mary asked as Ed struggled to his feet, "Are you okay? What was the clue?" Mark said, "Forget that for now. Odin is here. We have to get these ropes untied and get our ass out of here." Ed said, "Let's move, I will show you the clue in the car." Mark pulled up the rope, wrapping it around his shoulder. Ed went and untied it and said, "I will rewrap it later, let's

move."

They headed back down the path to the van. When they got there, Odin was waiting. Joe and Robert were pulling rope out of the van and untangling it. Cherry yelled, "Hey, team what the hell is your name, Team Three or something. How did it go?" Mary said, "Don't talk to them." Mark said, "It is a beautiful day. We are in the home stretch. One more payout and we are done." Dawn said, "Hey, you are kind of cute. Would you like to change sides?" Ed said as he reached the van, "I thought the rules were we don't speak." Robert said, "No, we can't work together. Like you couldn't give me the clue for, let's say, $500." Ed said, "Five hundred dollars? You can do better than that." Robert said, "Okay, a grand then." Mary said, "Come on, boys, we have to be headed back up north."

Mark hopped in and started the van and asked, "Up north where?" Ed said, "You don't even know the clue. You lied." Mary asked, "What is the clue?" Ed said, "Let me dig that clue out. Here it is, you figure it out." He handed it to Mary. She read it, "Isthmus, rotunda. That's it." Ed said, "Rotunda? That has something to do with a building, right? Text the clue to the girls and tell them we are on the way." Ed said, "Okay, rotunda is a round building, especially with a dome. And an isthmus is a narrow strip of land with a sea on both sides that connects two larger land masses." Mary's phone dinged. She said, "Madison, it's the capitol." Mark said as he punched in Madison on the GPS, "This will be a straight shot. I have a feeling this is the last clue. There it is, 268 miles. It should take four and a half hours."

They went and picked up Johnny and the girls. Mary pulled out a pack of cookies and gave them to Johnny. Mark asked, "Hey, could I have one of those?" Johnny asked, "Is your penis long enough to reach your asshole?" Mark said, "It sure is." Johnny said, "Good, go fuck yourself." Mary grabbed Johnny by the back of the neck and said, "You apologize right now." Johnny said, "I am sorry. You can have some of my cookies." Mark said, "I was going to stop for ice cream but screw you, buddy." Ed asked, "Did the child go to the restroom? If he didn't, we should stop at the next gas station." Johnny said, "I don't have to go." Sue handed Johnny her iPad and said, "Johnny, play a game and be quiet."

Jane asked Sue, "Would you like a couple of kids?" Mark said from the driver's seat, "I will impregnate both of you, might take a few times trying." Mary said, "I thought you said you had a vasectomy." Johnny asked Ed, "How do you spell that?" Ed said, "V-A-S-E-C-T—" Johnny said loudly, "Ouch, they cut your balls off. It says they do it right in the doctor's office, and there is a picture." Mark said, "Look on YouTube. You might be able to watch the surgery." Mary said, "Don't be looking at that." Johnny said to Ed quietly, "Mom is such a fun sucker." He then asked loudly, "Where do sharks go on vacation? Finland. Where do sheep go on vacation? Baaa-hamas. Where do hamsters go on vacation? Hamsterdam. How about cows? They go to Moo York." Jane said, "You had to give that to him, didn't you?"

Johnny asked, "How do rabbits vacation? They take a hareplane. What do frogs drink? Croak-a-Cola." Mark said, "I have one. When the red river is a-flowing, take the dirt road." The car quieted down and Mary said, "God, you're a sick bastard." Johnny told Ed, "I don't get it." Ed said, "You are not supposed to get it. Mark, do not explain it." Johnny said, "I have to pee." Ed said, "Told you. We have been on the road for a half hour." Sue said, "Really? A half hour? It feels like five hours." Johnny pointed and asked, "What is that?" Ed said, "It is a big blue ox in the campground." Johnny asked, "So what is a campground?" Mark said, "It's pretty much a bunch of people who don't live in a trailer park but like to vacation there."

Odin went up the trail to the dome of the Old Man in Dalles. Robert said, "Watch closely. Team Three just came through here." Cherry asked, "What the hell, Geronimo, you think you can track them?" Dawn asked, "Did you see that team has a couple of new players?" Robert rolled his eyes and said, "Shall we just focus on the task at hand? We need to know where they tied off." Joe said, "Let me take lead." He looked at the path and started the climb to the top. He found where the rope was tied and asked, "So who wants to go down? Not on me, the clue should be almost fifty feet down." Dawn said, "Like anybody would go down on you." Cherry said, "I think a guy should go down." Robert said, "Fine, I will do it." Cherry said, "No, that is fine. I will go, it will just take a minute."

She wrapped the rope around her and repelled off the rock face, dropping ten feet at a time. Then she ran a few feet across the face to the clue. She grabbed it and got the clue. She yelled up, "Okay, pull me up." Joe and Robert pulled her up. She walked up the side as they pulled. Dawn asked as soon as she got up, "So what is the clue?" Cherry said, "What is green and has a big dick?" Robert said, "Ha, very funny." Cherry said, "I really don't know what this is." She handed the clue to Dawn. Dawn read it, "Isthmus, rotunda. Now a rotunda is a room, right?" Joe said, "Here we go. An isthmus is a stretch of land with a sea on both sides and a rotunda is a building or room especially with a dome." Robert said as he looked at his phone, "It has to be Madison. Look, there is a lake on both sides." Cherry said, "Let's roll. This could be the end of the game." Robert said, "Finally. Joe, you still up for that mountain climb in Seattle?" Joe said, "Well I do have a couple of weeks before school starts." Cherry said, "Let's go, guys." She jogged down the trail to the van. Once they got into the van Joe said, "Well, back to Mad Town. Killed off a few brain cells there." Dawn said, "It's a party town. We will have to find out when the tours are."

Team intel pulled into the parking lot just as team Odin was leaving. Randy asked, "What the hell time do you white folks get up in the morning?" Gloria said, "A hell of a lot earlier than you.

We should have been out of the hotel by nine." Scott said, "Let's get this done. We are not that far behind. If we get this quickly maybe we can catch up." Darwin jumped out of the car and lit a cigarette, taking a long drag. Gloria said, "Be careful with that. It is dry and we don't want to start a fire. That is such a disgusting habit." Scott said, "Okay, I will get the ropes. Are we sure it is going to be on the cliff?" Jeremy said, "Well I would presume so. That is what this place is." Scott asked, "Has anyone rock climbed?" Randy said, "You're not getting my ass down there." Gloria asked, "Even if I said please?" Scott said, "Fine, I will go. This

sucks. Let's find out where they went over the edge."

They followed the trail. Darwin stepped off the side and took a leak. Gloria asked, "Couldn't you wait?" Darwin said, "The world is my urinal." They walked up and down the trails. They found a few guys rock climbing and asked them if they had seen the question mark. One guy said, "Yeah, it's downriver, two hundred yards or so." Randy asked, "Could you guys climb down to it for a hundred dollars?" A guy said, "A hundred bucks? Not a problem. It is an easy climb." Randy pulled a hundred out of his wallet and said, "We are in kind of a hurry. You need to put a key in it and get a clue for us."

The rock climbers grabbed a rope and some gear. Scott said, "If we get this done quickly, there is another hundred when you are done." The three climbers led the way. They came to a spot and one of them said, "Well this must be it, looks like they tied off to this tree." The climbers quickly set up. They laid down a mat over the edge to protect the rope from fraying on the rocks.

Darwin said to Gloria, "Did I ever tell you my dick was in the Guinness Book of World Records? The librarian caught me and told me if I didn't take it out she was going to call the cops." Gloria asked, "Did anyone tell you you're one sick man?"

The climber repelled off the side of the cliff. Jeremy held on to a small tree and looked over the side. Randy asked from ten feet behind him, "So how is it going?" Jeremy said, "He is at the clue. It took him four hops and he was down fifty feet. He is on his way back up."

Randy took Gloria's shoulders in his hands and he started to massage her shoulders. He said, "It could be great between me and you." She said, "You do know this is sexual harassment?" Randy said, "Oh come on, we could hook up once and see where it goes." Scott said, "Her ass meant no. What don't you get? You know what I am doing after this game? I am going to Vegas to get laid, everything legal done professional, and catch a show or two." Gloria looked at him and said, "Really? You're a good-looking guy. You shouldn't have trouble picking up a gal." Scott said, "You would be surprised. And the drama, I don't need that crap."

The two climbers helped the one up and over the edge. He walked up to Scott and asked, "Was that quick enough? It is an easy climb." Scott pulled out a hundred and exchanged it for the key and the clue. He read it, "Isthmus, rotunda. That's it. So an isthmus is a strip of land with water on both sides, and a rotunda is a round building with a dome." Darwin asked, "How the hell do you know this shit?" Randy said, "Oh come on, everyone knew that clue. Didn't you go to school?"

Jeremy said, "Let's get this game done with. I hear I am going to Vegas to get laid." Gloria asked, "Aren't the two of you going to do your secretary?" Scott said, "That's right, we can do her every day till she is with child. That should be different." Jeremy asked, "Now I have thought of this. Shall we do her in the office or the lab?" Scott said, "Oh, in the office. We can take turns sitting at her desk. It should be fun." Gloria said, "You are going to be creating a person. That's a big responsibility." Jeremy said, "No, it's not. We are just going to knock her up. It's like a sperm bank but we deliver." Jeremy said, "I have donated sperm before. They look for an IQ of over 120. And when you hit 140 they are pounding on your door." Darwin asked, "So is 140 smart?" Randy said, "Anything over 140 is considered a genius. Jeremy, are you over 140?" Scott said, "That's just a number. And he did break the plane." Jeremy said, "We're going to do the test again." Gloria asked, "What is going on here? Did Scott beat you in an IQ test?" Jeremy said, "Let's move. We have the clue and are in last place." Randy said, "So Scott is smarter the Jeremy, who knew." Scott said, "That is on paper, means nothing." Jeremy said, "He does make more money than me. I think that is why, and he kisses ass like a whore." Scott smiled and said, "You have to slip it the tongue if you want to hit the sweet spot. We are trying to change the world."

Darwin leaned forward and whispered in Gloria's ear, "You know I am actually quite handsome. When you are drunk and the lights are low and there are no other dudes around and you have very low standards." Gloria turned and said, "I never said you were ugly. You are not bad looking, you clean up nice. But you stink and are disgusting. I mean come on, you're hiding from the law, you abandoned your wife and kids." Darwin said, "But I am free, and it feels so good." Randy said, "You make people think it would be nice not to have to worry about bills and money. They probably learned their lesson. Why don't you call your ex-wife and give her a chance?" Darwin said, "Fuck that. She is a money-grubbing whore. She has a sugar daddy and is burning through his savings. She would love for me to get a divorce so she could take him to the cleaners. I keep an eye on her in social media." Scott said, "So did you give the guy a heads-up?" Darwin said, "No, why would I? She is great in bed, and she probably puts out three times a week. Just wait, it will slow to once a month if he is lucky." Gloria said, "Really, once a month?" Darwin said, "If he is lucky. When you are married you only have sex when she wants to. Then you find out she wants to with someone else."

CHAPTER THIRTY-FOUR

To the State Capitol

Team Three got to Madison. The traffic was terrible. Mark said, "So we are going to make the 3:00 tour. Let's do this in one shot." Johnny said, "Wow, look at that, it's the White House." Ed said, "Johnny, that is not the White House. That is Wisconsin's state capitol, looks like the capitol in Washington, DC, but it is shorter, I think. Anyway, the White House is where the president lives, it is not the capitol." Johnny said, "That's not true. Everyone knows what the White House looks like." Ed said, "May I have a show of hands? Who know the White House is where the president lives?" Everyone raised their hand. Mark said, "And you don't have to be white to live there. That is kind of racist, isn't it?"

Mary said, "I heard there are tunnels connecting everything." Ed said, "Well there is a bowling alley, a florist. Hell, there are a lot of rooms, secret tunnels. It's a fricken maze down there." Sue said, "It sounds like you have been there." Ed said, "Me? Oh no, just rumors I have heard." Mary turned to look back at him and asked, "Who are you really?"

Mark said, changing the subject, "Hey, there is a Hooters here. Can we stop for a bite?" Johnny looked at Ed, who said, "It's a restaurant where women wear short shorts and show a little cleavage. They have good wings there." Mary said, "This should be a payout, ten grand or better. We eat later." Mark said, "But where? See, the girls here are cute and friendly. I used to go at two fifteen. That is when they cleaned the lights, cheap entertainment." Jane said, "You dog, you." Mark said, "You know what they say, young, dumb, and full of cum."

Ed glanced down at Johnny. Johnny smiled and said, "I know. I watched porn with my dad." Ed said, "You do know that is illegal? He could have been put in jail for that." Mary said, "Not in that town." Jane looked back and said, "Ah, poor baby." Johnny said, "It just makes you look at girls differently." He raised his eyebrows and smiled. Jane said, "That was creepy."

Ed said, "Johnny, my boy, sex is hardwired into our system. Everyone has a sex drive. Yours isn't turned on yet. Once you hit puberty you will think in a different way. Sex is dangerous. People carry a lot of diseases. You kiss a girl and you are kissing every boy she has ever kissed. And sex lasts for a few minutes but can ruin your life." Johnny said, "That can't be true. If you kiss someone, how do you kiss everyone she has kissed?" Ed said, "Okay, if I spit in a glass and I have, let's say, HIV, which is a sexually transmitted disease. I put some water in it, you take a drink. Now you have HIV. You hand the cup to Jane. She takes a drink. Now she has the disease, and she shares it with your mom. Soon the whole car has the disease except Mark, because nobody is going to drink out of his cup." Mark said, "Hey, what are you trying to say?"

Mary said as Mark parked, "You know, if I wanted to tell Johnny about the birds and bees I would have done it myself." Mark said, "Birds and bees, hell, your old man had him watching gay porn and some really sick shit I wouldn't even watch. And were where you? Out supporting his ass." You could see Mark struck a nerve, tears started to flow down her cheek. Sue said, "Mark, that was rude." Mark said, "I am sorry. I know you did the best you could. Love is blind. Now we need a game plan." Mary said, "Love at first then it was survival, just trying to keep a roof over our heads. He left and we lost that too."

Sue said, "Okay, they have tours damn near ever hour, so let's go inside and see if we can catch the next one. I haven't seen any other teams." Ed asked, "Mark, where are the other teams?" Mark stood on the sidewalk and said, "They are both on their way. Odin is an hour out and Intels just left the cliff." Ed bent down and said, "Give your mommy a hug and tell her you love her." Mark said as Johnny hugged his mom, "And tell her hair smells nice." Ed looked at Johnny hugging Mary with his head just above her belt. He smiled and shook his head.

Jane said, "You are such a sick fuck. You were right though, she should have left that loser."

Ed picked up Johnny, slid his arm around Mary, and pulled her close. Johnny put his arm around his mom's neck and put his head on her shoulder and said, "I love you, Mommy." Ed hugged her and said, "Everything will be fine. Just have a little faith." Johnny said, "Let's go get the money."

Once they got to the steps they looked up. It was huge. Sue said, "Rotunda, I think it is in the lantern room." Mark said, "Okay, where the fuck is that?" Mary shot him a look. He rephrased that, "Where the heck is that? Better?" Ed said, "Right at the very top. It isn't on the tour." Sue said, "Great, this could be a bitch." Jane said, "This could be over ten grand, tax free." Ed said, "I would claim it, if I were you. A lot of people are watching."

Mary grabbed him by the shirt with both hands and asked sternly, "What is your deal? Do you have money riding on this?" Everyone stopped and watched Ed pick his words. She looked him right in the eye. You could see she was stressed to the breaking point. Ed calmly said, "Yes." He paused then said, "I have a hundred grand riding on us winning, and I would like to help you get on your feet." She buried her face in his neck, then she pulled back and kissed him.

Mark said, "I thought it was a million dollar buy in, Come on, we have to catch the next tour." Johnny pulled on Ed's leg. Ed bent down and Johnny asked, "So when you kissed my mom you got the germs from everyone she has kissed?" Ed said, "Well kind of. See, your mom's immunity system kills off most of the germs, but there are some things it can't kill like sexually transmitted diseases. They get transmitted through bodily fluids."

Mary said, "Wow, look at this place." Ed said, "Looks like Vegas." Mark said, "That's it, all the polished marble. I went to

Caesar's Palace early in the morning. They turn the lights down. It looked like a lake with statues sticking out of it."

They got in line for the tour. The guide started with, "This is not the first capitol, the first was in Belmont." Mark said, "Shit, could we be in the wrong place?" Sue said quietly, "The clue is 'isthmus rotunda,' this is the place." Ed put Johnny on his shoulders and said, "Now you can see." Johnny said, "This is great. I have a question. Is this bigger than the one in Washington?" The tour guide said, "That's a fun fact. The capitol building is 284 feet, and the nation's capitol is 288 feet." Ed said, "Now look for a question mark or a monument."

The tour went on. Ed told Johnny, "Stay with your mom. I have to ask a question." He stepped up to the tour guide and introduced himself and shook her hand. She peeked into it to look at the bill Ed slipped her. He asked as he showed her his phone, "You wouldn't have seen a question mark like this or a monument like this? For some reason we think it is in the lantern room." She said as she pointed to the monument, "This one. And you are right, it is on the very top of the dome." Ed asked, "On the inside?" She smiled and said, "Of course it is inside. How could you get to it on the outside?" Ed than asked, "Is the lantern room on this tour?" The guide said, "No, I am sorry. You will have to submit a form for a special tour." Ed said, "That was a hundred. How about four more Benjamins to go with that?" She looked at him and said, "Deal. Let me get another guide to take over. When we get to the door I will take you up."

Johnny stepped up to a man in a suit and asked, "Are you a politician?" The man said, "Yes, little boy, I am a senator." Johnny said to his mom, "Is he a senator? He says he is but his lips were moving, so he is lying." Mary asked, "Why do you say that?" Johnny said, "Mark said you can tell when a politician is lying if their lips are moving." Mary said, "I am sure he was a senator. Don't take Mark seriously. He means you can't trust people in power."

Johnny walked over to Mark and said, "My mom says that all politician are not liars." Mark asked, "What is the difference between a politician and a flying pig? It is the letter F. You get it? Flying, you drop the F and it spells *lying*." Johnny asked, "But where does the pig come in?" Mark said, "Come on, Johnny. Ed is motioning us to move to the rear."

The team came together. Ed said quietly, "We are going upstairs. This tour guide is going to take us up to the lantern room. There are going to be a lot of stairs. This is not open to the public."

Johnny was making faces at an old woman. She walked over and Johnny hid behind Ed's legs. The old woman said to Johnny, "You know, little boy, when I was young my mother told me if I made faces like that my face would freeze that way." Johnny smiled and said, "Well you can't say you weren't warned." Mark laughed. It echoed in the hall. He said, "Damn, that was a good one."

They started to walk around the first observation deck. A man took over the tour. The girl worked her way back to the team and said, "Okay, here is the door. I hope everyone has a good pair of shoes. There are quite a few steps. The lantern room is 244 feet and 6 inches from ground level. The view should be beautiful today."

Everyone followed her up the stairway to the next observation level, then to the great mural. The guide said, "If you look over you will see the decorative floor of the Rotunda it is 184 feet and 3 inches below. We must keep moving. This isn't a scheduled tour. Now the higher we go, there is one staircase that rocks. Do not be worried, it is supposed to move."

Jane said, "Johnny's not going to make it." Johnny said, "Am too." He hurried to catch up. Soon they were to the top. You could see the city and the two lakes. The monument stood right in the center. Mark asked the guide, "Have you ever come up here and had sex?" Her face turned red and she said, "No, of course not." Ed said, "That is good because if you look in the corner, a new camera is mounted. It has a live feed to Las Vegas." She said, "They just put this up here a few weeks ago, but I will warn my people."

Everyone got out their key and put it in a keyhole. Mark said, "Okay, Johnny, slowly count backwards from five." Johnny counted down, "Five, four, three, two, one." Ed said, "Turn."

They turned the key. The bundles of cash had "Winner" on the top. Mark said, "Well, that is that. We won." Jane said, "We came in first six times, so we made around eighty grand in three weeks. Not bad. Let's go find a hotel and have a couple."

Mary's eyes watered up. She crouched down and took Johnny into her arms. Johnny asked, "What's wrong, Mommy?" Mark mocked him, "Mommy? Is that your mommy? Oh, is the little boy going to cry?" Johnny looked over his mom's shoulder and said, "You are such a dick." Ed said, "Now that is rude. Call him a *putz* or a *shmuck*. They both mean *dick*, just sound better." Sue asked, "Isn't a *putz* a whale's penis?" Ed said, "I think you are right." Johnny said, "Whoa, whales have a ding dong. That must be huge." Mark said, "YouTube it." Mary said, "Don't tell him that."

Johnny asked Ed as they went down the stairs, "Why are there young guys running around?" Ed smiled and said, "Those are pages, and they are not all guys. They run papers around, get coffee, do stuff for the politicians. They learn how the government works."

Jane said to the guide, "There are two more teams coming, so watch for them. Maybe you can make a few bucks." Jane asked Sue, "Are you ready to start a new life? I can work anywhere." Sue said, "Let's take a cruise. I can sell cars anywhere, then we can figure out where we want to live." Johnny asked, "Are you going to get married and have kids? Well you can't have kids." Mark said, "Oh yes, they can. And if you want, I could throw them a couple." Ed said, "You tried that already. They know you have been snipped."

Sue asked Mary as they got to the van, "So what are you going to do?" Mary said, "Well, I am going to have to get my car and find somewhere to live, then find a job." Ed said, "I could hang around and help you get on your feet. Johnny needs to get tested and find out what grade he should be in. Two weeks should do." Mark asked, "Are you going to slip her the bone?"

A voice came on the speakers and said, "Too damn late now. Well, Team Three, well done. You have won the game." Mary asked, "What do you mean too late to do Ed?" The voice said, "I had ten grand on the two of you sleeping together." Ed asked, "This is Lance, right? Okay, we need to know how to exit. What do we do with the van and do we have to claim this money? It is all cash?" Lance said, "I would claim it. The game got a bit out of hand. There are a lot of investors in it. Let me tell you I did not bet on you winning. And the ones that bet on Sue and Jane hooking up, they made a pile of cash." Mark asked, "The van, what should we do with it?" Lance said, "Leave the keys with the front desk of your hotel. Someone will pick it up."

As they were leaving the capitol, they met Intel. Ed stepped over quickly and said, "Gloria, it's nice to see you." Gloria said, "Edward, how are you doing? Or should I say, who are you doing?" Ed smiled and said, "Nobody since I had you. What are you up to after the game?" She said, "Back to the old grind, crawl back into the office. I will have to take the boyfriend out for a ride. It was fun. I wish I'd been on your team. It would have been a blast. By the way, where is the clue?"

Randy walked up and asked, "Is this white trash bothering you?" She smiled and said, "We were just saying goodbye for the last time. Hey, you want someone great in bed? This guy could teach you a few lessons." Randy said, "What you talkin' about? You don't know what kind of a ride you are missing." Ed said, "See that was your first mistake." He stepped in close and kissed her a long, lingering kiss. He gently rubbed her muffin, then said, "You have a good life. Focus on the good. You are one hell of a girl."

The whole team was watching. Mary looked like she was ready to cry. Mark said, "That is one hell of a girl. If she is sleeping with the black guy, she will be all stretched out." Ed said, "Oh, he wishes." Jane said, "That's an old wives' tale. All black guys aren't hung." Johnny said, "They used to do that with the slaves. They would hang them from the trees." Mark said, "Back then they hung horse thieves, and that was a long time ago. You're going to have to reread that. Slaves were property, they were worth money. Did I tell you the joke about an Indian, a black guy, and a cowboy? The Indian said, 'Once we were many, now we are few.' The black guy said, 'Once we were a few, now we are many.' The cowboy said, 'That is because we haven't played cowboys and blacks yet.'"

Sue said sharply, "Mark, you're an asshole. The black race has done so much for our country." Ed said, "Come on, guys, let's go. Johnny, you did get the joke, right?" Johnny said, "Yeah, cowboys and Indians. The cowboys killed off the Indians." Ed said, "Well, yes and no. The white people brought a lot of diseases the Indians didn't have before and millions of them died. It was mostly smallpox. Many races have died off because of the spread of the Europeans. The world keeps getting smaller."

Gloria got a text from Ed, "Lantern room, $500, THANK YOU." Gloria said to Scott, "Let's take the tour. It is in the lantern room." Darwin said, "This is not good, they have cameras all over." Randy said, "So what?" Darwin said, "I am out of here. They are probably using facial recognition software." Jeremy said, "We need your key." Darwin said, "I need my stuff. Don't worry about me, I can blend in anywhere." Scott said, "Just don't look up. I will walk you out to the van." Darwin held out his hand and said, "Thank you so very much, and good luck." Scott said, "The same. Here. Have you ever thought of moving south for the winter?" Darwin said, "I have thought of saving the money and flying to Hawaii, but I would never make it through security."

Scott got a text and jogged back into the capitol. He met up with the team. Jeremy asked, "Do you really think the cops are looking for him?" Scott said, "The computers are. He has a beard, long hair, I ready don't think they will pick him out."

They started on the tour and got up to the first observation point.

The guide they paid off said, "Okay, team, if you would follow me."

She opened a side door and said, "Keep up please, it is quite the hike.

We are at ninety-two feet, the lantern room is at 236 feet."

They got to the mural. This thing was huge. They were listening to the guide. She said it was thirty-four feet in diameter, painted back in 1912, and is suspended. Jeremy said, "Did you see that guy with Gloria? He fucked her." The guide said, "Please watch you language. With the curvature of the mural, you can hear someone talking all the way across." Scott chuckled and said quietly, "Let's catch up. It looks like a lot of stairs." The tour guide said, "About a hundred more steps. Let's go, boys." Randy asked, "Did slaves build this? There must be blood of my ancestors spilled on these walls." The tour guide said, "Now see, I don't know about this one, but the capitol in Washington they did. There is a plaque honoring the slaves that helped." Gloria said, "You know, I am getting a bit sick of you complaining about how your people were treated. You could get on a plane and go back to your homeland and walk three miles a day for dirty water. And they are always starving over there. Climate change is really hitting them hard." Randy said, "That's not the point. The point is they kidnapped us, put us on a boat, and sold us. They whipped my people, made them work for nothing." Gloria said, "And look at your people now. Hell, one of your race was even a president. And what have you done? You say the white people treat you with disrespect, well maybe if they would follow the law of the land things would be different." Randy said, "Now what the hell does that mean?"

Gloria stopped to catch her breath and said, "There are more black people in prison than whites. You want to know why that is? I will tell you. Because they broke the law more. Watch the news. Are you shocked when a black guy robs a place?"

Scott said, "Why don't you guys just let it go? We get this last clue and we are done." Jeremy said, "Now, Randy, have we treated you any different? We should have because you are a dick. You do the job and get paid the same as us. Just cut the shit." Scott asked, "Is this safe? The whole staircase shakes." The guide said, "The staircase is suspended. It is built this way, it always shakes."

They got up to the lantern room. The guide said, "This is 236 feet, and the top of the statue is 284 feet." Scott said, "We need you to turn a key for us, and we need to do it all at once." The guide said, "This wasn't in the deal now, you paid me to take you to up here." Gloria said, "How about another hundred?" Randy said, "Okay, three, two, one, turn."

The door opened on top and Gloria took out five packs of bills and handed them out. She took a hundred from the last stack and handed it to the guide. Jeremy said, "We will split that one up in the van, and whatever is left of the petty cash."

The headed back down to the van. Randy said, "I really was hoping for a million dollars." Jeremy said, "The game paid out a million. If we were in first place every time, our team would have got a half million." Gloria asked, "So what are you to going to do?" Scott said, "Monday it's back to the lab. We have a lot of work to do." Jeremy said, "We have to impregnate the secretary. That should be fun." Randy said, "I just don't know about you white folks. I have some money, I think I am going to get back out there and play engineer." Gloria asked, "So do you like that job?" Randy said, "It's not bad. I don't get my hands dirty and get to boss around white guys." Scott said, "There we go, you lost your job because you are a racist, wasting more time showing you are better then everyone." Jeremy asked, "So, Glo, what are you up to?" She smiled and said, "Vacation, still have some summer left, then it's back to teaching, computer classes. I could go back to school so I can teach college."

Team Odin got to the capitol. Joe said to Robert, "Last chance to see if you can find a leprechaun." Cherry said, "Come on, aren't you going to let that go? But have you noticed the queer look in his eye?" Joe said, "I don't think taking it up the ass is going to turn him gay." Robert said, "Thank you. And can we get this clue and call it a game?" Joe said, "Now we have to be careful. This has high security. We ask everyone and find out where it is." Cherry said, "Let me ask if they have a private tour up to the top. I have read there are stairs all the way up to the top and you can look out of the lantern room over the city."

As they climbed the stairs, Joe said, "This place is huge, and you say the lantern is right below the statue?" They got inside and found the tour. Cherry walked up and asked for a private tour of the lantern room. The girl said, "That is not on the tour. Are you with the treasure hunt? If so, that will be $500." Cherry said, "Yes, we are. We are the Odins." Dawn smiled and asked, "Do you have any leprechauns here? Robert here is looking for one." Robert said, "Let's just get this over."

The guide said, "Now we must be quiet. How many teams are there?" Joe said, "Three, us, the Intels, and Team Three." The girl said, "Well your team is in last place then." Cherry said, "Well it is five hundred bucks. Let's get our ass up there and collect it." Robert asked, "Who is the broad that is on top of the dome?" The tour guide said, "There are a few stories about that, but the statue was made in 1914, weighs more than three tons. It represents the state motto 'Forward.' She is fifteen and a half feet tall with outstretched arms. In one she holds a globe with an eagle perched on it. On her helmet there is a cluster of grapes and the state animal, the badger." Cherry said, "Shall we get on our way? I have a date waiting for me." Dawn asked, "That Jim guy? The accountant?" Cherry said, "He is making me an offer. I have to meet his kids. There is no way I am going to be a stay-at-home wife." Robert asked, "You're thinking of marriage? You knew the guy for one night." Cherry said, "What can I say? He is building a case. We are talking about Vegas, getting married by Elvis, in a gondola." Dawn asked, "But what would you do?" Cherry said, "Get a job, settle down, have a couple of kids. And he is a sweet guy with a big dick."

The tour guide said, "We have to pick up the pace and be quiet." The team climbed the staircase all the way up to the lantern room without saying a word. The tour guide said, "Here we are at 236 feet overlooking Madison. And here is your monument." Dawn said, "Oh my god, it is beautiful."

Robert asked the guide, "Could you help us? We need a fifth person to turn a key." She smiled and said, "Yes, of course. The other team gave me a hundred bucks to do it." Dawn said, "See we are not the only team that has lost a member." The tour guide said, "Team Intel lost three members." Joe said, "No shit. Jack, he was mauled by a tiger. It sounds insane but that is what happened."

Robert said, "Okay, when I say turn, turn your key clockwise. Three, two, one, turn." The door on top opened. Dawn reached in and took out the stacks of money with one hand. On top was a note, "Third place." Joe said, "Loser. Oh well, it was interesting. What did we make, like $26,000, in three weeks? Not bad." Dawn counted her stack and said, "This payout is ten grand." She pulled a hundred out of the pack and handed it to the guide. She held up the stack and said, "We will spilt this up in the van."

The guide said, "Well we should shove off then. It's a lot faster going down." Joe said, "You could go down on me anytime." The guide said, "That, sir, is sexual harassment." Joe said, "I was just joking. That line has never worked." Cherry asked, "Are there bats in here?" The guide said, "Nope, the snakes ate them." Cherry eyes popped open wide as she said, "There are snakes in here?" Robert said, "I take it you don't like snakes? There is nothing for them to eat in here." The tour guide said, "We have to move. I have a tour in twenty minutes."

Robert said as they went down the stairs, "Be careful. We made it through the hunt, we don't want to fall." Dawn said, "I might go on the road with that basketball player. He keeps on texting me, wanting to hook up." Joe asked, "Can you travel with the team?" Dawn said, "Oh hell no, fly first class, baby."

They got to the van and Robert booked a hotel for the evening. Lance came on the speaker, "Well, Team Odin, you came in last, just three hours late. Not bad. Clean out the van, leave the keys at the front desk. We will have someone pick it up in the morning." Joe said, "Thank you for the opportunity to play the game. I had a good time. Now I have some cash. I think I am going to hike Yosemite Park." Lance said, "You did a fine job. A lot of people bet on your team to be the winner." Cherry asked, "Who won, may I ask?" Lance said, "Oh, the house won. That was a good game. Team Three won. They got first place in a lot of the clues. Speaking of that, what would you have changed in the game?" Robert said, "Well, the clues were lame. Why Wisconsin? It was a very nice treasure hunt but a long distance for the clues." Dawn said, "I thought it was great. We got to go to great places, do some weird shit."

Cherry said, misty eyed, "Well I guess this is it. One more night together and we go our own ways in the morning." She gave Dawn a hug. Dawn kissed her on the cheek. Cherry went to give her a quick kiss on the cheek. Dawn turned her head quickly and their lips met. Cherry didn't pull away. She slipped her the tongue and then said, "It has been nice to know you. We are going to have to keep in touch."

Robert asked Joe, "Are you flying to California and renting gear to hike Yosemite?" Joe said, "That was the plan. You want to come?" Robert said, "Always wanted to climb El Capitan, but that is too much for me." Joe said, "I would like to hike around it, but that is out of my league too. It looks beautiful in pictures."

Cherry said, "Book your flights now. you could leave tomorrow morning and it will be around $400 round trip. That's cheap. Then you need to rent a car. The trip will run you around a grand apiece, not bad." Joe said, "You're a climber, why don't you come?" Cherry smiled and said, "I am going to cum alright, just not with you two. I have to put my life together." Dawn said, "He is a nice guy." Cherry said, "His house is up for sale. He is closing on another. This will be our house. I get to decorate it and buy everything. I shit you not he is selling his house furnished." Robert said, "But he has kids you haven't even met." Cherry said, "Oh, fuck the kids. We will get along. If not, send them to the mother's. Who cares. We are going to start our family. We are going to have three." Robert said, "I think you should throw on the brakes, slow down, this is a big step." Dawn said, "Live the dream, enjoy. Life is short." Cherry said, "The game is done, back to reality."

The End